JIŘÍ KRATOCHVIL

THE VOW

A REQUIEM FOR THE FIFTIES

TRANSLATION OF THIS BOOK WAS SUPPORTED BY

THE VOW: A REQUIEM FOR THE FIFTIES
by Jiří Kratochvil

Translated from the Czech and introduced by Charles S. Kraszewski

**Translation of this book was supported
by the Ministry of Culture of the Czech Republic**

First published in the Czech as *Slib* in 2009

Proofreading by Stephen Dalziel

Copyright © Jiří Kratochvil, 2009

Copyright © Druhé město – Martin Reiner, 2009

Introduction © 2021, Charles S. Kraszewski

Cover art: Carl Spitzweg 'The Poor Poet' (1837)

Author photograph by Jef Kratochvil

Book cover and layout by Max Mendor

© 2021, Glagoslav Publications

www.glagoslav.com

ISBN: 978-1-914337-55-0

First published in English by Glagoslav Publications in December 2021

A catalogue record for this book is available from the British Library.

JIŘÍ KRATOCHVIL

THE VOW

A REQUIEM FOR THE FIFTIES

Translated from the Czech
and introduced by Charles S. Kraszewski

GLAGOSLAV PUBLICATIONS

JIŘÍ KRATOCHVIL

CONTENTS

IN THE NAME OF KAMIL MODRÁČEK?
JIŘÍ KRATOCHVIL'S IMPERFECT GOD

Tadeusz Kantor once said that one doesn't enter the theatre with impunity. Ezra Pound said that a book should be like a ball of light in one's hand. Both these great writers, whose lives were impacted by the horrible events of the mid-twentieth century, a portion of which make up the background to Jiří Kratochvil's novel *The Vow* [Slib], imply that those who engage with dramatic or literary art ought to expect to be challenged by the artworks. Texts are not made to entertain, or, at least, not merely to entertain. They are to pose questions to us — sometimes uncomfortable ones. *The Vow* is just such a challenging work. As such, the questions it asks are many; perhaps as many as there are readers. As a translator, I have been engaged with this book for several years. But it was only very recently, once the translation was completed, that it finally became clear to me what question it was confronting me with. Just in time, as I was about to begin work on this introduction.

It came to me at Mass.

It was a Sunday morning, at a small parish not my own, in upstate New York, near a lake. Before I go any further, I ought to confess that whereas I love the Mass, I loathe sermons. They're usually overlong, ingratiating, and full of platitudes, repetitive, poorly constructed, and not at all inspiring. Just like introductions, the cynical reader might smirk. Perhaps.[1] At any rate,

....

[1]   I myself am of two minds concerning introductions. On the one hand, I think that translators especially should feel obliged to explain to the reader how they understand the text they are recreating, which may be different from the manner in which others do. On the other hand, introductions are spoilers, and the reader who reads the introduction before the story itself not only runs the risk of ruining punch-lines, but also of subjecting him or herself to someone else's guidance and direction. I have long been convinced that introductions should be

for me, sermons are a waste of time. I'd like to say that this is because I'm a Catholic, not a Protestant, and 'we Catholics' or 'Catholics of my generation' don't go to Mass for sermonising, we go for another reason entirely — to be present at the Holy Eucharist, in which God Himself is not symbolically, but actually, present. But while there's something in that, the real reason is — probably (I'd like to say that this is an occupational hazard, but that would just be another excuse) — the real reason is probably that I'm just a prig, a snob.

Anyway, I almost missed the question entirely because, with what I've just admitted, it won't be a surprise to You, Reader, that I don't pay much attention to what the priest is saying during his sermon. Sometimes, I'm even lucky enough to drowse (and luckier still if my wife doesn't notice me drowsing and elbow me awake). But on this particular Sunday, maybe it was because the weather was nice, or the setting was beautiful, or the trip was enjoyable — I was more conscious than usual during that part of the liturgy. The Gospel was taken from Mark (10:46–52) and dealt with Timaeus, the blind man, who called to Christ while the Lord 'was leaving Jericho:' 'Jesus, son of David, have pity on me.' To His question 'What do you want me to do for you?' the blind man replied 'Master, I want to see.' The sermon that ensued was just as dull, boring, predictable and pedestrian as all the rest I've ever suffered through. Predictably, the priest tossed some bland rhetorical questions out at the congregation, such as 'What is it that blinds *us*? What is it that stops *us* from seeing Christ in our neighbour?' after which he spooled off onto a digression, the dimensions of which would have sufficed for a sermon of its own, with questions like 'What takes the place of God in *our* lives?' At (long) last, he brought that digression to an end with some groaner of the sort 'I've never seen a Brinks truck follow a hearse to the graveside.'

As I looked about the church that day, it occurred to me: *There's not a single person here who isn't thinking right now: 'I'm not blind; no, not me. I see Jesus in everybody. My stomach's not my God; nothing takes the place of God in my life; I'm not one of those materialistic fools to whom passing things like belongings or money mean anything...'* And what a wonderful world it

<hr>

read only once the reader has finished the story on his or her own. To avoid the situation of the blind leading the one-eyed, as Byron once put it, I suggest, dear Reader, you skip to Kratochvíl's text, right now. This introduction isn't going anywhere. Read it later.

would be, if all that were actually true. So, this is when the question that Kratochvil's novel is posing to me, particularly, hit me. Permit me to hold you in suspense about that for a moment, but I will tell you that I was helped on to the answer, almost immediately, by recollections of two quite different writers: St James and Tadeusz Różewicz. But, with your indulgence: of that, a little later.

WE'RE ONLY HUMAN. UNFORTUNATELY

Kratochvil subtitles his novel 'A Requiem for the Fifties.' This has the ring of finality to it; something akin to what John Lennon said in one of his last interviews: 'Wasn't the seventies a drag, you know? Well, here we are, let's make the eighties great because it's up to us to make what we can of it.'[2] There are a lot of such milestones we impose upon history, as if to say: well, now that's over, and we don't have to worry about it any more. But although Khrushchev may have denounced Stalin in February 1956, that no more put an end to totalitarianism and government oppression (of all stripes) than George Bush's 'Mission Accomplished!' speech in May 2003 put an end to the troubles besetting the world since 9/11. There are no full-stops or 'thick lines' — to use another frequently invoked metaphor — in history, because people do not change. The same human material that gave rise to the problems besetting the characters in Kratochvil's novel in the 1950s is walking around today, in the clothes that you and I wear, and it's only a matter of time until it gets this poor suffering planet into more serious trouble. Woes such as Kratochvil describes don't come about because of something in the air or the water in a given decade, a given place on the map, they come about because of something in you and me and all of our kind, whether we consider them our brothers and sisters or not, whether we're able to see Christ in them or not. My tradition, after Augustine, understands it as the 'spiritual syphilis' that still inclines us to evil, a residue of Original Sin. Depending on what your tradition may be, you may just want to say 'Man's a bastard.' Yep. No argument here — brother. The grime that infects our world doesn't carry an expiration date. It'll be around as long as we are.

....

2   Cited on johnlennon.com, http://www.johnlennon.com/about/ [accessed 23.10.2021]

Kratochvil himself toys with the idea of original sin when he brings in Nabokov's short story, the Czech translation of which sparks Kamil Modráček's imagination on how to even the score with the State Security Services (StB) following the death of his sister. In the Russian tale, a family captures a KGB officer, imprisons him in their bathroom after pronouncing a life sentence upon him. And then:

> The family […] arrive at the determination that, when he attains an age older than that of his gaolers at present, they will pass him on to their children's care, and then, perhaps, on and on, to the children of their children — passing him on like an inheritance from generation to generation.

What is this inheritance, but a binding of all future generations to slavery, to an inherited guilt? To say nothing of the fact that, in this fictional world of Nabokov's, the present family and their descendants are condemned to life imprisonment as well. Obviously, someone has to remain stuck in that apartment as warder and turnkey, as long as the 'guilty party' is imprisoned in the bathroom. It is hard for us to imagine the manner in which our debased human nature holds us in thrall; it is hard to get our minds around the great freedom that our first parents enjoyed before the Fall, which St Augustine sums up in the laconic truth: *possunt non peccare* — 'They didn't have to sin.' But once they made that decision *to* sin, the toothpaste, to continue with Nabokov's bathroom metaphor, couldn't be squeezed *back* into the tube, and here we are. Thanks a lot, Adam. Way to go, Eve. From Adam and Eve stretches a direct line through Cain to Kamil Modráček to…

At one point in *The Vow*, Kamil Modráček, the main character (not to say 'hero') of the novel, references Dante's *Divine Comedy*, ironically casting himself in the role of Virgil, Dante's guide. The difference is — as he himself notes with a wink — Virgil's not carrying a hammer to rap someone on the noggin with. 'Abandon all hope, ye who enter here' indeed. Also unlike the magnum opus of the great Florentine, this 'Virgil' will not lead us out of Hell and into the blessed region of Purgatory. He might also have quoted Marlowe's Mephistophiles in reference to *The Vow*, at that point where the devil appears to Faustus who, when (O, blessed naiveté!) he professes his belief in progress and doubt in the existence of Hell, responds, 'Why this is

Hell, nor am I out of it!' Given our tendency to evil, however you wish to explain it, which is as inseparable from us as our very flesh and bones, it is in this sense that Sartre's quip of hell being 'other people' is almost correct. Almost, because — again, in this sense — we just need to strike that word 'other'. For proof, I will just point to one more sermon, before I'm done: that which Fr Klenovský delivers in his underground church on the text 'Thou shalt not kill'. In the end, someone in his congregation (maybe even more than just one of their number), goes ahead and does just that.

In what way is the murder committed in Modráček's underground 'cathedral of silence' — a killing that some try to justify using Caiaphas' bloody reasoning (it is better 'that one man should die for the people, and that the whole nation perish not') — any different from the extra-judicial execution of a supposed enemy of the state in the nearby cellars of the Security Services' building? The answer is: there is no difference at all. In his book, Kratochvil helps no one to any 'high ground'; some people may be more victimised here than others, but… everyone is a perpetrator.

It would be nice to say that Kratochvil so constructs his novel as to set his characters in extreme situations, where they are forced to make a choice, or make choices, which they later learn from. This is hinted at once, when Ivan Sluka executes Lieutenant Treblík in the cellars of the StB station on Běhounská:

> Once again the basement came to your mind, along with the burning match falling along Treblík's trouser leg, and what was slipping out of it. And how your dick swelled and stiffened right at the moment when you readied yourself to pull the trigger — just as if it, too, wanted to shoot its load into Treblík, and how then you struck your last match so that you could see where you were shooting, and how you then pulled the trigger four times, and how between the first and second shot you heard Treblík cry out softly Mama, mama! before he crumpled along your legs, rustling to the ground, and how you pulled your left shoe out from under his body with a quick jerk. And how immediately, horridly sick to your stomach you became, hurling the contents of your stomach into the darkness, probably onto Treblík lying there at your feet. My God, you whispered through your sour and sticky lips, I've just killed a man. But then you got a grip

on yourself, left the scene of your deed, and emerged from the cellar over those endless steps.

But Kratochvil is too good a writer to write so predictable a story. As we shall see, there are various narrators in the complex novel *The Vow*, and here it is significant that Sluka's thoughts are not being reported in the usual third-person omniscient voice; rather, we have here a sort of legal protocol. The paragraph above sounds like a prosecutor's summation, rehearsing the facts to the guilty party. But — no verdict is pronounced, no jury votes, and after this undeniably dramatic moment, Sluka will disappear from our purview. Of great importance here is how even Sluka's conscience seems to abandon its role as Fury; or, more precisely, is overcome, shrugged off the perpetrator's shoulder, as soon as he 'gets a grip on himself and leaves the scene of his deed.' For — and this is the great strength of Kratochvil's writing — it is not the fictional characters who are being challenged; we are not being invited to sit on the jury here. No, it is us who will be in the dock.

But more of that, later. To return to the characters in the novel, it is for this reason, among others, we hesitate to call Kamil Modráček, or anyone else in *The Vow*, a 'hero.' Jiří Kratochvil's *Vow* is a multi-layered narrative of some thirty-one chapters. Although not every character in the work is afforded the chance to narrate a chapter, various parts of the story are told from different perspectives (although it very infrequently occurs that the same event is shown from different angles). A third-person, omniscient narrator leads us through a full third of these chapters; next comes Modráček himself, who presents nearly that many, for eight are given over to him to narrate. The private eye / SNB second lieutenant Dan Kočí's voice dominates four, and then Modráček's sister, and various other main characters (Fr Klenovský is an exception) are given one chapter each. However, there is no real difference between any of these voices. No one among them — not even, perhaps, the omniscient third-person narrator — is a moral paragon. The amount of space, so to speak, that Kratochvil allows his narrators is not intended to direct us to any conclusions about who is more worthy of our respect or our attention. To speak merely of the characters who figure in the main trunk of the book, the chapters dealing with the 1950s, the quantitative ranking has nothing to do with justice, but rather — the amount of naked power the given character wields over others.

The Vow displays the manner in which the fates of people are strongly influenced, if not determined, by forces beyond their control. Again, 1950s Czechoslovakia is a convenient background, against which matters of free will and compulsion can be shown in high relief. However, this is only a vehicle to confront us with our own situations. To what degree are we free in our decision making? What is it that compels us to this, rather than that, decision? Is it fear, or hope of gain, or a determination to do what we know is right, even if it hurts? In Kratochvil's novel, it is fair to say that just about every one of the characters seems to be in control of his or her fate, only to have their control proved an illusion, sooner or later. We've already given the starkest example of this in that self-assured true believer Ivan Sluka, who is in control, not only of his own fate (he decides to take his turns at the twelve-hour night shifts at the station, which he has instituted, to be a good example to his men) but also of another man's life (the presumed guilty Lieutenant Treblík), only to find that, after executing him — without anger or hatred, but 'for the good of the working class' — something changes deep inside him and he cannot function properly anymore. In the aftermath of a drastic, but well-considered action, he is by turns gripped by catatonia and vomiting; his mind itself is completely clouded over (he undertakes a midnight journey to a home he no longer lives in, to visit parents that no longer exist).

And everyone answers to someone; power devours us all. Given the historical setting of the novel, the height of Stalinism/Gottwaldism in 1950s Czechoslovakia, the 'power' that compels most of the characters is that of the State, in the person of its instruments Ivan Sluka and Lieutenant Láska. This introduces the theme of compulsion to collaborate (something which we, naively perhaps, feel sealed off safely from by those illusory temporal milestones of ours!). At the start of the novel, Modráček seems a stock character from anti-totalitarian narratives centring on the victims of Nazi or Communist exploitation. He is a victim, and the justification for his collaboration with SS Gruppenführer Wagenheim on the construction of his macabrely-shaped villa in Brno is an understandable one — if not to say 'noble.' He wishes to spare the life of his sister:

I was ready to declare myself Albert Speer if it would only buy me some more time to talk with him, to keep trying to fight for my sister's life. So I risked it and just clenched my jaw and said, You're looking to build something? I can build anything, from a doghouse to an opera to a hockey rink.

This same desire motivates his willingness to collaborate with the Communist security forces who have taken over from the Gestapo after the war:

As soon as I found myself outside it occurred to me that I should have stressed how I was simply bursting with desire to collaborate, sure, to the very separation of soul from body, anything to convince them that into the care of such a comrade they could safely entrust his little sister; that it was unnecessary for them to hold her any longer in some dark and cold cell.

And so, Kamil Modráček is a cringing doormat during the Nazi occupation of his city, and following its 'liberation' by the Soviets. As Ladislava Galusková puts it (though perhaps a bit harshly), he 'navigates the régimes swimmingly without a single pang of conscience.'[3] He will design a villa for a Gestapo officer in the early forties; less than ten years later he will participate in the metaphorical destruction of the family across the hall from him by agreeing to be a snitch for the StB. Is this enduring trait of his — grovelling sycophancy — a flaw in him, a weak human being, or the rational practicality of a man who has but one move out of checkmate? It is, presumably, easier to stick to one's morals like a self-assured Antigone, *usque ad sanguinem,* when the only thing the martyr has to lose is his life. But when the gun, so to speak, is pointed at the head of someone we love? 'Modráček fell victim to a hectic frenzy, such as he'd never before experienced all his life long. Even though he knew that he liked his sister very much, that he was really attached to her, he never imagined just how fatal a force in his life this sibling love was.' Unlike Winston Smith, the hero of

<hr>

3   Ladislava Galusková, *Poetika míst v díle Jiřího Kratochvila* [The Poetics of Place in the Works of Jiří Kratochvil] (Brno: Filozofická fakulta, Ústav hudební vědy Masarykovy univerzity [Bakalářská diplomová práce], 2010), p. 28.

George Orwell's much darker *1984*, who begins screaming 'Do it to Julia! Do it to Julia!' when he is faced with torment, so as to spare himself, there is something (again, it is difficult to use the adjective 'noble' here), admirable in Modráček's willingness to sell his soul to at least have the chance to save that of his sister. Considering the atmosphere of the entirety of the main, 1950s, portion of the novel, the second possibility mentioned above seems more suitable to Modráček's situation. For Kratochvil shows us that oppression is a food chain; there is always someone above you, and someone in turn above him. Or, it is an ouroboros: no part of the serpent's body is safe, when the head is swallowing its own tail. Rudolf Švarcšnupf, alias Lieutenant Láska, must watch his own step:

> Švarcšnupf, Švarcšnupf, the chief was asking for you before he left. What did you tell him?
>
> That the devil only knows where you've been running about.
>
> But you knew I had an interrogation! And the interrogated party was a stubborn cuss — and this drew the investigation out enormously!
>
> Enormously! Chovanec laughed. Where'd you get that one from, enormously! That's a beaut, that is! Just be careful — that's not an imperialistic term, is it?

As we said above, no one is exempt from blame. Even as positive a character as Dan Kočí, as far as anyone may be said to have 'positive' characteristics in a novel so pessimistic about mankind as *The Vow*, exploits whomever is in his power:

> Just the same was he cheered by the realisation that, at last, he would be using his Leica again, and without having to respect the persons of his subjects overmuch. On the contrary — he was again being empowered to shamelessly strip them to their underclothes in an attempt to eternise them in flagranti, after which, in his darkroom, he would see what intimate details would emerge from the developing pans, captured by his camera… and perhaps he would play with those intimate details under the enlarger… (The private eye had his own private collection of intimate details, worked up by the enlarger.

Should anyone take those large format obscenities in hand, they'd never guess that he was glomming at a stable of prominent, highly placed promiscuous mares.)

What is Dan Kočí's private collection of smut if not his own way of using people, no less repulsive for its 'virtual' nature (the camera 'capturing' his victims at their most vulnerable moments) as Modráček's underground 'city'? In another place, we read of him, setting off on a case: 'Ants began to crawl all over his back — something he only felt these days right before bedding a heretofore inaccessible partner, whom he'd had to chase after for a long time.' So, no matter what Dan suggests about his 'professional ethics,' the connection he makes between the stimulation provided by his investigation and sexual arousal suggests that he is little more than the classical idea of a pornographer, or addict to pornography, who sees not the whole person in his photos, but only body parts. What is more, Dan's self-description is just as predatory as any Kamil Modráček prowling the streets of Brno with a rag and bottle of chloroform in his breast-pocket; he too is a 'hunter.'

WHOSE FAULT? / WHOSE BUT HIS ALONE? INGRATE. MATE IN TWO

If this is the case — dog eat dog eat dog — perhaps everyone is inculpable? Perhaps the world is nothing but an inimical corrosive soup, in which we thrash about, without any hope of reaching shore? Does Modráček speak for us, when, at a particularly nerve-wracking crossroads, he exclaims: 'What was I thinking, after all? That I'd be able to cheat fate?!'

At times, the world presented by Jiří Kratochvil in *The Vow* seems a trap. The story of Konečný the builder, who controls Modráček for an entire week, and from afar, like some tantalising god, might be offered in evidence of this fact. His mind is that of a chess-master, always at least one step ahead of his opponent:

Konečný led me over to one of the empty tables. He set up Nabokov's mate-in-two, and after a short pause, which he evidently relished, he stretched out his hand, set it on the white bishop, and moved it to C2. Careful! I wanted to call out, but the builder, who even heard my unexpressed cry of alarm, immediately showed me how marvellous a move it was, and what resulted from it. […] See? smiled Konečný the builder, and then, with a tiny flick of his finger, he executed the king as if beneath a tiny guillotine. Then he said that he was very sorry, but that the painting would not be changing hands.

I understood then that he had known all along that I hadn't the slimmest chance of lighting upon that solution, and that he wasn't taking the slightest risk of losing his Le Corbusier.

Then, in the game of his life, as he attempts to cross the 'green border' into the free West, lugging his valuable painting with him, he is 'checkmated' at the border, and falls under a hail of bullets just as surely as he flicked over the king with his finger.

The story of the builder and the 'Russian Roulette' game with the Le Corbusier is one of the many digressions to be found in this *stromata* of a novel. At first, it seems to be merely a fleshing-out of Modráček's character, the introduction of something into his life that would provide it with a ballast of human interest (he loves something other than his sister), something that could give his cringing life a direction, as he puts it: 'I don't just admire Le Corbusier, immensely; for me, he's something of a saint. And with him in my atelier, I'd be ashamed to commit those indecencies of mine before his eyes, that mass production of architectural dwarves. For such magical values a person is willing to pay any price.' But when we come to the end of the story, and see how it ends, finally and dramatically, for Konečný, the game of chess expands into a metaphor of life, free will, inescapable destiny. The world, it seems, is a prison — Alžběta Hajná, one of Modráček's 'tenants' describes the 'subterranean horizontal city' in which she is imprisoned as a 'delightful Alcatraz.' Perhaps the story of builder Konečný (whose last name suggests 'finality' in Czech, and as *konieczność* in the kindred language of Polish, 'necessity') is meant to teach us that, even if you scale down the drainpipe and make it down to the shore of the bay, the currents are too strong, you'll never make it to freedom?

Cages and imprisonment are a constant Leitmotiv in Kratochvil's *Vow*. The bear-cage, with which Modráček (unintentionally) initiates the construction of his 'delightful Alcatraz' is introduced right after the circus investigation with 'electric Belinda,' whom Dan Kočí tracks down on an adulterous bed in the middle of the big top, with a fierce tiger circling about to ward off intruders. And here we have another marvellous, and marvellously subtle, metaphor. This is as much enjoyment and freedom as we can hope for: lovemaking in a tightly constrained space, sex in a tiger's cage. We will perhaps call this metaphor to mind in the later parts of the novel, when Luděk explains to his lover Petra: 'at the time, for our folk sex was the only available route to freedom that the puritanical comrades (and their street gangs) weren't able to control.' Alas, as enjoyable a freedom as it may be, it was also an illusory one; sex leads to children; the hooking up of Mrs Modráčková and Láska, both imprisoned in her husband's 'underground Utopia,' leads to the birth of little Eduard Láska. And while, in his benign insanity, Modráčk announces to his prisoners, as Hajná puts it, that 'we should take the birth of our first child as a joyful sign that we have accepted our new tasks as passengers on Noah's Ark' — as a kind of underground Virginia Dare — it is Fr Klenovský, the only character in the novel who represents a world-view that rejects predetermination, who protests:

> even though you provide for us in this reality here, the fact remains that we are in a prison, which is, let us assume, merely one pocket in the straitjacket of that much greater prison, into which the entire Czech nation has been thrust, but we needn't understand a prison within a prison as some sort of enclave of freedom, [...and] even if, like it or not, we were to accept the fact that we ourselves are to spend a certain amount of time here, that doesn't mean that you have the right to imprison children as well, you cannot justify such an act in any way.

These words should be understood in a broader manner than just as the particular situation intimates. The idea of a good, loving God, who loves man so much as even to refuse to impede his freely-willed choices, even when they are harmful (and thus we begin this segment with a citation from Milton's *Paradise Lost* III: 96-97) is incompatible with the idea of any sort of acquiescence to the evil determinism that would condone the propagation of children into a prison — this particular one, governed by Modráček, or the wider one, governed (seemingly) by Calvinist-Hegelian-Marxist historical necessity.

The voice of Fr Klenovský, especially here, is one of the most important, if not the most important, in *The Vow*. This despite the fact that all evidence seems to point to the contrary; we constantly find ourselves in the environment of power and imprisonment. The novel moves from 'legal' constraint (Modráček at the beck and call of Láska) through his sister's imprisonment, to Kočí's circus investigation and cages both literal and figurative (the bear and tiger cages, Kočí's Leica), to the purchase of the bear cage, the virtual imprisonment of Láska, and then Modráček's collection of people in his underground city beginning with Láska himself. Finally, we have (as Fr Klenovský points out) the Czechoslovak Socialist Republic (ČSSR) as an inescapable prison (since both Konečný's and Modráček's escapes are foiled)… It would be reasonable to assume that the universe is being described here as God's toy box, and human history the story of the compulsion He exerts on us, no less irresistible as the will of the chess-master who takes a pawn in hand.

Even ignorance is its own form of prison. Consider the story Anička Fraccaroli, Láska's daughter, relates to Petr Luňák during their interview:

> Supposedly, Dad reported that the entire case against the architect's sister had been fabricated, and he kept on insisting that this was murder, categorically demanding an investigation. He was taken off the case, and a few days later he vanished completely. So, it's all quite clear, isn't it? A word to the wise suffices.

She has no idea that it wasn't the StB who did her Dad in, but the architect. There is no one to explain the truth to her now, and so she — this is important — is constructing an image of the world that has very little to do with the actual truth, no matter how convincing it seems. Remember Fr Klenovský's objection! In a very similar way, Modráček himself is incarcerated in the prison of ignorance:

> I went down into the cellar every morning and evening, in order to satisfy the ever more ravenous Lieutenant Láska. It seemed as if he had decided to compensate for what had befallen him by a fantastic gluttony. And to punish me for having imprisoned him by devouring all of my grain and meat stores. I still couldn't quite figure out wheth-

er or not something had happened to his brain, or whether it was all a trick with which he was assailing my compassion and polite upbringing. Some days he said nothing at all, while on others he babbled on endearingly before falling into some quite incomprehensible tongue.

In exactly the same way — if what Fraccaroli tells us is true — Modráček serves out his own life sentence of ignorance, never coming to know the truth of his sister's death, which he might have learned that very moment that Láska, by chance, rushed into the foyer of his building to escape the pounding rain. Modráček never gave him the chance, thwacking him on his noggin with the hammer, twice, having prejudged a case without being in possession of all of the evidence.

A similar case is that presented by Dr Pešek. This is all the more eloquent as possible evidence of predetermination than the foregoing. For Pešek is not going to be metaphorically imprisoned by ignorance, he is going to become Modráček's second victim, imprisoned in the underground after stumbling by chance upon the architect at work constructing his prison in the mediaeval vault. In what is perhaps the one passage of dry Czech humour in a basically sombre book, Pešek's imprisonment at Modráček's hands is directly caused by the actions he takes to avoid being imprisoned by the authorities!

> And so, still barefoot, I'm walking around the flat, near the glass-paned bookshelves when my good guardian angel turns my head in that direction and — what do I see but — horror of horrors! Masaryk's World Revolution, the Black Band of that émigré Hostovský, Beneš's Memoirs and all the books from the Anglo-American Bookstore. What, as if I didn't know how Venhoda flits his eyes about? I don't know that just one book of that sort could turn my life upside-down, and after Venhoda's visit, the next guests to show up at my door might be some SNB goons, just as it happened at the Kratochvils? No, I definitely can't play around with that. And so I immediately set my hand to the task.

Had he not overreacted to the impending visit of a Communist official who was to drop into his flat the next day, he would have never pulled those books off his shelf, never gone down into the building's basement at midnight. 'I had no wish to be part of the idiotic vacuum,' states Dan Kočí when he comes upon his friend Radek staring blankly into the distance. And yet that's exactly how he'll end up too, swallowed by the vacuum along with Pešek who preceded him there, when he goes off cockily, without backup, after Lieutenant Láska.

The fact that it is Fr Klenovský who is proven right in the end, and not the determinists (of Calvinist or Marxist stripe) is borne out by the manner in which time is dealt with in *The Vow*. For although primarily set in the 1950s, a significant portion of the novel takes place in the 2000s, when we are with Luděk and Petra, who discuss the deeds of Modráček and other amateur turnkeys from the distance of our own day and age, and — this is most important — at least a full two decades after the Velvet Revolution saw the prison walls around Brno and the entire ČSSR come tumbling down. So again, Fr Klenovský's urging of his fellow prisoners to be patient, for 'in two or three days they'd be free anyway,' has an eloquence that exceeds the particular situation in which the words are uttered. In the large sense, they are eloquent of a faith and hope that were proven true in the end: not only was Modráček's prison door to be opened, but the 'Communist Utopia' up above was fated to disappear. And, in a still larger sense, the manner in which time is handled in *The Vow*, which brings in the free Czech Republic of the twenty-first century as the Communist prison that was Czechoslovakia in the fifties, testifies to change, to progress. Determinism is a prison, because it excludes change, it is a continuum. No child should ever be born into that, and, as history and Fr Klenovský prove, no child is.

Another proof against determinism is provided by Modráček himself. Although (as we will see) he feels himself to be 'moved' to his mission by a power outside of himself, the truth is that he takes all of these aberrant decisions himself. And why? He feels trapped, and he wishes to take control, to act out in some way against the horrid chains that seem to bind him.

Consider, for example, the aftermath of his sister's death, once the initial numbness has passed, and he begins to busy himself with the disposal of her body. Although 'neither he nor his sister were believers' in the Christian God, Modráček arranges a 'funeral Mass and Catholic burial ceremony' for her, because — he 'felt that he had to do something.' It is this feeling of being obliged to 'do something,' perhaps anything, that is at the root of Modráček's insanity, and is to be blamed for the harm he inflicts on other people. For it is not 'something' that we need to do, in order to 'somehow transcend everything that had happened' — which in this case and all others is selfish self-therapy, something that *we* need — but the *right thing* that must be done, to help others. The former attitude is inward thrusting, the latter, outward. And, as another positive character in the book, the physician Dr Štefl well knows — first, and above all, *do no harm.* When we don't know what is the right thing to do, when others come into the equation, it might just be better to do nothing at all, even if that means that we must live with our own helplessness. It is better not to help ourselves, than to harm others.

Here, perhaps, it might be fitting to introduce one of those writers who helped me to an understanding of the question posed by Kratochvil's *The Vow* just the other day at Mass (as I continue in this question to put the cart before the horse). In his long poem *Recycling*, Tadeusz Różewicz poses the rhetorical question:

> Skąd się bierze zło?
> jak to skąd
>
> z człowieka
> zawsze z człowieka
> i tylko z człowieka[4]

> [Where does evil come from? / what do you mean where // from man / always from man / and only from man]

And Różewicz, whose entire postwar poetic career can be read as a long polemic with God concerning justice, agrees at least so far with traditional Christianity. It's as simple as that.

....

[4]   Tadeusz Różewicz, *Zawsze fragment: Recycling* [Always a Fragment: Recycling] (Wrocław: Wydawnictwo Dolnośląskie, 1998).

                                          CHARLES S. KRASZEWSKI

KAMIL MODRÁČEK, THE PUNY GOD

Of course, if Modráček were wise, or sane, enough to realise this, we would have no novel. And so, now let us turn to this most important figure of all, in more depth. For, above, all, it is Modráček who is at the centre of *The Vow*. It is the vow he made to his sister — however meritorious or lacking in merit that vow may be, however reasonable or insane — that is the motor to the entire story, and it is he who deserves most of our attention in a discussion of a novel so deep — no pun intended — that a discussion of all of its characters and motifs would require a book of its own.

Kamil Modráček is a loner. He is estranged from his wife, he has no friends to speak of, his sister (in whom he has perhaps an unhealthy interest) is taken away from him by Láska, and that one constant relationship of his life, which he shares with his 'invisible wife,' can hardly be called a human relationship of love. And so his creation of the underground city can be understood as a desperate attempt to collect a group of people who will love him, for they must. He is not just Noah with his ark, he is a morally ambiguous 'god' trying to create an Eden where there will be no fall, where he might walk in the garden in friendship with his creatures. Of course, this is naive, to say the least. For he is not God, to Whom man owes obedience and love and gratitude for His having brought him to life; no, Modráček is more or less a puny, negative image of God — he created no one's life, he ended the lives of twenty-one persons, as far as any of them could tell, by stealing them from the lives they led aboveground, with people whom they loved, to lock them up in a mediaeval vault deep underground. Where God intends freedom, Modráček imprisons, enslaves (they were, after all, forced to help him in the construction of his subterranean opus). So his dream for a little paradise may not be crazy as much as childish, or crazy in an innocent way: the very wrongest realisation of childhood longings for a peaceful world of friendship and harmony. That it had no chance of being realised is something that he himself perhaps sensed. As he is about to leave them for good, their ordeal nearly over, he wishes to bid them farewell:

Turning around, standing face to face with the half-circle that the people now formed, he assayed a friendly smile. But that smile didn't quite work. He had sensed that this farewell of his with them wouldn't be worth much, but he had no idea that it would actually be impossible. Right now, he wanted to say something, but his tongue cleft to the roof of his mouth and — why not admit it? — his chin nearly trembled. But on their faces, there was no movement whatsoever.

Well, maybe he is a little crazy. After all, he was stunned at the manner in which 'somehow none of [them] were taken with the thought,' when, in apricot season, he offered to cart down bushels of the fruit so that twenty-one adults might 'make preserves until [they] keeled over!' Váša the lifeguard from the Zábrdovice baths puts his finger right on it when he snaps, 'What, when you were a little boy, did you experience a big apricot boil at your grandmama's and now you want to spread the joy among us?' Certainly, one definition of insanity is to be so overcome with your own *idée fixe* that you are literally unable to understand the effect that your actions have on another person; how any 'reasonable' person might be unable to comprehend the logic of your progress, or how, really, you have your victim's best interests in mind. It is for this reason that, as innocent as the apricot boil idea seems to be, we cannot have sympathy for Modráček. A good portion of his insanity certainly is his lack of empathy for others. Consider, for example, what he says about his appropriation of and use of the gold and jewels left behind in the cavern by its previous inhabitants, whether Germans or Jews, or Germans secreting the wealth robbed from the Jews of Brno during the long night of the Holocaust. Modráček has a tinge of conscience at so liquidating the wealth of others for his own benefit, but he rationalises his behaviour immediately:

> For that reason I can perhaps consider my discovery an inheritance from those who had to abandon everything when they tried to find some path, some way, to remain at least a little alive. And after all, I hadn't broken into this mediaeval vault, this their underground place of refuge, by force, like some burglar. No, I'd pierced into it by pure accident, during that wild frenzy of mine, which perhaps they themselves would be able to understand, just like all outcasts and outlaws who fight back against institutionalised hatred in explosions of helpless rage.

Yet, in reference to his own 'tenants,' he doesn't understand that for them *he* is a hated institution, which projects, if not an institutionalised hatred, at least an institutionalised unconcern with their wills and rights. Modráček's lack of empathy is actually infuriating. During the apricot-boil episode, he says to his prisoners with a smile: 'All you need do is ask [...] just tell me what you need and I'll bring it all down here for you, I'd be delighted to.' What they need? They need their freedom. But that can't be 'brought down here,' and so it's out of the question.

Modráček's obtuseness is, or has become, a pronounced trait of his character. He — like we all — has a healthy terror of prisons, something that is made clear when he describes his attempts at tracking down his sister after her arrest by the StB. Stonewalled by everyone he queries as to her whereabouts:

> Modráček wanted to try his luck in the prisons of Brno, as well. But the mere sight of those huge, gloomy edifices filled him with terror. He'd never before considered how deeply prison architecture might depress a person: the whole intention of which was not to include in its design anything slightly uplifting or aesthetic, but to create a dead monolith of spiritual emptiness!

How strongly these words strike us when we recall that, whatever he choose to call his 'subterranean horizontal city,' it's still a prison, and the people who populate it didn't volunteer for residence there — he literally plucked them from the street and incarcerated them within it. His childish regard for his 'tenants' or 'lodgers' as he calls them can be disarming — as Alžběta Hajná reports: 'Mr Architect indulged us with a little grass down here and some shrubs, even tulip beds, just about everything that can bear this hothouse regimen of ours without sky and much space,' but the fact remains: no matter how pleasant you make it, a prison is still a prison. And, as Hajná — happy enough to be incarcerated alongside Dan Kočí (again: sex in a cage) — develops her thought: 'but beneath this low cavern vault some days I feel that I'd be happy to trade Dan Kočí for a walk lined with chestnut trees or a gigantic kingly walnut or an even grander holm-oak of the sort I used to go visit in Lužánky.'

Another characteristic of insanity, I reckon, is the inability to understand, or accept, the fact of one's guilt, the inability to accept responsibility for one's actions, the blame for which one is quite happy to lay at someone else's feet. In the case of mad Kamil Modráček, he uses the same tropes of predestination which we've already debunked to exculpate himself from responsibility for something he knows, deep down, is wrong, convinced that he is under the influence of some will other than his own. He describes his extraction of his father's manuscript thus:

> One evening upon returning home I pulled out a large packet of my father's unpublished writings from behind some books on the bookshelves. To the very last moment, I had no idea why I was doing what I was doing; what was inducing me to ferret through those old papers at that very moment.

We will pass over the fact that nothing in the scene prepares us for a suggestion of supernatural agency here; this is not Dante's son having a prophetic dream about the location of the missing 'heavenly' cantos of the *Paradiso*. But Modráček is convinced that he is somehow being 'led' to the actions he undertakes. To give just two more examples, from among many, when he discovers the forgotten poster of the SNB operative, the destruction of which will reveal to him the fateful undergrounds of Brno, he says: 'Nearby, a pickaxe was lying on top of a large box, just as if someone had placed it there for me,' and later, after the discovery had been made: 'I knew that that mediaeval vault had revealed itself to me at precisely the right moment; that someone had carefully prepared it for me, just as I had been led to those bookshelves and induced to rummage through the writings my father had left behind.'

No. All of this is nothing but an attempt at rationalising actions which, deep within him, he knows to be wrong. If one is merely the instrument of a higher power (passing over, for the sake of argument, the rightfully discredited Nuremberg Defence), who is to blame for the evil one commits? There may be some tenuous, and perhaps none too convincing, yet all the same comprehensible reasons for his decision to pronounce a sentence upon the head of the person he blames for the death of his sister, but is there any excuse for the composition of his human menagerie? As explained, from a distance, by Luděk, the contemporary student of Russian philology whose interest in Modráček's history seems something of an obsession itself:

> In the end, Modráček understood it all as a vocation, a mission. On the one hand, he kept the promise he had made to his dead sister, his vow to snatch her murderer and punish him with a sentence of life imprisonment, while on the other, by a chance set of circumstances, and random motivations, he broadened that mission of his by degrees: to preserve some sort of pattern of humanity from that which threatened them up above.

This is a megalomania bordering on a god-complex, which (as my entry for the understatement of the year award), I will state is a rather problematical attitude. If we are looking for proof of anyone's insanity, this sort of thing is fairly convincing.

But if Modráček is a 'god,' is he a just god? The very fact of his imprisoning people who have done him no harm is evidence enough of his injustice. Even stronger evidence against him is presented by his initial motivation to impose his (punitive) will on another human being. At first glance, the motivation to take vengeance upon a criminal who is otherwise untouchable seems rational. It is, after all, the common theme of the great majority of black-and-white-hatted Hollywood vengeance trash. It is so understandable as to be almost syllogistic: a) Lieutenant Láska's role in my sister's death deserves to be punished. b) The apparatus of 'justice' in this country protects criminals such as Lieutenant Láska, so he will not be punished by the proper authorities. c) Therefore, I shall punish Lieutenant Láska myself. Or, as Modráček puts it: 'Láska must meet with a just punishment, such as refers to a higher justice, far removed from that of the inhuman Communist regime.' The problem with this is not only that Modráček is neither God nor cognisant of God's will in this matter, but that vengeance is not justice. Furthermore, there is the matter — not unconnected with the fact of Kamil Modráček's being far from omniscient — of Lieutenant Láska's humanity:

> Where's Anička?
> Playing outside in the courtyard, Marta answered. That's not an answer to make Láska very happy. The courtyard in question was full

of garbage cans and rotting mattresses, rusted and hole-riddled metal pots. Rats ran about there, and at nighttime drunks would piss down into it from the gallery running outside their doors. Láska fears for his daughter with a tormenting fear. Sometimes, during an interrogation, he'd grow suddenly still. His gaze would drift until his eyes came to rest somewhere, up on the ceiling, let's say… Once it even so happened that Láska's victim had to clear his throat once, twice, to jog the Lieutenant back into the present moment, so as to get on with the interrogation.

Láska's love for his daughter and his need to protect her is a perfect thematic rhyme for Modráček's love for his sister. By depriving Anička of her father for having first deprived him of his sister (even if this were true), Modráček is not acting justly — the strict 'eye for an eye' justice has been abrogated over two thousand years ago. To lift the matter out of the context of Judeo-Christian theology altogether, simply and philosophically put, one cannot set right one immoral action by perpetrating another action that is just as immoral. The two actions cancel each another out, as far as the balance of morality is concerned, and all parties are left with empty hands. Petra James' words concerning the subtitle of *The Vow* are worth remembering here:

> The book is thus conceived by the author as a requiem for the victims of the Stalinist era of 1950s Czechoslovakia, represented in Kratochvil's text by his mother (herself a victim of the communist persecution to whom the book is dedicated and who appears as a minor character in the novel), Modráček's sister, and the policeman Láska, unjustly imprisoned and punished.[5]

If Kamil Modráček is a god, he is one of those very unsatisfying ones we come across in our pre-Christian culture. As we know, the gods of the Greek and Roman pantheons were different from us in one thing, and one thing

5   Petra James, 'The Trauma of "Enforced Disappearance" as a Topic in Central European Fiction after 1989,' in Florin Abraham and Réka Földváryné Kiss (eds.), *Remembrance and Solidarity. Studies in 20th Century European History*, No. 6 (2018), p. 73.

only: they were immortal. This in itself is problematical, and cuts right at the root of any sympathy we may have for Modráček's situation, and how he deals with it. The Greeks, like Homer and Sophocles, seem to have accepted the sort of gods their culture presented them with in fearful reverence, if not, at least, with a shrug. Virgil, closer to our time, has a heart like ours. He wants his gods to be just; he wants them to be the incarnation of impartial justice, of goodness, but — his mythology will not let him. As close as he gets to shaking his fist at an incomprehensibly shoddy Olympus is in his *Aeneid*, where, upon painting the perfect portrait of the evil, arbitrary god in Juno, who, although she knows that she cannot forestall the founding of Rome, kicks and scratches all the way, sacrificing entire nations of people — even those she supposedly favours, like Dido and Turnus — to her pride, gasps, *Tantaene animis caelestibus irae?* [Can such anger reside in breasts divine?, I.11]. Modráček is such a petty 'god.' He has nothing but power. A chilling hint of this is given earlier on in the work, in the words that Modráček directs at Lieutenant Láska during the first of the interrogation sessions that we witness. He is discussing the manner in which the Germans understood the word 'work':

> They had a completely different understanding of the word 'work,' just as they had in the case of a whole bunch of other words. After all, you're quite aware that above the gates of the concentration camps they placed the words Arbeit macht frei.

In the context in which we find these comments, we take them to be sarcastic, a pinch of biting back at the hand wielding the whip, the iota of snarky rebellion that the powerless victim feels himself enabled to indulge in. And so does Láska interpret them: 'You want to lecture me now?' Later on, however, toward the end of the book, when Luděk and Petra are discussing the matter with the (chillingly) cold interest that makes documentaries about murderers so riveting (and which itself says a lot about our human nature), the words take on a completely different meaning:

> Now, I still don't understand how he was able to keep control of those twenty-one lodgers — why they didn't rise up in revolt against him.

By force, obviously. Every Utopia is a concentration camp. [...] Let us not forget that, among the items he had discovered in that subterranean German hodge-podge there were also two pistols: a 7.65mm Walther and a 9mm Smith and Wesson. He did his best to remove any doubt from their minds that he would not hesitate to use them.

With this in mind, it seems that Modráček was not necessarily speaking in a manner which sets the Nazis on one side, and himself on another, i.e. how 'they' understood things as opposed to how 'we' or 'I' do; he was giving voice to one possible manner of human expression, such as he would put into practice himself if it so suited him. To return to Alžběta Hajná's account, we find Modráček actually using the same sort of euphemistic imagery to cover his evil as that found in the showers of Auschwitz, with their gay decorative tiles of water sports:

> I managed, the architect said, to squeeze into an area that is none too large everything that you need for a comfortable life, and I did everything that was in my power, I really like it when you say things like that to us, Dan Kočí said at that, we worked like slaves at this avant-garde architectural opus of yours, just like the slaves that built the pyramids while you just strolled about with a pistol at your hip and we considered ourselves fortunate that you didn't urge us on with whips and cat-o-nine-tails.

It is in this very aspect of his story, where it doesn't even occur to Modráček that his 'underground Utopia' doesn't just mirror the Communist 'Utopia' above, but actually Buchenwald, Theresienstadt and Auschwitz, that Kratochvil's story explodes beyond 1950s Czechoslovakia to reach us — overcoming me, as I said at the outset, in a small church in upstate New York.

HI, I'M KAMIL. PLEASED TO MEET YOU

Modráček's story is bigger than him. Kratochvil will not permit us the comfort of using the architect as a scapegoat. To return to the sociological/psychological eloquence of *The Vow*, it is patent that this is a novel which is a deft, and depressing, psychological study of human nature. Although I beg not to be misunderstood here according to the jargon of contemporary liberal sociobabble, *The Vow* is a study of relationships of power.

> Whenever I would enter the stationhouse on Běhounská I would submit myself to a process, which had something of the invariability of strict ritual to it. The StB goon who served as porter had to call upstairs and wait for confirmation that, indeed, I had been summoned. Upstairs, of course, they always took their time. So I would stand there, and in the interim, which sometimes stretched into quite a long period of time, while the StB functionary seemed to take no notice of me. But God forbid that I should make the slightest movement in any direction. No, I had to stand there rooted to the spot. At most, I might shift my weight from one foot to the other, or flex my fingers and toes. Then, at last, the phone would ring and it would be confirmed from above that I had been summoned.

As we have said, the oppressed become oppressors in their turn. Whenever the torturer-in-chief cedes his place, one of the previously tormented is more than willing to jump behind the controls and administer the same voltage to those further down the food-chain. Could this be learned behaviour? Or is it, as I suggested at the outset, something endemic to human nature?

Most shiver-inducing of all is the way that, for each 'rebel' like Dan Kočí, who won't allow Modráček to get away with that kind of thing, as Alžběta tells us, there are collaborators down below, too: 'constantly there are found amongst us people such as cooperate with Mr Architect.' That is to say, there are Capos in Modráček's Concentration Camp Eden, who not only accept the new reality, but take their oppressor's side. Whether this is Stockholm Syndrome or a pragmatic desire to reap rewards rather than face punishments is rather beside the point. What we see here is the horror of human nature — the facility to adapt even past self-defence. Another question we might pose (but not wish to consider too closely!) is: Does the experience of being imprisoned in an exploitative, and threatening, environment such as a concentration camp or an 'underground Utopia' such as Modráček constructed, and the consequent decision to cooperate with one's exploiters, signify a change in a given subject's personality, or a discovery of the same? The humanist would prefer the first, exculpatory, version: had this or that person not been put in a situation in which he or she felt that survival depended on morally disreputable behaviour, he or she would never have indulged in it. The realist, or pessimist, will say: opportunity makes the thief. Perhaps Alžběta's words concerning the rather repugnant character of the rather *fauve* chef can be extended to all of Modráček's tenants: 'I'm certain that he was no different before Modráček snatched him.' Despite all the fantastic and 'magical-realistic' qualities of Kratochvil's writings, *The Vow* is firmly grounded in reality. Quoting Aleš Haman, Michaela Wronová reminds us that:

> In his work, Kratochvil does not employ motifs that would shock the reader with strong improbability. Rather, while maintaining the characteristics of fantasy his fiction remains firmly grounded in realia that do not surpass the limits defined by the possibilities of our sensory perception of the world as it is.[6]

And this goes both for improbable, but still conceivable situations in the physical world, such as Modráček's construction of the first part of his underground city by himself (who helps him to bring down, and set up, the armoured door?) and in the moral sphere of his characters' actions.

Perhaps it can be extended to us, too. Kratochvil deftly insinuates the 'puny god' who lives inside us all when he has his narrator set a thumbtack on the floor, point up, not once, not twice, but thrice over the space of less than three hundred pages. The last time this occurs is in 'our' twenty-first century:

> Luděk, it's eight minutes after midnight. Can I open the window?
> Sure.
> And Petra got up out of bed naked, and trotted over to the window. But the narrator, who's already taken a liking for this, has set a thumbtack on her path. Sharp end pointing upwards.

....

6   Michaela Wronová, 'Fantastické momenty v české metafyzické detektivce' [Fantastic Moments in Czech Metaphysical Detective Writing], in Tereza Dědinová (ed.), *Na rozhraní světů. Fantastická literatura v mezioborovém zkoumaní* [At the Interface of Worlds. Interdisciplinary Research into Fantastic Literature] (Brno: Filozofická fakulta Masarykovy univerzity, 2016), p. 304.

'The narrator's already taken a liking for this' sort of sadism. It is a petty sort of god, unworthy of anyone's worship, who traps flies in order to pull off their wings.

Yet — is that not the sort of 'god' who lurks in each one of us?

It is a premise that can be entertained. At any rate, as we said, by his manipulation of time, Kratochvil will not allow us the comfort of holding this perversion at arm's length, of saying 'sure, in 1950s Czechoslovakia, maybe, but not here, not now,' as people in the West used to do when confronted with Orwell's description of 'thoughtcrime' before the imposition of expected uniformity of liberal attitudes led to 'cancel culture.'[7]

He achieves the same thing 'geographically,' and culturally. For Kratochvil spreads his idea of housing as incarceration — that 'underground horizontal city' — beyond the borders of Czechoslovakia and the Iron Curtain with his reference to Le Corbusier's 'honeycomb' construction in Marseille, from which Modráček first drew inspiration. Le Corbusier's Unité d'habitation is described in the work as 'a comfortable and elegant human apiary' and thus: a housing conglomeration for drones!

And the first time Modráček penetrates the underground, his description of a portion of it reminds us of Notre Dame du Haut: 'From there I discovered a cavern, a sort of transverse cave interrupting the smoothly running wall, which somehow suggested that it had been used for cultic purposes. An underground chapel cut from the rock, with stepped altar and hardly discernible, blurred frescos?' Ronchamp is also planned so as to recreate the experience of a mysterious underground cultic centre, such as Les Trois Frères, with dimly-lit interior accessed only by 'squeezing' one's way through a barely perceptible entrance. And so again Kratochvil is not

....

[7] An American football coach, Jon Gruden, was 'outed' in late 2021 for having made disparaging comments in private e-mails that were leaked to the press. In her column, 'Football Made Jon Gruden. Now the NFL Must Reckon with its Creation' in the 12 October 2021 issue of the *Washington Post*, Sally Jenkins considers the fact that Gruden expressed himself thus *privately* while acting differently (politely? civilly?) in public to be an exacerbating circumstance: 'He wrote those things between the ages of 47 and 54, some of them as recently as 2017, and it matters not at all that they are private expressions. In fact, that only makes them worse — there's an unnerving divergence from his chatty charm-boy act for cameras that won him such rich contracts. He has spent his life culling rewards in a public-facing business, in which 70 percent of player-colleagues are Black and nearly half the audience is women, in which he had every opportunity to grow a respectful heart.' Basically, she suggests that the real criminality lies in his thought, not his actions, as he never expressed himself thus publicly — just the opposite!

allowing us in the 'free world' — be that beyond the Iron Curtain in the Communist days, or in post-1989 Brno for that matter — the luxury of saying: *Oh, that's over there, that has nothing to do with us,* as people in the West used to do with books like *Animal Farm* and *1984,* before the 'progress' of technology made it so that we all carry around telescreens in our pockets, all the time. The entire thrust of the novel is once more emphasised: This can happen anywhere; don't be afraid of that Kamil Modráček, who was burnt to a crisp in a car accident in the 1950s, be afraid of the Kamil Modráček who's inside you, right now.

AND IN THE END MCCARTNEY'S RIGHT AGAIN

(I cited *Paradise Lost;* can I not cite *Abbey Road*?)

Time in *The Vow* exceeds the 1950s and the 2000s to disappear into eternity. And that's where I was sitting when Kratochvil's question flashed in upon me, for, as Mircea Eliade reminds us, the boundaries of sacred space — such as a church — don't just divide the sanctuary from the street, they are a *limes* that, on account of the presence of the sacred and the sacrament enacted within them, lift the persons congregated inside out of vulgar, temporal time and into eternity.

When, at the beginning of the work Modráček addresses us, he does so in full knowledge of how his history has played out. Thus, he addresses us from eternity, for he is dead. He appeals to us, his 'imaginary

judges,' which seems an honest thing to do, but actually, slyly, he's inviting us to be who he was: judging others, acting like little gods ourselves. And wasn't that exactly what I was doing when that sermon was being delivered, and I pronounced my verdict concerning what 'all those others' were thinking (thoughtcrime!)? The question, therefore, that the book presented to me at that point was: how much of Kamil Modráček is in you?

It's a clever ploy in which Kratochvil indulges in *The Vow,* and when you see what he's doing in presenting the history of Kamil Modráček to you, it hits you like a punch to the solar plexus.

When, at the end of the novel, in an example of what Lubomír Machala notes as Kratochvil's tendency to create the 'novel as a system spread wide,'[8]

....

[8]   Lubomír Machala, 'Petrovské prozaické kvarteto jako zrcadlo současné literární situace

                                        CHARLES S. KRASZEWSKI

the author, who had inserted himself and his family's story into the fictional world of *The Vow*, appears in his own voice and tells us about 'extracting' Modráček's 'tenants' from their underground prison, this is no facile Deus ex machina. Rather, in his disrobing of the usual fictional suspension of disbelief in order to reveal himself, the writer, as the 'creator' of his fictional world, he is putting Modráček in his place: there is a 'higher power' in this novel just as there is a higher power in the world; it is not for us to take such decisions and judgements. Zbyněk Fišer's general comment on Kratochvil's moral approach to literature seems spot on here:

> Kratochvil both feels and clearly shows that the weak and the decent were, are and will always be the most endangered group in human society. Therefore, he takes the side of the good and believes that evil will be punished — even if it takes supernatural forces to effect this.[9]

The fact that he 'assures' us of the safety of characters we are (presumably) concerned with is an appeal to our better angels. If we can have concern for figments of a writer's imagination, what should be our attitude towards the real men and women of flesh and blood who are sitting next to us, passing us on the street — or, especially, towards that idiot on the highway riding on our backside and flashing his high-beams at us. How dare he? Does he not know who we are? Well, do we ourselves?

The problem may be: he knows exactly who he is: Kamil Modráček, self-important, puny, vindictive god.

Oh, yeah, that other writer. St James. In his letter, when he's discussing the matter of faith and works (and stressing the fact that the former is rather insufficient without the latter): You say you believe in God? 'Thou dost well: the devils also believe and tremble.'

....

(Nad knihami Jiřího Kratochvila, Petra Ulrycha, Alexandry Berkové a Michala Viewegha)' [The Petrov Prose Quartet as a Mirror for the Contemporary Literary Situation (on the Books of Jiří Kratochvil, Petr Ulrych, Alexandra Berková and Michal Viewegh), *Česká literatura*, 2001, Vol. 49, No. 6 (2001), p. 646.

9   Zbyněk Fišer, 'Fantastično a postmoderna: role fantastična v díle Jiřího Kratochvila' [The Fantastic and the Postmodern: the Role of the Fantastic in the Work of Jiří Kratochvil], in Dědinová, p. 273.

In that sense, I believe in Kamil Modráček.
And I tremble.

ONE QUICK NOTE ABOUT THE TRANSLATION

Our translation is based upon the original version of *Slib,* published in 2009 by Druhé Město of Brno. The poetic construction of *Slib* is elegant, shifting, and so carefully crafted as to enjoin upon the translator the same great care in his work, so as not to disrupt any significant formal element found in the original. In this endeavour, I may have erred on the side of caution by scrupulously hewing to Kratochvil's presentation of direct speech as hardly ever set off from the general narrative flow by punctuation, whether that be inverted commas or dashes. Likewise, I have tried to reproduce the author's rather idiosyncratic use of italics. In the original, italics seem to be used only sparingly, for emphasis. Foreign words, which I would otherwise italicise, are left in normal type in the original, and so they remain here. The one concession to English usage that I have made is the italicisation of the titles of books and films. Hopefully, these remarks will provide a sufficient explanation to the reader of what might otherwise seem a cavalier approach to typesetting.

Williston, VT
23 October 2021

THE VOW

A REQUIEM FOR THE FIFTIES

*This novel is dedicated
to the memory of my mother,
the real person
behind the events described.*

PART ONE

THE VILLA WAGENHEIM

But now we have to step back just a bit. Brno at the beginning of the fifties. Not a pretty picture, believe you me. My studio on Kounicová — by then Lenin St — had been turned into an affiliate workshop of the Municipal Design Bureau. So I wasn't an architect any more — just another office drudge at a draughting table. And there were rows of such tables in our 'workers' collective.' Our collective task was, among other things, the further development of the barracks in Židenice, and the construction of an apartment block in the Socialist, and so perhaps more or less Neoclassical style, on Botanická St. I didn't allow myself to get pally, to say nothing of becoming friends, with anyone in that collective, for I considered them all to be intruders. They had confiscated my studio and assigned six other fellows, two of them jabbering old grandpas, unremarkable old school architects, whom in the old days I had never come across at dinners or vernissages or garden parties, just rubbish blown in from somewhere on the peripheries of the trade. The other four were kids, who clearly gave me to understand that they were of that generation who were to build those 'sunlit cities' that were supposed to spring up here suddenly like mushrooms after the rain. To tell the truth, we were a sort of factory of building projects — a fact testified to by the additional deployment among us of a gang of girl cartoonists (I used to call them cheerleaders), whose job it was to copy our drawings, just like a conveyor belt, with ink and mechanical pencils via tracing paper. And down below we had doorkeepers with time cards, and if I were even only five minutes late, there would be serious consequences, which with that ugly smudge on my copybook from the days of the Protectorate, I simply couldn't afford.

Now this smudge of mine, yes, I must begin with it, has a name: the Villa Wagenheim. Which is also my dubious, disreputable claim to architectural fame. I had the privilege of selecting a prime location for it: between Leopold Bauer's Villa Russig and the Villa Tesařová of Bohuslav Fuchs, that is, on Hroznová St, on the site of the once renowned vineyards of Brno. Yes, it was there that I created my strange masterpiece, architect Kamil Modráček's Villa Wagenheim.

Jawohl, Kamil Modráček, that's me, at your service. Of course, Gruppenführer SS Günter Wagenheim didn't enjoy it for long. A mere two years after the villa was approved, Wagenheim was executed by the Nazis themselves, for being implicated in a conspiracy against Hitler, after which the villa was made over into the third central Brno office of the Gestapo (the two previous ones being the Löw-Beer Villa and the law faculty of the university). These days the building is peacefully occupied by some notable Communist potentates, who don't seem to be bothered by the fact that it is laid out with its four wings forming a great Hakenkreuz. This can especially be noticed from a bird's eye view. Not too long ago, during an air festival, an aeroplane full of working-class youths took off from Slatina for a sightseeing turn around Brno. As soon as it drew near Pisárky and was about to fly over the Villa Wagenheim, stewardesses covered the eyes of the children with some black blindfolds, which had been specially prepared against the event. Since the number of kids was greater than the available blindfolds, the stewardesses dutifully covered the eyes of the last two children with their own hands.

So where did we leave off? said Lieutenant Láska, and I watched as he shuffled his papers, to pull out, at last, always the same questions, which I had answered again and again over the space of several months. It's possible that he was counting on lulling my attention to sleep so that by the gruelling repetition of the same questions I would let down my guard and give perhaps a different answer, to my detriment.

Does the name Gruppenführer SS Günter Wagenheim mean anything to you?

It does.

You have met with him?

I have.

Once, twice, or more than that?

Rather more.

And you would meet with him in the Gestapo building on Veveří St, or in his apartments in Stalin Gardens?

Back then it was not called Stalin Gardens, but Koliště, Deblingasse. But you're correct about the rest. I would meet up with him both in the Gestapo building on Veveří, and in his apartment on Koliště.

And so one might say that you met with him frequently?

For a certain time, which didn't last too long, I met with him frequently enough.

Now, don't tell me that you didn't know that he had the blood of Czech patriots on his hands — that he compiled the lists of those who ended up being executed in the courtyard of the Kounicová student dormitory. And that you were therefore meeting with a German beast.

I didn't.

How is it possible that you didn't know, since he trusted you so much as to meet with you in his own home?

We never spoke of anything besides the construction of his villa in Pisárky. When he needed to speak with me about the villa, he would send a messenger for me. And when it so happened that he was not at work in the Gestapo building on Veveří, that messenger would take me to his apartment.

And you call what he was doing 'work?'

Pardon me? I don't understand your question.

You said, 'when it so happened that he was not at work…' So you call that 'work,' drawing up the names of those who are to be executed?

They had a completely different understanding of the word 'work,' just as they had in the case of a whole bunch of other words. After all, you're quite aware that above the gates of the concentration camps they placed the words Arbeit macht frei.

You want to lecture me now?

I don't.

So then, answer me this fundamental question. Why did you choose a giant swastika for the footprint of that villa?

At the request of Gruppenführer SS Wagenheim.

You might have refused him. You might always have found some technical excuse to refuse him that.

Once I accepted the commission, I had to accept it in full — and so the swastika layout as well. It was too late to back away. He wasn't stupid; he wouldn't have swallowed any such excuse. And anyway, I couldn't refuse, because I didn't want to put my sister's life in danger.

Aha — the life of little sis, Láska smiled. So, tell me, how did it go with the life of that sister of yours?

I think I've told you already, several times.

You want to lecture me, again?

My sister Eliška, a painter and graphic artist, fell into the clutches of the Gestapo because some leaflets had been reproduced in her studio and on her press. They tossed her in gaol, and she would've ended up either in a concentration camp, or executed herself. And so I went to the Gestapo, and they referred me to Günter Wagenheim. But he had no intention of chatting with me, and the whole affair would have come to a swift end had it not been for a serendipitous coincidence. I was already on my way out when a secretary appeared at the door with some business on which the Gruppenführer was obviously waiting with much impatience. He was a Jew, she said, and he's already been gassed.

Wagenheim gave out a furious growl. Another Jew! So, what — all the good architects around here are Kikes?

At that, I turned around at the threshold and said that I'm an excellent architect myself, and I'm no Jew.

Was anyone speaking to you? But he motioned me to a chair. How do you know that you're an excellent architect?

I was ready to declare myself Albert Speer if it would only buy me some more time to talk with him, to keep trying to fight for my sister's life. So I risked it and just clenched my jaw and said, You're looking to build something? I can build anything, from a doghouse to an opera to a hockey rink.

I don't need a doghouse or an opera or a hockey rink.

But it was clear that I'd succeeded in changing the tenor of our conversation. I had him. And that's how I learned that he wanted to build in Brno (Operation Barbarossa was still in its early stages, and he still believed in the triumph of the Reich), and that he'd already found himself a lot in Hroznová St, or Traubengasse. I offered to build him the most beautiful villa the world had ever heard of there, and for my payment I asked no honorarium in return, just my sister's release. At the start it looked like he would explode and tear into me, but he just grew quiet for a moment and then he said: I'll let you know.

A week hadn't passed before they released Eliška, and I met with him and set to work. I built a villa for a Gestapo man, but by the same token, I not only saved my sister's life, but also fended off the danger of her revealing under torture the names of the other people involved in that leaflet action.

Come on, don't tell me that the Gestapo would just let their prey escape like that.

And yet I am, it so happens, an excellent architect. This was placed on one dish of the scale, and on the other — those couple of clowns with their leaflets. Certainly, they'd already come to the conclusion that those paperboys didn't belong to any sort of armed insurrectionary group, but that they were nothing more than harmless idealists — hundreds of whom they'd put to death anyway, as it was. So they let my sister go, but for sure they continued to watch her. And I didn't take a single crown from the Gruppenführer for that villa, notwithstanding the fact that he insisted on some honorarium.

But you did construct the building which is the city's shame, having as it does the Nazi symbol for a floor plan.

It can always be demolished, just as the German House on Red Army Square was.

You will know that, unfortunately, the villa is also one of the architectural jewels of Brno.

The same building can't be both an architectural jewel and a city's shame.

You're going to lecture me again?

Right after the war, when somebody wanted to blame me for the work I did for the Gruppenführer, the participants of that leaflet action immediately came forward and declared that, without a doubt, I had saved their lives — and no postwar court even lifted a finger against me. But you already know that, for sure.

If I were you, I wouldn't appeal to those leaflet clowns, as you just termed them. Two of them are already in gaol. They had been preparing a coup d'état in collaboration with the American central espionage agency. But I wanted to ask you something else. How is it that such an excellent architect, as you've just declared yourself to be, is living in some low-grade flat in a tenement on Běhounská? How is it that you've not built yourself a villa in one of the more exclusive neighbourhoods? Since that's the case of any Brno architect (here he glanced at his papers) that you'd care to name: Kalivoda, Kumpošt, Fuchs, Polášek, Kroha?

Back then I still thought, and that for a long while, that Lieutenant Láska was just playing a game with me. Maybe he didn't have anything better to do, and so was just practising his chops on whatever material had come to hand: this case of mine was nothing more than an amusing exercise. There were other indications in support of this. For example, the design bureau where I was employed was located quite near the Ministry of the Interior on Lenin St — where all of those under investigation by the StB[1] were summoned. Now in my case, as luck would have it, I was summoned to the police station on Běhounská, which was a fair haul from the design bureau. But on the other hand, this was only two doors down from Běhounská 3, where I lived on the third floor. Which of course wasn't worth shit to me, as I was always interrogated during working hours, and after which I had to return to the office. And Lieutenant Láska always noted down the hour and minute of my departure from the interrogation session on the pass. And at the porter's back at the office the timecards awaited me, so upon arrival I would hand the pass over to the porter, who was certainly an StB stooge himself, and he would compare the time of my arrival with the departure time from the police station. And when it seemed to him that my road from the interrogation took longer than it should he would tell me that he had to report that somewhere, and that if I'm going to continue to fritter away the working day like that, it might well happen that I'd have a surprise waiting for me upon arrival. I knew that those weren't empty words he was speaking. And so I never had a chance to drop in at home. The only thing I was able to do as I passed Běhounská was to ring out 'Four Little Shepherds' on my doorbell downstairs in the foyer, as a signal to my wife that I'd survived the interrogation safe and sound, and that everything was OK.

And now I must confess that however troublesome it made my life, that StB game was actually almost pleasant. Now, I don't want to exaggerate here. I want to say that I didn't bitch and moan about it, because it humanised Lieutenant Láska for me. *Ludo, ergo sum.* See, I told myself, if that bastard

....

[1]   The State Security apparatus; in Czech *Státní bezpečnost* or StB for short.

has the ability to play, he can't be such a monster, and so the most you can fear is that he'll have a few more nasty chuckles on your account. Well then, have at it, you StB beast, as long as it's nothing worse than that. And so in this way I had even come to an understanding with it all, except that in reality everything was much, much worse. I had no idea of what was waiting for me.

THE TRAMWAY DREAM

Daniel Kočí sold meat in the butcher shop on Josefská St. He was an unskilled labourer in the trade, because he didn't like the job at all, and determined to devote no more time to it than was absolutely necessary. Actually, he would much rather have spent his time behind a counter selling buttons, pins, and thread, or tiles, flooring materials, and roofing shingles, if he had to be a seller of anything. But he'd come across nothing better, and there were no open slots anywhere save in the butcher shop. Basically, he was unhappy in this line of work; it was hard for him to bear the sight of all of those innards torn and chopped into portions, the bodies of animals turned inside out, and the hooks from which hung the remains of those pleasant and basically friendly creatures. And yet one might have thought that all this shouldn't really bother him, given that in his former profession he had often had to look upon the bodies of dead human beings — sometimes also abnormally torn by all those Brno Jack the Rippers. True, Dan was never quite thrilled when he was called to investigate bloody crimes, but, when it was necessary, he endured it rather well. Unlike the corpses of animals intended for human consumption, he was able to examine the dead bodies of people disfigured by wounds of murderous passion with a professional interest, which might have been mistaken by a chance passerby for professional delight. But it was decidedly nothing of the sort. Dan's real bailiwick, and perhaps even professional pleasure, were cases of marital infidelity. He liked snooping after unfaithful wives, and errant husbands as well. And then there were the occasional highlights: when, armed with his Leica, he succeeded in capturing an adulterous pair in flagranti, developing compromising photos from the film.

But now the end had come, officially, for private eyes. The communist régime had not only nationalised banks, mines, and factories, but, in very short order, all private enterprise as well, including that of private investigators. Just like any other person with an extraordinary ability, a unique talent, which was now stifled, and which he was supposed to just let go, Dan could not come to terms with this state of things. Whenever he caught sight of a woman on the street hurrying somewhere, he was able to distinguish, with a great degree of probability, the one who was rushing off to a hasty cuddle with a secret lover from the one who was on her way to pick up some shoes after they'd been repaired, or the one off to a real hen party with café Vienna and blueberry tarts. At such times he always sensed a very pleasant tickling somewhere in his abdominal cavity. But then he had to force his eyes away from the woman hastening to her adulterous games; whether he wanted to or not, he had to turn away, and the pleasure he'd felt was quickly transformed into a sourness, a knot in the stomach, which remained for a long time. It lasted so long that he began to wonder whether or not he ought to get that checked out, lest it be the symptom of some nasty illness or other. But of course that's just what it was: a disease, that fierce, stubborn, importunate talent that, denied again and again, turned at last upon its owner. For on the other hand, whenever he took on a case, illegally, on the black market, as it were, the blissful feeling would remain, while the sourness in his gut would disappear, and in his bowels there would reign again a harmonious relation between his somatic and psychic spheres.

Dan lived on Orlí, in a kind of rental block with an avant-corps on the corner, in which his second-floor bedroom was located. Most of the time, he shared that bedroom with a taciturn woman with naturally highlighted hair. And it was just that hair of hers, something quite exotic at the time, which had first attracted him to her. When, one day, he caught sight of those highlights in a crowd on a busy street, it was all over for Dan, amen; the same as it would have been for Odysseus had he not stopped up his ears with wax and had himself lashed to the mast in time. They weren't single, as it were, but they weren't living together either, or, as one put it back then, shacking up. The girl with the highlights in her hair — Brighty, he nicknamed her — was married; she belonged to a different household entirely. But what she shared with Dan, this was always stolen time, hours carefully scrounged and saved, and that in such an inventive manner, that the people who carried out that famous train robbery might well be envious. Besides all this, Dan had other women too, of whom the girl with highlights in her hair was well aware. They shared quite a peculiar bond, those two, but more of that later.

The butcher shop was literally just around the corner. Every morning, Dan hurried off to work, his head filled with nothing but delightfully shady scenarios. Still, time flowed hopelessly on. Until one day the phone rang. Dan got up from his supper (eggs and dumplings, with fresh lettuce from the nearby Zelný Rynek) and trotted out of the kitchen and into the foyer, where he made for the flower stand. It was only then that he pulled up short in surprise. For he didn't have a telephone. Never did. (In those days, only such civilians as physicians, governmental clerks, managers or, eventually, their deputies, had telephones.) He stood there musing for a second before returning to the table.

Something happen? asked the woman with the naturally highlighted hair.

No. No — I don't know…

Stomach ache, again? she asked, surprisingly. But then again, not all that surprisingly, for Dan had noticed, for some time now, that she was not only possessed of that uncommon, naturally highlighted head of hair, but also of the faculty of knowing things he'd never confided to her.

No, no aches or pains.

And then he just tried to explain it away. A day later, his boss at the butcher shop sent him off to the post office. He had gotten his receipt signed, and had just stepped outside, when, from the Alfa shopping centre across the way there emerged someone, with a wooden horse on wheels under his arm. This person visibly stiffened when he caught sight of Dan, pulling up short and staring at him. Dan was surprised at the sudden encounter as well, but he was certainly not as shocked as the other man. They stood there like that for a moment, each on his own pavement, looking at one another.

Then, Radek Stolař accompanied Dan all the way back to the butcher shop and waited until Dan had spoken to his boss, after which they went off to the café and sweet shop next door, which, even after the communist takeover, was still known as U Sedláčka.[2] Radek set the wooden pony down on the empty chair next to him, and at that split second — noticing a bent nail protruding from one of the pony's nostrils — Dan was struck with a

---

[2]   At the Little Farmer's — with its connotations of land ownership.

                                                                JIŘÍ KRATOCHVIL

lively sense of how far the two of them were now from their maturity exam, which had brought their schooldays at the Královopolské Gymnasium to a close; immortalia ne speres, monet annum et almum quae rapit hora diem, he thought, recalling those two lines of Horace about the passage of time, which somehow by oversight managed to remain in his head from those years of sitting at the school desk.

Radek Stolař raised high his arm and waved his hand until, at last, the waiter, who had been chatting up the girl at the coat check, deigned to approach their table. When he had ordered for Dan and himself, he returned to the matter that he'd already broached along the way: You know, I own a stonecutting workshop at the graveyard — right near the gate. Last evening, on my way from the workshop, I stopped in at the tavern U Mrtvoly.[3] I settled in there a good while, and then I fell asleep in the tram. It was just a little nap — I woke up when the tram bumped twice along the rails — but the way it is with me these days, just that little nap was enough for a longish dream. The only thing I remember from it was that I tried to contact you, to call you on the phone.

What? exclaimed Dan. Could you repeat that, please?

Last night, in my dream, it seemed to me that I called you on the phone.

That's what I thought you said. Can you tell me what time that was, more or less?

Radek grew a bit alarmed. Is something wrong? Did something happen?

Nah — it's stupid. Sorry. It doesn't matter what time it was. Anyway, I don't own a telephone.

Obviously I can't remember exactly when it was, but it could have been around 7:30, give or take ten minutes. Can I go on with my story?

Who's stopping you? Go right ahead! Dan glanced at what the waiter set before him and, to the great surprise of Radek Stolař, he proceeded to plunge his finger right into the thick cream that topped his café Vienna, after which he lifted it thoughtfully to his lips. Then he came to himself, licked his finger clean and wiped it on a paper napkin. It occurred to Radek that, at that moment, Dan had been a thousand miles away. When he returned, he carefully folded the napkin, set it in the ashtray, snuffled once with his

....

[3]   At the Cadaver. The same pub is mentioned in Jan Balabán's short story 'At the Communists,' collected in *Maybe We're Leaving*.

nose and said: So you called me on the phone. What did you want to talk to me about in that tramway dream of yours?

You didn't pick up.

I couldn't. Like I told you, I don't have a phone.

Of course. But I was only calling you in a dream. However, I was calling you for a very concrete reason. I wanted to ask if you still operated that old business of yours.

Yes?

And so now I'd like to take the occasion to ask you in person: Are you still active in that old job of yours?

Eh — you see for yourself what sort of job I'm active in now. If it was that you needed some offal meat for a stew, or a bone for your dog… You know yourself, damn it, who has the monopoly on murders these days, both great and small. Or maybe you don't? To get back in that business I'd have to worm my way in amongst the pigs, and that's one place, I hope, that you'll never find me.

No, you don't understand; it's not about that. This has nothing to do with any murder, great or small. And back then, you specialised in something quite different.

At this, of course, Dan's face lit up. Silently, he fixed Radek with his stare. Then he shook his head again. I'm not doing that any more either, of course. All jobs, you might say, have to be kosher these days.

He took a sip of his coffee, scalded his tongue, then chuckled: All right. I'll do it. But it's going to cost you. There are expenses in this line of work, and in order to take it on I'll have to ask for an unpaid holiday from my job.

But in order to talk it over fully, a chat in the pastry shop wouldn't suffice. On the contrary, both of them felt uncomfortable discussing it there, especially with that wooden horse on wheels constantly staring at them, as if with the eyes of Radek's youngest son.

They met again the next afternoon at Špilberk.[4] Eight times they climbed the hill to the fortress, and eight times they descended, just to go back up another eight times, all the while tearing everything apart and putting it

....

[4]   A thirteenth century Moravian hilltop castle in Brno, which was converted into a prison during the years of the Austro-Hungarian Empire.

back together again — that is, the case of Radek's wife. Radek laid out all of his bad suspicions, and in this way Dan came to know all he needed to know — above all, the fact that Radek wasn't looking for a divorce. No, he just wanted to be certain whether or not his wife was cheating on him, and, if so, then, with whom. So it all had to be carried out with the utmost discretion, and no cameras. Radek was in need of no corpus delicti for future use; all he was after was trustworthy information about how things stood.

One of the unwritten rules that, you might say, directly bear upon the ethics of this specialisation of Dan's was that he should warn his client to drop the matter right there; to stop worrying about getting to the bottom of it all, knowing the truth; to let sleeping dogs lie. Because that which in the light of all proven facts might appear to be something catastrophic, might well, from another perspective, turn out to be nothing more than an insignificant nothing — a speck of dust behind the eyelid, on account of which there was no good reason to pluck out the whole eye. And even though Radek stated that he didn't want to break up his marriage, didn't intend to at all, still Dan knew quite well that when a client finds himself faced with a reality that brooks no discussion, this can change him, unrecognisably. And so today's fact, which might turn out to be something totally different two weeks from now — after all, marital infidelities are mere sparks, which very seldom develop into raging infernos — can, when pitilessly dragged into the open, explode and sweep away an entire relationship, which before only needed a little work to repair. But this time, Dan offered no such word of warning, because he absolutely did not wish to discourage his client. Just the opposite: he was happy that, at last, he was again poised to practise the craft for which he had been put on this planet in the first place. And all things considered, the fact that he had heard the telephone he didn't even own ring in the foyer after Radek, in his dream, called his number, he took as a sign that he was doing the right thing. It never crossed his mind that it could be quite the other way round, and that that signal might also be a lure, tempting his feet on to the path that leads to Hell.

THE BUILDING ON BĚHOUNSKÁ

The building on Běhounská 3/5 is a standard four-storey rental building. But still and all, thanks to that historicist, eclectic façade, it fits within the long, nostalgic carnival range of architectural styles from the turn of the twentieth century that make Brno Brno. It was built by the Kletzl brothers, sons of a master mason, as their ambitious flagship structure. A building designed for rental flats, conceived on the plan of a modest urban palace composed of three horizontal sections, of which the middle sports a bay with a balcony and columns with Ionian capitals — simply put, a *bel étage*, as one said at the time, with a cordon cornice, and it was here the brothers set up shop. Above the balcony is a grinning face — a so-called mascaron — little gilded suns and an ambitiously imaginatively stylised decor. Sure, all of this outside stuff works, but just come in, and you are confronted at once by an uncomfortable stone staircase (obviously worn by the tread of that host of souls, now long past, who lived out their meaningless lives in this place), cast iron railings with leafwork designs, ugly walls like those of a prison, like those of some repulsive citadel, broken violet tiles, black electrical wiring boxes and — of course — no lift. The flats to the left are somewhat more spacious — of four rooms, their balconies opening out onto the courtyard shaft; the flats to the right are of three rooms, and are quite cut off, ungainly parcelled. In just such a flat on the third floor lives Kamil Modráček, the architect, joylessly at anchor here his whole life long. He has his studio in the largest room looking out onto the street, ever since they nationalised that one on Lenin St. Since we find ourselves alone in the room, let's make the most of the occasion. Let's go over to the window (I remind you that these are the early fifties) which looks out toward the restaurant U Cajplů across the way, and have a little chat about our architect.

First something pleasant, so as not to put you off him from the very start. And so, in the eyes of the new lords of thunder, the mortal sin of architect Modráček was not merely that villa he'd built for SS Gruppenführer Wagenheim, but above all his political convictions. For he did not belong to the prewar architectural left, but was, so to say, one white crow amongst all the red ones.

Well and good, but why was it that he was living in a tenement, at a time when other Brno architects such as Kumpošt, Kroha, Fuchs, Polášek and Kalivoda, for some time already had their own villas in the better parts of the city? Now, you might find the reason for this entertaining. For architect Modráček was never satisfied with petty things. He always aimed as high as possible, convinced that he had no right to think otherwise. He hadn't the slightest interest in mediocrity. And this, of course, discouraged clients and contractors. People who have a lot of cash are often swine. And because their boundless sense of their own importance fosters in them a taste for kitsch, and what's more, they are so certain of the rightness of their viewpoints, a good architect doesn't stand the slightest chance with them. And Modráček was aware of the fact that even a good architect, in order to engage in his profession, must aim to please his client and descend to his level, carefully avoiding all experiment, suppressing and denying his inventiveness. Modráček found a deterrent example of this in the person of Leopold Bauer, the architect who won fame as the designer of the first modernist domicile in Central Europe: the robust and at the same time elegant villa of the lawyer Reissig — an admirable toast raised in honour to the American architect Frank Lloyd Wright. For just ten years later, at the request of the manufacturer Hecht, he built — in the same Pisárky neighbourhood and even on the very same street — a conservatively planned building, a neoclassical patchwork, the stylistic decay of which so caught the eye of the Soviets, that they located their consulate here after the Communist seizure of power. Because Russians find kitsch as irresistible as blowflies dead bodies.

The interior of the tenement in which Modráček lived was nothing to brag about, yet it was not getting any worse, either. Each day he walked up to that third floor (plus mezzanine) with the conviction that, if ever he were to have a family, he would not want to have it here. He would not want his pregnant wife climbing to such heights over such difficult stairs with her precious cargo. He dreamed of having his own villa — a unique architectural wonder — somewhere in the Černá Pole or Úřednická neighbourhoods, or in Pisárky. But time was slipping by, and such was his professional intransigence that he only had the occasion to build one villa on the outskirts of Olomouc, and a family home for his little sister in the Žabovřesky section of Brno. This house was sort of a tentative variant of his own dream villa, but for all that it sucked in everything that he had earned from his work in Olomouc. Of course, he made a name for himself with those two villas, as Günter Wagenheim himself verified before entrusting the design of his Brno villa to him — which in turn certainly saved the life of Modráček's sister, but was no help at all to his plans for building his own home. However, just as soon as the war ended, he decided at last to realise his dream, and to start earning money in order to build it. And thus, in the end, did he retreat ingloriously from his 'aesthetic aristocracy' to sprinkle around Brno some 'adorable architectural dwarves,' as architect Kroha, Modráček's friend, gleefully commented — envious all the same of the kingly honorariums he was raking in for that postwar architectural rubbish. This was in 1947. But just as everything was beginning to fall into his lap, suddenly something went wrong; the window on Modráček's future closed forever, and he found himself imprisoned in the apartment block at Běhounská 3/5.

THE CASE OF RADEK'S WIFE

For the first three years following the end of the war, I still ran an ad in the papers: *Dan Kočí, alias Stanley Pinkerton Detective Agency. Services eminently professional, and eminently discreet. All types of investigations, as well as highly specialised tasks.*

For the longest time, my only sidearm was a camera with a flashbulb. But when I used the flash — and here I'm speaking of those *highly specialised tasks* — the adulterous couple caught in flagranti were well aware of the fact that the jig was up, and that the next step was divorce proceedings, in which the plaintiff would be cutting the adulterer off from any little portion gained through marriage or dowry. But more frequently, it so happened that my client didn't want the flash used, but merely expected the most discreet as possible establishment of the state of things.

Radek Stolař the stonecutter lived not far from the train station, in one of the rental blocks on Hybešova St. Along with his address, he provided me with three photographs of his wife, since, of course, he couldn't introduce me to her in person. She was an extremely attractive blonde. To this I hasten to add that Radek himself was a good looking fellow. His hard work at stonecutting and his boyish doggedness kept him in shape and young. They really made a beautiful married couple, but I can imagine that life can untwine even the most stunning married couples.

I took a leave of absence from work so that I could scope out in detail the daily routine of Radek's wife. From Radek I knew that she took care of both the house and a little garden walled in among the buildings; that she played the piano a bit, and took the dog on walks.

That's not very much, I think, to keep a woman as young as her busy, when you're away all day at the cemetery.

You're right. But I've also bought her a subscription to the People's Book Club. Last year they published *The Story of a Real Man*,[5] but they also brought out some sort of French novel, Madam Batory or something like that.

Madame Bovary?

O, that's it. A nice selection, right?

Suppose so. But don't ask me. Ask your wife.

Lucie. Her name is Lucie.

Hybešova is quite a busy street. Along it trundle, from the train station to Mendlák,[6] and from Mendlák to the train station, trucks piled with all sorts of stuff, from coal to crates of greens to barrels of beer from the nearby Starobrněnské Brewery. I calculated which window on the second floor belonged to the Stolař apartment, and took up such a position so as not to be in a direct line of sight. I didn't want to be seen at first glance should the lady of the house chance to pass by the window. But even so I shifted my observation post. Now I leaned against a parked greengrocer's delivery van, while concealing myself behind large sheets of newspaper, in which I'd cut two holes for quick snapshots; now I took up a position in some uninviting passageway or other, where I killed time by reading long vertical lists of names pasted beside the building's doorbells. Some of them were real beauts, that remain stuck in my memory. For example, Vladimír Šuplík, Zdeněk Kančibuch, Anna Lepuvzdorná or Richard Zápecník.

When I finally caught sight of Lucie in person on that first day, I immediately became cognisant of all the things that mere photographs can't capture. At first sight, she was an elevated being, a queenly beast, whose God-given beauty was not only a gorgeous, but transparent covering, beneath which some slimy creatures swam about.

She left the building to go on a walk with a large shaggy dog — a Čuvač[7] I reckon — and I set off quietly after them. They went along Vaclavská to

---

[5]   A novel by the Soviet author Boris Nikolayevich Polevoy (1908–1981), based on the true story of Soviet fighter pilot Aleksei Petrovich Maresyev (1916–2001), *Povest o nastoyashchem cheloveke* (1947).

[6]   Local slang for the Mendlovo náměstí, or Mendel Square, named for Fr Gregor Mendel, the geneticist who lived and died in Brno.

[7]   A large all-white shepherd dog native to the Tatra and Carpathian regions.

Mendlák, then up Pekařská and on through the streets of Brno — with heads constantly turning as she passed. But she, obviously, held them all in contempt, those glances (she was, you might say, elevated above them all). She passed on through the midst of these endless glances, cast by women as well as men, catching the eye of passers-by on the sidewalks as well as those of people in the cars and transports passing along the roads. Yet it seemed as if she didn't even notice them. Then she returned home, without having exchange a singled word with anyone — not counting the woman behind the counter in the deli, where she bought some buns, butter, soft cheese and something in a little box, the contents of which eluded me. But even though, in the course of that rather indifferent stroll of hers, I didn't observe the slightest hint of a response to any of those glances tossed her way by men, even then I knew, with professional certainty, that only Radek's athletic body was strong enough to bear such delightful horns as that divine dam, that ruttish anima mundi, that priestess of sex, might fit him with. It was on the third day of my surveillance that I obtained confirmation of my professional assessment.

I had just lit a cigarette, bending aside so that the wind wouldn't blow out my match, when I heard her footsteps on the pavement. She went — this time without her dog — to a fashionable shop. She didn't go inside, she just stood there, waiting.

I have such a prodigious photographic memory, that I believe I am not exaggerating when I compare it to a granary filled to bursting with recorded faces. Some of them are arranged in a system — let's call it a card-catalogue for memories. The reason for this is that there is something in me which continually organises, systematises, everything I come into contact with, so that it should be at my immediate disposal in my work as a private detective — even though I hadn't been practising the métier for some time now. I am here, my dearly beloved and unbeloved, I am here for the purpose of keeping close tabs on you, deducing from your behaviour any inklings of anything that might fall within my competence as a private eye.

But to return to the matter at hand. From among all these thousands of human faces, I have barely a thousand, I figure, systematically arranged, whereas the rest of them just lie about in a jumbled heap — yes, just like grain in a granary. And this is why what happened to me then could happen in the first place.

The subject under surveillance (Lucie) was meeting someone in an open-necked summer shirt, with an official sort of briefcase. As soon as I saw him, I recognised him as someone I knew from somewhere. But I couldn't find him in my systematised 'card catalogue.' He simply wasn't so classified in my memory that I might immediately place him. But all the same I had no doubt that he was known to me.

So Radek's wife approached the light-shirted fellow with the briefcase and quickly, almost imperceptibly, tapped him on the elbow with two fingers — oh, just like this — index finger and middle finger. As soon as she'd done so, she backed away from him, as if she hadn't done anything of the sort. Then they both went off at a brisk pace, together, but all the same with a noticeable distance between them, as if they had nothing in common.

From the get-go I realised that this couldn't be some insignificant little clerk. The finger of Her Bestial Majesty would never graze the hide of so wretched a peon. So this was some exceptional, important official who was probably out on some sort of official business, which of course he was only using as a pretext.

But while I was pondering this matter, a large moving van suddenly appeared and cut off my view of them on the opposite pavement. And because, as ill luck would have it, that damned van was crawling along at a snail's pace, I realised that I would have to cross over to their side of the street if I didn't want to lose sight of them. But these plans too were crossed as, my ill luck continuing, a large boxy military van turned onto the street, followed immediately by a long flatbed truck. Just then I heard the engine of a passenger car rev to life, piercing the thumping of the moving van, military truck and flatbed like a flute soaring above thunderous tympani. I feared the worst, and so it turned out. Just as my line of sight came clear again, the car disappeared past that long turning on Hybeška. And along with that car, without a doubt, the subjects of my surveillance. I ran as fast as I could past the curve of the street, but there was neither hide nor hair to be seen. Shit! Fucking, shitty shit!

✦

GENTLEMEN'S URGES

Dan Koči returned to his post opposite the main entrance to the apartment house. He waited there a little more than an hour, until he got what he was waiting for: Lucie returned. But not by car, as he had been expecting, perhaps, but by tram.

He began to consider what his next move should be. If the same thing were to happen next week, he'd know for sure that Lucie's copulationer (or should that be copulator?)[8] comes to pick her up in his car, which he parks a little farther away, in the direction of Staré Brno. Covered, perhaps, by the ever-present brewery trucks. But what good would it do him, even if he were to get a close look at the car, and note down its mark and plate numbers? Even back in the good old days it was quite a chore to pry information about the owner of a car from the Traffic Division. To say that the police were averse to cooperating with private Sherlocks would be an understatement. And now, in this Socialist paradise, such a thing was completely out of the question. He knew no one from whom he might borrow a car to follow the pair over the cobblestones. And to attempt the task of surveilling the lovers' car from a taxi, well, in 1950s Brno, that was just as absurd an idea as it would be to turn to the zoo with the request of borrowing a python so as to strangle one's mother-in-law. And thus the only meaningful modus operandi was to make use of what he already knew. The fellow was some very important official, and Dan was already familiar — somehow — with his mug. But how might he find the proper context for that face? How could he find a place for it in his 'card catalogue'?

Then he got an idea. At that time, among civilians, cars were doled out only to physicians and, besides them, such as had been awarded the Order of Labour. And in the case of the latter, only those who held important

---

[8]   *Luciin kopulovčík (nebo snad kopulátor?)*

economic positions. So he really was a very important official: most likely, the director of one of the large enterprises located in Brno.

Then he knew just where to go. On Jezuitská St, the State Film Lending Library was located. Its holdings were only available to Socialist organisations and professional associations, but even the butchers and sausage makers had their own Professional Club, and welcomed cultural initiatives from among the ranks of its members. And so, at Dan's initiative, the butchers and sausage makers of Municipal Region I gathered at their hall for a film. It was the eve of the birthday of some Communist bigshot (and such anniversaries were ready-made occasions for cultural manifestations). They sat themselves beneath a hand-painted sign bearing Lenin's words: 'Of All the Arts the Most Important is Film.' Hands stained with the blood of our four-legged brothers and sisters were folded on laps, so as to discreetly shield any spontaneous swelling from eyes nearby should Alina Mandlová or Lída Baarová appear on the screen — which had supposedly been promised them. But promises and guarantees are things in which only dolts believe. And this time the celluloid menu consisted entirely of three newsreels from First of May celebrations from 1949 through 1951. During the screening of the first two, the butchers and sausage makers began to evaporate quietly, so that during the projection of the third, only the fireman at the door and the projector in the booth were present, along with Dan Kočí by his lonesome in the audience. Dan was convinced that he would see the directors of all the Brno factories marching at the head of their enterprises in the First of May parades. Indeed, his patience was rewarded, but the real surprise came a few minutes later, when the First of May pilgrimage schlepped its way onto Red Army Square. There Dan met up with his boy — on the grandstand set up before the statue of the Red Army Soldier. He was delivering a speech to his comrades of both sexes, in his role as the secretary of the Municipal Committee of the KSČ.[9] Now Dan, who always pushed politics away to the farthest edge of his perception (he had no room for politicians in his 'card catalogue'), had a hard time coming to terms with the fact that he'd have to sherlock around a bit on an individual like that.

....

[9]   *Komunistická Strana Československa* — the Communist Party of Czechoslovakia.

He located the secretary's address in the telephone book (at the beginning of the 1950s their addresses were still the public property of the workers), but he already knew that next week he wouldn't be waiting for the secretary on Hybešova, in front of Radek's wife's apartment, but in the Jiráskův quarter, in front of the secretary's own little villa. He calculated the hour that the car with its erotic cargo should arrive there, and on the determined date he took the tram to Náměstí Míru,[10] from which it was only a short stroll to Havlíčkova St and the functionalist villa in question (probably the design of Ernest Wiesner).

But when he arrived, he realised to his surprise that someone had got there before him. And this was no goon squad[11] watching over the security of a distinguished apparatchik, but, on the contrary — investigators keeping their eyes on the backside of someone who'd apparently fallen, or was about to fall, out of favour. Dan was quite certain of this, or, actually not completely certain, but above all he was aware of the fact that those two fellows were greenhorn thugs — quite unsophisticated as far as the profession was concerned. Dan guessed that they had been recruited from the ranks of the working class and that, unlike him, that is, Dan, they probably were adept at operating jackhammers in slag pockets and pouring ingots in cast-iron moulds (poor Dan had no idea what a cast-iron mould even looked like, whereas the narrator of this tale has only a cloudy conception of the same, having been for a short while at age eighteen a brigade worker at the Klement Gottwald New Foundry), but for all that they didn't know shit about surveilling a suspect person. Their behaviour suggested that they were to keep Comrade Schildberger and his house under observation without him catching on. But all this remained rather in the sphere of hypothesis than reality. For they were clumsy dolts, who, instead of being inconspicuous, were on the contrary as conspicuous as judges in their robes on a carousel, no, not that, I want to say like hickeys on the Queen of England's neck, no, not that either, but that'll have to do, if we want to move on. In short, Dan was pissed off at their doltishness. He couldn't abide amateur blunders in his profession.

....

[10]   Peace Square since 1950, formerly Babákovo Náměstí (for Eduard Babák [1873–1826], a Czech physiologist from Brno.

[11]   *Papalášská ochranka.*

One of these investigators loitered in a supposedly casual manner in the vicinity of the villa, while the other was stationed in a rented flat directly across the street, where he waited at the window with a camera. From time to time they made signs to one another — from the window to the street and vice versa. And so everybody on the street (as well as everybody in the streets nearby) was aware of the dark clouds of fate gathering over the head of Schildberger the apparatchik. (This was back in the days of the show-trials where various 'conspiracies' were uncovered.) Only the secretary himself was unaware of what was going on. But this should not surprise us. Condemned people quite often are afflicted with such blindness that they walk straight on, as if through a fog as thick as pea soup, straight into the clutches of their waiting executioners.

Dan took care lest the men on stakeout should become aware of his presence, which, after all, wasn't hard to do in the case of such boobies. Then he heard the secretary's car approach. Again I must remind you that in those days, personal autos were as rare as hen's teeth, and since very few delivery vans appeared in the Jiráskův neighbourhood, even the long ears of the boobies pricked up at the sound. The car paused for a fraction of a second somewhere past the corner, but then immediately came on again, turning now into Havlíčkova from Rudišova St — and Dan immediately surmised what that brief pause, just beyond his, and the investigators', field of vision signified. Then the apparatchik drove up in his car, alone.

Without a moment's hesitation, Dan hurried off to the transverse of Soukopova, then turned another corner to Sedlakova St, and there his expectations were fulfilled. He was just in time to catch Lucie as, in the shade of a wide spreading linden tree, she opened the gate to the large garden that abutted the secretary's villa on the southwest side. Meanwhile, to the northeast, the secretary was just getting out of his car. He opened the garage, whistling the hit song *Our Spring's Not Over, After All.*[12] Submerged in his erotic visions he saw neither the investigators nor the clouds of fate that kept gathering over his head.

Why was it, then, since he knew nothing of the men surveilling him, that he let Lucie out of the car past the corner, sending her around to the other side, having her enter through the garden gate? Back then, in

---

[12] 'U nás jaro nekončí,' a popular song by the crooner Karel Gott.

its infancy, totalitarian Communism was one of the most puritanical of régimes. An eminent apparatchik might well occupy a villa confiscated from the family of a factory owner, and live there in a certain luxury, justified in this by the great demands and responsibilities of his Party functions, but his private life, as well as his address, was at the time the public property of the workers. In this way, Breton's terrible surrealistic dream of 'glass houses' came about in reality. And so the secretary might well have a gentlemen's urges, but if he wasn't able to control them, and netted somewhere a beautiful concubine, who on top of it all was another man's wife, he should at least have sense enough in that 'glass house' of his to stretch an opaque screen around those urges, so as not to unnecessarily untune all those lathe and milling machine operators, drivers of tractors and milkers of cows.

Dan knew that he had no more than a half hour — which he decided, at last, to spend in what at first glance seems a rather dubious manner. Instead of clambering over the little wall and finding a tree in the garden, from which he might be able to peer through one of the windows at the secretary's antics with Radek's wife, he just crossed Sedlákova to Foustkova St, then went down Wilson to, of course, the Jiráskův Wood, where he spent a few moments looking for an appropriate place. When he found one, at last, he brushed the ground with a little branch and spread out a handkerchief. Then he knelt down on the ground, and set his head inside the top corner of the isosceles triangle, the bases of which rested on his elbows. Then, setting his head on the ground in such a way that his interlaced fingers would provide the support of resistance to the back of his skull, he raised his pelvis and, with tiny steps on tip-toe, drew his knees close to his trunk. Next, he shifted the weight of his body and his entire centre of gravity onto his forearms and the crown of his head, slowly raising his legs from the ground, while his head remained as fixed to the earth as if it were attached by a screw. Slowly, he balanced his legs until they were perfectly in line with his trunk, perpendicular to the ground.

Dan was taught this position many years previously, by a Indian shopkeeper, for whom he clarified the matter of his brother's alleged suicide, which turned out actually to have been a murder (this was the so-called Case of the Sapphire Serpent, but of course we have no time to go into that now). Back then, Dan discovered that this position, so similar to the shirshasana of yoga, opened imaginative vistas for him into just-solved cases. Which, practically speaking, is something quite useless — it could never be introduced into court, of course, but all the same it is definitely worth taking note of.

And so, after a few minutes in this position similar to shirshasana, Dan quite distinctly saw the room in which the secretary had just gone to his knees before the wide-spread Lucie, placing his head at the top of her bushy, and moreover isosceles, triangle. Then Radek's wife slowly lifted her legs until they were perpendicular to her supine trunk, while the secretary raised his pelvis, and, with tiny steps, tip-toe, drew close so that, with Lucie's aid, he might slip his Johnson into her pussy. Then he transferred his weight, and his entire centre of gravity, onto his forearms and pelvis, in such a way that his head remained set on Lucie's shoulder, as if it were fixed there with a screw, which shoulder, that dick (I mean, his head) bit into. But now the secretary had pushed forward, pumping, slowly at first, and then ever more quickly. Finally, immediately after it had all played out the way it should play out, and the snorting secretary had pumped his load and slipped himself back out, Lucie got up, glanced at her watch, and went into the bathroom where she had a shower, got dressed, and fixed herself in front of the mirror. Then she caught sight of an eyebrow pencil resting on a glass shelf. It had been forgotten there by the secretary's wife, who was away for two weeks now, somewhere in Konstantinovy Lázně. Lucie grabbed the pencil and, suddenly turning directly to face Dan in this imaginative vista, she looked him straight in the eye. She made a mark on his forehead with the pencil: right there where the nose meets the brow. Then she winked at him, put the pencil back in its place, and at that moment the dream-screen went blank. *Kanets fil'ma.*[13]

Slowly, Dan lowered his legs and transferred his centre of gravity back to its previous position, got up, picked up his handkerchief, glanced at his watch and set off at a brisk pace back up Wilson, through the Jiráskův Wood, of course, then back through Foustkova and then Sedlákova. It was there on the corner of Rudišova that he ran into her.

....

[13]   Russian: The end of the film. Following the author's usage, we transliterate the sound of the Russian words, rather than their spelling.

She was going down to the tram stop. As they passed, Dan saw, close up, really very close up, a little black mark on her forehead, right where the nose meets the brow. But Radek's wife didn't take the slightest note of him, passing by nonchalantly, indifferently. For her, in this real world, despite all those imaginative vistas, he simply existed no more.

PUNCTURED SOUL

The question as to why I, amongst all the noteworthy architects of Brno, should live in a humble flat in an ordinary, dime-a-dozen tenement — that question, I say, is such an obvious one that no one's ever really asked it. Obviously, I don't include here my Mephisto, Lieutenant Láska, but let's set that aside for now. Those who assumed to know me probably arrived at the conclusion that, in reality, I was already building a villa for myself in some secret corner, and that soon I was going to surprise everyone. I confess that there have been times when I was not far from similar thoughts, that is, that there would come a day on which, quite simply, I'd sit down at the drawing board one fine morning, and before the sun had sunk in the west, I'd have that villa of mine completely planned out, in every detail, including interior furnishings, and that the only thing left to do would be to buy a well-scoped out plot in Černá Pole or the Žabovřesky region and start building. But when that day finally arrived, I realised that something in me had, well, jammed.

I had turned that villa over and over again in my head for some six or seven years. Dozens of different designs had occurred to me — and it appeared that all I had to do was to choose from among them the variant which had the best chance of success. I missed my chance to do it before the war, and then the German occupation trod on the throat of all architectural song. Then later, in 1947, when I had quickly amassed all the means necessary, and actually sat myself down at the draughting board, I realised that I didn't have it in me. That I didn't know how to transfer all those dozens of promising designs onto paper, though I thought that they were all at my beck and call, right down to the last detail. Something had happened. All of a sudden, I wasn't up to the task of designing my villa.

Of course it also occurred to me that my inability to determine a final, congenial, design for my villa was the price I was paying for all of those abominations, all those vile villas I had built in Brno right after the war to satisfy my wealthy and kitsch-loving clients — which I had done in order to amass the means indispensable to the construction of my own villa, that wonder of architectural invention. But where had my inventiveness come an end? To put it simply, someone just let the air out of it. But what am I saying, 'someone?' That someone was me — I was the one who punctured my own soul. And now I was merely rolling along on my rims, waiting for my wobbly ride to end up in a ditch full of nettles.

Can it be that we are always strictly punished for betraying our talent, and that it's only when we finally find ourselves at the very bottom, flat on our backs, that we realise our treason? Is it then that we understand just what it is that we've lost, gone and buried forever? But where then is that soul of mine, since I went and sold her for some three thousand eight hundred and ninety-four bowls of lentils, or however else one might assess the worth of that kitschy *vileness* that I scattered around here?

Sure, the beginnings of the collapse of my talents might well be marked by that Wagenheim villa. Granted, it is an unquestionably noteworthy building, architecturally speaking, to which the only reproach to be made is in the Nazi symbol incorporated into its footprint. But then it occurred to me: might it not be all the more noteworthy, for that very reason? For did I not take that on as a challenge? I had to wrestle with that Hakenkreuz just as I'd have had to come to grips with any other commission involving treacherous terrain — such as if I had been required to put up a villa on waterlogged ground, or beneath a cliff where slides presented a constant threat. Yes — I remember well how often that problem would wake up in the middle of the night. How I'd go over to the window and gaze down upon Běhounská street — empty in the dark hours long before sunrise, like a shaft somewhere deep under ground. I struggled to find a way to discharge the commission with honour. And not just with honour. I wanted to carry it off, somehow, in a way that would outsmart that Nazi swastika like the fox outsmarted the crow with the cheese in his beak. And so, not only did I make four fully functional residential wings out of those four legs of Hitler's long johns, but on top of that, I rotated the construction in relation to Hroznová St in such a way that two spreading wings made the other two arms of the broken cross invisible. So much for the façade. But even from the side, these other two wings, those other two arms, were all but invisible, since they were covered with the mature greenery of the landscaping in which I had set them. And so, only an aerial view would reveal Wagenheims's original requirements. (And yet the Wagenheim villa had such good fortune that when the Allied air forces bombarded Brno toward the end of the war, their missions didn't extend to Pisárky, and thus they didn't have their way with it.)

Above all, I designed each of the four wings with such obvious functional applications, that it had to be clear to all that, just like a bird its wings, so this villa needed all four of its wings for its full, intrinsic existence. Because the actual residential areas were located in them, and the cube, out of which they grew, was nothing more than the joint which allowed the wings — if such a thing might be imagined — to start moving, waving, rotating. There remains the fact that, at the extremity of each wing, a sort of mini-wing was attached, at right angles, as is the case with swastikas. These I utilised for such areas as required their own entrance ways. And because they were at the extremities, and even past the corners of the wings, they were discreetly aloof from the main residential and representative area — four smart little rooms, detached from the common traffic.

When a delegation of Finnish architects came to Brno right after the war to inspect the exhibition grounds and other functionalist construc- tions, with the intention of making Brno, this surviving fragment of the erstwhile avant-garde, into a centre of modern European architecture, they paused in front of the Wagenheim villa too — despite the fact that none of the Czech organisers of the excursion had included it in the excursion route. Of course, it would have been difficult to sidestep it, located as it is in the immediate neighbourhood of the Fuchs and Wiesenthal villas. So they paused before my masterpiece, baffled that no one amongst their Czech architectural colleagues had noticed it. They paused in front of it like mushroom pickers face to face with a gigantic boletus, chattering at first in technical terms, pointing at the wings broken into smaller winglets at the extremities; but then they all grew quiet with something like a sacred reverence, fixed to the spot like a petrified flock of speechless admirers. Of course I was not there myself. I heard of this later. Above all, I heard of the frightful consequences of their visit. For when they returned home, to the land of lakes and forests, the homeland of Alvar Aalt, they spilled architec- tural swastikas around the country, without a single one of those lunatics realising what it was that they were planting in the Finnish soil.

Still and all, I'd like to believe that with my Wagenheim villa, I was able to outsmart the devil. If such is not the case in reality, of course; if it is that it wasn't the devil himself that led me here in the first place, to the suggestion that I outfoxed him (and not vice versa).

THE STUDIO ON ELIŠKA MACHOVÁ STREET

I suspect that when Kamil decided to build my villa on Eliška Machová street in the Žabovřesky neighbourhood, it wasn't just because he'd come across a chance lot, where an earlier structure had been demolished, but because of the jolly fact that Eliška Modráčková would be living on Eliška Machová. Surely, that also played a role in his choice of locations. Kamil is ever susceptible to all sorts of sudden flashes of inspiration, ranging from admirable and mostly unrealisable intentions to the most cockamamie idiocies. So it is all the more mysterious to me that, although he is doubtlessly one of the best architects of Brno, as well as an inventive sort positively ill with creativity, still he hasn't the foggiest idea of what I'm up to at the moment. And I'm not only talking about my painting here. Not all that long ago, he was leafing through a Dutch publication concerning Kandinsky and Malevich when, suddenly, he thrust it quickly away. It's not that he ever criticises me; no, he takes special care never, God forbid! to hurt my feelings. I look upon these efforts of his with a bit of gleeful amusement. A quiet laughter begins to bubble up within me at such times — of which he knows nothing, or, at least, of which I think he knows nothing. He'll walk about my studio turning round the paintings that I have there leaning face-first against the wall, and stand there considering them in deep thought. But because it would trouble him were he to lie to me, most of the time, he'll say nothing. And when — to toy with him a bit — I ask him about them, directly, he'll praise one for its interesting composition, or pat me on the back for my courage to be constantly attempting something new. Only at rare intervals is he unable to restrain himself. Then he asks me — only this — why it is that I no longer paint those magical surrealistic landscapes, in which a gigantic crab claw suddenly grows out of a little roadside chapel, or where a flaming comet falls upon a field of grain. Or why I've abandoned that long series of realistic portraits, on which each of them something surprising may be found. Like that portrait of a dandy in a fashionable black jacket, on whose shoulder sits a huge blowfly. Or that other one depicting a beautiful and chic young woman chewing the enormous nail of her middle finger.

But the fact is that I remember quite vividly — something that he's already forgotten, it seems — that when I was painting such things, he wasn't particularly enthusiastic about them. Then, too, he tried to conceal what he thought. But I could read it in his face, how irritated he was by those very small quirks on the portraits, which denied them their otherwise forgettable loveliness in such a blasphemous manner, as if someone had exchanged the ewer containing holy water in church with a spittoon.

Now, what I've just said about those portraits is really an attempt on my part to see them through the eyes of Kamil, or the eyes of just about anyone who is not me. Because I would not call them small quirks, nor did I sense any blasphemy in my placing them there. The question also once occurred to me whether I belonged to that group of people who exist here on earth as mediums for something inexpressible; or whether I'm not just a piece of small change quietly falling through the galaxies. But no — that's stupid. Stupid and also presumptuous — forget I said it.

For some time now, Kamil's life has been poisoned by this StB goon. He tries not to take that dick of a cop too seriously. He has even wondered whether or not the cop's been just yanking his chain, having some fun at his expense. But today when he came by, his hair was veritably standing up on his head. He paused before my new painting, the Diagonal Series, and stood there for a moment. I could tell just by looking at him that he couldn't even see the picture his eyes were fixed on. He had something to say to me, and he was searching for the first sentence, to get the ball rolling. At last, he began telling me about the StB goons that suddenly materialised behind him when he set his foot on his stairs.

I heard them behind my back. They were swearing because there was no lift, so they'd have to hump it up the stairs on foot. They caught up to me as I was plunging the key into the lock. I turned around, but they were already standing with their backs to me, ringing the doorbell of the flat across the hallway. The Kratochvil place. There's a window onto the passage there, too, and behind it, a little room where the maid was supposed to live. The curtain in that window was pulled aside. Mrs Kratochvil's old father slid one of the panes half open and asked the two men what they were after. We've got a search warrant for the Kratochvil apartment, one of them said, and so loudly, as if he also wanted me to hear. You can always recognise them by this exhibitionistic arrogance of theirs. Some sort of defiance took hold of me then, and I kept on standing there a while at my open door. But when one of them turned on his heel and looked straight at me, my defiance quickly evaporated, and I shrunk inside. As I was closing my door, I heard the door opening across the way. It was two o'clock in the afternoon. Mrs Kratochvil was still at work, I guess. It then occurred to me that I hadn't seen her husband for quite some time. A long time. She was living in the apartment with her two sons and her elderly parents. But lately I've noticed that it's a little different. I sat down on the bench in the foyer, and was taking off my shoes when I heard some movement from across the hallway again. I walked over to the peephole on bare feet and had a peek out. At the door across the way stood one of those two sons, a ten-year-old boy with a large glass pitcher in his hands. He closed the door behind him and ran downstairs. I took myself over to the window and looked out. After a few moments, I saw the boy run along the sidewalk opposite and disappear into the U Cajplů restaurant. The first thought that came into my head was that those cops had sent him out for beer. If they were going to give the Kratochvil place a proper tossing, then certainly they'd have to paw their way through a great big teacher's library — Kratochvil is, as far as I know, a schoolmaster — and then, probably, they'd be lifting up the mattresses and grubbing into some old trunks they'd find in the closets and maybe they'd even have a look under the beds, so that they'd have swallowed so much dust in the end that they'd have to wash it down with something. But then I realised that they dare not drink while on duty. That's probably why there were two of them — to keep an eye on each other, and to squeal on each other, when necessary. So perhaps it was rather that they just permitted the old man to send the boy off on an errand somewhere, so that he needn't witness the 'plundering of the family hearth.' It is possible, after all, that even the most unscrupulous, calloused StB goons are capable of being considerate to children — even the children of their class enemies. But then I also noticed that there was someone standing down below near the entrance to the building, because now he drew back a bit to the edge of the pavement in order to communicate with someone leaning out of the window of the

Kratochvil flat. The cop up above explained to the cop down below that he was to keep an eye on that boy with the glass pitcher who had run along to the restaurant, and make sure that he spoke to no one there, passed nothing on to anyone.

Then Kamil grew silent. Suddenly, he got up from his chair and set Vít the cat on the floor (his name is Vít because he greets everyone who enters the studio).[14] He made his way over to the shelving and pulled a plug from the socket, to which half a brick was attached by wire wound round it.

Eliš, don't get upset at me, but you're crazy! What is this? he asked, lifting the wired brick.

You don't know? You've never seen anything like that? I use that for heat. The wire wrapped round the brick gets nice and warm, and makes for very cheery heat. But the socket blew and there are no fuses to be had.

Kamil unwound the wire from the brick and, tearing it from the plug, inspected its frayed end.

Something like that could electrocute you, kitten. Or burn down the studio. And with the proper stove you have, after all! If you ran out of wood or coal you know who to turn to! He looked about the room. You wanted a nice atelier, and then you go and warm it so lousily! Well, it's not cold any more once the early morning's past, and we'll think of something before autumn rolls round again.

Then he went to have a look at the fuse box. He unscrewed one fuse after another, nodded that all were in order, and came back. How long have these sockets been acting up?

Three days now.

I'll send someone by. Today even, or tomorrow.

But don't go yet. You haven't finished what you were saying.

What? There wasn't much more. I stood there near my open window, so I heard what the two were saying to one another. It seemed that the one in the window was afraid that little Kratochvil might pass on a message to someone waiting for him at the restaurant. That's how StB goons think. It's drilled into them, and they're paid to think cautiously like that. And so the

....

14   A pun in Czech. Vít is a man's name (Vitus); the Czech verb 'to greet' or 'welcome' someone is *vítat.*

one down on the sidewalk took off into the restaurant after the Kratochvil boy. Yeah — and one more thing. Last night I ran into Doctor Pešek in the hall. He lives in the flat beneath me, you know. My wife is his dentist. He told me that in the building they're saying that Kratochvil's emigrated. And so each one of us ought to expect to be questioned, one after the other.

Well, but that has nothing to do with you, after all. Old Lieutenant Láska is taking care of you. But you're avoiding me now. You still haven't told me the most important thing — why you came here in the first place.

Now, this was a shot in the dark. But that unease of his, which led him here and set him up in front of my painting, to stare at it like that without seeing a thing, and then his concern with my electrical situation… all of those tiny behavioural tics that only a loved and loving little sister would notice, and tip her off that something wasn't right — all of this provoked in me the suspicion that there was something else, something much more important than what he'd just confided to me.

He looked at me and turned back into the room from the door. For a while he stood silently near the shelves. Then he slowly swivelled round on his heel, took five steps forward, then five back again, and at last sat down in the wicker chair. I followed those manoeuvres of his and all the while that silent laughter was bubbling up in me again. Out with it, bucko, I urged him, taking up a position behind him and placing my hands on his shoulders.

OK, then. Towards morning, I had this dream. It was here in your studio. There were a couple of policemen here, in uniform. And another one outside.

Lieutenant Láska?

I think so. God knows what his name is, after all is said and done. I've heard that they use aliases.[15]

Doctor Pešek again?

What?

Is he the one that told you that they use aliases?

Well, yeah.

So, go on, buddy. What else happened in your dream?

They were… bothering you.

How precisely, brother? Were they grabbing me?

....

[15]   The lieutenant's alias is ironic: in Czech, *láska* means 'love.'

Yes.

Undressing me?

Yes.

And themselves, too?

No, they keep their uniforms on.

So, they forced themselves upon me? Where the hell was your dream-censor when this was going on? But hold on — you're holding something back from me. Something else happened that you're not saying.

I kept standing behind him, pressing his shoulders. I began massaging them. He said nothing. I kept kneading his shoulders for a while, and he kept quiet. Then a garbage truck came rumbling along Eliška Machová, and I suddenly realised that it was nine o'clock on Thursday morning, and I still hadn't put out the trash, and that in a moment's time it would be too late.

Where were you, little brother, while they were raping me? I asked him softly. Admit it — You weren't by chance one of them who were dishonouring me so?

He jumped to his feet. What are you saying, Eliš? And then: I don't know where I was when that was going on. Maybe I was nothing but the eye that was seeing it all transpire. I couldn't intervene.

I laughed. Don't take it so seriously, Kamil. After all, it was only a dream.

I'll send someone along to have a look at those sockets. Today even, if possible.

At the gate, I embraced him and gave him a kiss. He's not at all fond of such public displays. I have an endlessly bashful brother. I really knocked him for a loop with that question of his taking part in my rape. Sometimes, quite often, actually, I'm a monster like that.

I didn't get the trash out in time. They had already gone down Šmejkalová. When they paused, I yelled to them, and tried to sign them from afar to come back up and take my rubbish. One of them replied with an obscene gesture, which infuriated Kamil. He wanted to run after them. I had to use all my strength to restrain him. He was in the grip of such fury that I had a hard time of it to convince him not to run off after a garbage truck — to the gigantic hilarity of all who should happen to see him. To say nothing of the fact that it was a rather extravagant hope on my part, to expect garbage men to return up the street they'd already cleared just to empty my bins. I understood that Kamil had invested the garbage man's vulgar gesture with much more meaning than that latter originally intended. He had invested it with his fresh dream experience, and — poor fellow — wanted to prove to me how he would rush to my defence.

I returned to my studio. I went over to the picture I had been painting, and repainting. I touched those portions of the canvas covered with impasto, feeling them to be veins and warts; feeling the pulse of its life. I wasn't able to work any more that day. It occurred to me that Kamil, not me, was the one who needed a protector. He needed somebody to defend him. He's unable to come to terms with this world. He has no strong grounding at home. His wife seems to me to be the most superfluous creature, empty and lacklustre, and when he lost what really mattered to him — the possibility of constructing those dream buildings of his, he had nowhere to turn, nowhere to escape to. I work two shifts in a huge cabinetry factory, and then I have an afternoon, or, like today, a morning, free to spend in my studio. But Kamil is stuck in a design office doing work he despises, and otherwise doing nothing else; he's become resigned to it all. I guess I'm afraid for him. As if I had a presentiment that someday, something horrible would happen to him, something that I wouldn't be able to prevent.

COMRADE, YER A SWINE, YOU ARE!

I walked through the main entrance and had a look around. To the right, next to the cemetery wall, huddled a little building with a low roof, but long — like a covered bowling alley. There it was — Radek's stonecutting workshop. The door was wide open. Radek Stolař was sitting on a little stone sculpture, reading the paper. Only when I got near him did I see that he wasn't reading at all, but sitting there motionless, paper in hand, staring out blindly into the idiotic vacuum. And because I had no wish to be part of the idiotic vacuum, I took care to avoid his glassy stare; only when I stood right near him did he snap out of his trance and take cognisance of me.

Did you read today's paper? he asked, with terror in his voice.

Nope. But I know what you've got in mind. I heard it last night on the radio.

What's going on? I don't understand.

I reckon that they explain it quite clearly there, no? Last night on the radio they said that State Security had caught hold of the threads of an anti-government conspiracy, and this time they led all the way to Brno. The enemy of Socialist progress, who has wormed his way into the highest organs of the State, has stretched his claws even unto our little town. You know what? The hell with it, bud. Fuck it. In my opinion, ours is not to wonder why, you know.

Because the ceiling of Radek's workshop is so low, and I had to stand there with my neck bent, he motioned me to sit down on the base of a marble cross to which a crown of thorns, fashioned from rusty wire, was attached. I sat down, taking extra care not to get my hair tangled in that thorny crown.

I — Radek bravely confessed — I knew that secretary somewhat. David Schildberger was from this large Jewish family. They have a family plot here. His parents and all of his relatives perished in the camps. But he wanted me to carve all of their names on the lid that covers their grave, even though they'll never be buried there — all of their ashes remain somewhere in Poland or Germany. He's an immensely chivalrous fellow, he is. He helped us to get our place on Hybeška, and brought Lucie this gigantic bouquet of flowers, and told her something strange and beautiful — a citation from Dante's Divine Comedy — I don't recall what, but Lucie will know. Those Jews! They carry whole libraries around in their heads! Now they've grabbed him too, and carted him off to Prague, last night. I've been thinking this through and — I've come to the conclusion that we've probably seen the last of him.

I nodded. He was one of theirs, and they deal mercilessly with renegades. It's possible that even his ashes wouldn't return to Brno. When I narrowed my eyes (As I did at that moment, and an image really did suddenly appear before me), I saw a lonely street on a rainy night, a car, and someone's hand stretching out the window, spilling out ashes from a canister…

I opened my eyes and blinked idly for a few moments. Radek stared at me in fear: Do you sometimes have visions?

I've never told you about them? Of course it's not that my talent as a private investigator stands and falls with them, but sometimes something kind of jabs me. It's a sort of visual intuition, which is always associated with the cases I happen to be working on.

But Schildberger isn't associated with any of your cases.

How, not? I mean to say, Yes, of course not! But even that happens sometimes. Sometimes my intuitions, so to speak, overflow their banks.

We never met with him again. But I'll never forget how nicely he behaved towards my wife. Her eyes were shining long after he'd left. Those magnificent words of his, especially that quote from the Divine Comedy, lit her up from the inside, and that light continues to glow in her eyes… I feel beholden to him. If anything were to happen to him, I'd carve his name on that gravestone, even if no one were to ask me to. Alongside the names of all of those relatives of his who were murdered in Dachau, in Auschwitz, in Buchenwald and who knows where else…

We sat there for a while in that cemetery stonecutter's workshop, saying nothing. I, with a marble cross and rusty crown of thorns at my back, and he on a stone angel, who was covering his face with his hands.

I broke the silence with a cough. Listen, Radek, just so I don't forget. I came here to tell you that I've brought your wife's case to a conclusion.

Yeah? he asked. At which I realised that in that first moment he didn't know what I was talking about. So I paused a bit until it came to him.

I can assure you that your wife has no lover. (I really should have said she *no longer* has any lover. They've already taken care of that lover of hers. And I could also have added, with certainty, that she wouldn't be having a lover again for some time. For that pussy of hers was so tightly shut with alarm and distress that you wouldn't be able to force a blade of meadow foxtail in there. And if her tussling with the secretary were to meet the public's ear — as they were in the habit of bringing about — well, that clamp of anxiety would keep her cunt shut for some time yet. Of course, after a while, it'd open up again, and she'd do her best to make up for all she'd been missing out on. But that would no longer be any concern of mine, as I was determined never to take a case from Radek again.)

You know, Dan, he confessed, I knew that, obviously. Lucie would never do something like that to me.

OK, so tell me, why did you hire me, since you already knew? Why shell out for something you already had, for free?

My buddies over at The Cadaver were constantly on my back about it. Saying that a beautiful woman like that always has another somebody, somewhere, to give her a tumble.

Right. Maybe you'd be better off finding new buddies. Or a new joint to drink in.

Radek pulled out his billfold and I at once felt awkward, accepting the honorarium from him. For sure, I had carried out a thorough investigation, yet… well, I skewed, somewhat, the final conclusions. Let's just say that we gave a spin to our diagnosis, in the best interests of our patient's ability to get a good night's sleep. Sure, what I did wasn't entirely kosher, but in this instance, the truth might've derailed Radek entirely. And if I had declined the previously agreed-upon honorarium, this would have led him to suspect that something fishy was going on. Furthermore, I'd put in a full day's work on his account — more than I'd ever done. After all, I'd insinuated myself into pretty risky company on his behalf. In spite of my professional perfectionism and the obvious unprofessionalism of those 'secret' policemen, I could still have made a wrong step. And then I'd've caught it proper. After all, to snoop around that 'anti-government conspiracy' of theirs, while they were sniffing around too in hopes of uncovering some additional advantage to themselves, well, I was literally risking my neck. And so I let him pile that honorarium onto my palm in a little pyramid, which I then thrust into my pocket. And one more thing. I could indeed assure Radek that his wife had no lover. But I quite well couldn't warn him of the fact that, her pussy being clamped tight with anxiety, his wife wouldn't even be letting him in for the next few days, or even weeks. But as far as that's concerned, the boy would have to come to grips with it on his own.

Despite the fact that I doubtlessly know my Pappenheimers[16] and so I had nothing to fear from the part of those who had been surveilling the secretary's house — for example, that they'd have registered Lucie's cautious arrivals and departures — and despite the fact that I'd made out that the window looking into the secretary's bedroom, where he'd been squeezing Lucie, gives out onto the garden, and thus well out of the range of the agents' eyes and telephoto lenses, nevertheless, I preferred to watch over the house on Hybešová.

Yes. Despite the fact that the case was closed and the honorarium paid, nevertheless for fourteen days I still hung around the Stolař hearth, making sure that Radek never caught sight of me there. For if they had found out that the secretary had been humping Lucie, they would have already come for her as well by now, or they would at least have had her building under surveillance. But after the passage of those fourteen days I kicked it all to the curb, sensing that everything was OK and that Radek had nothing to worry about any more (at least as far as the StB was concerned).

But Lucie did cross my mind again, about a month later, while the trial of Schildberger and the other conspirators was going on. For one day my boss brought round to my work station a petition signed by all the butchers and sausage makers, which demanded the noose for the former Party Secretary

---

[16]   *Znám svoje pappenheimské.* A Czech idiom derived from Schiller's play *Wallensteins Tod.* In this context, it means 'I know the people I'm speaking of; I don't trust them, but they can't fool me; I'm one step ahead of them.' It eventually derives from Gottfried Heinrich Count Pappenheim (1594–1632). A military leader of the Holy Roman Empire, he was on the side of the victorious side of the battle of White Mountain (8 November 1620), which saw the Czech lands swallowed up by the Habsburg Empire.

of Brno, among others. I put down my knife and set aside the little blades used to portion chickens, but, when I set myself to sign the petition too, a little chicken blood dripped onto it. I wanted to wipe it off, but merely succeeded in smearing it all the more. My boss's eyes rolled in his head like billiard balls. Dear God, Comrade, what a swine you are!

WARNINGS AND RECRUITMENT

Lieutenant Láska smiled in an almost friendly way. And there was more. As soon as Modráček entered the interrogation room, Láska turned on the hotplate and offered the architect a cup of coffee, to which he added a thin, but nevertheless dense, cigar — the smoke of which began to choke him as soon as he lit it.

Please — you don't have to smoke it, if you haven't got the taste for it.

Relieved, Modráček set the cigar aside and waited, nervously, for what would follow.

So then, Comrade. I've called you in today, above all, to let you know how much all of us respect the work you do for us. Great respect we have! Immense! And here I'm speaking on behalf of the entire collective of interrogators, investigators, and… inquisitors. That was a joke there, Comrade. Obviously. And here Láska spread wide his hands, as if he wanted to show Modráček that here we have no inquisitors, and also what a jolly good sense of humour the long arm of the law has, here at the Běhounská precinct station.

So you're building a large apartment block on Botanická Street (he glanced at his papers), numbers 37 to 45. Is that correct?

Not entirely. I'm not building them. I just had a hand in their design.

You're going to lecture me again? the lieutenant laughed.

But because Láska continued to smile — as best as he knew how to — Modráček wasn't quite certain of himself. And so he chose his words carefully: Besides the design, I've also been entrusted with certain other technical matters concerning the project. But it's all mainly in the hands of the young architects.

Truth be told, Modráček was above all entrusted with making sure that the residential block shouldn't fall down; that its foundations were sound and counterbalanced, that it had a high-quality core — and all of this most definitely did not end with tabulations. Basically, the building was Modráček's work, and only its external appearance of a Socrealistic vertical was left to the young architects to earn their spurs on.

You're too modest, Comrade, admit it. You'd like to leave all the credit to others. But we know what we know. Without you, that building wouldn't have a prayer of being built. Those young architects of yours, they're just small-fry. And so I wanted to ask you if you wouldn't mind telling us a little bit about that. For instance, about the ways in which (and here he glanced once more at his papers) our new, revolutionary way of thinking, our new ideological content, enters into the traditional architectural forms of our nation. And I in turn will tell you, for example, a little bit about our own work. I'd be happy to convince you that, just like you, each of us is hard at work on the little acre that has been entrusted him, and indeed, the best (again he glanced at the papers) upon the national field that has been passed down to us.

But Modráček wasn't in any mood to talk about what was spoken of back then as the Socialist Neorenaissance or Neoclassicism, and so he merely expanded upon façade decorations, frescos, sgraffiti and colourful bas-reliefs with motifs of workers and children; in other words, upon things that he really had nothing in common with.

Láska listened to him for a while, or, rather, pretended to be listening to him, so that he might unexpectedly interrupt him in mid-sentence with: So I hear tell, Modráček, that some sort of Kratochvils live across the hall from your flat, is that right? (He glanced at his papers.) Anečka Kratochvilová and her sons, Jiří and Josef. And her parents, too — František and Emilie Žyl. You're aware of the fact that her husband has emigrated? And this is why we have to devote some special care to that family, so that nothing... sinister should befall them. That's what our job is, obviously. And then it occurred to me that you might be helpful to us in all this...

Láska fixed his eyes on Modráček and grew quiet, so quiet, that one could even hear someone rolling about the examination room next door, as if on roller skates, maybe, bumping into the furniture.

Look here, Comrade, Láska said, crushing out his cigar in a large cast-iron ashtray. Just so we'll understand each another. Enough joking around. The main reason I called you here has to do with something different. We have our eye on your sister, too, so that nothing sinister should befall her, either. After all, you are well aware of the fact that we've already had to lock up two of those paperboys, who got themselves mixed up in something nasty. There still remains a third one, and he continues to visit your little sister regularly. And now I'm going to reveal something to you, just so that you know that you have our complete trust. That third paperboy, the one who snores alongside your sister, works for us. So look, look, Láska smiled. I've got to warn you, too, right away. I've got my money on you, that you're not going to run right off and blab to your sister what you've just learned. On the contrary. I'm betting that right now you will be of the most help to us. Now, your sister, obviously, is very talented. Really. She's got talent to spare — explosive talent — but someone needs to rein it in already. Because somehow it spurs her on strangely, and she goes galloping who knows where.

Láska got up from his desk and pointed to some landscapes that were hanging on the walls. He walked from one to another, explaining that he was a great admirer of the painter's art. I'd be very pleased to hang your little sister here, too, but right now, I just can't. Because rather than employing her talents to provide us all with unforgettable experiences, she pours poison onto her canvases from her palette — for sure — American poison, which one calls abstract painting…

Here Modráček tried to protest. As we know, he himself wasn't all that ecstatic about how his sister painted, but that wasn't important at the moment — he had to protect her from that dangerous accusation, blunt the arrow — and so he drew the lieutenant's attention to the fact that it was no American imperialist standing at the forefront of abstract painting, but the Russian artists Kandinsky and Malevich.

Well, look here. Again you're going to lecture us. It looks as if your sister's trained you well, Láska nodded. But let's not forget that we've been trained too. Yours is a pretty sad case, Comrade Modráček. Every time we seem to be approaching an understanding, you take a quick step backwards and to the side. You're incorrigible. But that's enough for today. Just wait a moment, don't get up; I'll call the duty officer, and he'll see you on your way.

THE BRASSIERE

The door opened a crack, and in peeked the cleaning woman, pulling behind her a vacuum with a long cord: Comrade Švarcšnupf, may I tidy up now?

I passed my tongue over my lips and commanded: And thoroughly at that, Comrade! Yesterday I found dust in my drawers.

She barked back: Don't be vulgar, Comrade! I'll complain to the chief.

Immediately, I realised that she was Comrade Slepec's aunt — well set up in the party cadres she was — and so I rushed into an explanation that I wasn't joking, that the drawers I was referring to were not what she had in mind. But it didn't matter. She still didn't believe me.

It was high time for me to be off to my Russian lesson. But before I could, I still had to pop in at the chief's office upstairs for my instructions for next week. Because he was leaving for Dresden that very day. From behind his desk in the antechamber of the chief's office, Comrade Chovanec made a face at me: Who's late to the game has only himself to blame.[17] Švarcšnupf, Švarcšnupf, the chief was asking for you before he left.

What did you tell him?

That the devil only knows where you've been running about.

But you knew I had an interrogation! And the interrogated party was a stubborn cuss — and this drew the investigation out enormously!

Enormously! Chovanec laughed. Where'd you get that one from, enormously! That's a beaut, that is! Just be careful — that's not an imperialistic term, is it?

I've always known that Chovanec was a dangerous type. He seems to be joking all the time, but in reality he's got his eyes on us, constantly. For example, what happened to Comrade Zhořelec? He lived here like the rest

....

17   *Kdo pozdě chodí sám sobě škodí.*

of us, interrogating his subjects, drawing up his reports, keeping his eye on his suspects — I'd say he was the picture of conscientious industry — and suddenly, wham! He disappeared. And only later did we learn that the chief had summoned him one evening, interrogated him all night long, and then, in the morning, they carted him off somewhere, and he never returned. It turned out that he was a subversive element. He passed himself off as the son of a small craftsman, but then at some sort of party Chovanec got under his skin and squeezed out of him that his father was once the owner of a plumbing firm with eleven employees. Eleven exploited workers! Once, the chief said to us: You can lie as much as you want, Comrades, but never, never deceive the party!

But now I had to run. My Russian lesson starts at four. The lady that gives me lessons lives on Poštovská St, and that, fortunately, is just around the corner. Varvara Puchliaková's flat has four doorbells, one for each room. She's an old grandma, hard of hearing, so she has to have a bell hooked up not only to the main room, but to the kitchen, the foyer, and the jakes, too. I lay my palm across the buttons and rang all four at once. I waited a moment, and rang them again. I took a step back and cast a glance up at the window on the second floor, but it didn't open. And then the doors of the building flew open wide. I just had time to jump aside, at the last moment, otherwise I'd've been flung out onto the street and under the wheels of a big Tatra that was just then lumbering past. It was Comrade Klouček who came flying out. His lesson was an hour before mine. Just wait — you're in for a treat! Today the babushka reeks like Tsarist shit!

Don't open the window, Tovarich Švarcšnupf, it's cold! And she shooed me from the window. We stood there looking at each another, while the old hag kept on stinking on all cylinders and I couldn't help breathing so soon my lungs felt like they were full of shit.

Have a seat, Tovarich Švarcšnupf, she invited me, in Russian.

I sat down on a creaky chair, opened my book, found the page, and strove to hack my way through the primordial forest of Cyrillic letters. But I had no machete, and so I was just flailing away hopelessly. At last, I gave up, and Varvara Puchliakova began reading to me, while I repeated after her, sentence after Russian sentence:

Varvara: Ah, girls! How hot it is!

I: Ah, girls! How hot it is!

Varvara: Listen, after our lessons, let's go swimming!

I: Listen, after our lessons, let's go swimming!

Varvara: Oh, girls, I can't go with you!

I: Oh, girls, I can't go with you!

Varvara: Mama has forbidden me to swim in the river!

I: Mama has forbidden me to swim in the river!

Varvara: In that case, we won't wait for you!

I: In that case, we won't wait for you!

We were getting on well. I'd say that soon I'd be speaking Russian as well as the chief. And when vacation comes around, I'll go to the Crimea, to the Black Sea. O, girls! I'm going to go swimming in the Black Sea! And then I noticed that the old lady didn't stink so much any more.

On the opposite wall there hung a bulletin board, and on it all sorts of large and small pictures — mostly Russian saints with golden aureoles and, among them, that holiest of holies, a colour plate of Comrade Stalin. Under the board a rack was fixed, on which a candle was ever burning, dripping its wax into a little bowl placed beneath it on the floor. Once, Comrade Klouček had explained to me that the bulletin board with the saints and Stalin was called an iconostasis.

I live on Pekařský street, in a poor, confiscated flat. Two rooms in a house with a gallery. It used to belong to a composer of music, who had run off abroad. Sometimes I have the feeling that he did it on purpose. As if he knew that State Security would seize it and assign it to me. The walls are damp. A paradise of roaches.

The nameplate by the doorbell reads Rudolf Švarcšnupf. Here, everybody knows me merely as Švarcšnupf, the quiet, somewhat sheepish relative of that composer. A rumour that the chief allowed to spread, so that nobody'd get wise to the fact that, in reality, I'm a cop. Lieutenant Láska.

I fit the key in the lock, but the lock wouldn't budge. I've been meaning to have it changed for quite some time now. So, once more I've got to ring.

NABOKOV HERE

The father of Modráček the architect, Docent Zdeněk Modráček, taught Introduction to Philosophy and Logic at the University of Brno. But shortly after the occupation of Czechoslovakia, he died, following a rather banal operation for a pulmonary embolism.

Docent Modráček was chiefly interested in Christian philosophy. More precisely, in that branch of the same, which had been influenced in a decisive manner by Vladimir Solovyov, that most noteworthy representative of religious philosophy in Russia. He had translated Solovyov's fundamental works into Czech: *The Crisis of Western Philosophy*, and *Lectures on Divine Humanity*. Among the followers of Solovyov, he was most interested in Nikolai Berdyayev, that metaphysical existentialist. From among his works he had translated Philosophy and the Free Spirit. While he was working on this translation, he contacted Berdyayev, who was living in Paris, by letter, and in this way he came into contact with other members of the Russian diaspora there. And because the Russian diaspora in Paris was closely interconnected with the Russian diaspora in Berlin, it became unimaginable that the contacts of Docent Modráček should not widen to include the significant Russian personages in Berlin. And it was in this manner that his correspondence with the writer Sirin, that is, Vladimir Nabokov, came about.

In this way, Zdeněk Modráček became the first Czech translator of Nabokov. At first, indeed, he felt it awfully difficult to skate out from the translation of philosophical essays onto the thin ice of the literary arts, and belles-lettres, but at last he succumbed to it. He brought over into Czech several of Nabokov's poems and short stories, and then, he set himself to the translation of the novel *The Luzhin Defence*, with verve. From this bold enterprise, there remain only thirty-four, by now quite yellowed, pages among Modráček's literary remains. Yet from his epistolary contact with

Nabokov there developed a certain friendship, supported above all by the fact that, at Nabokov's request, Modráček visited the writer's mother, Yelena Ivanovna, née Rukavishnikova, several times after she moved to the Smíchov quarter of Prague after the assassination of her husband (Nabokov's father) in Berlin.

For, when Hitler became Reichskanzler, life in Berlin became even more dangerous. After all, Vera Yevseyevna, Nabokov's wife, née Slonim, was a Russian Jew. Still and all, a full four years passed before, at last, Nabokov bestirred himself, and in May 1937 sent his wife and three-year-old son Dmitri to Paris, under watchful escort. He set off himself after them, choosing a roundabout route through Vienna, before Hitler's Anschluss of Austria. Before doing so, he sent Zdeněk Modráček a letter in Russian, of which I permit myself to cite but one small fragment, in my own rough translation:

'…I'm escaping from Berlin, which has now sufficiently been transformed into a trap that might snap shut any day, and for good. I'm still going to make a quick stop in Vienna on my way, so as to visit my friend, the entomologist Fritz Bölsche. (If you were a little more interested in entomology, my dear friend, you'd be aware of the fact that there exists a species of butterfly known as the Ladoga Camilla Bölsche, a fairly significant mutation of an otherwise widely dispersed type already known to Carl Linnaeus. But I really can't expect such knowledge of You, because the mutation Ladoga Camilla Bölsche, which is named after my good friend Bölsche, is known only to real experts of entomological taxonomy.) Still, immediately I must confess to You, my dear friend, that I don't intend to merely visit my good friend Fritz Bölsche; I'm planning to kidnap him. That is, I'd like to try and convince him to join me, because I've got a nasty suspicion that Hitler's going to have a yen for Austria before too long. While we're on the subject, my dear friend, I'd like to take the opportunity of asking You — and this was my first design in writing this letter (a design which was covered over by other, consecutively arising, designs, because I write letters to You with the same appetite I have for peach preserves, which remind me of the Sunday dinners of my childhood in our country house in Vyra) so, again, I wanted to ask You, my dear friend, if you'd have anything against me and my friend Bölsche attempting the route from Vienna through Brno. After all, the proximity of the two places to each other, and the kinship of the two cities, simply cries out for them to become a twin-city in some distant, idyllic future. We'd only really stop at your place to say hello, before racing onward — because I'd also like to consider passing through Prague, to say hello to my mother and — particularly — convince her to join us as well. But her correspondence makes it abundantly clear how immensely delighted she is with Prague; after all, just as Brno is similar to Vienna, believe it or not — Prague is similar to Saint Petersburg. Not so much architecturally speaking — no, probably not at all similar in that respect — but for all that, similar all the more on account of a sort of dark, stark dreariness that both cities share…'

To this fragment of Nabokov's letter I'd like to add a note: the Ladoga Camilla is — as I've confirmed by a glance at the corresponding encyclopaedia — a butterfly of the Nymphalidae family, that is, of the same species as the emperor and monarch butterflies. It's also found in our area. We know it as a Double-Row White Admiral, such as you can often meet up with around blackberry blossoms and flowering bramble. This of course is not the case with the aforementioned mutation named in honour of the Viennese entomologist Bölsche. That one is not to be found in our neck of the woods, appearing as it does only in the southern suburbs of Vienna.

LIEUTENANT LÁSKA IN THE FAMILY CIRCLE

Lieutenant Láska, alias Rudolf Švarcšnupf, slid the key into the lock. But the mechanism was stubborn — even maliciously so — and thus Láska had to ring. The door was opened for him by a tall, slender woman — let's acknowledge the fact that her name was Marta, even though Marta Švarcšnupfová has a chilling sound to it. But such is life.

That lock will drive me crazy, complained Láska, turning the useless key over and over in his fingers. What a horrid day it's been. Sometimes I think I'd've been better off as a barber or a shoemaker than what I am. But you only leave State Security in a pine box. Where's Anička?

Playing outside in the courtyard, Marta answered. That's not an answer to make Láska very happy. The courtyard in question was full of garbage cans and rotting mattresses, rusted and hole-riddled metal pots. Rats ran about there, and at nighttime drunks would piss down into it from the gallery running outside their doors. Láska fears for his daughter with a tormenting fear. Sometimes, during an interrogation, he'd grow suddenly still. His gaze would drift until his eyes came to rest somewhere, up on the ceiling, let's say… Once it even so happened that Láska's victim had to clear his throat once, twice, to jog the Lieutenant back into the present moment, so as to get on with the interrogation. At least it still wasn't common for the interrogated parties to complain to the chief about the absent-mindedness of their interrogators.

Five-year-old Anička is a particularly childish creature. It's true she's slow, as we say today. But she isn't autistic. On the contrary: she's highly sociable, she even clings to people. When it so happened that she should find herself amongst a large group of people, this only aroused in her a veritable explosion of affection. For example, should Švarcšnupf's relatives, or those of Marta, or both, come down for the holidays, if anyone at all showed up, immediately she would rush to them yearningly, behaving like a cuddly family pet. She would tangle herself among everyone's legs and crawl under the table, where a whole forest of such limbs was to be found. She would embrace them one after another, every now and then popping her head out from underneath the tablecloth, distributing smiles left and right like a model on the sunken runway of a fashion show, or some party boss at a subterranean podium. In the space of her four years she'd only mastered a few words, which came forth in a stream of otherwise incomprehensible sounds, and in such a way that even those words she knew would fly off and get lost in that auricular gale like butterflies on some blooming meadow. The only ones who could understand her (and not all of the time, at that), were Láska and Marta.

Did you happen to notice the rather poetic metaphor I used for that otherwise disturbing dissolution of words in a stream of incomprehensible sounds: butterflies on a blooming meadow? In this particular case, it's fitting. For in Anička's speech, such an ordering *agent* got the upper hand that ordered her expression according to laws different from those of linguistic communication.

One of the things left behind by the original occupant of the flat, the composer Maňoušek, when he hightailed it out of the people's republic, was a piano. An upright piano, to be precise: a black box of no great dimensions, resting against a wall. This was the most valuable thing abandoned by the scampering musician, if we don't count the mirror-like imprint of his soul, which continually hovered about the piano like some blurry stain of light, which the new mistress of the flat couldn't do anything with. When little Anička first discovered the keyboard of that piano, by chance, she began hammering at the keys with her whole hands. But soon enough, her fingers uncurled from her fists, and those fingers began to organise themselves, in their own unique way, until they had worked out a system concomitant to an actual sonic pattern, which we might, perhaps, call music. And it was this that was present in her speech as well, organising, in its own deconstructive way, comprehensible words into incomprehensible sounds. But if this was music, it was the mere presentiment of a music as distant as the rotations of the galactic system are distant from the rotations of the gears and wheels in some factory machine.

Láska and Marta strove in vain to get their little daughter to plunk out the simplest folk melodies on the piano with two fingers. So they gave up. And because they didn't put too much value on the old black crate themselves, they abandoned it to her tender mercies, to be whanged out of tune, made to yelp and whine, with a final view to the scrap-heap. Only the limitless love they had for her enabled them to bear the endless hours which their daughter sometimes spent at the piano. While she was at the keyboard, it was as if she were striving to extract from the howling entrails of the universe their pain: the scream of intestines, the moans of the liver, the sighs of the kidneys, the squeaking of the gallbladder, the sorrow of the spleen, the melancholy of the stomach, the choler of the urinary bladder.

(Kindly remember all of this concerning little Anička. It'll come in handy much later on in the story.)

Láska was quite aware of the fact that, as far as the distribution of confiscated real estate went, he had gotten the short end of the stick. It was both logical and understandable that the chief and his deputies should divide amongst themselves the apartments of the old factory owners of Brno… Did I say apartments? Ha! Rather, all their modern villas, furnished with everything that just such luxury villas in the West are tricked out with today. And the Láska family had been dumped into this reeking tenement with a gallery overlooking the courtyard. Now, a flat of better quality might certainly have been found — but then what was the chief to do with his pet (or, perhaps 'pets' is the better term, for as far as sex was concerned, the chief was insatiable).

But there were still quite a few class enemies in Brno planning to take to their heels. Sometimes, they were successful. Other times, some heel got wind of their plans and turned them in. So they would end up in the interrogation room — from which they would never return. Either way, the housing market would still grow with the newly freed-up homes of the families of those Brno factory owners who still survived from the old days, like trilobites, beneath their Barrandov Terraces. There would be a constant supply of apartments freed up by the mimeographers of anti-State flyers, by conspirators and renegades in the party ranks, or by those against whom collaboration with the régime of the Nazi Protectorate had been sufficiently proven, or by those who stubbornly refused to collaborate with the present régime. And so Láska knew that all he had to do was to keep his eyes peeled for the slightest trembling of the stalks; or, should the occasion serve, to give the wheel of someone's fate a little nudge in the right direction, himself.

Láska, standing at the door where we'd left him, lightly pushed aside his spouse and hurried down into the courtyard. As if she had been waiting for him, Anička was squatting amongst the dustbins, toying with some sort of rusty tin, scraping an iron nail against it so as to produce that characteristic squeal which makes a person's skin crawl. She raised her head and trained her shining eyes on Láska. He ran over to her, and swept her up from the ground and into his embrace, along with the tin and nail, which she refused to part with.

Láska was aware of the fact that his little daughter was mentally retarded; that there was something not quite right about her. But he didn't dwell on that; for him she was a magnificent, fabulous little human creature, who, he was sure, had her own fine place in this world's hierarchy of merit and treasure; that this tiny little body, now blissfully swaying in his embrace, would one day enchant everyone and become a shining ruby in a golden crown. That his little Anička's place was first in line amongst many of the rulers of the most powerful states on earth; before all of them, whose names even then filled the headlines of the newspapers and were printed on gold-embossed calling cards of real and not-so-real celebrities; before those who assume themselves to be the torchbearers of the radiant future. He also knew that it was his, Láska's, duty to protect that wonderful, sweet little mite from evil and all the dangers that the world presented. Likewise, he knew well that he was prepared to do absolutely anything so as to comply with that duty.

And so he bore that fragile little body (along with his official briefcase, and the rusty tin and nail) up the stairs to their flat.

And there in the room, little Anička sat at the piano and waited, a little impatiently that day, for the smudge of light to appear on the ceiling — the tender fluorescent soul of the musician who had spent hours, weeks, months and years at that same upright piano, until the day that somebody from the Union of Musical Composers denounced him for kowtowing to the atonal music of Arnold Schönberg. And inasmuch as he was well aware of what might occur in consequence of that denunciation, as soon as he became aware of it, he attempted to flee the country. Nevertheless, after successfully getting across the border, he tumbled into a deep open sump belonging to one of the manors near the Bavarian border, and before night turned to day, he was suffocated by the aggressive bio-gases.

◆

NABOKOV ARRIVES

I recall how wild, yes, let's put it like that, how completely wild my father grew in anticipation, as the date of Nabokov's arrival neared. At the time, we were still living in that big apartment on Augustinská St, which abutted the high wall enclosing the Augustinians' monastery garden. Of course, when the communists took over, they renamed the street Jaselská.[18]

It was in May 1937 — a very warm May it was — and at my father's request I hurried home from Olomouc. At the time I was putting the finishing touches on my first independent project — a villa in the suburbs for the automobile racer Nusek. And I had the strong, pleasant feeling of satisfaction at having succeeded in bearing to Olomouc the torch of functionalism — which was slowly beginning to grow dim, perhaps, in Brno. And who. knows, today, what might have happened had not the war and the German occupation intervened? After all, the 'aerodynamic villa' built in Pisárky for Augustin Tesař is proof positive that Bohuslav Fuchs' imagination was certainly not on the wane, and that the late thirties/early forties might well have become a further significant stage on the road of Brno architecture. But that's another story.

Three days prior to the writer's visit, my father hired an efficient cleaning lady, who transformed our apartment into such a 'battlefield' that I escaped from there to the 'owl's roost' — the flat belonging to my intended bride in Černá Pole. Two days before Nabokov's visit, he also hired a woman who worked in the kitchen of the Hotel Slovan. He sat long hours with her, debating possibilities for the menu. It was as if he were planning a month's victualling for some grand restaurant, whereas in fact we're only talking about one single supper, breakfast, and dinner. And then the cooking, fry-

---

[18]   In recognition of a battle near the Polish town of Jasło, during World War II, in which Czech troops took part alongside the Red Army.

ing and baking began. This all grew into such a wild copulation of cooking, dusting, and vacuuming that whenever I dropped in back home, even for a moment, my eyes grew as wide as those of some pimply kid on the brink of puberty, who for the first time in his life stumbles upon an unbridled orgy, such as up until then he'd only sensed goes on, somewhere.

My father also took it upon himself to make sure that Nabokov's entire visit would be documented in precise detail. His Leica was in constant — irritating — action, even though he didn't quite know how to use it properly. This began already at the Brno train station, where Nabokov, with courteous good will, agreed to pose in his dark blazer, white shirt and polka-dotted cravat, with one corner of a white handkerchief poking out of his breast pocket — such as no exemplary gentleman sets out on the road without. He sat himself down on a large trunk, holding another between his knees, with an impish expression on his face. From the twenty-four hours, more or less, that Nabokov spent in Brno, there remain a handful of photographs. His figure appears still athletic, although the autumn of his age was now upon him. Still, after all, he was also, among other things, the goalkeeper of a football team made up of Russian emigrants in Berlin. He was no mere cataloguer of books and — like my father — a translator; he was also a passionate butterfly collector and an engineer of chess problems, again, rather unlike my father. At first, the plan was for Nabokov to have arrived along with some sort of Viennese entomologist. Consequently, this travelling companion of his had also figured into the calculations for supper, breakfast and dinner. And I'm not just talking about victuals here (with which my father had so filled pantry, icebox and cellar that we would be nourished for months on them, like mice on Emmental), but also borrowed silverware. However, the fellow didn't come along in the end. It seems he didn't consider it necessary to escape the Nazi hydra, which was seething and rampaging just beyond the fence of Austria. Although once, Nabokov implied that he had that Austrian entomologist in that large travelling chest of his. But I rather imagine the belly of that gigantic trunk filled with books, manuscripts and dictionaries.

These twenty-four hours (more or less) with Nabokov are etched in my memory as one gigantic euphoria on my father's part — a euphoria as big as a whale gliding through our apartment, through the dining room and out the door, all the way to Komenský Square. I was fully aware of my father's conversational bliss: they spoke Russian, French and German, mixing the three tongues with obvious relish. My father spoke them all, almost as well as his guest. I, on the other hand, understood only the German, and a little bit of the Russian. The German portions were the fewest, and merely touched upon uninteresting organisational matters. They spoke Russian when talking about literature, and French when the conversation turned to food, women, or butterflies. It soon became apparent to me that their method of communication was strictly apportioned, for both of them suffered from an obsession with order. This is what brought it about that each sphere, each topic of their conversation, was dominated by, given over to, a certain language. As if each of these tongues had been strictly defined, God Himself having created each one of them for that one sphere of human activity or interest alone, and it was only the frightful shambles that pervades this world that has people use each of them indiscriminately, pell-mell, for everything and anything.

It would be fitting, perhaps, for me to describe here in all its sumptuous details that evening dinner party in our apartment on Augustinská, but I'm afraid I'm simply unable to. It's embarrassing, but I cannot even recall what was served — not even one dish from the various courses. This is certainly due to the fact that I don't speak French — that one tongue proper to descriptions of food, women and butterflies. But wait — my apologies — there is one aspect of that celebratory evening that has stuck in my memory, although it has nothing to do with food. My father also hired a server for the evening. I can no longer be certain whether or not she too was from the Hotel Slovan. But for all that, I clearly remember — you simply can't forget something like this — that she was rather a stand-in for a real server (such as in those days were impossible to come by), but what a stand-in she was! Although my father was upset at the fact that he was only able to hire that 'cabbage patch princess,'[19] well, she was a girl of about thirteen, if I had to guess, with a button nose, freckles, and a little violet stain on her bare neck that looked as if a fairy-tale vampire had been nibbling there. And there we are. How is it that I remember her in such detail? How is it that I have been able to carry her vibrantly colourful image with me, clear across

....

[19]   *Nánynka ze zelí.* A reference to a Czech folk song, 'Šla Nanynka do zelí' [Nanynka went into the cabbage patch].

the abyss of the years that divide me, today, from those still idyllic times? Perhaps for this reason: that she was something quite extraordinary and, in her presence, I felt ashamed, felt something bordering on shyness. For this most childlike of creatures already — I kid you not! — was in perfect possession of all the finesse of a woman; she had the entire repertoire of the female arts down pat, and wasn't at all shy about showing them off to us, if only in hints and suggestions.

Now this teasing display of hers had nothing whatsoever to do with the tasks she was hired to perform. But it's also important to state that this in no way impeded her impeccable service at table — it was something in addition to all that — but only now does it occur to me, in the dim flash of recollection, that I see, as if on a stage lit up for a second by the flash of a shorted light — the four absolutely gorgeous limbs of the girl so like the legs of a crouching colt — only now does it occur to me that our 'cabbage patch princess' was perhaps playing this role for the benefit of our guest; as if she wanted to tell him something important, communicate some sort of message incomprehensible to the rest of us.

We were at that very moment talking about atonal music (we were milling through simply everything that evening); about Schönberg and his path to dodecaphony, when suddenly, Nabokov halted in the middle of a sentence and remained motionless, holding his fork in the space before him, staring at the waitress. Then, after the passage of a few seconds of glomming like that, he set aside his fork and his knife and ran his hand over his face. It was as if he were tearing himself out of a trance in that way; as if he wanted to efface something inappropriate. Then he picked up his utensils again and finished the interrupted sentence. And as unbelievable as it may sound, I remember that sentence quite clearly, at least its basic framework. It's as if for that one passing moment there had been present some sort of peculiar preservative fabric, which mummified it for me. The sentence was expressed in German. I hasten to add that it was also appropriate to speak of music in German — as if that subject, too, belonged to its everyday, practical and organisational affairs. We can also assume that philosophical discourse pertains to its particular sphere of expression. So here it is, that sentence in its entirety, at your request not broken into two halves: Überzeugt, der Musikgeschichte mit seiner Zwölftonästhetik weite Perspektiven eröffnet zu haben, erklärte Arnold Schönberg, dass durch ihn die Vorherrschaft der deutschen Musik für die nächsten hundert Jahre gesichert sei.[20]

There is a post office at the corner of Augustinská St. First thing next morning, Nabokov trotted off down there to send a telegram to his mother in Prague, to let her know that he'd be by to see her that very evening.

In the forenoon we showed him around the city a little bit. Above all, I drew his attention to the architectural and urbanístic similarities between Brno and Vienna — about which he already knew something, in theory; but I was certain that he would be glad of the opportunity to compare the recent developments of the two cities in person.

Despite my father's best efforts at communicating to me — via gestures and faces made behind Nabokov's back — that he didn't feel it would be proper to bore our guest with an architectural lecture in German, I suggested it anyway, and tried to explain to Nabokov that, parallel to the case of Vienna, in the first half of the nineteenth century, Brno underwent a transformation from an enclosed, fortified city into an open one. The city ramparts disappeared, as did the battlements and bastions of the Baroque age, and in their train, the city gates as well. And then came the time for the boulevards, ringing the old town.

Once more my father made himself known to me from behind Nabokov's back, sending in my direction one of our familiar household signals, a warning, so much as to say: 'If you don't cut this out right now, I'm going to kill you!' I pretended not to see this warning signal, and continued on, convinced of the fact that Nabokov was now hooked, and anxious to learn, in excruciating detail, how it all came about that Brno opened up and outward into its Ringstrasse.

At the moment, we were standing on Komenský Square, where, like a traffic cop at an intersection, I could spread wide my arms and point out to Nabokov the direction from which the link road ran, between the obelisk in the Denisové Gardens and the Lutheran church, that is, one of the compositional axes of the ring road, crossing Eliščiný Square, that is, today's

....

[20]   I am convinced that, with his twelve-tone aesthetics, Arnold Schönberg has opened wide the perspectives of music, and thereby confirmed the supremacy of German music for the next hundred years.

Komenský Square, perpendicular to Joštová, which of course during the time of His Imperial Highness was known as Archduke Eugene Boulevard.

I hastened to stress the fact that this whole project of the ring road truly fulfilled the vision of the urban identification of Brno with Vienna; after all, the creator of the project was none other than Ludwig Förster, who played a key role in the Vienna Ringstrasse as well.

By now, my father was entirely disgusted with me for boring his guest to death. But I'd lay a wager on it that jealousy also played a role in his emotions. For this was one of the most important encounters of his life — and on top of that, one with severe time limitations, and here I was appropriating his guest entirely to myself. But whatever he was really feeling, he continued to bob into my field of vision from behind Nabokov's back, sending in my direction more and more of the ancient signals of our clan (dear God! What a clan we were!) culminating in gesticulations which meant to convey the following sentiment: 'I'm about to jam my arm right down your throat, grab hold of your innards, and pull them all out into the daylight!' This, as one might deduce, was a much more serious signal than the one which merely indicated infanticide. Now, this warning gesture was used only in exceptional circumstances. Actually, it was one that we rather avoided using. After all, it was something along the lines of a family curse. But since it had already been tossed out into the open, it would have been unforgivable to ignore. And so I just made a slight bow with my head as if to indicate that the lecture had now run its course, and I handed Nabokov back over to the tender mercies of my Pops.

Today, as from this great distance I look back upon that long-past visit of Nabokov's, there also comes to my mind the rather large disappointment that I felt at the time. However much my father always gave pride of place to the philosopher Berdyayev, he was no less a great admirer of Nabokov's. He considered him one of the greatest writers of the age. But he also admired him as a man. And for that reason, I had been expecting something extraordinary — a little wonder of the world. At least something along the order of Prince Bolkonsky in sables, with the Medal of St Dmitry (Third Class). As it was, the disappointment that made its appearance then, I brought about myself, through my obtuseness.

When Vladimir Nabokov went away the next morning, he presented my father with a gift that he was to treasure until the day he died. (Unfortunately, that day was none too far off. Even then, death was treading on his heels, pacing on the other side of the door, and so impatiently — as if, the bitch, she had somewhere more important to be, and my Dad was holding her up.) It was the manuscript of his short story *Zdes govoryat po-russki*. My father translated it over the next few days. Today, I know that his Czech title, *Zde se hovoří rusky,* is a little inexact, for the original is a reference to a sign on the door or storefront of a shop somewhere in Berlin, advertising to the Russian emigrant or tourist the fact that inside he could conduct his business in Russian.

At the time, I was enraptured neither with the tale, or the entirety of Nabokov's visit. A whole lot of water had to flow under the bridge before I came to realise that both the visit, and that gift, were actually meant for me. And that it was the gift of gifts!

But let's not get ahead of ourselves. Let's not be like death, who so impatiently treads on one's heels and paces just on the other side of the door.

◆

LÁSKA SETS THE HOOK IN MODRÁČEK

Whenever I would enter the stationhouse on Běhounská I would submit myself to a process, which had something of the invariability of strict ritual to it. The StB goon who served as porter had to call upstairs and wait for confirmation that, indeed, I had been summoned. Upstairs, of course, they always took their time. So I would stand there, and in the interim, which sometimes stretched into quite a long period of time, while the StB functionary seemed to take no notice of me. But God forbid that I should make the slightest movement in any direction. No, I had to stand there rooted to the spot. At most, I might shift my weight from one foot to the other, or flex my fingers and toes. Then, at last, the phone would ring and it would be confirmed from above that I had been summoned. The StB porter would then lead me to the lift, call it down, open the door and accompany me to the level indicated, where Láska would already be waiting by the elevator shaft. The porter and he would greet one another with Praise to Labour, at which the porter would deliver me into Láska's care. This of course took place wordlessly, but it too was no doubt a ceremoniously serious official act. So Láska would take me in hand and lead me down a corridor panelled waist-high with shining marble. Along the way we would meet with other investigators; on the day in question we actually came across two, who were just leading my neighbour, Mrs Kratochvilová, from interrogation. Each of them were supporting her gently on both sides. It was then that I clearly saw how advanced her pregnancy was. And this, certainly, was the reason why she was summoned to the Běhounská precinct: so that she wouldn't have to waddle over to the big station on Leninka, with such a big belly, where otherwise she might have been expected to be summoned, according to the category of her offence, i.e. being the wife of an emigrant.

For if I understand it correctly, and I believe I do, the investigative offices on Běhounská dealt with the usual police matters, such as the interrogation of thieves, rapists, and traffic offenders. On the other hand, the huge head-quarters of the Czechoslovak State Railways Administration, on Leninka, which after their takeover the Communists had appropriated, was given over to the struggle against their class enemies. Mrs Kratochvilová and I were clearly exceptions that proved the rule. In her case, it was a gesture of humanity, an expression of the state security service's thoughtfulness, whereas in mine it was, I guess, one more example of StB drollery. But certainly it was also because Láska was officially stationed at Běhounská (where they had a small detached workplace), and he carried a torch for me for some reason — it was that sort of predisposition that the police sometimes feel, which along with paedophilia and necrophilia, belongs among the steamiest passions known to man.

When Láska and I passed Mrs Kratochvilová and her two investigators in the corridor, I nodded a slight greeting in her direction, as it seemed inappropriate to wish her a good day in such surroundings. But she didn't see me. She just walked on, with her head bent low. Perhaps she couldn't even see what was at her feet, for she tripped on a tile and her two investigators had to catch and steady her from both sides. But my Láska greeted those other two Láskas with a loud Praise to Labour, Comrades, at which both of them replied, Praise, Comrade.

Láska led me into the chamber, had me sit on the chair, but this time he offered me neither coffee nor cigar. Instead, he walked right over to the window and stood there, staring out into the street. I waited there, thinking that it'll be the whip today, not the sugar. But even though I thought myself more or less prepared even for the words, still — I didn't reckon on what happened next, what he said — even in my worst nightmares. For he just hauled right off and pummelled me in my most sensitive place, all the while just standing at the window with his back to me, speaking to me from there. At first, it occurred to me that he was having fun at my expense again, and that, again, I'd fallen for it. But suddenly I was gripped with terror. I sat there, paralysed with shock so, that in the first few moments I couldn't even breathe. I still don't quite know how long it lasted.

You know, we were discussing whether or not to lock you up, too. Because, how can we be sure, after all, that you're not mixed up in it all? But in the end, I didn't agree. I vouched for you, because I think I know you well enough to venture that you don't approve of your sister's activities. But of course a man can always misjudge things. After all, we thought that your sister's boyfriend was on our side — as I told you in confidence last time — and what does he up and do, but try to high-tail it through the long grass with one of her paintings rolled up in a tube. He told us that he was planning on selling it to a gallery. But in the meantime your sister herself admitted that it wasn't an artwork at all, but rather a camouflaged map of the Brno armoury. What's more, all of her so-called abstract paintings are actually works of espionage: maps, plans and schematics of industrial and military objects.

I tensed. It took all my strength of will to stand up and declare: Please don't get angry. But I know, without the shadow of a doubt — I stake my head on it — that her paintings have nothing to do with espionage, but are really and truly abstract paintings!

Láska turned from the window and motioned me with his head to sit back down. Ah, Comrade Engineer. Have you never heard that one mustn't ever enter into a wager with the devil, risking one's head in the bargain? He was standing there now with his hands in his pockets, and an amused expression on his face, carefully looking me over as if I had begun to show clear signs of apoplectic stupor. I'll pass over in silence, today, the fact that you're wanting to teach me lessons again. So, amongst your many talents, you're also able to distinguish abstract paintings from camouflaged schematics of industrial and military objects? If indeed you are so possessed of this valuable faculty, you might be quite useful to us. And as it is, you're about to receive the opportunity to provide us with evidence of your usefulness.

Láska wasted no time in developing his thoughts concerning my usefulness. I wasn't quite able to follow him at first, because I had before my eyes the clear image of my little sister in a dungeon, as I remembered such from the Vilímek engravings that illustrated an edition of The Count of Monte Christo that I'd read. But I was ready to do anything, understand? simply anything if only to somehow help my sister out. And this was quite in line with Láska's concluding instructions. He charged me with the surveillance of the Kratochvil family's flat, and all the comings and goings thereat. He stressed again that he had placed his own men there too, But you, as their long-time neighbour, have such opportunities as our people can only dream of, if you catch my drift.

Slowly, he pulled his hands out of his pockets, approached the table from the opposite side from where I was sitting, and fished some papers out of a drawer.

So we'll just draw up a little agreement now, he proposed.

I'd like to see my sister first. I'd like to talk with her.

Of course. You can count on it. But not right away. Everything in its proper season.

At this he lifted up my numb left hand and placed his own fountain pen therein. Then a thought crossed his mind; he said Pardon me, my mistake, and transferred the pen from my left hand to my right. There, that's better, he said, pleased with himself, and proceeded to direct my hand to the concluding paragraph of an official agreement, which had most likely been prepared long ago. But as my hand remained motionless, he gave my ear a light flick with his finger as if to snap me out of my stupor. Then he followed with his eyes as the pen began meandering over the paper.

Carefully, he dried the ink of my signature with a rocking ink blotter, picked up the phone and called the officer on duty, who led me out of the interrogation room, and took me down to the ground floor in the lift. Once there, he opened the door, motioned with his head, and let me out into the street.

But as soon as I found myself outside it occurred to me that I should have stressed how I was simply bursting with desire to collaborate, sure, to the very separation of soul from body, anything to convince them that into the care of such a comrade they could safely entrust his little sister; that it was unnecessary for them to hold her any longer in some dark and cold cell. And so I turned to the officer on duty who had let me out, wishing to convey that desire of mine to him in the sincerest terms possible… But at the moment, I couldn't get a single word out of me. And from all the beastly effort at coming up with something, a huge bubble of snot swelled from my nostril, over which an iris of colours played, until it burst — and that before the officer had time to skip out of the way.

◆

BACK TO DAN KOČÍ

At the moment, Daniel Kočí was changing the ideological embellishments in the shop window of the meat provisioning cooperative (as butcher shops and delis selling smoked meats were called back then.) Such tasks were also part of his duties, since at the time sausage makers didn't have their own window dressers. He was on his knees, hovering over piles of tinned paté, installing righteously appropriate slogans (*Hands off Korea! The Struggle for Peace — a Blow against American Imperialism!*) and all the while he felt two eyes burning holes in his back. Careful, he thought, that's how paranoia begins, but when at last he turned around to clear up the unused coloured paper and cardboard letters scattered among the gesso sausages and plaster kielbasas, he saw that there was indeed someone standing near the display, who was now raising his hand in greeting.

> I'm afraid I'm going to have to disappoint you. I'm not in that line of work anymore.
> But Mr Stolař told me —
> You can just forget whatever it was he told you. He shouldn't have told you anything.
> I can pay you well. I know it's a difficult task…
> But I have nothing to offer in exchange for your money. Wrong number, my good sir.

Then some customers arrived. Dan sliced them some cheap, mealy salami, sold them tins of lard, and promised them, that, next week, probably, there'd be something more than bones and skin for soup — but that stubborn client just kept on standing there to the side, waiting patiently for the butcher to make some time for him.

He turned out to be the director of the Elektrodom on John St. Now, because there was a large ED over the entrance to the store, the people called it The Edison — and this was what caught the attention of the powers that snoop, who then proceeded to order the director to take the letters down. But he, surprisingly enough, dug in his heels in defence of Edison, arguing that the National Artist Vítězslav Nezval,[21] who had just been awarded the gold medal of the World Order of Peace, had written a narrative poem in praise of Edison, which had just been reprinted in the latest of many editions. The monitors, who were not used to backing down, hesitated this time: Nezval was Nezval, after all; even they had heard of him; and so in this way the letters ED were allowed to remain over the entrance to the Elektrodom.

Now, I'm mentioning this simply because I wish to arouse in the reader some sympathetic feelings toward the director of the Elektrodom, trusting that these will in turn migrate from the heads and hearts of my readers to the head (and heart) of Daniel, and our story will be able to continue. Which — see? — is what is actually happening. For how else can you explain the fact that, in the end, Daniel Kočí gave up, surrendering to the insistent urging of the Elektrodom director, and took on his case?

This was a completely different case from that of Radek Stolař. For the director of the Elektrodom wasn't looking for relief from unpleasant suspicions, nor did he need to prove that his wife had no lovers. On the contrary, he wanted to have evidence in hand, such as would allow him to divorce her, with her as the guilty party, thus enabling him to hold onto his most treasured possession: the splendid villa that Modráček the architect had built for him right after the war.

At which we hasten to add that it really wasn't quite so splendid a villa after all. No, it was one of those kitschy stillbirths in Modráček's postwar style, which stuffed his pockets full until the triumph of the working class screwed tight the taps of the moneyflow.

....

[21]   Vítězslav Nezval (1900–1958). Czech surrealist poet; active in the Communist Party, he received the gold medal mentioned here in 1953. The narrative poem 'Edison' was originally published in the 1930 collection *Básně noci* [Poems of Night].

And so we find ourselves in that villa, which jumbles a wannabe neoclassical tone of the sublime with a then-fashionable riff on an English cottage, it all resulting in a monstrous bourgeois fish-fowl.

It is a late summer evening. Outside the window is peaceful Klecandova St, in that most peaceful quarter of Brno, Černá Pole. But even so, the director of the Elektrodom closes the two shutters on both sides of the windows; perhaps so as to give himself an excuse to switch on the gigantic crystal chandelier, which hangs from the high ceiling of the hall on the parterre, a hall surrounded by a gallery that runs around the first floor. Gazing about the hall, Daniel Kočí, who inhabits a modest flat on Orlí St, realises with satisfaction that, at last, and after such a long time, once more he has the sort of client he deserves — the sort he was used to before the war and during the first months of the Protectorate — an elevated sort of person who, even in these rather unpropitious times, has succeeded in preserving his societal niveau. Just the same was he cheered by the realisation that, at last, he would be using his Leica again, and without having to respect the persons of his subjects overmuch. On the contrary — he was again being empowered to shamelessly strip them to their underclothes in an attempt to eternise them in flagranti, after which, in his darkroom, he would see what intimate details would emerge from the developing pans, captured by his camera… and perhaps he would play with those intimate details under the enlarger… (The private eye had his own private collection of intimate details, worked up by the enlarger. Should anyone take those large format obscenities in hand, they'd never guess that he was glomming at a stable of prominent, highly placed promiscuous mares.)

She has a brother who is employed here in the Brno Armoury. Every now and then he picks her up and takes her to see their parents in Vysočina.

And that's where she is now?

The director of the Elektrodom nodded.

And you suspect that what we have here is no innocent visit to Mum and Dad, at all? And that maybe that it's not to Vysočina that he's driving her?

The director of the Elektrodom nodded again.

A richly laid table stood in the middle of the hall. The crystal chandelier hung directly over it, like the summer sun above a fat pasture, and the private eye's hand swam out somewhere among the ham sandwiches (at this time, ham was as rare as an outbreak of tropical malaria in the Lednice-Valtice region, and this was something that Dan knew a little bit about, so the director of the Elektrodom must be selling a lot of lightbulbs), while the latter poured some fragrant English tea, fortified with something or other, into their cups. Around the crystal chandelier fluttered two exceptionally obese moths (lobster moths), striking against the small decorative crystal pieces and setting off a gentle tinkling. In such a way the fragile music of the spheres was drawn down into the professional consultation that was taking place between the private eye and the director of the Elektrodom, seconded by the drumming of Daniel's fingers, which were smeared a bit by the yellow condiments of the sandwiches.

I didn't quite hit it off with my wife's parents — to put it rather gently. Between me and my in-laws, someone has, so to speak, lain a sword, said the director of the Elektrodom in answer to the unasked question.

Now Dan, caught off guard by the flowery language, didn't quite know what to do at first with that sword. You mean to say that you never take your wife to Vysočina yourself?

You've hit the nail right on the head, Elektrodom praised Dan. But once it so happened that I had to speak to my wife, urgently. It was such an urgent matter that I couldn't wait until she got back. So I hopped on a bus and took myself to that hole in Vysočina, Sněžné it's called, and sped directly to my wife's parents' house, as quick as baked partridge to the mug of a squire. (Ah, you should've been a poet, thought Dan.) As a matter of fact, they have a rather large house in the country, with a barn, so you might actually call it a little estate. They greeted me in a way that I won't describe to you now; it's not that important anyway. At any rate, I learned that my wife had gone off on an excursion with her sister, and her parents didn't know, exactly, where, or when she'd be back, other than the fact that it'd be more than two days until she returned. But as I was about to go back to the bus stop, I turned around once more to cast my eye at the house my wife grew up in, and what did I see through the mansard window but her sister.

And there's no mistake in that? It couldn't be another one of your wife's siblings? Maybe she has two sisters? One that went off with her Past Seven Mountains and Seven Rivers, and another, who preferred to stay home reading Karolina Světla?

Of course not. Don't mix everything up. As long as I've known my wife, she's only had one sister. I remember her quite well from the wedding. Those eyes that she shot out at me from the mansard window in Sněžné were the same as those that pinned me to the wall of the banquet hall when I got married. It took an effort, I tell you, to keep myself from being crucified by them then and there. So, while I was waiting — for an hour — on the next bus from Sněžné, pacing the grassy platform overgrown with nettles and smoking one cigarette after another, furious, I knew with certainty that it wasn't to her parents in Sněžné that that brother of hers was giving my wife a lift — but on the contrary, who knows where? Most probably to the ready-spread sheets of some adulterous bed where who knows what sort of bastard was waiting for her. But you'd probably like to take a look at my wife's room? Maybe there's some trace there that only the eye of a professional might see.

The private eye wiped his fingers and his puss in the napkin that the director of the Elektrodom handed him. Then he followed him up to the gallery above the hall, where the director of the Elektrodom pointed to a door. Entering, he pulled down the venetian blinds and flipped on the light.

Before the private eye there opened a vista upon a woman's world so stuffed with divers items that I'd not wish to catalogue here for all the tea in China. But Dan was not flustered. Immediately, he began to scan it all with the eye of a professional. From all of his Pre-Protectorate, Protectorate and Pre-February detective cases he'd developed such experience as we might describe according to the 'Purloined Letter' of Edgar Allan Poe. That is, what we're searching for, what is most often its most important trace, is always somewhere right under our nose. And so those looking to hide something cleverly and well, seem to know, intuitively, that the principle of the 'Purloined Letter' is the very best way of hiding something from the eyes of all — except those of Daniel Koči.

Dan stood there in the centre of the room for a moment, slowly turning round on his own axis, searching for that one thing that somehow sticks out from everything, yet still appears to be part and parcel of the everyday female world. And then he saw it. Pinned on the inside panel of the door, a poster from the Circus Belinda.

Despite the name, this was a Czech circus. On the poster was the picture of a tiger jumping through a hoop — a fiery hoop at that, which the tamer was holding over his head. At first glance, you might think that it was this magical representation of the exotic that was the reason, the one and only reason, why the wife of the director of the Elektrodom (let's call her Belinda from now on. Because her real name, just like that of her husband, is so revolting that it would ruin your day if I mentioned it. And here we might well wonder: was the director of the Elektrodom so miserly that he refused to part with the nominal legal fee required to change it? Or was he fanatically attached to family traditions? Or was there some sort of perverse coprolalia at the bottom of it all? At most, let's add the adjective electric to the name Belinda, since her husband is the director of the Elektrodom); so, as I've just said, it might occur to you that this is the one and only reason why electric Belinda hung that poster in her room. But Daniel had already ventured a guess at the real reason.

Dan was not in the habit of immediately yielding to his first impressions, his first stroke of intuition, even though in most cases it so turned out that the first thing that came to him was the right path to follow. And so he let it settle in overnight, sinking through and impressing itself on his dreams; when he awoke, he carefully crawled over his yet sleeping partner, had a look through the double window of the avant-corps, casting one eye on the fresh morning of Josef St and the other on the still fresher morning of Orlí St. Then he set the water on for coffee in the kitchen, having time to swallow down half a bar of baking chocolate, bid good morning to the retired officer from the flat across the hallway, whom he met in the passage (at the moment, the latter was busy attaching a love note to the little rose-coloured box on the collar of his cat, whom he employed as a Cupid of sorts, before sending him on his way two floors up) after which he loped down the stairs, opened the door, which was as heavy as the lid of a sarcophagus, and then found himself out on the street. A garbage truck was just then passing by; he made a deep bow, yes, a deep bow to the garbage truck, spreading wide his arms, a sure indication of his excellent mood, after which he swerved round the corner and in a twinkling found himself at the counter of the butcher shop on Josef St.

Of course you can have the time off. But you understand, old chap, that this way you'll have burned through all your vacation time, and nothing will be left until the butcher's socialist work brigade leaves for Rügen?

Dan nodded; he understood. Then he went back to his place for his pad and pencil, immediately going out again to bum around the streets — he was so churning with inner energy that he wouldn't be able to stand or sit or do anything else with himself, and the telephone exchange at the post office wouldn't open until nine.

Then, at last, he had the Prague telephone directory in hand, wherein he found the number of the headquarters of the Czechoslovak Union of Cabaret and Circus Artists. He dialled, and when someone picked up on the other end, he identified himself as the presiding officer of the cultural committee of the local chapter of the Revolutionary Union Movement, and that he was interested in learning about the present tour of Circus Belinda — the schedule of each of its stops. He learned that, at the moment, the circus was on the outskirts of Brno, encamped by the river Svratka, on the Jindrov side. Upon learning this, he asked for a detailed rundown of each of the dates when Circus Belinda was in the Brno area — spring, summer, and early autumn. These dates he wrote down, day by day, into his notebook.

The director of the Elektrodom was not only burdened by an odious name, the likes of which simply cannot be expressed in a novel of genteel aspirations, but also by an equally odious systematical predisposition, and a bureaucratic devotion to order. For the time being, we shall pass over this, in silence, otherwise our story would be spinning its wheels for quite a while. Now, the director of the Elektrodom also had a list of all the dates, all the days, on which his wife had supposedly been visiting her parents in Vysočína. It did not surprise Daniel at all that these dates dovetailed exactly with those on which Circus Belinda was in the Brno region. Spring, summer, fall. So, every season, she's a sleazin', Dan thought to himself.[22] But in reply to the question whether or not he had any ideas, he would say indeterminately that he might be close to something, but he really couldn't say yet.

Above all, Dan knew that he daren't drag his feet now, since according to his information concerning the present tournée of Circus Belinda, he knew that they were to pack up tomorrow and set off to Gottwaldov,[23] then to Bratislava and Zvolen.

....

[22]   *Takže kvartálnice, kvartální nevěrnice.*

[23]   So was Zlín known, in honour of the Communist leader Klement Gottwald, from 1949 until 1990.

                                                        JIŘÍ KRATOCHVIL

When he got out of the tram at the Jundrov stop and set out along the dusty path, he could see from afar the tall marquee and, coursing over the sloping meadows, the colourful triangular flags. And immediately he felt that peculiar trembling, such as he knew well from those days when the detective's craft was his daily bread. Ants began to crawl all over his back — something he only felt these days right before bedding a heretofore inaccessible partner, whom he'd had to chase after for a long time. Or when he stood before the paintings of Chittussi.[24]

24   Antonín Chittussi (1847–1891), Czech impressionist painter, specialising in landscapes.

A SAD CHAPTER

From time to time, Modráček the architect would request permission to visit his sister. Again and again he presented his appeal in writing, addressing it to the police station on Běhounská, even sending it by registered mail. But he never received any reply. It occurred to him that, perhaps, his requests didn't fulfil the conditions required for such an appeal. After all, it was possible that there might even exist a certain kind of form that one had to fill out and attach to the petition, without which Sesame would never open. So he turned to the porter at the police station, but only received the curt reply that a request for such a visit must be made directly to the Ministry of Internal Affairs. So Modráček followed up with the question, whether specific forms for such petitions existed, to request permission to visit an imprisoned loved one, and the answer he got was, of course, such forms exist, but they have to be obtained directly from the Ministry of Internal Affairs. Finally, Modráček further inquired as to whether he might be so bold as to ask where his sister, Eliška Modráčková, was being held — whether in Brno, in Prague, or somewhere else yet? But the porter made no reply to that question, ignoring it, as if it hadn't even been posed. And when Modráček repeated it, a little more loudly, the StB goon at the other end of the passage silently detached himself from the wall and, coming up to Modráček, ejected him from the station with a rough push.

Then Modráček wanted to try his luck in the prisons of Brno, as well. But the mere sight of those huge, gloomy edifices filled him with terror. He'd never before considered how deeply prison architecture might depress a person: the whole intention of which was not to include in its design anything slightly uplifting or aesthetic, but to create a dead monolith of spiritual emptiness! What is more, the prison in Bohunice was the first example of Socrealism in Brno. Just think: Socialist Realism commenced its career in

Brno with the construction of a prison. But just as in Cejl, co in Bohunice they wasted no time with Modráček; they didn't react to his questions. It was as if he hadn't asked any at all. He even went to have a look at Špilberk. Even though he knew that, since the end of the war, there was nothing there except for barracks and museum spaces, and maybe some gaol cells for soldiers. Because he also knew that the Communists needed, and will need, ever more prisons for their class enemies: let's say six hundred more Špilberks crammed with class enemies. Perhaps that would satisfy their bloodlust.

Modráček also tried to contact Lieutenant Láska. He worked up a detailed report on his surveillance of the Kratochvil family, but, suddenly, Láska was unavailable, uncontactable, unreachable. It was as if he'd never existed. Ah yes, ah no — did any such person as Lieutenant Láska ever really exist?

Modráček fell victim to a hectic frenzy, such as he'd never before experienced all his life long. Even though he knew that he liked his sister very much, that he was really attached to her, he never imagined just how fatal a force in his life this sibling love was.

He tried to recall whom he was acquainted with in Prague, to whom he might turn to fetch that damned form for him from the Ministry of Internal Affairs. Some old fellow classmates of his, one guy and two girls, lived in Prague. Some time ago he'd even received wedding invitations from the girls. He didn't go to Prague for the weddings in person, but he did send them congratulations by telegram. He'd been quite close to both of them; they were super friends of his. With them, he'd experienced everything that could be squeezed out of such a friendship; as a matter of fact, even then it was mind-boggling to him that he didn't marry one or the other of them himself, instead of that current wife of his, who was so featureless and unspectacular, that he was hardly aware of her existence at his side. Even though he still thought about having children with her, some day, he had stopped sleeping with her some time ago, abandoning the bedroom they shared, with the window onto the courtyard, for the room next door — his office, with the window looking out onto Běhounská St. Simply put, she grew transparent. He stopped even seeing her. She would take on a more material consistency, he mused — only when a fierce conflict would erupt between them. But both of them were careful to avoid that. Now, when the moment ripens to fruition, we are going to witness just such a materialisation. But right now, let's return to those two girls.

Certainly, they would be more than willing to help him out. They really were fantastic people, those girls, but he'd thrown away those wedding invitations long ago, and no longer had any idea of their married names, or their Prague addresses. He felt at the time that, with those weddings, they'd cut themselves off from him once and for ever. It had never occurred to him that they might be of use to him again. The only option was that male classmate. But he had vivid memories of how he and others had had a field day back in school with that last name of his — Bachař,[25] of all things! So, so much for that.

But then — the most obvious solution? To go to Prague himself! For many reasons, this was not only the most obvious, it was also the best solution. He could not only pick up the form, he could fill it out on the spot and submit it — and as long as Eliška found herself in some prison in Prague, maybe he could even visit her, then and there! Of course, for many reasons, this was the best plan, but for one, decisive reason, it was unfortunately impossible. Even so impossible that it never, I mean never, even seriously crossed his mind.

The construction of the building on Botanická was drawing to its conclusion, and so it was completely out of the question for him to run off anywhere at such a time. The construction of this, first, socialist koldům[26] was supposed to be the gift of its builders, in honour of some proletarian anniversary or other, and thus was so tightly bound up in the knots of socialist commitments that there existed the danger of something important being neglected because of the feverish tempo imposed. For this reason, not only the builder, but the architect as well, had to be on the spot, to make sure that it didn't all come tumbling down like a house of cards. At such a time he simply couldn't allow himself to disappear, and risk smearing his cadre reputation with even more shit — which would also make his sister's situation so much the worse. But on the other hand, while nowadays he had to get up so early in the morning so as to be the first one at the site, and

----

[25]   'Screw.'

[26]   In Czech, *koldům* was a typically socialist abbreviation for *kolektivní dům,* or 'collective dwelling.'

                                        JIŘÍ KRATOCHVIL

constantly squabble with any old cretin, including the builder, barking at him, bawling at him, mixing in the proper honorific 'comrade' with bestial titles (… you swine of a builder! Don't you know that if you don't shore up the load-bearing wall, it'll come crashing down on us?…) this also had one undisputed benefit: for when he returned home late in the evening and fell upon his bed still half-dressed, to come to again only in the morning at the sound of the rampaging alarm clock, he simply hadn't the time to torture himself with thoughts of his little sister. Even though, of course, he couldn't ever quite budge her out of his head, and she ran rampant through his mad dreams in all possible incarnations and the most unbelievable disguises.

He had decided that he would go off to Prague on the very first day that they could do without him for a couple hours at the site. But then, everything turned out quite, quite differently.

Before he was able to free himself up for a trip to Prague, he was called in for further interrogation. For the very first time, he was actually pleased at such a summons — it was just what he was hoping for.

He was, however, surprised at the fact that this time he had not been summoned to the station on Běhounská as usual, but rather to the Ministry of Internal Affairs on Lenin St. While he was seated amongst the other adepts on the long bench in the corridor near the lift, it occurred to him, obviously, that it would not be Láska waiting for him here, but some other StB agent, who was now assigned to his case. Because after Eliška's arrest it really was a case, and not, as before, some sort of game, in which for their sadistic pleasure, the StB goons played on his nerves, trying to see, probably (perhaps with a view towards gathering evidence for some statistical research project of theirs) how much an ordinary chap could bear.

But this time it all went like a whirl. He outdistanced everyone who was seated on that Bench of Záhoř,[27] for no sooner arrived had he and set himself down on a free edge; no sooner had he begun to toss a thought or two through his head, than the elevator doors opened, someone called his

....

27   An ironic reference to the ballad 'Záhořovo lože' ('The Bed of Záhoř'), a fantastic narrative poem about a brigand named Záhoř, by the Biedermeier poet Karel Jaromír Erben (1811–1870) collected in his popular *Kytice z pověstí národních* (*A Bouquet of National Folktales*, 1853, 1861), one of the signal works of late Czech Romanticism.

name, and took him up to the second floor, where he was entrusted into someone else's hands, at the door to the interrogation room.

Have a seat, the StB agent said, without even bothering to introduce himself to Modráček or wasting time on ritual pleasantries. No, he got right to the point. But this wasn't to be an interrogation this time; rather, it was an imparting of information.

But when the information had been imparted, at first, Modráček seemed not to understand a single word of what had been said. It was immediately apparent to the anonymous agent — who had merely been entrusted with imparting information, and as such, was nothing more than a nameless messenger — that he would have to repeat it all from the top. And so, once more, he imparted his information:

She hanged herself in her cell. You are hereby authorised to take away what she left behind. You are similarly authorised to dispose of her body according to your customs and preferences. The items she left behind her will be transferred to your possession at the porter's on the ground floor, upon your signing the paperwork. However, the villa where she had lived has been confiscated by the state, along with all of its furniture and contents. Its current tenant will decided which of these objects will be handed over to you, in detail, and in what manner such transfer is to take place. We are obliged to inform you that you are forbidden to approach the villa and its surroundings; otherwise, you will be liable to arrest.

A shoebox was waiting for Modráček at the porter's grate. It contained a few trifles: stockings, handkerchiefs, and a small pack of cotton, which she had been using as sanitary pads.

The coffin had been sealed, so Modráček had no chance of seeing his sister now. After the funeral Mass and Catholic burial ceremony (neither he nor his sister were believers, but Modráček felt that he had to do something, which would somehow transcend everything that had happened), he took a leave of absence from work without even giving a thought to whether or not he was still needed at the building site, and when his wife attempted to say something, when she wanted to be helpful with all that was going on, he heard her even less than before — if such a thing were even possible. And when she stretched forth her hand and placed it on his arm, tenderly, he flicked it off as if it were a speck on his sleeve before hurrying off to his rendez-vous with fate.

He got on the tram at Svoboda Square. He changed at Red Army Square and then rode through Žerotín Square all the way along Veveří and then through Konečné Square until he got to Žabovřesky, where he got off near the chapel on Burian Square. Then he walked along Šmejkalová until, as he drew near Eliška Machová St, he slowed his pace, and slowed it yet again, until he was really dragging his feet, step after step. When the corner of Šmejkalová and Eliška Machová came into sight, he stopped and stood still. It's hard to believe, but, looking back, he wouldn't be able to say whether he'd stood there for three minutes, or perhaps a whole hour.

The first thing that came to his mind when he turned into Eliška Machová was that they'd anticipated his coming. Even though they'd forbidden him access to the house he'd built for his sister, they knew that he wouldn't listen to them, so they'd prepared accordingly. An StB agent, in parade uniform, was pacing before the house: ten steps this way, ten steps that, the holster with his pistol slapping him and slapping him on the backside as he strutted.

Modráček crossed the street so as to avoid the StB agent, and to get a good look at the villa. It was then that it happened. Standing on his sister's balcony was Lieutenant Láska, and next to him, a woman — clearly his wife — who was holding a child in her arms — a little girl. A little family, peacefully nested in the house left by his murdered sister.

Modráček didn't return home until the next morning. He wandered about nocturnal Brno — at the time we are speaking of, the early fifties, it was as dark and empty as if under martial law, or threatened by bombing raids. It was in this dark and emptied city that he first met with that frightful thought. But, at the time, it possessed neither soul nor matter. It was just some sort of nocturnal insect, buzzing about his sick head.

APERITIF AND MAIN COURSE

When I got off the tram at the Jundrov stop, I set out along the dusty path and soon the circus tent, the place where the caravan wagons were parked, and the cages of the animals met my eyes. I felt that peculiar, chilly thrill which I know well from the days when the detective's craft was my daily bread. Once more the ants began to crawl over my back — something that I otherwise only feel right before bedding a heretofore inaccessible partner, whom I'd had to chase after for a long time. Or whenever I find myself in front of a painting by Chittussi.

I bought myself a ticket for that evening's performance, and because it was still early, I wandered around the circus animals' cages, the circus wagons, and, along with the other curious folk, I poked my nose into the corral where the Arabian stallions were kept (that is, insofar as they are Arabian stallions. Horses aren't my strong suit.)

It often so happens to me that, when I'm conducting an inspection of something, the thing I'm looking for, insofar as it is hidden in some inconspicuous detail, well, I don't have to see it immediately. Rather, later, I notice it with — so to speak — retroactive actuality. That is, when I allow the whole path I've just trod over to roll once more before my eyes, as if I'd filmed it with what you might call my inner camera (for I have an indubitably unique visual memory recall, so requisite an aspect of my professional kit), it turns out that sometimes I experience what I call imaginative transparencies. I was initiated into this process by a certain Indian shopkeeper, out of gratitude for my getting to the bottom of his brother's supposed suicide (in reality, it turned out to be murder, and I was even able to point out the murderer to him, even getting his photo into his hands). Yes — I'm referring to the so-called Case of the Sapphire Serpent, which won me a certain amount of renown in my professional circles, but which today, of course, has faded away completely, like ripples spreading over the surface of a pond until they vanish.

So then, even today I make use of this well-established and trusted procedure, which, if I'm in luck, will yield me an imaginative transparency into the matter at hand.

At the moment I'm speaking of, I took myself away from the circus premises and found myself a little spot near the bank of the Svratka. There I broke a branch from a thorn bush and brushed clear a little space, whereon I spread out my handkerchief.

It was a late summer evening. The fall was just coming on; it was such an evening as one might even call delightful, if one were to judge it by the feathery clouds, buxom and indecently white, the uppermost portions of which had the appearance of cauliflower, such as meteorologists — if I'm not talking rubbish here — call cumuli. Well, another moment and I'd be seeing them even more distinctly; I only had to assume the position, whereby I'd be glancing through the Lord God's windows from the perspective of a frog.

I knelt down on the ground, and set the top of my head inside the uppermost corner of an isosceles triangle, the sides of which were formed by my arms and elbows. Then, setting the crown of my head on the ground in such a way that my interlaced fingers would provide firm support to the back of my skull, I raised my pelvis and, taking tiny steps on tip-toe, drew my knees close to my trunk. Next, I shifted the weight of my body and its entire centre of gravity onto my forearms and the crown of my head, slowly raising my legs from the ground, while my head remained as fixed to the earth as if it were attached by a screw. Slowly, slowly, I balanced my legs until they were completely vertical, perfectly in line with my torso, squarely perpendicular to the ground.

But just when I'd accomplished all this and was waiting — if I were in luck — for the imaginative transparency I was after, it all came to an abrupt end. For there erupted at that moment a raucous round of applause, which wrenched me away from it all. When I lowered my eyes from the fluffy clouds, just now licked by the rosy tongue of the alpenglow, I found myself surrounded on three sides by a group of circus-goers. Obviously, they took my shirshasana for a circus trick. For who back then knew a jot about Buddhist yoga? So there was nothing for me to do but get back on my feet, make a deep bow on all three sides, sign a few autographs, and beat a dexterous retreat.

The lights around the amphitheatre dimmed, while the ring, that gigantic doughnut pinpointed round about with floodlights, that Gulliverian flying island of Laputa, began to glow brightly in the darkness, and from the sawdust there arose the pungent aroma of sweating animals being put through their paces.

Then the entrée sounded, and there came on a long series of circus performances, with high-wire artists, Olsen's Flying Pleiades, alternating with earthbound gymnasts, clowns in tiny cars, plate-spinners and other jugglers, illusionists, mind readers and a large family of artistes lithely leaping onto one another's shoulders and heads, human pyramids and bears on bicycles, until, at last, the clown musicians gave way to the tigers.

And at that moment, when partitions made of strong metal bars were being set up around the ring, fastened together with screws and special metal hooks; while the whole tent resounded with the busy noise of construction, and sellers of eskimo pies and chocolate pastries[28] were hawking their wares amongst the audience members, I saw — at that very moment — a young woman climbing up onto the little stage raised over the entrance to the ring. In one hand she was holding a tiny chair, and in the other, a little pillow decorated with roses and hearts. I recognised her immediately, even though up till then I'd only seen her on photographs — one of which I always carried with me, the way soldiers in the First World War used to carry around little photos of the Emperor Franz Josef. It was electric Belinda in the flesh. And so I wasn't wrong after all. What I'd seen on the poster in her room, that gallant tiger-tamer in his costume with the gold braid, holding over his head the fiery ring through which the tiger was sailing, was — I was sure of it — the quarterly lover of electric Belinda.

She set the little chair down at the very edge of the stage, and, after placing the pillow upon the seat, she sat down on it herself. As soon as she did, she began to systematically nibble the fingernails of her left hand. My delicate sensory nerves, always particularly sensitive to everything concerning the case at which I happen to be at work, quite clearly heard — even through the clamour of construction in the ring — the chewing noises made by her teeth and the tiny ring of the chewed-off nails falling into one of the musical instruments that had been set aside. And I understood that this rodent-like

....

28 *Ledomedo* — an ice-cream cake, actually; the name derives from its mascot, an 'ice bear.'

              JIŘÍ KRATOCHVIL

ritual of electric Belinda's was eloquent of her fear and anxiety concerning the anticipated danger that her lover would soon be facing amongst the wild tigers. But it was also clear to me that this ritual functioned as a sort of aphrodisiac as well — the gnawing of her fingernails mobilising in her, I reckon, all the erotic essences she contained, in anticipation of her last night together with her lover. Yes, indeed — this was the second and last night that the Circus Belinda would spend in Brno. I had no doubt that the nails of her right hand had been chewed off last night, and that if the circus were to remain here for one more day and one more night, electric Belinda would be obliged to take off her right shoe and stocking there on the little chair onstage, lift up her foot as high as she could, and run her rodent-like teeth along her toenails.

The musicians had returned from their snack, still brushing clean their furious Biedermeier whiskers[29] and greeting electric Belinda with a slight nod of the head. When the metal safeguard was firmly in place around the ring, the musicians took their places and emptied their instruments of Belinda's fingernails, the rheostat began to dim the coloured bulbs above the heads of the audience, the spotlights were trained on the ring and the strictest silence reigned: the eyes of all were fixed upon the tunnel-like cage, through which the tigers were to race into the ring. The director lifted his baton.

I found myself standing before a riddle I didn't know how to solve. When, before the night's performance, I had inspected, as thoroughly as I know how to, all I was able to inspect, it became clear to me that there were terribly few circus wagons around. The entertainers had to be jammed in them like sardines or herrings. The tamer of tigers slept in a wagon with three other artistes, and if he wanted to fuck electric Belinda there, he'd have nowhere to put those others. After all, even the main wagon was packed full of that whole tribe of family gymnasts. There was, indeed, an inn called 'Na Piavě' in Jundrův, near the river, but it had no rooms to let.

....

[29]   *Furiantské kníry.* The adjective is built from the word *furiant,* which denotes a Slavonic folk dance beloved of Czech composers in the nineteenth century, some of whom, like Smetana and Dvořák, created orchestral works around it. It seems that the adjective here alludes not only to the business of the whiskers in question, but also of the somewhat outmoded, traditional, 'Biedermeier' look of the musicians sporting them.

And so after the performance, while the spectators of the circus were going off home, gradually, in crowded trams lit up from within so that they looked like mobile aquariums moving through the dark night, and even after the frazzled circus performers had thrown themselves in the sack — I went on yet another reconnaissance among the wagons and cages. I was quite surprised at the fact that no one was keeping watch there. But just as soon, I realised how unnecessary that would be. The tigers were in their cages, of course, but nevertheless no one from the outside would dare invade this space at night — the very presence of those beasts was like a protective hand stretched out over the encampment. To tell the truth, I wasn't feeling very cheery myself. But — as strange as it sounds — the caged animals didn't react to my presence in the slightest. Obviously, I kept myself at a respectful distance from the tigers, but all the same, not so far away as to be unnoticed by them. And I found myself there at an hour when nobody from the outside would be hanging around the place. But perhaps they were so benumbed and fed up with many-headed human nosiness, day after day, that they ignored my presence out of mere contempt.

And even so I took a few more trembling steps in the direction of those cages — but the black shadows behind the bars didn't even twitch a muscle. This emboldened me to take a few more steps, until I was so close that, in the light of the moon I saw that there were only three tigers there. Two in one cage, the third spread out in the one next door. This one opened his huge yellow eyes, looked me over, yawned in annoyance, and turned over onto his other side. But from the performance in the ring I remembered that there had been four tigers. In one of the climactic numbers, three tigers formed a shaggy wheel on a lowered trapeze, through which a fourth leapt, to and fro. I still had the stirring applause in my ears. But where was that fourth tiger now?

Well and good; what else can I do anyway? I set my Leica down somewhere in the dark and, without even sweeping a circle about myself with a branch, I spread my handkerchief down on the ground where I'd rest my head, and in a trice — in the darkness before the tiger cages — I performed my shirshasana. With one arm sunk in camel shit, or whatever, I saw, for a few brief seconds, Electric Belinda with her animal tamer: A little lantern standing on a crate of oranges cast light on their bed of love: in the midst of the circus and on a tarpaulin, among eiderdowns and pillows, the trainer's arse was convulsing, while Electric Belinda was wildly thumping some invisible drum with her heels. It was then that I saw the fourth tiger. Guarding them from the curious, prying eyes of the circus staff, those nudgers and winkers, he was pacing through the little tunnel of cages set right beneath the circus tent, and then I understood that he had been ordered by his master to react at the slightest movement nearby.

I lowered my legs to the earth, used the grass to wipe clean my arm, smeared to the very wrists in the shit of that camel, or whatever it was (just because this particular circus hadn't a single camel, that still doesn't mean that it couldn't have any camel shit), I located my Leica in the grass and boldly made my way toward the big top.

But I had no sooner drawn close than a dark growling emerged from within: it was a warning to me, not to take a single step forward, and also to those two, that somebody was prowling about in the vicinity.

The presence of the tiger served more than one purpose, and the role of watchdog, so to speak, was, perhaps not the most important one. For who among the circus troupe would venture to disturb the tamer at his most intimate business? It's true that circus-folk are godawful beasts, and practise all different sorts of monstrosities upon one another, but who would dare set himself up against the authority of the tamer? Lion and tiger tamers enjoy a certain prestige in circuses. And so that watchdog of a tiger was rather nothing more than snobbery, like the red-coated guards outside Buckingham Palace… Or, of course! A female aphrodisiac! I can still clearly remember what it was like near the end of the war — the furious screwing that went on in basements and air-raid shelters: the propinquity of mortal danger is the most potent aphrodisiac for women. Electric Belinda, chewing her nails, awaiting the tigers' gig. And now, just the same, in her lover's embrace, exposed to the sight, smell, and hearing of one of the most bloodthirsty of wild animals. That tamer understood not only tigers, but women too, and here he showed himself capable of squeezing the maximum output from Belinda!

And this does not exhaust by a long-shot the possibilities presented by the combination of tiger, lover, and Belinda together beneath the big top of the night. Above all, what a magnificent setting! Just imagine the otherworldliness of it all: a tiger walking round and round a couple making love! Such crazy shit can only be thought up by such fools as hot-blooded lovers! All the same — more's the pity — there was that first-class watchdog circling round. There was no question of me documenting them in flagranti. I won't get no pictures here.

And so I took the night tram to the nearest city quarter, that is, Žabovřesky.

Four hours in the U Kozáka Hotel, and then the morning tram back. The dawn was just breaking, and a squadron of bats was on its way back to the cliffs of a distant promontory. The mist was just beginning to steam off the Svratka River, but the circus was already up and abustle. I could hear from afar the circus workers taking down the big top, and they'd already started up the tractor that was to pull the caravans. At first I thought that I'd only come to bid farewell to the opportunity that had now hopelessly disappeared, the chance that I'd fucked up. But then I met up with them, and in the end, I was rewarded.

The tamer was accompanying electric Belinda from the circus camp to the tram stop. As we passed, I lowered my eyes so that they would not read anything in them, and I greeted them just as one does when coming across a random person on a lonely road in the fields in the early morning. But as soon as they passed, I doubled back and went on after them.

They weren't aware of me following them. Surely, they reckoned that I was still heading in the direction of the loud noises of the camp being dismantled. Electric Belinda was dressed in sweater and trousers, just as she had been for that excursion to Vysočina. And then I saw the tamer slide his hand down into those trousers. He slid it down deep indeed and kept it there, possessively. I saw quite tangibly how he slid it between electric Belinda's cheeks and persistently kept it there. I opened the case of my Leica, checked to see if the flashbulb was on, and started to think up a quick plan of catching them at it.

'That sure was sharp of you to catch that swine in the act — that detail there — and at the same time to get her to turn around and face the lens, just as the flashbulb popped...'

I presented him with the burnt bulb along with the photo. He turned it over and over in his hand, happily. After all, it was worth all he had: a childless marriage dissolved on the grounds of the wife's infidelity — what more could a person ask for, who needed to get rid of his spouse on the cheap?

I took my percentage of his wealth, at which no spendthrift was going to be nibbling any more, and immediately knew what I'd be doing with it. There's this secondhand-goods store in the Jiráskův quarter, where my obsession, my mania, for Chittussi is well known. Some time ago, they let me know that two of his paintings were waiting for me. Of course, the cost was a bit high for someone who works the counter in a butcher shop, but they were willing to wait a bit, because they well knew that, sooner or later, my mania would scrape together the necessary funds.

The shopkeeper smiled in my direction as soon as he saw me in the doorway. Even though he couldn't wait on me right away. He was busy with a client who was at the moment purchasing a very strange gold-plated thingamajig resembling a railroad wagon folded down to somewhat more manageable proportions. Now I, being by nature a fellow willing to pitch in and lend a hand, skipped forward with the shopkeeper to help the client get that whatever-it-was onto the rack of his car. After this was accomplished, he smiled at us in friendly wise, told us to wait, and plunged into the interior of his car for something or other, returning with a box of Cuban cigars. He unsealed it and gave us one apiece. Cigars from the island ruled by the dictator Batista are held in high regard among us, and despite the fact that I'm not really much of a smoker, I accepted the gift as a sort of aperitif to the rich main course awaiting me.

But before the time for that main course, or, should I say, those two main courses arrived, the shopkeeper told me a thing or two about that thingamabob that looked like a railway wagon. It was actually a gold-plated, collapsable bear cage. A rich Jewish shopkeeper named Schlesinger used to have it at his villa in Pisárky, and kept a real bear in it. For you see, he was the owner of a firm called Bär und Sohn. Then it all ended for him, along with his son, in a concentration camp, and during the Protectorate some Gestapo officer or other lived in the villa, while the bear wasted away. After the war, Schlesinger's Jewish relations who waited out the war in America inherited the villa, and sold the empty cage.

So, did the happy new owner of the cage buy a bear as well?

The shopkeeper shrugged. I'd blundered up against the ramparts of his mercantile discretion and loyalty to his clients.

And then came the time for my two main courses. Soon, I was the happy owner of two paintings by Chittussi: the smaller one depicting a small fishpond in southern Bohemia at sundown; the other Devět skal in a wintry mood. I brought both of the paintings into the light and looked them over: the signature was right, as was the Chittussi's reassuringly familiar impressionistic palette. Everything seemed to be in order. I laid out a sum for which I could've bought a Jawa 250.

I'll deliver them to your home, day after tomorrow at the latest. That's 18 Orlí, right?

No, no. I'll take them away today. One under each arm.

The shopkeeper wrapped them up for me with care and then opened the door to let me out into a world where, all the same, real art means less than a smear of dogshit.

These were my fourth and fifth Chittussis. I wandered around my flat trying to decide where to hang them. At last, I hung them with the rest in that room in the avant-corps, where I sleep, dream, fuck, solve my intricate detective cases, and think through my life strategy.

Admit it. You've got a new girl. Or a new Chittussi, said Hanička when she showed up at the butcher shop for some liverwurst.

The second. Two Chittussis.

There it is! Because it's been a long while since I've seen you so happy. And when will my dreams come true? When are you going to sell me a proper hunk of pork? When will there finally be enough meat?

I glanced around the shop and then leaned forward to whisper in Hanič-ka's ear:

Soon, soon my girl. It's on the way. They say that on the black market they're already portioning up the meat from that anti-state spy-ring they executed.

Hanička made the sign of the cross and drew back quickly from the counter.

SYNCHRONICITY?

My sister was, most probably, the most important being in my life. Even in childhood, and ever onwards, I felt for her something more than the mere responsibility of an older brother. And because I received the news of her death the way I did: dully, unmoved, in a stupor; because I was unable to resist when they commanded me not to open the casket, warned me not break the seal with which they'd locked her in, for the rest of my life I will be justly locked up in my own prison of stupor. As punishment for not protecting my little sister, for not being able to stand up to them.

When I attempt to recall those days immediately following my sister's funeral, they flow together so, that I can't tell them apart. Work was coming to an end on the foundations for the apartment block on Botanická, and at the same time an annex to the barracks in the Židenecký quarter. But I can't fish out a single moment, a single detail from those days. I did the work they wanted from me, but I did it unconsciously, as if instead of me I'd sent some sort of mechanical double in my place, an identical android. Something had happened to me, and it looked to be irreversible. I fell into a sad despair with which it was unbearable to live, but which all the same kept me living on and on. And for me life was a punishment, a constantly pro-longed punishment. I was paying the price for something I couldn't undo.

But then in the midst of this something happened, something I'm un-able to name. Suddenly, it broke. Unbelievably, it just broke. But perhaps it was really just a coincidence, because as we know, coincidences are like wild beasts; you can be shot dead by a ricochet, or some chance occurrence can really mess up your head. Or, as in my case, a coincidence can calmly decide the rest of your life:

One evening upon returning home I pulled out a large packet of my father's unpublished writings from behind some books on the bookshelves. To the very last moment, I had no idea why I was doing what I was doing; what was inducing me to ferret through those old papers at that very moment. Only when I found it did I realise — this was the reason, and that somehow from the very beginning I knew all about it, after all, and it was only that I was unable to name it, express it.

It was Nabokov's manuscript *Zdes' gavaryat pa russki*, with the dedication to my father. And along with it, held together by a great paper-clamp, my father's typescript translation entitled *Here You Can Speak Russian*.

I read through the first three sentences of the translation: 'Martinchek's news-stand was found at the corner. That's what the world is like: news-stands are found in corner buildings. Martin Martinchek's shop was doing a thriving business there.'

Thereupon I slid my stool closer to the bookshelves, so that I might rest my back against them, and thus I remained until I'd read through the entire typescript. When my wife passed by and saw me sitting there, engrossed in reading something, she stopped short, surprised, as this was something unheard of for me in those days.

My father, I reckon, was a good translator of the philosophy of Solovyov and Berdyayev, but living speech, narrative, was a bit beyond his talents. His Czech here was quite gritty. I had the sense that this translation wasn't worth much. That's the first thing that occurred to me concerning that story of Nabokov's as presented by my father. It felt just like when you want to cross the street and a passing car makes you stop for a moment. Immediately afterward, after the passage of a few seconds, I become aware of the meaning of that tale, entirely: that fantastic, but for me at the time, so intimate a story. That short story of Nabokov's, even in my father's poor translation, gladdened me, greatly. But all the same that was everything I could expect of it, all that I wanted of it.

In the room with the view out onto the courtyard, that is, in the room that used to be our bedroom (and in which, I remind you, only my wife sleeps now) the cornice on one side came loose. The ceiling here is high, and so, in consequence, are the windows too, and thus it wasn't a matter of just climbing up on a chair to reach the space. Here, I needed a ladder. So I grabbed the basement key from the hanger on the foyer and went down into the cellar. Our part of the basement is found at the very end of a long vaulted passage, which recalls a casemate. I unlocked the padlock and went inside our cubby-hole, in which I had to slip gingerly between the wall and a gigantic heap of coal. The stepladder, which was the object of this expedition of mine, was, for some incomprehensible reason, found at the very back of the place, behind marvellously messy piles of things. I pushed stuff aside, the existence of which I'd forgotten long ago: whole heaps of my old draughting boards, boxes, crates and coffers so heavy it seemed as if they were full of gold bars. There was the skeleton of a bicycle, a metal washbasin, the frame of a smashed aquarium, and a filthy garden parasol. To top it all off, this little cellar of ours was illuminated by a single lightbulb near the entranceway, locked within a little wire protective cage, so that the rear of the cellar was as dark as midnight and I had to use an electric torch. I lit up the ladder and prepared to just grab it deftly and retreat with it. But when I'd wriggled my way to that little space, the cone of light fell upon a poster hanging on the back wall. At first, I didn't know how it got there, but then I recalled that I had hung it up myself some three years ago, after removing it from a wooden fence shutting off a gap on Kozí St where a crater had been made by a bomb during the war. At the time, the poster made me laugh. In stirring colours, it depicted an StB goon, a member of the NSU — the Communist National Security Units — and beneath him ran the caption *The People and the SNU!* beneath which in turn some wag had added in red ink: *As if we needed a good screw!*

Then something unexpected happened. For when I caught sight of that poster — just a portion of it, the legs of the goon in his military boots — the torch began moving of its own accord, sweeping over his body, revealing the details of his uniform, and at the same time I felt something begin to swell in me. That earlier rigid torpor of mine, that mental immobility, that sort of spiritual catalepsy into which I'd plunged following the death of my little sister, now swiftly, suddenly, was transformed into its polar opposite: a sharp fury.

Yes, that's exactly what happened. I fell into a rage. All of my hatred of those who had tormented Eliška, hounded her to suicide, or simply and straightforwardly murdered her, exploded then and there. I dropped the ladder. Nearby, a pickaxe was lying on top of a large box, just as if someone had placed it there for me. I picked it up and hurled myself at the paper goon. Again and again I swung that pickaxe at the figure on the poster, striking him now in the face, now in the chest, and again and again and again.

But then something happened that took my breath away: the wall swayed, and a large hunk of it fell into a darkness beyond. I laid the pickaxe down and picked up my torch, which before my attack on the paper SNB man I'd lain aside, still lit, on some little shelf, and shone it into the darkness beyond the broken wall. A great space stretched out there, which my flashlight was unable to penetrate very far. That light of mine was like a little pebble tossed into a gigantic black lake.

I had heard, of course — who hadn't? — of the undergrounds of Brno. I'm not speaking here of any sewer system, cloaca, but rather mediaeval underground corridors, only partially accessible in the shape of the broad vaults of various pubs in the old core of the city, or beneath the episcopal consistory and under monasteries. And it was also common knowledge that near the church of St James, under Jakubské náměstí, there are most probably wide spaces in which church crypts connect to gigantic vaults with charnel houses from the former graveyard around St James. Běhounská St connects Jakubské náměstí, or St James Square, with the Náměstí Svobody, or Freedom Square, and because the church of St Nicholas used to stand on Freedom Square, there must be some underground passage below Běhounská that leads between St James and St Nicholas. And so again, most likely, ossuaries or crypts.

But at that moment, I didn't give much thought to all that. It wasn't difficult at all, now, to clear away the rest of the partition that separated my little cellar room from the underground, and to slip inside. I found myself in a long, broad corridor, partially hewn from the natural stone massif on which the city is built, the spine of which stretches beneath Běhounská St like the petrified body of a gigantic buried reptile. But here I must say that I didn't discover everything I'm going on about now and will continue to relate during this initial penetration of mine, as I strove to get my bearings in those dark spaces by the insufficient light of my electric torch. (Today all of this has run together; I'm unable to distinguish what I took in from that very first look around me with nothing but that little flashlight, and what I saw later, in the glow of the spotlights I'd hung there.) The barrel-vault was damaged in places, but nowhere to such a degree that it might collapse. But I often came across sections lined with brick, or with brick and quarried stone. It was evident that this was no ossuary. I never trod upon the smallest bone, but on the other hand I kept running into gigantic blooms of mould, shining in that darkness like the white trunks of some sort of rampant vegetation in an underground garden.

There was no doubt about it that this broad, vaulted space dated from the Middle Ages, though later on it served the most various purposes. Underneath the vault, for example, I discovered the remains of some peculiar chains, from which, I assumed, some sort of foodstuffs had been suspended in baskets and pouches, to keep them safe from voracious rodents. So, a sort of gigantic mediaeval refrigerator? From there I discovered a cavern, a sort of transverse cave interrupting the smoothly running wall, which somehow suggested that it had been used for cultic purposes. An underground chapel cut from the rock, with stepped altar and hardly discernible, blurred frescos?

An interesting phenomenon awaited me in the dim distance of this broad and long corridor. At the very end, this mighty mediaeval barrel vault, or what have you, ended in a smooth stone wall, which obviously signified both the end of the passage, and the fact that it was connected with no other further underground labyrinth. I estimated that, here, I'd got as far as somewhere beneath Svoboda Square, but still fairly far away from the former crypts of the destroyed church of St Nicholas. And here, imagine that — I came across something that, at first glance (and by the wretched light of a flickering, dying electric torch) seemed like a hastily and chaotically assembled public bar that had been suddenly abandoned. Stools, chairs, little tables, couches, even beds with mattresses, blankets — some even with eiderdowns, as well as armoires, crates and coffers… It was a real hodgepodge of furniture and trappings, from battered Empire furnishings to modern functionalist designs. So, at some point in time, a group of people had frequented this place — perhaps the underground area served them as a bomb-shelter during the last phase of the war, when bombs were sometimes falling on the city — for example, on neighbouring Kozí St, which was not far away at all.

Here, they were outfitted in all the essentials. There was a large barrel of water off to the side, on a table, and some other ones in an armoire. On some chairs, heaps of largely dirty tableware were piled, and even some plates with hardened scraps of food into which spoons had been sunk. Completely to the rear were some covered buckets, into which I supposed they relieved themselves. My flashlight was almost completely dim, but I still made out an open, upturned book on one of the chairs. Some sort of *livre de poche.* I thrust it into my pocket, scolding myself for coming so far into the caves with weak batteries in my torch.

That will-o'-the-wispy light of my flashlight sufficed just enough for me to make my way back to my cubby-hole, by carefully sidling along the wall. As I locked my grate, I had time to satisfy myself that the junk that I'd piled up with difficulty in my quest to reach the ladder now served as a screen blocking the view to the rear of my little cellar space, and the entrance to the underground. It was then, when I'd locked the grate and dropped the key into my pocket, that the thought first occurred to me. I stood there for a moment, rooted to the spot. But then, when I'd dragged the ladder to the stairs, the idea had settled, taken on firm contours, so that when I finally stood at the door of my flat, I knew that that mediaeval vault had revealed itself to me at precisely the right moment; that someone had carefully pre-pared it for me, just as I had been led to those bookshelves and induced to rummage through the writings my father had left behind. People call things like this coincidences, but perhaps one could also say synchronicity? When two different things occur, which in special circumstances fit together, be-long together, clearly — but which a person only realises when he witnesses them occurring simultaneously.

I lugged the ladder into the bedroom, set it at the window, and climbed up. My wife handed me the hammer and the staples, and when the cornice was level once more, I climbed back down and recalled the *Taschenbuch* in my pocket. I pulled it out. It was something by a certain Arthur Schnitzler called *Flucht in die Finsternis*, that is, *Escape into the Darkness.*[30] Then I called to mind something I once heard from Dr Pešek — that during the Protectorate, quite a few Germans lived in this building. But in the last days of the war, when Malinovsky's army was thundering near Brno, all of the Germans disappeared from the building. And so, those underground spaces were used not only as a bomb shelter, and to escape the artillery barrages trained on the city centre, but, most probably, also to hide from Russian patrols who, along with the so-called Revolutionary Guards, were combing through and 'cleansing' the city. But why then did all of them abandon their vaulted chambers, and what happened to them — this only

----

[30]   Arthur Schnitzler (1862–1931) was a prominent Austrian writer. That he should be unfamiliar to the narrator is somewhat surprising.

                                              JIŘÍ KRATOCHVIL

God knows. One thing, however, was certain: they counted on returning here, and for that reason they left all of their possessions in the vault, and carefully walled up the entrance to the underground, putting a seal on it, as it were.

And one more thing: are we to call this mere coincidence, or synchronicity? When two things occur, which belong together, in truly peculiar circumstances, which become quite clear, that is, that reciprocal belonging, only when they occur at one and the same time. If I had uncovered the entrance to the underground without having read Nabokov's story a day earlier, or, vice versa, if I'd read the story, but didn't discover this path to the mediaeval vault, I wouldn't have had that sudden idea — I wouldn't have become enflamed with it. But the story and the vault came into contact, sparked, and immediately I knew what I had to undertake in order to save my soul.

Above all, I needed a car. It was inconceivable that I would be able to transport it from the far-off Jiráskův quarter, from Sedlákova St, by hand-cart. But first, so as to not get into an unnecessary frenzy, I went off to make sure that it was still there.

It was a little antique shop that one entered via stairs leading to a basement. There was a bell above the door, but it hadn't rung for ages. Someone had spitefully paralysed that little heart of metal.

I've come to see if you've still got that bear cage.

But of course, Mr Modráček! Who on earth would buy it? It's destined to end up on the scrap heap.

No, it won't. I'll come by for it later today — tomorrow at the latest.

But for heaven's sake! What will you do with it? It's almost as if you told me that today or tomorrow you'd be bringing me a Cuban cigar!

Exactly. Wait and see — you guessed it! I laughed.

Nearly right across the street from the building in which I live, on Běhounská, a Health Centre is located. My wife's boss, the head of the entire place, is Dr Štefl. He's one of the people for whom I'd built a villa right after the war, according to their awful taste, and who, when they finally gazed upon the finished product, were captivated with bliss.

I need to borrow your car[31] for an hour or so. Don't worry, I've got a licence.

He gave me the key to his garage and a few little pieces of advice.

The garage was located in the Hybešova quarter. But now on our way to the garage it occurs to me that I still haven't mentioned something very important. Out of shame, or caution. All the same, this story could hardly have progressed as it finally did, had I not discovered in that mediaeval vault not only the temporary refuge of the German tenants of my building on Běhounská, not only their furniture, beds, and all sorts of other mouldering junk, but also a certain coffer into which — before they set out on their careful recon of the terrain, or whatever it was that tempted them from their relative security — they placed, sicher ist sicher, all of their jewellery and more exceptional valuables. Oh, how certain they were of returning for it all! Since that time, seven years have already passed and, of course, they never came back at all. Today, they're either all dead or living somewhere far away from here. For that reason I can perhaps consider my discovery an inheritance from those who had to abandon everything when they tried to find some path, some way, to remain at least a little alive. And after all, I hadn't broken into this mediaeval vault, this their underground place of refuge, by force, like some burglar. No, I'd pierced into it by pure accident, during that wild frenzy of mine, which perhaps they themselves would be able to understand, just like all outcasts and outlaws who fight back against institutionalised hatred in explosions of helpless rage.

Even the Nabokovs were escapees like them. But now we've arrived at that further point, about which I want to speak. We've come to that story of Nabokov's, *Zdes' gavaryat pa russki*:

It concerns a Russian emigrant family in Berlin, into whose hands, by chance, a KGB agent, ostensibly an official of the Soviet consulate in that city, has fallen. They decide to set him before a hastily improvised tribunal and pass sentence on him — as one of those who imprisoned, tortured, and murdered their relatives and friends, and finally chased them off into banishment. They hesitate between a sentence of capital punishment and

---

[31]   The Czech text reads *Hadimirška* here. Deriving from the 1931 comedy film *To neznáte Hadimiršku* [Well then, You Don't Know Hadimirška] this was a popular nickname for the Tatra 57.

life imprisonment, and decide on the latter, more humane sentence, for, after all, they're not like him. And so they convert the bathroom in their flat into a gaol cell and lock their lifer inside. In this way, they become gaolers, and assume the obligation to care for him in their prison. And because their prison is a humane one, not at all like those in the Soviet Union, they keep him well nourished, and, as an exceptional privilege — such as those so-called class enemies daren't even dream about in Soviet gaols and prison camps — the prisoner will be permitted to read books, to improve himself, and have the opportunity of experiencing some aesthetic pleasure by engaging with the masterworks of literature. He sleeps on a mattress in the bathtub, regularly receives clean laundry, and slowly even gains a few pounds in the elegant bathrobe provided him in place of prison togs. The family then arrive at the determination that, when he attains an age older than that of his gaolers at present, they will pass him on to their children's care, and then, perhaps, on and on, to the children of their children — passing him on like an inheritance from generation to generation.

So you really did come back for that bear cage? And are you going to buy a bear for it, as a present for your wife?

No, not quite, I laughed, and the antiques dealer asked no further questions. Discretion is just as much a part of his profession as a leather muzzle on a bear's snout. He went off to retrieve the crate from his storeroom. It was a collapsable cage, but all the same of impressive dimensions. He cleared some space by pushing aside Empire chairs, Sezessionstil chests of drawers, and Biedermeier end tables, until he'd made enough room to set up the cage and demonstrate it to me. It was still a gorgeous, gilded thing. I crouched, knelt, and stretched my hand between the bars of the cage to touch its metal floor, and when I pulled my hand back and lifted it to the light — there on three of my fingers, index, middle, and ring finger — were a few ruddy ursine hairs.

Well, for Pete's sake! the shopkeeper exclaimed, peering at my hand from this angle and that.

I reached for the billfold in my breast-pocket while he loped to the back to retrieve a large ledger, which he paged through before pronouncing the price. I paid him, and helped him to fold up the cage again. We stood there over it and exchanged a few more words. He grabbed hold of it to help me load it; but then this helpful sort skips over, who up until then had just been looking on. I backed on up the stairs to open the door for them and let them pass. Then out in front of the shop the dealer and his assistant helped me fix the cage to the roof of the car. And when we did (just picture it for yourself — that 57 with a bear cage atop it! — just picture a turtle with an elephant sitting on his back!) I motioned them to wait a bit, and went to pull out of the car the box I'd set on the seat so as not to forget it. It was a box of really fine cigars, rare Havanas — yes, straight from the island ruled by the dictator Batista. I'm no smoker, but I got them still before the February victory of the working people from another of the lucky ones for whom I'd built one of those kitschy postwar villas. I tore off the wrapping paper and gave one to the shopkeeper and another to his assistant.

O mordidiu! O sakrablu! the antiques dealer exclaimed, gaping wide-eyed at the cigar before vanishing back into the store with that assistant of his, or whoever he was.

I still fiddled a bit, securing the cage onto the luggage rack of the little Tatrovka,[32] and when I set off with that gilded monstrosity delicately atremble on the canopy of the little auto, I looked like a waiter carrying a gigantic, poorly balanced tray crowded with tall sundae goblets.

I took down the cage and dragged it over to the corridor, unlocked the door to the cellar and dragged it onto the stairhead immediately behind the cellar door, which I then locked from the inside, leaving the key in the lock. Then I went down to clean up my little compartment, and to widen the entrance to the underground. Then (after an hour that seemed endless), when I had manoeuvred the cage over the narrow staircase and into my cubby hole, and then farther, through that space and through the opening into the underground vault, I had the palpable sense of what it must have been like when Jacob was wrestling with the angel.

And there, in those subterranean spaces, in that immense strongbox of stone, I unfolded the cage to all its bearishly beautiful dimensions.

Then I cleaned up, swept up the cellar stairs, and everywhere I'd bumped or scraped the walls on the way down with the cage, after which I piled all

....

[32]   Tatra is a Czech vehicle manufacturer; *tatrovka* is a Tatra car.

the junk back into my cubby-hole, setting it up in such a way as to once more construct a screen impeding any sight of the entrance to the vault.

I sat myself down on the uppermost cellar step with the feeling that I'd done everything that was in my power to do. For I had discovered that mediaeval vault, transported the bear cage and set it up inside, fulfilling in this way some sort of purely symbolic act, a ritual, a ceremony, wherewith I'd lifted a burden from my soul. The gaol cell had been made ready (even though it would remain forever empty). There you have it — such is the power of symbolic actions. Now that chapter was closed. Now I would be able to go on peacefully with my meaningless existence, and my sister's absence would now become, with time, just a palpable wound, scarring over.

◆

A WOMAN'S HAT

The Creature known as Brighty — and sometimes Brighty Highlights (because, as we've already mentioned, she had natural highlights in her hair, which at the time drew Dan to her the way the fragrance of wild honey attracts a bear) — was resting in bed with her back against a pillow, running a wet finger around the rim of a wineglass. To his Welschriesling, Dan added his cigar. He set his glass down on the night table, bit off the end of the cigar, and lit up.

Where'd you come across that stinker?

You ask a lot of questions, Brighty. Some two months ago, at an antique shop in Jiráskův. I helped a fellow load some junk onto the roof of a little Tatra, and he gave me this cigar as thanks. I've kept it for two months, and today, its hour has come.

I said stinker, but it actually has a pleasant aroma.

Because it's no stinker at all. It's from Cuba — the island of the dictator Batista. There's whole cigar plantations there, where blacks and mestizos and creoles and mulattos and all sorts of coloured fellows slave away. And this here cigar is a crown jewel. A real smoker wouldn't hesitate to sell his own mother in order to get his hands on it. And today's the day. I don't have to go back to the butcher shop, Brighty. I've got a real gig now. I'm a detective in the criminal section.

So you're SNB now?

You're getting your terminology all mixed up, Brighty. SNB goons are the ones that pound the pavements — beat cops. It's true, my job also falls under the National Security Corps, but I'm in the criminal division, and that's a whole other ball of wax. And I've already got my first case. But I don't dare tell anyone about it.

So get on with it then, said Brighty, since you've started. 'Cos in a little while you'll have other duties to attend to.

　　　　　　　　　　　　　　　　　　　　　　

No, I don't know… I'm bound by professional secrecy.

So, come on, show me the knot. I'll undo it for you.

Stop it, Brighty, quit goofing off. Are we here to gab or shag?

You know, I heard of one chap though, really, who had such a long one that he could tie it into a knot.

You heard, or you saw?

No comment.

Instead of knotting his hankie, he knotted his willy?

Exactly, Daniel.

OK then, I'll tell you. But only if you vow that it will remain between us. If they found out that I was carrying out secrets, I'd be out on my arse. If not worse. So, all right, it happened through the good graces of the director of the Elektrodom, who put in a word for me. I was just finishing a pyramid of tinned meats on the display case and —

You know what, Daniel? Who gives a toss about those pyramids? Don't start ab ovo, plunge right in. Don't torment us with suspense. But hold on, hold on — a little tongue first. Don't forget your manners.

And Brighty was gazing off somewhere into the far distance: both intensely present and intensely absent, and when she finally got there — she didn't cry out, she merely moaned softly, and shuddered for a good while yet with these repeated electrical twitches until the breakers were tripped and she finally went motionless. The private eye, on the other hand, took a long time in coming; sweat was dripping from his face, which Brighty wiped off with a pillow. Just as if they'd switched roles, it was Dan who gave some loud yelps while Brighty watched him from below with her large, amused eyes.

So where did we finish, then?

That you got your first case and that it all began with the director of the Elektrodom coming over at the very moment you were making pyramids out of tinned meat…

So you see how careful I am with details — I noticed that the fingers of his right hand were all yellow from nicotine, like those of an obsessive smoker. Something's up with him, and he's a recent client of mine, but I can't let him rake me one in the kisser with that, I'm thinking. Maybe there'd occurred what I call the paradoxical effect; maybe he'd made an unfortunate mistake when he wanted to get rid of his wife. I've already seen things like that before. A fellow gets rid of his missus because she's unfaithful to him, and then he wakes up to find that he can't live without her. So it's like he's coming to lodge a complaint or something, and what can I do about that, I mean, after all I did what he wanted me to do, but at least I have to hear him out even if it's just to say, well, you know, it sometimes turns out like that. So I told him to come over and see me that evening.

When he comes, I invite him in and ask if he wants coffee or tea. I put the coffee on, sit him down comfortably, and he starts off. And he tells me that he's in a bad way, but that has nothing to do with why he came to see me. He's just got some difficulties at work. 'Cos you see it's no walk in the park to have the sort of socialist crown jewel like the Elektrodom on one's back, what with looking after all the employees, and all. But that's not why he came to see me, he said again; I couldn't help him with that. What I could do for him, on the other hand, had to do with this best buddy of his, Honza Rychlík. Honza has a woman who's slinking about on him with the boys, and he's the one, the director of the Elktrodom, who caught her at it, by chance. And it won't do, absolutely not, for him to just up and tell Honza himself, because he's so nuts about that woman of his that, if he doesn't see it himself, if there's no hard evidence, no corpus dilecti, he just won't believe it, and what's more, he'll blame him for spreading rumours.

And so here I asked him if maybe it wouldn't be better to just let sleeping dogs lie, since this Honza Rychlík doesn't know anything about anything and is living happily ever after, and most likely that boyfriend of hers will fall by the wayside anyway all of a sudden; it's probably only a meaningless little fling such as happens in every marriage — we're humans after all, not angels. But no, he responded, with heat, Honza's wife is the bane of his life — a complete monster who treats him badly, wipes the floor with him, and now, at last, here's the perfect opportunity to get rid of the millstone around his neck that's pulling him down into the depths.

I wanted to suggest that maybe Honza Rychlík likes to be treated like a rag and that the bane of someone's life can be just as irresistible as anything else. But I kept my tongue behind my teeth, I said nothing at all, and I accepted the commission, the job, even though it went against one of the fundamental rules of my ethics, which is, to take on as a client, as a customer, only a party directly concerned in an affair like that; never to take on a case second hand, without the knowledge of the injured party. And you see, I'd never gone against that ethical rule. Earlier, whenever anybody approached me with the request to take the case of some relative or acquaintance like that, I simply showed him the door. Because nobody has the right to rummage through someone else's dirty sheets, whether it be brother or sister or ever so best a buddy. But those were the days, Brighty, when I had a secretary and people were queuing up for my detective services. But now I didn't want to let that case slip away, and so I let him speak.

So, supposedly, this is how it happened. The Elektrodom has some sort of warehouse in Žabovřesky, and he was held up there until 5:30. Then when he was walking past the Lucerna Cinema, he saw that they were showing *The Watch on the Amur*, this old Soviet chestnut, and he thought it was time to nourish the soul a bit. So he bought himself a ticket and was looking at a display of Soviet film posters in the lobby. The screening room was still empty — there was still a half hour to go before the show was to start, but the doors were already open — they were airing the place, and he happened to take a glance inside. A rather unusual slide was being projected onto the screen, probably a holdover from the days of the First Republic — a reminder to women in the projection room to kindly take off their hats before the film begins. And just such an old fashioned hat, complete with peacock feathers and flowers, was drawn on that slide. And that slide, from the days when one still called one's female comrades Ladies, and those ladies wore bourgeois hats just like that one, moved him so, that he went inside. Immediately, he heard the sound of a movement at the other end of the room. He turned around just in time to see the door of the projection booth ajar, and this chap come out of it, probably the projectionist himself, followed by a woman who was still hurriedly buttoning her blouse.

He intuited that the booth served other purposes as well as throwing images on the silver screen. He sat himself down at the end of a row with his back to them, but then he heard a little voice that seemed familiar. So he turned around once more to cast an eye on them, and for a moment in the light coming from the booth he saw the woman's face, a little puss with eyes closed, little pursed lips, pressed against the mug of the projectionist. They remained like that, blissfully, for a while. Then the projectionist released her from his embrace and led her out of the screening room (the director of the Elektrodom spun around quickly, so that she wouldn't recognise him) then returned to the booth and turned off the slide.

Later that week, the director of the Elektrodom met up with Honza Rychlík at the pharmacy. Cleverly, he led the conversation round to the latter's wife. He learned that lately she'd been coming home later and later from work each Wednesday — supposedly some sort of urgent action was going on at the Post Office.

But he wanted to be sure. So he went back to the Lucerna Cinema on the following Wednesday. This time the Soviet epic *Admiral Nakhimov* was playing. It was around 5:30 again, and once more that same slide reminding the ladies about taking off their hats before the picture began was up on the screen. It occurred to him that this was perhaps a signal for the crew at the cinema — especially perhaps for the projectionist whose shift was to begin next — not to enter, for obvious reasons, the booth, the door of which it was forbidden to lock for safety's sake (frequent fires caused by the self-combustion of highly flammable celluloid). And it all played out exactly as it had the week before — taking into account some minor variations in the basic script. This time, Rychlík's wife was adjusting her garters in front of the projection booth, and once the farewell ritual was played out, the projectionist ushered her out into the lobby before returning to his booth and shutting off the slide for the ladies with the hats. And all this the director of the Elektrodom prudently observed, this time pressed behind a column along the wall.

So then, there's your case. You'll run along there next Wednesday to catch Rychlík's wife in flagranti.

Bloody likely, Brighty! That was no case. That was a trap. A trap set for Dan Koči.

At that moment, right beneath the window of Dan's avant-corps room at the corner of his building, a horse and wagon loaded with fodder and scrap for animal food was rolling along Minoritská St, while from the other side, from Josefská St, a heavy truck with spare parts for tower-cranes, what they call 'Wolfáks,' was rumbling up. The truck's exhaust pipes backfired twice. It sounded like shots from a cannon, and the horses began to rear in panic, whinnying like crazy. Dan leapt out of bed and ran to the window and pulled back the drapes. He saw the carter[33] spring down from the coachman's seat like lightning in an attempt to calm the horses and get them

....

[33]   In Czech, curiously enough, *kočí* — which is Dan's last name.

back under control. It's worth mentioning here that, at the time, the centre of Brno was as covered with horse apples as the breast of Marshal Masturbov with medals, and tractors and horse-drawn wagons passed through the historic core of Brno just as often as Škodas and Tatras. Meanwhile, down at the intersection of Orlí, Minoritská and Josefská the situation was growing complicated on the account of an enraged carter and a furious truck driver. Dan Kočí, surprisingly enough, took the side of the carter, but perhaps only because the truck driver, who was standing face to face with the carter, was wildly jabbing and whirling his hands in the carter's face in a manner that reminded Dan of an aunt of his from Buchlovice, who just as rapidly and deftly wielded her knitting needles — and this was thirty years ago already — so that it made little Danny's head spin. That's the way it is with childhood memories sometimes — they glide along throughout one's life like processions of monks on their way to the cloister garth and there's nothing we can do about it. On her part, Brighty's hackles rose as, from the bed, she had a clear view of all the traces made by the fingernails of Dan's other girlfriends on his back during their escapades. She called out:

So are you gonna tell me about it, or perch there like some giant horned owl?!

It's difficult for anyone to imagine what this craft of mine means to me, this mania of mine that pierces me to the marrow — or how without it I am slowly devoured by this ghostly longing, and feel such helpless emptiness that my very heart seems set to shut down. And so, even though I was warned by a not insignificant foreboding, I was drawn to this new case by a desperate force. And the director of the Elektrodom proved just how concerned he was that I should catch Rychlík's wife in flagranti by placing in my hand nine new flashbulbs for my Leica. Each flash burns through a bulb, Brighty. It's like every time you have an orgasm, you wear out your lover and need to find a new one.

I'd kind of like that — for each of my orgasms to burn my lovers to a crisp.

And so these nine new flashbulbs made it perfectly clear to me that I have to hash up as many photos as I can, compromising Mrs Rychlík in all her naked obscenity.

It was raining since the early morning, and I couldn't decide whether I should take an umbrella or a raincoat. Both of these have their pluses and minuses. I was a bundle of nerves. That foreboding was gnawing at me, though I tried to ignore it. Three times I put on that raincoat and three times I took it off again, to put it on a fourth time and then plunge off in the direction of the Lucerna Cinema. Even though I felt like Skafander Fox[34] in it.

I found everything just as the director of the Elektrodom had described it to me. Wednesday, a bit before 5:30 in the evening, I bought myself a ticket to *A Ruddy Glow over Kladno*,[35] and because the cloakroom was still closed, and I had nowhere to set aside my wet and loudly swishing raincoat, I rolled it up into a little wet cocoon, which I then jammed into my pocket. That was a mistake — as you'll soon see. I should also have been suspicious at the fact that, although the lobby was wide open, there was no ticket taker, or anyone else, to tell me that it was still too early to go in. But that's how it played out in the story told by the director of the Elektrodom, so I shook off all my doubt and crept into the cinematic sanctuary, setting myself up right near the swing doors. Through the round, porthole like windows, there was a clear view onto the screen on which the aforementioned slide reminding the worthy ladies about removing their headwear was projected. So, in a word, I was in like flint: the newts were in the tank, the ball bearings in their grooves, the eggs in the frying pan! I got my Leica ready, slipped quietly into the screening room, and immediately turned to take a look behind me, toward the projection booth. I saw the door slightly ajar, and the dimmed light that spilled out over the steps leading to the booth. I slid my way along the wall until I got right near the booth. And it was only here that I noticed two spectators sitting in the fifteenth or sixteenth row, their eyes glued to the screen with the woman's hat. And when I got completely to the rear, right beneath the pair of little windows through which *A Ruddy Glow over Kladno* would soon be spooling through the inverter, I crouched down — quite unnecessarily, as the windows were high above me. I was now right in front of that slightly open door. And what I saw there exceeded all of my expectations: On the floor of the projection booth there was a mattress spread with a checkered eiderdown, just like at Mum's, from beneath which two tousled heads poked out: ah, dark-haired Jeníček and a little blonde Mařenka! The woman's face was without a doubt the same as that on the

....

[34] Protagonist of a cabaret song by Jiří Voskovec (1905–1981).

[35] *Rudá záře nad Kladnem* (1956), directed by Vladimír Vlček.

                                                    JIŘÍ KRATOCHVIL

photo given me by the director of the Elktrodom. And if up until now I had ignored the bad feelings that had accompanied me all the way to the Lucerna Cinema and up to the very projection booth, now I was given one last chance, one last warning: how else might you explain the fact that the door was slightly ajar like that, where the couple were canoodling as if in plain sight? And yet I raised my Leica and the bulb flashed. And it was just as if this was what they had been waiting for. At that very moment, the two lovers tossed off the eiderdown, and I could plainly see that they were both completely dressed: two SNB goons, a male and a female. I lurched backwards quickly; I wanted to evaporate, but then, from the other side, that of the screening room, those two audience members — the ones I'd seen sitting in the fifteenth or sixteenth rows — were approaching me: plainclothes cops. I remained standing there between the two in uniform and the two in plainclothes, and only then, to my horror, did I notice that the wet raincoat that I'd thrust into my pocket had squeezed out a big wet spot along my left pants leg. While I'd been crawling up to the booth, I'd noticed nothing but the light spilling out over the steps, but now, in my helplessness, I became painfully aware of the fact that I was making a puddle — to the great amusement of those SNB swine, who thought I'd pissed my pants from fright. O, they had fun with that! There had never been any faithless Mrs Rychlík and maybe there'd never been any Honzo Rychlík either. Obviously, I was deathly afraid when they carted me off to the jug — who wouldn't be? After all, they'd caught me red-handed at private detective work, which, according to Communist law, is a much more serious crime than sewing someone a sports coat on the sly or filling someone's teeth outside of working hours.

But then Dan did something quite unusual. He went off to the pantry for a bottle of vodka. Whenever he'd have a drink with Brighty during a screw, it was always something of a proper vintage: Riesling or some French wine, in glasses set on a nice tray. Because whereas soft things grow hard with a good wine, in the case of hard liquor, the opposite is the result. But at that moment it was hardness be damned. He poured two liqueur glasses full and admitted that he'd much prefer drinking something better with her than vodka — but the last bottle of whiskey he'd been given by one of his clients from the pre-Communist days had already gone the way of all capitalist amenities.

Of course, I was shaking in my boots when they led me into the station on Běhounská St, but there they behaved quite properly in my regard—something you'd never have expected. It all had been a game, indeed: a trap for Dan Kočí, but — you might say — a nice trap. Kind of like when the missionaries snatch a bushman, and teach him not only the Ten Commandments, but also how to read and write. OK, Brighty, it's not the best comparison, but I want to say that if I hadn't been caught like that, I'd still be there at the counter in the butcher shop selling liverwurst and soup bones and responding to questions like When'll there be meat again, comrade…?

The Case of the Sapphire Serpent! this young captain — or whatever his rank was — said, extending his hand to me. My father used to tell me all about you and that sapphire serpent of yours. You're a living legend, comrade! And it's just such men as you that our young socialist criminal investigative units need! So then, we'll send Comrade Brkoš off to the U Mamlasů pastry shop for some treats. Of course, we can't toast your hire while on duty, so you can toast it yourself, in private, eh? Anyway, what's your poison as far as cakes are concerned? Cream puffs, pets-de-nonne, meringues, éclairs, cream-straws, Indians, cream-filled doughnuts, or pies?

But because I made no reply, and just stood there like that, Comrade Kristl told Comrade Brkoš to go get us two of everything, and because I just kept on standing like that, he nodded toward this comrade that I think is called Nedopusť and that one pushed a chair near me from behind, while Comrade Kristl came in front of me, and with a courtly smile and a stiff forefinger pointing at my chest bade me take a seat. Welcome to the Criminal Investigations Unit of the National Security Corps, the SNB goon / CI said, who had such authority in his voice that he couldn't have been just any old captain. But I don't know from stripes.

And then in the end I learned that the director of the Elektrodom — like all other directors and chiefs — was in collaboration with the Security Services. And that it was he that drew their attention to me, when it chanced that they were talking about them needing some outstanding criminal investigating detective for some pressing and intricate case, a real keen one, without whom they couldn't budge it. I do apologise about the trap we set for you — said the fellow who might also be a young lieutenant colonel, he had such authority and self-assuredness — I really do apologise, but on the other hand, well, that just was such a smart, clever, and devil take it well-thought-out little ploy that it really tickled the fancy. I really had to sweat to think it up — but we had a lot of fun with it, knowing that you can't catch someone like yourself with any old mousetrap. But all the same I was betting that even if you smelled a rat, to switch metaphors, and thought it might be a trap after all, still you wouldn't be able to withstand it. An exceptional talent like yours is something like a vice, am I not right?

I nodded my head, twice in fact, the first time in acknowledgement of the fact that indeed I had such evil forebodings, and the second admitting that, yes, this talent of mine is like an addiction — I can't withstand any such offer. And then I learned some other details concerning the director of the Elektrodom. It seems that on a tip from someone, the state investigators pounced on the Elektrodom, and — of course — found what they were looking for; those chaps always find what they need to find, and since he was in a real bad way, the director of the Elektrodom turned to the State Security forces for support. Now, they'd've just shrugged and let him drown if not for the coincidence that the Public Security station on Běhounská was turned upside down with a shaggy mess of a case that they couldn't manage. And so, while he was pacing the corridor waiting for the superior organ to receive him, by chance he overheard something from the SNB officers passing by. And he sensed his chance. He spilled the beans in front of them about everything concerning me, everything he knew, including how he hired me to help out with that circus act of his unfaithful wife. And guess what? It worked. There in the Criminal Investigations Unit Comrade Kristl recalled that sapphire serpent, that dazzling reputation of mine that kept paying my bills even for a short time after the war — and the director of the Elektrodom won out. The State Inspectorate moped away with their tails between their legs, and for a while he was untouchable. He helped them set up their trap for me, code-named Lady's Hat, and in this way I got the case that can set me up nicely now. True, it has nothing to do with any cuckold and his slutty wife or virtuous woman and her sleeparound husband; in other words, none of my usual sweet operettas, but, after all, I'm not so specialised as not to be able to climb on board a common criminal investigation. And after all, the case of the sapphire serpent, with which I won my spurs, was a case of missing persons and murder. So just imagine that, Brighty — now I've got a spanking new uniform, which I'm not going to have to wear, of course, because Criminal Investigations is a plainclothes unit — I reckon I'll only put it on for ceremonial purposes — but it's a second lieutenant's rank from the get-go.

So, you're no longer a private eye? I must admit that I liked you more as a private eye. You were able to slip away from national service quite cleverly — but you couldn't escape a bag in the end.

I beg your pardon — a private what? I used to work in a butcher shop. And if I did a little snooping on the side from time, that was only a little black marketeering, so to speak — for which, in the end, they might've sewn me up nice and tight. Listen, girlie, you've read too many movie magazines. In reality, you can only get real criminal investigative work done in a team, with roles assigned, and now I don't have to busy myself chasing peanuts of information in every case — that's what the gumshoes are for. They bring me what they gather, and then I plunge right into the heart of the matter.

Aha. On the sudden. Still and all, I liked screwing a private eye a lot more than some second lieutenant of the SNB. But I wanted to ask you something else. You haven't mentioned the name of that director of the Elektrodom. You mean to say he doesn't have one?

Of course he has, Brighty. But I wanted to spare you. It's a real ugly name. You don't want to know it. It's so bad that once, when a person heard it for the first time, when the director of the Elektrodom was plainly and shamelessly introduced to him, he had to find a porcelain god to worship.

Well, now you've piqued my interest. I don't mind such piety…

And then, after a moment of hesitation, Dan took a deep breath and pronounced the name. It hit her like a blow. Something lurched deep inside her — her cheeks puffed out and she leapt quickly out of bed and raced out of the room towards the foyer. She remained there a while. When she returned, she was hollowed-out, green.

One floor above them, in a room with an identical avant-corps, the doors of an old wardrobe creaked loudly, and Dan placed his finger across his lips, before pointing toward the ceiling. They remained silent like that for a full five minutes, listening to the voice of that cabinet. While they were thus intent on listening to the sounds above, Brighty slowly regained her balance. Only then was she bold enough to ask if she might venture another question. Even though I don't know if you'll answer me, I won't puke again.

Ask away, Brighty. Nothing else is going to turn your stomach.

Super. I'll survive. So tell me then, Daníček, what's this case they've set in your lap as first lieutenant of the SNB?

Second lieutenant, Brighty, at the moment. Well, this officer of the SNB, a certain Rudolf Švarcšnupf, alias Lieutenant Láska, has suddenly disappeared. Imagine that — he vanished, just as if the earth beneath his feet opened to swallow him. It's a case of a totally missing person. And I'm going to investigate it, Brighty.

PART TWO

THE STORY OF A REAL MAN

14 July 1952. Today is the anniversary of the French Revolution, the taking of the Bastille. There's no mention of this in any of the papers, even though the schoolbooks teach us that the bourgeois French Revolution was a rightful precursor of the Great Socialist October Revolution, and thus a necessary stepping stone. But of course this iron causality, the succession of societal orders, where the latter is raised upon the ruins of the former, the former enriching the soil from which the more progressive order springs, is not required of the journalist. It is, rather, the Hegelian and Marxist 'historical necessity' which makes use of nations and entire eras of humanity as mere necessary stadia, by which the grand process of world events ascends the spiral of history. Human fate must subject itself to this. As Hegel puts it: 'The history of the world is no path of happiness. Periods of happiness are nothing but its empty pages.' And for sure, certain things are better left untouched in common journalistic practice. For after all, that causality touches upon our own present state as well. If it hadn't been for the First World War, Verdun, and mustard gas, there would be no Soviet Union, which rose from the rubble of that war, and if it weren't for the Second World War, Hitler, and Auschwitz, the spark of Socialist revolution would never have leapt across to Central Europe. And from my work in Armaments I know that our entire industry is set up in preparation for a Third World War. That war is no less historically determined than the fact that, following it, there will be just one societal order all over the world — a completely just one, yet not at all happy. And these peace movements of ours are nothing more than a pia fraus: after all, it's written down somewhere that we're supposed to be as innocent as doves and as crafty as snakes. And what does this shitty little life of mine mean in this mill of history?

Of course, one would like to improve one's cadre reports, the foreman told me, but who can keep their eyes on you, who don't know how to set your hand properly to anything? All I needed was another scribbler here, he went on, and now I can just jam all those plans and projections right up where the sun don't shine.

And Kožík's putting out book after book although I still remember well how in the spring of 1943 the Germans made use of him in their anti-Soviet propaganda campaign, when they discovered the mass graves of the murdered Polish officers in Katyń. How can Kožík get away with that, while I can't even get away with the fact that my father once owned a bakery? Where is it that I made my mistake?

15 November 1952. I've started a journal. But if instead of that I'd established a kangaroo farm, the effect would be just the same. The days in the factory are a deadly bore. I have nothing to write about concerning that. And as far as what's going on in this country, well, I don't understand much of that at all. But there is one thing worth noting down. Modráček the architect paid me a visit. The last time we saw one another it was just before Christmas, in 1947, in the Barvič and Novotný bookstore, where I was signing copies of *The Adventures of the Wise Badger*. The book was selling well — which is usually the case with attractively published children's books just before Christmas. So I was in a good mood, cheery, as that long snake of my readers was brushing its tail up against the table where I was sitting (come to think of it: where does a snake's body end, and his tail begin?) and there among the last few was Modráček the architect. I asked him if congratulations were in order, since he was buying a children's book. He replied No, but that he was thinking about keeping that book of mine at home as bait for the stork. At which I told him that that's not where babies come from, you know, but if he'd wait a minute until I collected my things I'd take him to dinner at U Stopků, where I'd fill him in on all the details of how it's really done. We argued for a bit about who was going to pick up the tab, for, at the time, Modráček was making a nice pile with those villas of his in Brno, while I had just had my first real market success with a book. I stood fast — so in the end we agreed that I would invite him this time, and he me the next. This time at U Stopků we had pheasant (faisan en barbouille) — who could forget that! And after all, that night I felt as if I had just set my foot on the first rung of the ladder leading straight up to writer's Olympus. My cheery mood continued at U Stopků so that I began explaining at length the multi-volume novel I was about to embark upon. For his part, Modráček held his tongue for a long while. But I understood that. Back then, things were going on that shunted all sorts of plans to the side; then time lifted the curtain and, instead of finding myself on Olympus, I ended up in a factory.

So this time it was he who invited me to supper. Of course — At the Stopwatches again — U Stopků. Surprisingly enough, that old epicurean restaurant had outlasted all the revolutionary ferment and you can still eat a fine meal there. There wasn't any more pheasant to be had, but there was wild hare in plum sauce — in short, still a gourmet's dream such as I didn't dare indulge in for quite some time. When the next courses came in the wake of the hare, I wanted to pay my part of the tab — who doesn't know how dear things are these days — but he waved my offer away: now it's his turn, to say nothing of the fact that he's still an executive architect; meanwhile by some mistake or oversight they had shunted me off, temporarily, into some less than profitable dump.

21 November 1952. To return again to my supper with Modráček three days ago. I can't seem to get it out of my head. At the very least, it was an interesting meeting and a peculiar conversation. First, he asked about that saga of a novel which I had gone on about in that good mood of mine over our pre-Christmas pheasant. And even though it was immediately clear to me that he hadn't invited me to supper to talk about the novel, I still couldn't resist plunging in da capo. Work on the book had been stuck in place for a couple of years — but that happens sometimes with novels. I haven't given up on it; I just have to work it over a bit. You see, I'd given the lead role in the partisan struggle on Vysočina to a parachutist sent our way from London. Right after the war, I'd even met with one of our pilots from the RAF to consult with him on the details. But now I know that the leading role in the partisan struggle must be entrusted to Soviet paratroops. And it is also for that reason that I've been working in the Armoury for three years now. Among the workers, there are several former partisans.

Excellent. I'll be very pleased if you succeed in bringing your novel into tip-top shape, Modráček said, bringing this part of our conversation to a conclusion. Of course, I wasn't surprised at all when, after ten minutes of seemingly rapt attention, Modráček clicked the stop button and moved on to the reason he'd invited me to At the Stopwatches. But when I heard what he wanted to talk with me about, that did surprise me. I always knew that he was an outstanding and most likely very successful architect — in many ways my complete opposite — a practical sort, who always proceeds rationally. And so I never would have expected him to be interested in such particularly literary questions as the relationship between fiction and reality. At first, I misunderstood him, and assumed that perhaps he was thinking about writing something himself. Most successful people are convinced that writing is a kind of hobby that they can take up with their left hand, so to speak, if the yen comes upon them.

So, at first I thought he was interested in the distinction between 'Dichtung und Wahrheit' in a literary text. But I was mistaken. For some reason, incomprehensible to me, he was interested in whether something that had been written before, something that exists merely as a literary text, say: a story even, might also come about in real life. Or, as I might phrase it: whether reality can steal something from literature, the same way literature steals from reality.

I raised my eyes from my plate. As a matter of fact, I set my knife and fork down and looked at him quizzically. He really had taken me by surprise. When I asked the comrade architect why exactly he was interested in such a thing, he merely shrugged — he simply was. And so I alerted him to the fact that there do exist several significant proofs of the fact that reality sometimes does steal from literature. Goethe wrote *The Sorrows of Young Werther* and evoked a whole series of suicides imitating that described in his novel. And Dostoevsky's *Crime and Punishment* has on its conscience a whole host of philosophising, murderous Raskolnikovs. But he only shook his head. That didn't answer his question. What if the event described in the story is really crazy? Can reality imitate even such a thing? This question piqued my interest all the more. I wanted to know what story he was talking about. He stared at me for a moment, then waved his hand and summoned the waiter.

U Stopků is really a high-class beer cellar, so it's not common to order a bottle of wine with your dinner. What's more, the waiters are always circling with trays full of Pilsner. The generous Modráček was always careful to make sure that I had something to drink, and this did not end with the wild hare. I understood that he wanted to consult with me about something of immense importance to him, but at the same time something was standing between him and his need to express himself. He was always gabbing away, but for all that, saying nothing. He wasn't himself at all, which was made all the more obvious by the way he kept tracing over his plate with his steak-knife, but picking nothing up. On the other hand, he placed his fork, covered in sauce, down on the clean tablecloth, without noticing what he was doing.

I attempted to satisfy his thirst for information, however disguised, trying to reply to his unexpressed question in such a way as if I were also just flapping my gums — sending a countercurrent against the flow of his own meaningless speech. Quite simply, I said, everything that has been written either has already happened, or is about to. You write a story, and you can never be sure if what you're writing isn't actually taking place two streets away from where you sit. You're working on a novel, but real life has a jump on you; somewhere in New Zealand that novel is playing out, with a two-hour head start.

But how can you tell — this is what interested comrade architect — what is just some writer's God-given invention? A writer writes a story, and how the fuck does he know that nothing like his story can ever happen? Or, on the goddam contrary — that it will? I reminded him of what Marx (or maybe it was Engels) said — that theories are only proven by praxis. It is only real life that crosschecks every story ever written down. And then I thought, enough is enough already, and I started to get up as if we'd come to the end of it all, but really I just needed to trot off to the WC — and when I returned, another course was waiting for me (sirloin on mushrooms).

Now, this was a veritably opulent feast, such as these days even several-time heroes of Socialist labour daren't hope for — so that I started to worry lest someone from the restaurant ring up the appropriate authorities and let them know what was going on here. While, these days, a proper working class family can hope for a meal with meat but once a week — since our economy has been hobbled by the recent activity of an anti-state espionage central — here we have a couple of fat cats who deserve a close look in the mouth ordering themselves up some wild hare, if you please — followed by two partridges, a suckling pig, and if we don't put an end to it, they'll still be calling for turkey, duck, goose, veal sweetbread, some Rhenish salmon, trout in champagne, lamb kebab, and maybe even some frog's legs to top it all off!

I can hardly remember anything of the last half hour of our luxury feast at U Stopků. After all, those barrels of beer and that mountain of plates grew so monstrous that I found myself transported to some misty region. I have a sort of foggy hunch — but I wouldn't bet my tar-, soot-, and coal-filthy soul on it — that, at last, comrade architect narrated the story that so vexed him, and the verification of which meant so much to him. But I remember no more of it than that it was very bizarre. Something about the imprisonment of a cop. But its bizarre nature alone does not explain why Modráček was acting so peculiarly, as if he wanted to entrust me with the patent of some sort of fireproof glue, or the very secret of the Holy Grail itself. It should have struck me by now that he had reserved us a table in what people call a 'bunker' — that is, this claustrophobic alcove, where we were separated from the traffic of the dining room as a whole, watching all the action there as one watches a whirl of sea creatures through the porthole of a submarine. What was there so provocative or even dangerous in that academic palaver of ours on literature that, whenever a waiter came near our niche, Modráček would clam up, suddenly cutting his speech off in mid-sentence, not to proceed with his story until we saw the waiter's back?

We left the luxurious beer-cellar only at closing time, when the maitre d', alternatively spreading wide his arms and bowing deeply, had led us out onto the pavement to bid us a servile goodbye. It was there that, after the manner of communist bigwigs, we embraced and kissed one another warmly on the cheeks before each going his own way home. With a heavy tread I relocated myself to the tram-stop at Koblešná and took the night tram home. I fell into bed like Robespierre's head into its bloody basket, and in my first sleep, which seemed to me to be still that poorly patrolled borderline between sleep and waking, I saw fiction puking up shaggy gobs of reality.

11 December 1952. I travelled to Prague for an exhibit of Masters of Socialist Realism, and while there I ran into Comrade Sklivec on the Národní třída.[36] We exchanged a few words just en passant, there on the pavement, and the strange thing of it all was that he recognised me, that he still remem-

....

[36]   Or National Boulevard, a main thoroughfare in Prague.

bered me. We'd last met up at some writers' event in Prague, but that was still before the February Triumph and, at the time, there were also among us several rabble-rousing writers, whom later the winds of emigration scattered throughout the world. In recent times, Sklivec's authorial career has been ascending like a rocket. He was one of the first to snatch the Gottwald Prize, for some novel or other about something I can no longer recall — it came out at the very same time that his reportage from the Soviet kolkhozes appeared in book form.

Why don't you write a story about a real man? he asked me amidst all that human jostling on the Národní třída. But where, I beg you, will I find a Meresyev here among us? Don't be stupid! It doesn't have to be about some double-amputee pilot, you know. You say that you're working in a factory — well, grab yourself some shock-worker there, some brigade leader of Socialist labour, and write his biography. That's what you need; that's what it's all about. We don't want fancy and invention any more, just real lives! The time of the novel is passed, and the era of real biographies has taken its place — which they publish in droves for every *War and Peace* or *Magic Mountain* or any other type of that horseflesh. He squeezed my arm — Sorry, but I've got to be off now.

I was lying, of course, when I told Modráček that I was working at the Armoury in order to consult my novel with the old partisans who work there, but all the same he didn't believe me. There aren't any old partisans there. On the contrary — that's one thing that became perfectly clear to me over the space of two years spent working there — because all of the workers there are more than happy to smear one another; that's their bad habit, and perhaps even the one source of joy in their lives — everybody there has a nasty bone from the Protectorate that others are delighted to pick. As soon as he took control, Reinhard Heydrich took some decisive steps to make sure that all Czechs employed in the armaments industry should enjoy some exceptional perks. Among the ways that they showed their gratitude to him was by collaborating with the Gestapo. When the war was over, the Brno armourers organised some kangaroo courts and lynchings of Germans, so as to cover up the sins they committed during the Protectorate. So there you have your 'story of a real man' from the Brno Armoury, which would be a real literary event, for which I might immediately be awarded the highest State award possible — the hempen noose. That's not a good joke. I understand that you need to keep your beak shut about certain things, for our Socialist society is surrounded on all sides by a hostile world and just one little misstep is all you need for the enemies of Socialism to raise their ugly heads. But I'm certain of one thing: there will come a day when the Socialist order will be strong enough to bear the truth.

◆

SUMMER 1952 — SUMMER 1947

A sunny summer day toward the end of June, 1952. When Modráček the architect was returning at noon from his control inspection of the housing units he was building on Botanická, he pulled up in surprise before the window-display directly across from Běhounská 3/5. There, right next to the U Cajpla restaurant, was a store selling board games and playing cards. What he saw there nearly knocked him over with shock. He moved up closer to make sure that he wasn't mistaken. No, right there in front of him, he saw a chessboard, and upon it, the pieces set up in the manner of a chess problem — a mate-in-two. There was nothing surprising in this fact, for the shopkeepers had got in the habit of setting up a problem on the chessboard, which — should one of the passers-by solve, they'd win as a prize a copy of some chess magazine that was also sold at the shop. But this particular problem, the one that was there right now, just one of all possible chess problems in the world, seized Modráček and held him there… At that moment, Modráček was bowled over; in that one instant, he was transported back over the space of several years — all the way back to one sunny day sometime in the summer of 1947.

Some sunny, summer day in 1947. In his atelier on Kounicová, Modráček had just fixed some onionskin to his drawing paper, in preparation for inking in the final copy of his design for attorney Pyše's family villa, when suddenly the doorbell rang down below. It was a curly-headed little boy.

Daddy sent me to you.

And who is your daddy?

Konečný the builder.

There was nothing surprising in this. At the time when Modráček was producing his litters of one doubtful villa after another, at the time when he was experiencing his commercial boom, he greatly aroused all the builders in Brno — all of them would have been more than happy to participate in that boom of his themselves. And so just such a message from Konečný was not unexpected. Modráček extended an open palm toward the boy. But the little child didn't reach into his pocket for his father's business card, on the reverse of which was an offer of cooperation, with the persuasive note that the construction firm of Konečný and Svátek was of the best, pre-war traditions on which architects and their clients alike could rely. The boy merely conveyed the message that his father sends his greetings and that he has something for you, something that will make you very, very happy. And that you're to come to the chess club that evening at the Avion. And before Modráček had a chance to say anything, the boy spun on his heels and vanished.

Modráček immediately dismissed it from his mind. It seemed undignified to bother himself with a message delivered just like that, in the doorway, by some little brat with patches on the backside of his trousers. But that evening, as he hurried from his conjugal threshold to that of his fresh new girlfriend, he took a detour through Česká and, going along the pavement by the Hotel Avion, passed a few metres beyond, before retreating, backing up as in a film rewound, and returned. He stood motionless in the doorway for a moment before entering. 'Daddy has something for you, which will make you very, very happy…' Curiosity, that intrusive cat-killer.

When he descended the stairs to the café, he glanced inside the room where the chess club was meeting. He actually recalled having met Konečný once. But that was a meeting that resulted in nothing —inconsequential. And so he wouldn't be able to recognise him now. But as soon as he'd poked his head into the side room, filled with chessboards, someone got up from one of the tables, smiled at him, and started over in his direction.

Ah, Mr Modráček, please be so kind as to wait just a second, until I mark the layout of the pieces. He showed me to a chair, then returned to his table to write something down on a slip of paper, which he then placed in the pocket of his vest.

Come with me, please. I live just around the corner, on Solniční.

Modráček wasn't too keen on being dragged away anywhere, but Konečný wouldn't take no for an answer; he had a very nice surprise for him, and he wouldn't be sorry.

You may be a little confused — why don't I just come right out and tell you what's waiting for you at my place? But let's just agree that it's to be a surprise, and I would spoil it if I told you anything.

It also crossed Modráček's mind that in some twenty minutes his girlfriend, so used to punctuality, would be standing at her door listening for the lift to hum as it left the ground floor. But that lift there in that building on Mášova St was either stuck in place, or on its way to another floor, carrying people to other embraces, while at the same time he was being borne upwards by a different lift in a different building — an eloquent bourgeois block of rental flats constructed sometime in the early twenties, and that it was inconceivable that the exchange of that lift on Mášova for this on Solniční was not based on something truly extraordinary. And we're just as curious, no?

The flat of builder Konečný was just as perfect as the building into which it was set (like a coloured facet of glass in a stained-glass window). Modráček looked around with interest. For him, architecture never ended with the roof; it included everything found under it, too: the furnishings of each flat. Figuratively speaking: if following some catastrophe nothing could be found of the building except for the merest wooden table of the highest attic studio, you should be able to reconstruct the entire building from that table alone. The pleasant interior of Konečný's flat did not only encourage Modráček's trust in the builder, it also assured him somehow that he would not be trying his girlfriend's patience in vain, for here some truly pleasant surprise must be waiting for him.

They passed through the foyer and living room, and then Konečný opened the door to his studio and motioned for Modráček to enter first. The first thing Modráček saw was a draughting table with orderly rolls of blueprints and documents stacked in piles, but there too stood a Sezessionstil bronze Diana with a deer at her thigh. Yet the builder was now leading him over to the right hand wall. On the wall hung a painting. It was no large canvas, let's say — more of a little picture. But the fact that outside of it the wall was empty, that the entire wall was as it were devoted to that one little picture, suggested that this was something truly extraordinary. Of course, that picture wasn't entirely unfamiliar to Modráček: that snail-shell and helix separating it from a male figure with wide-spread legs, but only when he drew a little closer and saw the signature in the corner, did he turn to the builder for an explanation.

You know, we call this game of ours 'Russian Roulette,' for fun. Now, chess is not a game of chance at all — none of us understand it in that way, but once a month our club makes an exception. But then you're playing, so to speak, for life and death. It's a very exciting evening — all attention is focussed on the table, one board, around which we all gather, and the game must be finished before the café closes. I'm not going to tell you what that 'Russian Roulette' chess match is all about — in the end, it's our club's secret. Nor will I tell you the stakes I risked — what I would have lost had I been defeated in that game. I will tell you this, though. The original owner of the painting was an Austrian emigrant of Czech extraction, who escaped to France following the Anschluss. It was there that he came into possession of the painting in a rather adventurous way. From France he went to America, taking it with him, and after the war he brought it back with him to Europe in a little trunk. Because he was both a gambler and an excellent chess player, he couldn't resist the suggestion to stake the picture in a Russian roulette match. And a nerve-wracking match it was, during which everyone was squeezing around our table, including waiters and waitresses — and he lost. This all happened exactly one year ago. He didn't stick around here too long after that. He didn't want to return to Austria, where there's still a Soviet zone, and last year's elections here, during which the Communists enjoyed a clear triumph, frightened him. He's convinced that what he's running from will soon catch up with us here, too. And so, that's why I'm turning to you now. I believe that you have something that I'd very much like to obtain, for which I'm willing to exchange this painting. What do you say?

Even though Modráček still had no idea what he might offer in exchange, he knew that he would, whatever it was. For what architect would not wish to be the owner of a painting by Le Corbusier? Along with Adolf Loos, Le Corbusier was one of the two boldest icons of the early years of the European architectural avant-garde. Their constructions initialised a new era in architecture, and as theorists, their views blazed the trail to functionalism. Besides this, Le Corbusier was also an artist, in both the fine and applied arts, a painter, all of which as he saw it constituted one whole along with architecture. But before Modráček could pose his question, Konečný had already provided the answer.

Because I came by that picture so cheaply, I'll let it go at a cheap rate. Easy come, easy go. I won it in a chess match, and I'll offer it to you in exchange for two mates-in-two.

I don't understand.

I hasten to explain. As I've just said, I believe that you have something I dearly want. I know that your father corresponded for many years with Vladimir Nabokov. He translated his poems and his stories and it seems that they even met once, briefly. Nabokov is not only a good writer — something that, as it is, I'm unable to judge — but, above all, he is the author of these truly spectacular chess problems, in which white arrives at checkmate in just two moves. And the solution of the best mates-in-two is always something that approaches the transcendent — a mystical experience, if you like. At the moment you uncover those two surprising moves that result in mate, something moves deep inside you, and you feel the skin on your back begin to tingle. Such is their beauty. It so affects you! And that's exactly how it affected me when I came across one of Nabokov's mates-in-two in an émigré Russian journal called *Sovremennyye Zapiski*. Now, I just can't imagine that Nabokov, as good a writer as he may be, but, above all, the author of these brilliant mates-in-two, I just can't imagine that he wouldn't brag about something like that to your father. So — tomorrow: same time, same place. You bring me two mates-in-two by Nabokov, and the Le Corbusier is yours.

Graciously released by Konečný, Modráček hurried off to his by now very impatient girlfriend.

Modráček couldn't even be sure if the painting was original. Or that this wasn't just some joke of the builder's, to get back at him for his not having invited him in for a slice of his construction pie. But he couldn't get it out of his head, and first thing next morning he went off to the offices of Prof. Krejcar. If there were any authority on such things in all of Brno, Modráček would place his hand to the flames and swear that it would be the architect Jaromír Krejcar.

And so you're the only person in all of Brno who didn't know about it. I wanted to buy that painting myself, but he wouldn't hear of it. If you have something that Konečný wants so badly, in your shoes, I wouldn't hesitate. It was then that Modráček knew that there could be no doubt about the painting. He went through his father's correspondence with Nabokov with a fine-toothed comb, everything associated with it, all of that writing, but he found nothing there that might have been a Russian note with a chessboard diagram, at least as he understood them from Konečný's descriptions. But all the same he took all of his father's correspondence with Nabokov to the

Avion on the night indicated, and there he sat to the side with Konečný as the latter went through it page by page covered by Nabokov's Cyrillic scrawl. Then Konečný went through the letters once more, page by page, backwards, after which he set them back in their stiff folder, closed it, and set it down on the table before Modráček.

I'm very, very sorry Mr Modráček. But you know what? he said, pausing a moment before resuming. You'd really like to own that painting, wouldn't you?

Who wouldn't?

He nodded. So don't go yet. Let's have one more drink, shall we? You might not quite understand me, but I'm not looking to exchange that painting for dough; I'd never sell it, not even at who knows what price. But it seems I've got a yen to get rid of it easily. So, let's try something else. You don't happen to play chess, do you?

Unfortunately, no. When I was a student I had a go at it. But somehow I've never really had the time.

You consider it a waste of time.

I didn't say that.

But if you did, you'd have been right. It's a game that simply devours time. So — when you sit down at a chessboard, not only do you not know what Evans' Gambit is, but perhaps you don't even know how the knight is supposed to move. Am I mistaken?

Not at all. I don't think I'd be too certain of how that piece is to move.

Please, for God' sake, there's no need to apologise.

I hadn't intended to.

And that's exactly what so pleases me. You're a chess virgin — never kissed by queen or rook. And so, my offer stands. We just need to tweak the game a bit. So let me ask you once again: Do you really want that painting? If so, this time we need to draw up a written agreement. And in that case, I beg you to accompany me back to my flat. Right — an agreement, but what are the terms? Well then. The Le Corbusier picture is yours if, before a week is out, and so, before one-hundred-sixty-eight-hour elapse, you can solve the one mate-in-two of Nabokov's that I have at home. Your signature will pledge that no one will help you. And my signature will affirm that if you bring me the solution to Nabokov's mate-in-two before the stated time runs out, I shall give over into your possession, immediately and without further conditions or delays, the painting by Le Corbusier. And not only will you obtain the painting, but in addition to that, the solution of this mate-in-two will provide you with a transcendental, or, if you prefer, a mystical experience, and the beauty of the solution will so affect you, that you will feel something move deep inside you. No, please sir, don't look at me like that; I'm serious. Finish your drink while I retrieve your hat from the cloakroom.

MATE IN TWO

I knew quite well that I was engaging in something unbecoming. For there exists a certain hierarchy, according to which the architect is obviously superior to the builder. But I was so possessed by that frenzy to win that painting that I was just about ready to turn somersaults in front of Konečný if that's what he demanded of me. And it couldn't have escaped my notice how much pleasure he was getting from his manipulating me like that. Yes, there's no other way of putting it. And yet I went right along with it. I don't think I need to overemphasise the point that I was not interested in that painting for its value, or as an investment. I don't just admire Le Corbusier, immensely; for me, he's something of a saint. And with him in my atelier, I'd be ashamed to commit those indecencies of mine before his eyes, that mass production of architectural dwarves. For such magical values a person is willing to pay any price.

I told myself that a mate-in-two can't be such a problem after all. You just need to test out all of the two-move variations leading to mate. And so I set myself to the task systematically.

If I could come to know not only the basic moves, but also the other regularities of the game of chess, then the number of these two-move variations couldn't be all that large. And if I set aside ten hours each day, six for sleep and four for other necessary things, then I'd still have ninety-eight hours left over from the 168 that make up a week. And if I reserved half of that, so, forty-nine hours, to familiarising myself in detail with the rules and regulations of chess, I'd still have forty-nine hours left for trying out all the possibilities of those two moves. The devil himself would have to be sitting on the lock for me to not be able to open the door to the secret of that chess problem.

I arranged my affairs so that I'd be disturbed by no one. It appeared to me like a pleasant week off, during which I'd take a little rest from the everyday routine of the building boom. And perhaps I'd even come to experience that deep inner movement, which Konečný said affects everyone who solves Nabokov's mate-in-two.

And so I dedicated those first forty-nine hours to a thorough study of chess, from all sorts of opening moves through the middle and right up to the endgame. I got myself a few (five) chess-boards, upon which I set up a few famous games simultaneously. Up until now, I'd never had even the foggiest idea that, for example, the theory of opening moves has such a complex structure. Of course, I did not overlook the Evans Gambit. I paid special attention to it, for I took Konečný's mention of it as a hint. And so I also learned from Otto's encyclopaedia that between the years 1831 and 1856, W.D. Evans was a captain of a merchant fleet, and during his interminable cruising of the Atlantic and the Pacific he always found time for chess matches with his first officer. Their chess pieces were outfitted with copper points on the base, which fit inside holes drilled in the sixty-four squares of the rosewood chessboard, so that Evans and his first officer could play on even during the most raging of storms, when the ship convulsed as if torn away from all harness, performing a mad St Vitus' dance.

I want to say that in the course of those forty-nine hours, that first half-week of time dedicated to the matter, I more or less learned chess, but only much later did I come to understand that the allusion to the Evans Gambit was an intentionally placed red herring. Konečný was certainly amused at the thought of me painstakingly worming my way through chess theory, whereas — as he knew quite well — there is a fundamental distinction between the game of chess itself, and mate-in-two problems. Had I been able at the time to conquer my aversion to Cyrillic and more carefully read through the letters that Nabokov wrote to my father, I would have learned that 'mates-in-two, that ravishing and at the same time worthless art, stands off to the side of the game of chess. Its relationship to the battle on the chessboard can be described thus: even the juggler makes use of certain physical properties of the sphere in order to conjure his fragile cosmos in the air. Chess players are not interested in these bizarre brain-teasers. They feel their beauty and honour it, but they are not capable of creating them themselves, for such problems are not a matter of experience or even chess technique, but rather of inspiration — a combined musical-mathematical-poetical inspiration.' And so, I'd entirely wasted the first half of the week. It would have sufficed, had I merely learned how to properly move the pieces on the board and immediately, after the first hour of the first day, at once set up the mate-in-two at its starting point. However, not being gifted with any sort of mate-in-two inspiration, I went on to waste the second half of the week as well — another forty-nine hours.

I am used to working with an immense deployment of forces, and am able to engage with problems in even quite unpropitious situations. However, never before had I experienced anything like this, when my determined drive resulted in nothing whatsoever. At the start of the second half of the week, I set up that mate-in-two at its starting-point on five different chessboards located in five different places of my flat. I sat down to that problem along with my breakfast and continued to contemplate it when I would wake up in the middle of the night, sitting on my bed, gazing confusedly at the little chessboard on my night table, lit up by the little reading lamp fixed to my bedstead, until I'd fall asleep again, only to wake up once more, perhaps an hour later, after having strolled in dream down a long avenue shaded by chestnut trees, in each of which there lurked bishop, knight, or even rook. In other situations, in a week's time I have been able to think up and design an entire architectural project from tip to toe, and so the interior design as well, down to the very last conceivable detail. But here I couldn't get past the first few scribbles and splotches. If, at the start of the week, I knew nothing at all about mates-in-two, at week's end I knew that there was no chance of me coming to know anything about them at all. The only thing I succeeded in doing was to burn this one into my mind, indelibly!

Konečný led me over to one of the empty tables. He set up Nabokov's mate-in-two, and after a short pause, which he evidently relished, he stretched out his hand, set it on the white bishop, and moved it to C2. Careful! I wanted to call out, but the builder, who even heard my unexpressed cry of alarm, immediately showed me how marvellous a move it was, and what resulted from it.

(This happened on 19 May 1940, at 2:30 in the morning, past the thick drapes that divided Nabokov's room from the rest of dark, stifled Paris. At last, after three hectic months and over the course of a few inspired minutes, he crafted his best mate-in-two, truly a work of genius, under the muted glow of a night-light. Right next to that nightstand his wife and son were sleeping; a child's toy truck was peeping out from beneath the pillow, while on his pillow were scattered newspapers bearing banner headlines announcing the German invasion of Holland.)

See? smiled Konečný the builder, and then, with a tiny flick of his finger, he executed the king as if beneath a tiny guillotine. Then he said that he was very sorry, but that the painting would not be changing hands.

I understood then that he had known all along that I hadn't the slimmest chance of lighting upon that solution, and that he wasn't taking the slightest risk of losing his Le Corbusier. And so, this Schadenfreude was his revenge on me, for not having invited him for a share of my boom?

This happened one summer day in 1947. Some sixteen months later, Konečný the builder attempted to cross the heavily guarded state border, and — as I came to learn from the builders' coterie — was shot dead during the desperate attempt. Among the valuables in his bundle, which were to help him survive the first few months in capitalist tyranny, was — I imagine — the painting by Le Corbusier. And where did its story end?

Five whole years now divide me from those summer days when I wasted forty-nine hours of my life upon Nabokov's mate-in-two. It is a sunny summer afternoon towards the end of June, 1952. I am returning from my control inspection of the housing units on Botanická St, and although dinner is certainly waiting for me at home (my wife, ignored by me and as it were invisible, still, despite her invisibility, does not ignore any of her own duties. Around noon, she never fails to hop home from her dental surgery to put the final touches to the dinner she'd begun preparing the night before), I decide not to resist the temptation to stop in for dinner at U Cajpla, where I'll also have a nice cold Pilsener to go with it.

(O you my listener, as full of patience as a lamb's shoulder of finely chopped mushrooms and mashed garlic, thyme, crushed bay-leaf and a stuffing of minced pork and veal and breadcrumbs soaked in milk, all the same just as invisible as my wife — even though you don't prepare my dinner or — sorry — are kind enough to kiss my arse clean, still, please know that I'm still quite concerned with you and take you seriously, and so, on your behalf, I shall now gather together some orientational information.)

The entrance to the restaurant U Cajpla is, so to speak, right across the street from the door of the building in which I live. To the left of Cajpl's, one door down, is the health centre where you can find my wife off the first staircase, in her surgery where, at the present moment, she is prising something out of some patient's mouth — please rinse and open wide again — while to the right of Cajpl's, and all the while we're facing the door with our back toward mine, number 3/5, or, if you prefer, toward the windows of my atelier — so, still until the spring of 1948 to the right of Cajpl's there was a jeweller and goldsmith's shop. It had belonged to the goldsmith Filip Roth, the only scion of the scattered Roth clan who survived the roundups of the Protectorate in Brno, because he left Brno in time for Newark, New Jersey — to which town he had hastened back just recently, following the triumph of the working class. For a while, that goldsmith's shop had the appearance of an excavated tooth, which my wife was about to fill with silver amalgam, bite down now, don't be afraid, bite down, until the year before last it was taken over by the shop selling cards and board games.

And so I'm returning from my control inspection of the socialist apartment blocks on Botanická St, and even though I'm on my way to U Cajpla, walking along the right side of the street from Svoboda Square, out of the corner of my eye I catch sight of something in the window of the card and board game shop that makes me halt and return a few steps, as we already know; I retrace a few steps to the shop window and there, slowly, I turn my face to what's on display.

As we already know, the shopkeepers peddling cards and board games had hit upon the idea of putting a mate-in-two on display there, a new one every week, and whoever among the passers-by should succeed in solving it would receive in exchange some sort of chess publication.

I went inside. When the shopkeeper raised his eyes to me from the paper in which he was wrapping up Hey Man Don't Get Angry for a client, I said to him from the doorway Bishop to C2. The shopkeeper didn't understand me at first. He gave me a blank look and said What? I repeated that white moves the bishop to C2. At last, he got it. The bells of St Jakub's began to peal midday from around the corner, a cart rattled by, and someone out on the street said '...it has an electromagnetic armature, that closes when the mercury switch is engaged...' and if someone had stripped me naked at that moment, certainly, he would have found on my body flaming stigmata in the shape of Nabokov's mate-in-two. Those murderous forty-nine hours, day and night, spent with that mate-in-two had so made me one with it that it was something like a marriage between us.

The shopkeeper indicated to me that I was to wait a second; he bound up the package with string, adorned it with the proper sticker propagating the Five Year Plan or whatever, took the money, bellowed at the cashier and then knelt down in the display window to retrieve the board with the chess problem and place it on the countertop.

I moved the white bishop and allowed it to be captured by the black pawn, at which the black king was throttled in checkmate.

I didn't expect that anyone would solve it. That's a real chess blockbuster.

I nodded and then showed him a few other illusory combinations hidden in that mate-in-two, like false banknotes in a roll. He gazed at me, enchanted, and asked how long I'd been familiar with that mate-in-two.

Eh — quite a few years already. That is, not so much a few years, as since another age entirely.

Aha, he said, as if he understood me.

But how did you come across it, if I may ask?

I found it in a Soviet magazine, which someone brought here because of that very mate-in-two.

I lifted my eyebrows in surprise. Then, what he set before me was an old number of the émigré publication *Sovremennyye Zapiski*. And then he explained that since he doesn't know Cyrillic, he had to figure out the letters one by one according to a table in a pocket dictionary published by the Central Committee of People's Russian Language Courses of the ÚV SČSP. And that he had to admit that that Nabokov, or whatever his name was, had thought up a truly extraordinary chess problem.

Ah, but Nabokov is not merely a genius of chess problems, I pointed out; above all, he is a marvellous writer.

Immediately he began to fall all over himself with apologies: These days so many new Soviet genius writers have appeared that it's hard to keep up with them all. But I'll certainly take a look at his work now, I will.

I wouldn't advise that. So, do you have any more periodicals of this sort?

Alas, I don't have any other Soviet periodicals here, but I'll do something about that, too.

I had no doubt as to the fact that the *Sovremennyye Zapiski* on the counter before me was the very same number of the Russian émigré journal from Paris, which that Austrian Czech brought back here along with that painting by Le Corbusier, the very same one from which the builder Konečný had fished out the mate-in-two.

Aha — your prize for solving the problem. And the shopkeeper offered me two books to choose from. One of them was a collection of chess matches from the tournament in Mariánské Lázně, the other Kotov's *Chess Heritage of Alekhine*. But I shook my head, replying that I'm really not the least bit interested in chess. As I left the store, I saw him staring after me in confusion. Let's just say that in his place, I'd stand there staring like that myself.

MODRÁČEK SNATCHES LÁSKA

And yet, surprisingly enough, it was only then, a little later, when I descended into the underground to have another look at that bear cage reigning over the depths — this time outfitted in the sort of flashlight that spelunkers use in their karst caverns — that it occurred to me that this second encounter with Nabokov was no coincidence. Yes — Nabokov waiting there for me in the display case of the card and board-game store was something like the ghost of Hamlet's father: This visitation is but to whet thy almost blunted purpose...

It really shook me, made my hair stand on end — this ever more clear chain of something, which by itself, that is, every link of which chain taken by itself, appeared to be mere coincidence. When I discovered that immense underground vault at the same time that I came across Nabokov's story among my father's literary remains, one link joined up with another. And when I'd set up the great gilded cage there, I first had the sense of having satisfied something through this symbolic act (man is a creature of symbols), of having fulfilled the vow made unto my dead sister: at the very least, I had erected the symbol of a prison for Lieutenant Láska. But then there was that odd encounter with Konečný the builder. After all, if back then he had not heard, by coincidence, that I was in possession of Nabokov's correspondence with my father, and if he had no picture by Le Corbusier at his disposal, and never offered it to me in exchange for mates-in-two by Nabokov; if he were not sure that I had no other mate-in-two by Nabokov and again if he were not so certain that I wouldn't be able to suss out the solution to the problem, even given a week's time, and if my hunger for that painting did not induce me to harness myself to that mate-in-two so tightly that its configuration should write itself into the table of my memory, where it all alone shall live unmixed with baser matter, it would not have happened that, coming across the mate-in-two again, years later, by coincidence and out of the corner of my eye, I should have been so shocked, as if by an electric current coursing through my frame.

Setting up the gilded cage in the subterranean chamber was certainly the first step, or, if you prefer, the first move in the mate-in-two. Exactly. This was also a mate-in-two situation — one that still gnawed at me. For now it occurred to me that with my second move I must somehow get Lieutenant Láska into the cage. Only then would my symbolic act be complete. But how to arrive at that point?

I even considered forcing myself upon him somehow, demanding a hearing, during the course of which I could 'grab' something from him. And that could be anything — even a crumb that might fall from his lips but, covered in his saliva, was a part of him, even his essence!

I went so far in these imaginings that I'd even have agreed to a long, incredibly long interrogation. And how the hours would drag from one I don't know to another I don't know, eh — from one dawn to the next, even — and so as to allow me no rest, so that the interrogation should not be interrupted, Láska would have to take his breakfast, lunch, and dinner in my presence. And while I'd be responding to his one thousand, seven hundred and eighty fourth question, he would open the brown bag into which his wife had placed some bread, take a slice and bite into it with relish. And so he's eating and putting his questions all the while, simultaneously, and crumbs are spilling all over the table. When he's finished eating, he'll crumple the bag and toss it in the bin. And sweep the crumbs off the table with his forearm. With the spotlight directed straight into my face I can't see the crumbs falling, of course, but — as is well known — when one sense is shut off, the rest are sharpened. And so I hear the crumbs fall to the floor and know exactly where they lie. And immediately I'm overcome, conveniently, with a fainting fit, and as I fall to the floor I land right on the spot where the crumbs lie. I feel them as they stick to my face; I fall on them with one side of my face and then the other, as if I'm gripped with fainting cramps, but then I get right up, so as to forestall Láska throwing some water on me, which would have washed away my valuable booty of crumbs. I lift my hands to my face, as one does following a fainting fit, and draw my palms over my cheeks.

Just after my 'fainting fit' and my 'cramps,' Láska lets me go, ending the interrogation, lest I find myself 'under the knife' in the end (as was probably the case with my sister). Have a bad day, yeah, get out of here, he says, and pushes me out into Běhounská St, which is just now waking up to the new day. It's four in the morning; I'm as exhausted as a baker's dog, but happy as a ground squirrel in fat farmlands. Why not? I've just gathered up two nice handfuls of crumbs cleverly wiped from my face. I go off with clenched fists, which Láska mistakes for my continued stubborn resistance to our socialist reality.

And here, first thing, I ask my invisible wife for the loan of a thimble from her sewing kit. It's in there that I place my crumby treasure, stopping it up with a crumpled tram ticket. I place this beneath my pillow and go to sleep. Then, when I awaken in the evening, I fish from out the thimble the most fitting (the porkiest, the fattest) crumb, gripping it with tweezers, sniffing it (yes — it reeks from a cavity rotting in Láska's bulldog mouth), take the speleologic lantern and, without a word to my invisible wife, who asks me no questions anyway, and so I don't answer her either, I descend into the depths.

I go into the underground chamber, open the cage, and set the crumb down on a stool I've made ready for the occasion.

Such are my daydreams these days.

But I'm quite aware of the fact that I'm not able to cross the border of this preserve of dreams into reality. Neither Lieutenant Láska nor any other StB goon has gotten in touch with me since my sister's death. They aren't concerned with me. It's clear that I'm of no interest to them.

And so in the end I do the one thing that's in my power to do. Since I'm not able to place anything that touched Láska's body, or any direct portion thereof, such as a nail clipping or some hair or whiskers, in the bear cage, I go at it a little more simply. I write *Lieutenant Láska* on a slip of paper, and grab the key to the cellar and the spelunker's lamp.

It had been clouding up since the early morning. And now, as I descend into the cellar, I see through the stairhead windows that the sky is completely black. As if it were about to rain blackamoors. And as I open the cellar door I hear the first peal of thunder and the first rush of wind. But in the cellar, here it's peaceful and quiet. I switch on my lamp and proceed in the blessed silence, where I can't even hear my own footsteps. It's as if I were treading on a carpet of cotton wool. There will come a time when I will call these spaces a cathedral of silence, but right now I just open the cage and place the paper with *Lieutenant Láska* written on it down on the stool I had earlier prepared. Then I close the cage and prudently camouflage the entranceway from my allotment of the cellar into the underground chamber. Already on the stairs I can hear it pouring outside — a real devil's wedding, as they say — or, this time, the powers of Hell were having an immense dance party, which then quickly devolved into a wild brawl, complete with demonic cries.

But when I opened the cellar door, I leapt back at the very first moment in shock and fright. The winds were howling and the rushing waters were pouring in through the open doors of the building, flowing all along the corridor to the rear, where, behind my back, the doors leading to the little courtyard and the dustbins were wide open. I knew that I needed to cut off that savage draught, and so I began wrestling with the doors leading to the courtyard, pulling and straining until I had succeeded in slamming them shut. Then I went along the corridor to the front door of the building. I could see that both leaves were wide open, and when I got close, I found that the latch that's supposed to hold the leaf of the right hand door had come loose. But now that I'd cut off the draught, the water was no longer streaming through the corridor; the only thing was, both of the leaves of the front door were flapping in the continuous bursts of wind, just as if the house were preparing to take wing. So I went back to the cellar for a wrench to try and fix the latch back onto the door. Thus I wind up a home handyman. But then, I immediately saw that I was mistaken. I was there, at that moment, for an entirely different reason. A tangle of circumstances and accidents set me at the right place at the very right time.

The windstorm was switched off just as suddenly as it had begun, until it had completely died away. But the downpour grew ever stronger all the same. It was like a downpour of lead out in the street; it sounded like the rumble of heavy artillery: in the sudden, windless air, heaven was bombarding the earth. And just at the moment when I had succeeded in getting the latch to lock and fixed the right hand leaf of the door tightly, at that very moment, someone ran in through the left, open half, fairly battered by the hailstorm, by that leaden shower.

At first I didn't recognise him, just as he failed to recognise me. In that first moment, he was just a person in need. Someone who slipped into the doorway in search of the closest shelter. And so I switched roles from home handyman to good Samaritan. But no — this was different. In the very next moment I saw that this person was none other than Lieutenant Láska, who had raced in through the open door — right onto my pitchfork.

Most probably, he had been running straight from the old Café Savoy to his office at the SNB pigsty, but that murderous rain had induced him to leap through the first open door he came across.

Ah, it's you, he said, when at last he was able to make me out. But I had the jump on him. Before he could get those words out of his mouth, I knew exactly what I had to do. The bafflement of the last few moments completely vanished and I began to operate like a perfectly calibrated, well-oiled machine. That mysterious, yet all the same perfect chain had caught me in its toils and I didn't even spend a second thinking of how to extricate myself.

Comrade Lieutenant, I was just getting ready to come see you. Well, not literally, as you can see for yourself — at the moment I was repairing the door to the building. But in the next couple of days, for sure, I would have come to you. Listen, it's still really ugly out there, coming down cats and dogs. So, if you like, why don't you come upstairs to my place? You can dry off and have a nice strong cup of tea. But first, I have something for you, which just can't wait any longer.

Now Láska was really knocked for a loop, naturally. He would have expected anything of me at all except such pleasant helpfulness. But maybe he thought at the moment — You see? All you gotta do is kill their sister or brother, their mother or father, and they climb onto the cross by themselves.

Anyway, I went on without pause, without having planned anything out beforehand (and how might I have done? Of course — such a situation had never crossed my mind). Still, I knew exactly what to say and what to do.

I've come across something in the cellar that will interest you. I'm sure that you've heard of the undergrounds of Brno. Well, it turns out that it's not all just the stuff of legend. And because it's always darkest right under the light-stand, well, let me tell you: right here, so close to the police station — ah, sorry, I meant to say the headquarters of the National Security Corps — some western agents have, most likely, gone to ground in those subterranean chambers. They've left some clear traces behind. But as to what degree this is all true — only you can judge for yourself.

Western agents is exactly the sort of thing that Láska would react to like Pavlov's dogs at the sound of the bell. He still distrusted me, of course, but let's not forget what he'd just been through. His mental resilience had been weakened by the helplessness into which he had been hurled by the strong winds and rain. And I had taken him in, with kindness.

Now, you just show me the human cattle who would not be at least briefly grateful to the person showing him some human kindness, just when things aren't going all that well for him, the beast.

And so I courteously opened the door to the cellar and, as Virgil Dante, led him to the gates of the Inferno and beyond. (I differed from Virgil also in this, that I made sure to take with me the spanner, which I'd been using to repair the latch, and a hammer.)

When he caught sight of the entrance to the underground chamber, and when I lit up the gloom with the light of my high-beam torch, in the glare of which glittered that gilded cage, and when he reckoned that he was standing face to face with something extremely suspicious, and most likely the work of some anti-socialist element, he forgot all about his being soaked to the bones; his trembling from the cold ceased, and his StB lust triumphed over all. And it was only when he had crept up quite close to the cage, precisely at the moment when his gaze fell upon the stool with the scrap of paper with his name (*Lieutenant Láska*) nestled therein, it was at that very wink of an eye that I brought the hammer down onto his head once, twice, properly, right on the noggin, just as you crack an egg. And thus, with that second rap — checkmate! — I solved the mate-in-two.

If up until then I had been acting in a sort of hypnotic trance, I came back to myself immediately in the following moments, awakening again to my old doubts, the uncertainty of how to cope with all this, now.

So I laid the unconscious Láska out on a couch that I had dragged to the cage — one of those things that had been left behind by the Germans — and I also covered him up in their blankets, placing on top of it all one of their Prussian or Swabian eiderdowns. I was really worried lest he come down with pneumonia on account of those cold stormwinds with their icy rain and hail — I wouldn't be able to deal with that. And after all, I hadn't set up that bear cage as some sort of gilded StB tomb.

When I went off to make tea, Láska was still breathing evenly, for sure. But I had no idea as to whether he'd last until I returned. I was afraid that maybe I'd exaggerated a bit with those raps to the skull. I came back down with a mug of tea and rum, which I had to carry wrapped in a towel, it was so hot. Over my arm I'd slung a net bag in which I had more tea in a large thermos. I was terrified of what I might find when I got back, but I was pleasantly surprised. Láska had come back around. He was sitting there with the eiderdown up to his chin, so the worst had not occurred. And yet before he said a word I knew, from the look in his eyes, that he'd be wandering a bit when he did start talking. And indeed, he spoke of being shipwrecked on an island surrounded by a raging sea. He must have dreamed of something like that, and it still held him fast upon wakening. This frightened me, on the one hand — for if this was to be his permanent condition from now on, I wouldn't be able to execute the just sentence I had passed upon him, since he wouldn't understand what was going on as punishment for a crime, but rather as some sort of adventure, like *Robinson Crusoe*. On the other hand, I was happy that, for the time being, I didn't have to engage with him.

The tea was still too hot. I set the mug and the thermos aside on a great stone block, of which there were many down there, everywhere, as if some giants had been using them to play checkers. What do I know, after all, about what had been going on down there?

I sat down on the stool near Láska's head and strove for many seconds to overcome my revulsion to touch him. At last, I placed my hand on his forehead and face to check if he was feverish. However, I wasn't able to arrive at any certainty. It seemed to me that he was hot and cold by turns. Láska watched what I was doing attentively, and smiled. I got up to see where we were with that tea — if it had cooled down enough to drink, and something unexpected happened. Láska gave out a big laugh, reached out with his arm and touched my backside with a hand he'd extracted from beneath his covers. When I turned around, I saw that he was holding in his hand the slip of paper (*Lieutenant Láska*) that had stuck to my pants when I sat down on the stool. He looked again at his name on the slip of paper (the first time he saw it was when he stood before the cage and looked in at the stool, at which moment I thumped him with the hammer, but then he really let loose with the merriment. I crawled out of the cage and picked the mug up off the stone block, lifted it to my lips to test the temperature, and found that here again I'd gone overboard, this time with the rum. Well, whatever. At least Láska will get some more sleep. But when I bent down and got back into the cage I saw that he was already fast asleep, card (*Lieutenant Láska*) gripped firmly in hand and a blissful smile on his face. I felt bad about the tea going to waste. For that reason, and also because I started to feel a little cold too, I drank the rum-with-tea myself and then, lo and behold, all that I'd gone through in such a short while, the whole course of events and my persistent effort to understand it as quickly as possible, hit me at once and I fell into a drowse with the empty mug in my lap.

I don't know how long I slept in the cage with Láska, my elbow even resting on his knee upraised from beneath the eiderdown. I might even have slept on still, had I not been awakened by the chill. The warmth of the hot tea had by then vanished from my core.

I think I've already mentioned that this underground chamber had once long ago served as a refrigerator of sorts where food had been stored: pork, beef, and mutton hanging from the hooks fixed high up in the barrel vault. In the meantime, some sort of warming of the climate must have occurred, because it was no longer cold enough for such storage down there any more. Underground spaces preserve a constant temperature despite the changing seasons, but for all that, their climate changes too, depending on various factors. The builder who is unaware of the fact that a cellar in which his grandparents preserved meat from the slaughterhouse might serve him now for an underground sauna is a complete idiot.

So a pronounced cold was no longer reigning down there, but some sort of coolness still lingered on. It was clear to me that I had to do something about that. Those Germans only held on there thanks to all those blankets, eiderdowns and furs of theirs, of which there were heaps. And that from the day near the end of the war when they became convinced that life on the surface was beginning to become very dangerous for them, all the way to that moment when someone gave them the all-clear and they crawled out of their burrow, leaving everything behind in the conviction that they'd be able to come back sometime and retrieve their jewels and other valuable little items, which for the nonce were as safe here as if in a treasury. Who it was and what sort of sign was given to them, so that they abandoned their underground asylum at that most unpropitious time, that I'll never know. But as I see it, that wealth was put there by whomever chose this path for me, along which he's now pushing me, to make sure that I would have everything I'd need along the way. And so it's like that, is it? I'm already believing in some sort of master of my story, some sort of fatal causality, from which I have no escape? Well, let's get back to practical matters.

If I installed some sort of heater that could warm the whole underground space — no, that'd be pure unreason, a superfluous luxury, to say nothing of the fact that something like that was beyond my means, both physical and financial, however swollen the latter had become at the moment. And thus I have no choice but to select an area in the midst of that vast underground space to wall off with brick partitions, constructing some sort of cavern room that I might heat with electricity. For while the Germans spent only a short while there— the cavern being something of a waiting room for them — Lieutenant Láska was going to spend the rest of his days down there, which might turn out to be an unimaginably long time. To calculate it according to a time-segment frequently bandied about these days, Láska's stay might rack up a whole long series of five-year-plans. So it behoves me to arrange some acceptable living conditions for him. Because I'd learned at least so much from Nabokov and my own moral conceptions: Láska must meet with a just punishment, such as refers to a higher justice, far removed from that of the inhuman Communist régime.

Of course, it also crossed my mind how easy it was for Nabokov to invent a story like that. But when a person decides to carry it out in real life, he meets up with a whole range of obstacles. Above all, he must keep asking himself, again and again, whether it all isn't just some form of insanity. If there doesn't stretch an impassible abyss between imagination and reality, into which I'd tumbled, right into its maw, into a cage that would now be my own prison?

Yet I didn't have time for all that at the moment, although I did think seriously that, sooner or later, I had to contact this writer I've known since the old days. And ask him to help me with these questions. A long time ago I was at his pre-Christmas book signing, and when I pulled his book from my shelves now — *The Adventures of the Wise Badger* — I found his calling card inside. He would be a proper expert in these things that were bothering me, thronging in upon me now. He should know the answer to the question whether one could lift a concocted, written work over the yawning abyss that stretches between fiction and reality. The trick is, of course, in speaking of this with him, I'd have to be extra careful lest something of this actual reality of mine stumble out into the open. Should I invite him to dinner (say at U Stopků?), and lead the conversation on to the question, just like that, casually; to pull right up to the border I dare not cross, and stop right there… I didn't want to put that meeting off, but right then I had my hands full with far more practical issues.

You simply can't imagine, O my imaginary judges, just how heavy a burden it was that I set down upon my shoulders when I appointed myself to the judiciary. I couldn't drag my heels too long with the construction of those partitions in the underground chamber. It did seem that Láska had not come down with pneumonia, but the unsolvable problem of other potential illnesses remained. Despite the fact that he was certainly the beneficiary of health insurance paid for by his employers, and the other fact that the socialist constitution guarantees everyone cost-free health care, even so, we couldn't quite take advantage of that in his case. He could kick the bucket on me due to the most banal sickness. I already had the feeling that something wasn't quite all right with him. I succeeded in trapping him, indeed, without causing any visible physical injury, yet… It was clear to me that from then on I'd have to look in on him daily, and that it was high time to take the first steps toward my construction in that Gothic underground. And that meant thinking it all through, perfectly, how to proceed, phase by phase, so as not to arouse anyone's suspicions.

I hadn't yet clued my invisible wife in on anything, even though I wouldn't be able to avoid that in the long run. Hour by hour it became apparent to me that I'd bitten off more than I could chew. And yet I couldn't spit it back out now, either.

Lying in bed at night and trying to fall asleep, I am frequently visited by the image of Lieutenant Láska, lying there on the divan in his gilded cage, staring up through the bars at the barrel vault of quarried stone, with that slip of paper (*Lieutenant Láska*) in his hand. And as those stupid hours drag on, before I take a sleeping pill, for example, I turn over on my stomach and through the mattress of steel wool on which I lie I gaze, my eyes piercing three floors and one cellar and one cavern vault until they meet with those of Lieutenant Láska. And those crazed eyes of his — I've already told you that something happened to him after I'd captured him with those two hammer-thwacks to the noggin? — seem to me eggs splattered on a frying pan.

In the morning, before I go off to work, I take a proper breakfast down to Láska. You ask what my sister's murderer has for breakfast? I don't know what he would eat in his life up to now, but these days he's nourished with abundant and healthy fare. That's in my interest, as well as that of the unimpeachable execution of this sentence. So then: bread and jam, a nice hunk of salami (horseflesh; in these early days, when socialism is just being built, we mainly eat horseflesh, which also happens to be the healthiest sort of meat), coffee substitute of the best quality, the sort that all of us drink at work, and always something warm on the plate reserved from last night's dinner: for example, yesterday there was pluck in cream. And of course, a jug of clean water. And that's got to hold him until I get back from work in the afternoon. In a corner of the cage I placed an old bucket covered with a lid and some strips of newspaper for him to wipe himself with. Whatever will happen to him, at least I'm taking care of his hygiene. I take the bucket off to a gigantic iron barrel that also remembers those Germans. But I'm going to have to think up something better, as time goes by. Just as the in case of a whole mess of other things.

I'm not eager to chat with him. I'm even at my wits' end about how to start. I still haven't written up a formal charge-sheet or a plea or anything pertaining thereunto.

On the first morning (after the day on which I'd taken him into custody) he had hardly caught sight of me coming in with a cord (which I hung for him from one of those hooks from which, in those halcyon days, hams, sausages and rings of kielbasa had hung) to which a mining lamp was attached, hooked up to my electricity in the cellar — after all, I had no intention of denying him light, even if I didn't know if it was denied my sister — hardly had he caught sight of me, I say, than he raised himself on one elbow and, to my surprise, greeted me with a smile:

Light, at last! My good fellow, I'd begun to fear that I'd be left here in the darkness like during an air raid. Come, have a seat. It's too early for sleep just yet.

Could it really be that had I rearranged him inside, with those hammer bonks to his head during that wild storm? Or was he just acting? Was he even in a condition to act? Or was there something acting up inside him?

Whatever the case may be, it won't make me change my attitude towards him.

For while Lieutenant Láska is lying there in comfort, all swaddled up in blankets and furs on a broad divan in a large, gilded cage, my sister's lying four metres underground in a tight little coffin that I dared not open for one last look. So this is my vow to you, little sister: as long as I live, Láska will not be getting out of here alive. So now, sleep well. Goodnight My Love.

After ingesting some barbiturates I black out into a dreamless sleep. It's like a thick curtain is pulled between me and this painful world.

ONE NIGHT IN THE LIFE OF IVAN SLUKA

The rainy day in the high summer of 1952 is just now coming to an end. You're standing at the window, a cup in one hand, and in the other a fresh croissant. Aha, of course — we still haven't said: you live in Pisárky, next door to the neoclassical Hecht villa, which now belongs to the Soviet consulate. The cosy little house with the big garden was assigned to you for that very reason, so that you'd be able to visit the consul with ease. The garden is full of fruit trees: apple, pear, cherry, plum, and chestnuts too, for variety. This orchard is a must for you, countryman as you are, transplanted into the city; you need it in order to breathe.

So then, a cup in one hand, a fresh croissant in the other. The nearby bakery, too, owes its existence here to the Soviet consul, who can get cravings at any time of day or night for fresh, crusty croissants and doughnuts still warm. You're sipping hot coffee, gazing out at that sublime chestnut in the garden, a tree to which you feel deeply akin, with its moving vital force, which delights you. So deeply, even, that you say to yourself that there inside, in that mighty wrinkled trunk beats your real heart, perhaps, while that which you feel in your own breast is just its faithful echo. And as always, at this precious moment, when no one dares disturb you, you're far away from where you're standing, in a little village in the Vysočina region, Křemka, images of which flood in upon you. Your parents: your Dad, a forest worker, and your Mama, a jobbing glover, led a life of poverty in a place where spring arrived later and later with each passing year, as if someday it was never to arrive at all. And even so you like to reminisce about your childhood. After all, that's what led you where you are today, and what you brought with you, what led you safely through the reefs and shallows of life to this office, where you have your impact on the fate of your land: that revolutionary flame of the ever-youthful world.

I won't be back in the morning. I'll be off to Prague as soon as the night-shift ends, you say to your wife at the half-open door. Take care of yourself.

At your command, work goes on in your office in two twelve-hour shifts, just as was the case at the time in any factory you'd care to mention. And because you strive to set a good example in everything to your underlings, you also take your own turn at those two daily shifts.

You open your umbrella at the stoop, only to close it immediately as an army truck rumbles by in the wind and rain. If only you so wished, they would send an official Tatraplán to pick you up, but you always prefer to take the tram. You still feel yourself to be one of them, a worker, whom the vanguard of the working class has summoned to other tasks, temporarily. It's still true: you can take any tool or machine in hand and wield it properly; you can still say with pride, putting your two hands forward, palms up: Here you go, have a look at these. Here are my two Party certificates for you! As you pass by the consulate, you glance up at its broad balcony resting on those Tuscan columns, where often at this hour stands Valentin Petrovich, hanging out rather, enjoying his first cigarette of the evening. Touched with spleen or, rather, a little out of sorts he gazes at the alpenglow over Brno, but now he lifts that hand with the cigarette to wave you a greeting. As we've already said, you visit one another regularly, but both know with a godlike certitude that even if you didn't see one another for long months, still nothing, absolutely nothing, would change the fact that you and the consul are profoundly kindred souls — the same way you are with that sublime chestnut in the garden.

It is no longer raining when you get off the tram at Svoboda Square. But it is only when you catch sight of the nightly garbage truck on the corner of Běhounská — they also work in shifts, but those lads are staggering around like drunks, and one dustbin just got away from them; it rolls away, spilling its contents right in your path — only now, meeting up with these lushes, do you admit to yourself that, ever since you opened your eyes today, you've been badgered by an evil premonition. But this can also be explained by the fact that today's the day of your monthly report, and so the still unsolved matter of Lieutenant Láska's disappearance will come up — which is perhaps the worst nightmare of your entire life. Anyway, you kick an empty tin of liver paste so that it describes a powerful arc, the apex of which reaches the second floor, at which the dustmen give out a loud whistle. You turn around and want to growl something at them, but you swallow it (your Adam's apple bobs with the effort) and all you do is point at the shambles they've made right in front of the SNB building, before slipping in through the door. As you sail into your workplace, Captain Nešť is busy sharpening pencils. He turns the little handle of the machine fixed to the writing table and then lifts his head toward you, his superior, Greetings, Ivanek! he is the only one here who dare speak to you in such a familiar manner. Nešť and you form what they at the Central Office in Prague call a 'duet.' But I don't have to remind you of that; the principle of duets is something you understand. There is an even number of SNB and StB operatives at every station, and whenever someone steps off the reservation for whatever reason the whole number is either increased or decreased so that the even number, that is, of paired operatives, is retained. And duets, in their own way, are even closer to one another than identical twins. Not only do they look out for one another, being reciprocally responsible for one another, but they cling together so, that, figuratively speaking, they could be strangled or patted on the head by one hand at the same time.

Captain Nešť gathers up the spiral shavings of pencil and, cradling them in the palm of his hand like the downy feathers of pigeon chicks, gazes at you fixedly, wondering what sort of day is waiting on him. Because he too had a premonition upon rising, and would gladly see it dispersed.

Ready? you ask, and while still on the way to the corner where you open your wet umbrella and set it to dry, you begin the dictation. Let's say that reports to the Prague Central always commence with some expected ritual phrases of an introductory nature, which you spit out automatically, but then it all slows down, to an ever slower and stuttering tempo, the while you pace about the room, twitching your left arm a bit, nervously, from time to time halting to ask Nešť if you're not going too fast? whereas you ought to know well enough that, on the contrary, it's the captain who's always waiting on you, who at last sets aside his pencil and begins searching his nasal cavity with curious fingers. But then you break off the dictation and ask: What's up with Treblík?

I spoke with him yesterday afternoon, Nešť reports. I think you were right. He's hiding something. He knows a lot more than he lets on.

(Treblík is Láska's duet partner, and so he knows quite well that he's responsible for his partner's disappearance. During the first few weeks he rang up all the hospitals in the region and, more and more despairingly, the morgues, asking after all the unidentified corpses. At last he began visiting the morgues in person, traipsing about the corpses going blue in search of Láska, ever more like some despairing lover.[37] But when time rolled on and the thought of Láska emigrating, stifled at first, floated to the surface like a crumpled plastic beer cup, Treblík landed in gaol. The recent scandal caused by a member of the Soviet counterintelligence, who defected to the other side, evoked fears lest a chain reaction occur in the other lands of the Camp of Peace. So, nothing at all could be overlooked here. A temporary detention cell was set up right here at the station on Běhounská in a narrow rubbish shaft.)

And what about Kočí? you asked, even though you knew well enough that that brainstorm of hiring a private eye would lead nowhere.

He hasn't yet shown up today. It's time you gave some thought to what's next for him, Ivanek. You know quite well that there was a fairly unpleasant reaction in Prague to that hire. He's nothing but a typical bourgeois snoop with a past in the First Republic and the Protectorate that can't be quite explained away any more. I think we'll soon have to toss him into some labour camp. Who came up with that idea anyway?

Treblík. Treblík's the one led him to us.

Aha, now I remember, Nešť laughed. And you know, at first, for a moment, I thought — imagine that! — that you were the one who came up with it.

(Now, admit it, major — at that point your blood ran cold.)

Lieutenant Treblík sat hunched in a metal crate hanging in the rubbish shaft. And despite the fact that he had more or less everything he needed, a bottle of water and something to eat, and even though he was let out at regular intervals to visit the toilet, something had already snapped inside

---

[37]   There is perhaps an untranslatable — double — pun in these lines. In the Czech original, they read: *Nakonec si do márnic vyšlápl osobně a probíral se tam modrajícími trupy hledaje Lásku, jak čím dál nešťastnější milenec.* The participle 'modrající' [going blue], comes from the same root as the name Modráček (who is the cause of Láska's disappearance), and the comparison of Treblík to a despairing lover glances off Láska's name, which means 'love' in Czech.

        JIŘÍ KRATOCHVIL

him, and he was ready to tell you anything. He was just waiting for you, at that very moment.

For in the end that malicious little chink in the armour of Láska's life, of which Treblík was aware, which he kept hidden from you, made its appearance. So you and Nešt' set your shoulders to the windlass and winched Treblík upstairs.

Believe me, comrades, I didn't consider it important, because Comrade Láska had no contact with him, never met with him; he had nothing in common with that scoundrel. He was nothing more than a very distant cousin.

So then, Láska's cousin is a pilot in the RAF? I can't imagine anything worse, actually, than that a member of our élite unit should have a cousin in the British military! You knew, comrade? Well, how could you know that they never met? And how do you know that he wasn't leading you around by the nose all this while?

And how can we be sure, Comrade — added Captain Nešt' — that you're not leading us by the nose right now?

Saying nothing, Treblík looked up at you, then at Nešt', his eyes racing from one countenance to the other. Hope, that malicious monster, still lived in him. As long as they're calling me comrade, things can't be so bad.

Nešt' shoved Treblík in your direction and then folded his arms across his chest. But then you pushed Treblík back to Nešt', because you had something else to do right now, and Nešt' needed to respect that. And so he uncrossed his arms and placed his hands on Treblík's shoulders (Just take it easy, take it easy, comrade), to hold on to him until you got back. In your office, you retrieved what you needed from a drawer before coming back for Treblík.

Things like this are not usually done here — actually they had never been done here, otherwise, there would be a person with the proper training stationed here. But because there wasn't, just as in the case of all extraordinary matters, this too fell to your lot, chief.

As you were descending into the basement with Treblík, you were ready for him to resist at any given moment. And so you kept him a step or two in front of you, so that you would be able to neutralise him in case he did, with a firm kick downstairs. But Treblík behaved in exemplary fashion. He did stagger a bit though. Due to the time he had spent in the rubbish shaft, he'd grown a bit weak, since in that metal box that served him as a cell it was impossible to exercise. And because he had been let out only for short spaces of time, for bathroom breaks, some of his muscles had atrophied a bit.

As is the case with all the buildings on Běhounská St, here too the basement is deep underground and you went on for a long while, quite a long while, until, at one moment, Treblík paused and turned to face you — with tears rolling down his cheeks. It was only a very distant cousin. I swear to you, he never met Lieutenant Láska. I swear, he whined.

No worries, Comrade, just keep on going, calmly.

Because you'd never done this before, it was no sure thing that you'd be capable of doing it now. What if Treblík starts to defend himself and what if, with death staring him in the face, some sort of anxious energy pumps enough vigour into his veins that he gives you such a kick that you're doubled over, gasping for breath, and he takes your revolver and shoots you three times in the gut?

When at last you'd reached the bottom, you were at a loss — there was no wall switch to turn on any light — or if there was, you were unable to locate it. And the light from the stairs didn't reach here. And so, you went through almost an entire box of matches before you found a suitable place. You used one match to have a look at your watch, as if that was at all important. It was eight minutes until midnight. And you were just preparing to set Treblík properly at the wall when you heard a kind of thumping coming from the other side. Three quick thumps and then a pause, then three again, slower. And then it repeated. What the…? you asked. And Treblík, to whom the question hadn't been posed, but who welcomed it as a chance to show his good will and readiness to reply to whatever questions you had, responded with That's SOS — Save Our Souls — tapped out in morse code. So, a telegraphic call for help. Then both of you paused a moment, waiting to see what would happen next. But the wall went silent, too.

Stand here. Face to the wall. Right. You can balance yourself against it. So, what — you were a ship's telegrapher, were you?

No, Comrade Major. I was a Boy Scout. They taught us morse code. They taught us to call for help that way.

Did you include that on your biogram? Did you know who it was founded the Scouts? Some militaristic baron…

Permission to correct you,[38] Comrade Major?

Sure. Correct away.

He wasn't a baron. He was a lord. Lord Baden-Powell.

So much the worse for you. At this moment, it's all the same anyway.

And then you undid the safety and struck your second to last match. And when the flame reached your thumbnail you dropped the still burning match and before it went out on the ground you saw that something was leaking from Treblík's pants-leg. And at the same moment you felt, to your great surprise, something go stiff in your own pants. What the fuck? you thought.

And then you struck your last match.

Just admit it: when they transferred you from the StB station on Leninka to assume your duties at Běhounská, you were, at first, discouraged. That place, chock-full of SNB gumshoes? And such a tiny space left for State Security... But you soon came to realise that, by chance, it had all been thought out pretty well — and everything was as well organised as a beehive or an anthill. A strict discipline reigned here, according to which the SNB officers were intended, above all, to assist you whenever you should need them. So now you sent a few down into the cellar to clean up. And you told one of them to take a chair and sit with his ear to the wall, listening carefully. You like that about them, that they're never surprised at anything and never ask any questions — obedience is deeply set in them.

Then came the time to finish the report. You related to the Prague Central that, in the case of Lieutenant Láska and Lieutenant Treblík, the most severe steps had to be taken. And then, when Nešť raised his eyes from the sheet of paper, quizzically, you finished with the phrase More information to follow by word of mouth.

And then Nešť lifted the phone off the hook to get Professor Kuhnert out of bed to cast an editorial eye on the report. The new chief in Prague is a pill for grammar and style (Style makes the man says that chief in Prague with his humanist education, whose hempen necktie, let's be candid, is already being plaited), and before you began working with Kuhnert, he would send all of your reports back to you. But every chief in Prague has his own

....

[38]   Treblík shifts to the familiar 'ty' here.

hobby horse, and they must be respected. Your dictation was written down in pencil; the professor will now do a bit of ghost-writing to correct the grammar and the style, and then write it out again in ink. And then you'll read it through and approve it and send it off to be typewritten, after which Nešt' will forward it to Prague by motorised night courier. And you'll go off there to headquarters, first thing in the morning, to make your oral report.

But Kuhnert not only corrects your reports for you, he also submits to you his own, concerning the situation in the Faculty of Arts. He's got his snoops and snitches, male and female, sprinkled throughout the school, and he takes good care of them. And he also tells funny jokes about the Jews: You see that smoke? That means I've just inherited two million from my Uncle Moses. What do you care about that, since in two minutes you're off to the gas chamber yourself? It's better to be a millionaire for two minutes, than never to be one at all.

For some time now, Daniel Kočí, private eye and now second lieutenant in the SNB, has been waiting at your door. And when at last he enters he brings a new brainstorm with him.

You know where Lieutenant Láska is?

Not just yet. But I'd like to give something else a try. It'll lead to reliable results.

Then I have no idea why you've been dragging your feet with it till now.

Well, you see, this is something I only use in extreme cases, only now and then, when all other attempts fail. Only as a last resort. But it's never let me down yet. An Indian shopkeeper's the one who let me in on it.

Great. So, quit standing there like a saint on Charles Bridge and get on with it.

There's a catch.

Shit on catches. You're a second lieutenant in the SNB.

All right. So I'll need the former workspace of Lieutenant Láska at my disposal.

But we've already gone through Láska's office with a fine-tooth comb. I set a special investigative team at it. But if you think you can come across anything we've missed, have at it.

I'm afraid you've misunderstood me. I don't intend to be looking for any physical evidence there. I did that on the very first day, before your investigative team, even. I subjected every mote of dust there to a thoroughgoing analysis. And yet, it's there that I need to be, to find something else. I want to find the place where Lieutenant Láska is right now.

Ah, you're a clever one, you are! — you laughed. To find the place where Lieutenant Láska is right now? Gosh, I would've never thought of that.

I'll use an Indian technique. And if this process is to have a satisfactory result, it must be performed in a place significant to Lieutenant Láska. I also need to be completely alone. I must be disturbed by no one. Otherwise it won't work.

I'm afraid, Comrade Second Lieutenant — you joked again — that this is not to be a materialistic-dialectical undertaking.

Now you've hit it right on the spot, Comrade Major. True, it's not going to be a Marxist undertaking at all. Kočí's eye sparkled with amusement.

So, well and good, Comrade, you replied to him. We'll turn a blind eye to your process, distant as it may be from our scientific world view — as long as it will bring the desired results.

The private eye made a slight bow, after which you told Nešť to lead him off to Lieutenant Láska's former office, ordering everyone milling about the place to scram for the time being.

You remained sitting there a little while yet, and once again the basement came to your mind, along with the burning match falling along Treblík's trouser leg, and what was slipping out of it. And how your dick swelled and stiffened right at the moment when you readied yourself to pull the trigger — just as if it, too, wanted to shoot its load into Treblík, and how then you struck your last match so that you could see where you were shooting, and how you then pulled the trigger four times, and how between the first and second shot you heard Treblík cry out softly Mama, mama! before he crumpled along your legs, rustling to the ground, and how you pulled your left shoe out from under his body with a quick jerk. And how immediately, horridly sick to your stomach you became, hurling the contents of your stomach into the darkness, probably onto Treblík lying there at your feet. My God, you whispered through your sour and sticky lips, I've just killed a man. But then you got a grip on yourself, left the scene of your deed, and emerged from the cellar over those endless steps. And upstairs, the first thing you did was to have a look at your shoes and pants-legs. Clean, no blood, no puke. And you sent some SNB chaps downstairs with bright electric torches to clean it all up. And one with a chair, to sit down and paste his ear to the wall. And just as always, no one was surprised and no questions were asked. But we already know that; we've already said as much.

Tomorrow in Prague you'll find out how Treblík's corpse is to be taken care of. Buried with full honours, as if he'd fallen in the struggle against the enemies of the state, or shovelled under like a dog, with an additional script concocted especially for him, according to which he himself was involved in the conspiracy of some anti-state espionage central? But that second option wasn't all to your liking, for then you too might get tangled up in it and, by bad luck, might also be dragged down into the bog along with him.

But now here's Lieutenant Stoula with his report from the building at Běhounská 3/5. You let him stand there, you let him spill it all out of him, holding nothing back, because in thought you are still far away from here.

We still have the Kratochvils under investigation. After just one interrogation, Mrs Kratochvilová ended up in the nuthouse, but she's back home again now. We show up there every week under some pretext or other, we keep Kratochvilová under pressure, and her kids too are under constant observation so that we're sure that they're not giving or getting any messages to or from anybody. So far we haven't uncovered any suspicious contacts.

So keep trying! And since he kept standing there waiting, you growl at him So, fucking dismissed, eh?

Professor Kuhnert. You're happy to see the old man, but I think that's already been mentioned, too. He's got this sort of trampled-on face, and a character to match. He's like your own personal clown and can always put you in a good mood, even if today — not so much.

First of all, I beg to report that all is calm and peaceful at the Faculty of Arts. And that everyone's accepted Stalin's Treatise on Linguistics, and many of them see in it, with relief, a further stage of the Leninist purge of linguistics, which the Caucasian linguist N.J. Maar so cluttered up.

You're interested to know whether That Zmar fellow, will he be executed?

Right now he's hiding among the shepherds of the Caucasus. Some evil tongues have suggested that he's disguised as a sheep.

Ah, yes, you cough.

And then Professor Kuhnert sat down and devoted his entire attention to your report to the Prague Central. He works silently and with concentration, and only inquires as to whether you will allow him to replace one of your phrases with a subordinate clause that will express more roundly what you state there so baldly, with one of the nominals in the sentence in question? He assures you that the chief at the Prague Central will certainly appreciate it. You get up and go around behind him to have a look over his shoulder, at which you notice that the back of his blazer collar has an ugly tear, and it immediately occurs to you that the situation at the Faculty of Arts isn't as idyllic as he'd have you believe. But today that's nothing to get excited about.

The duty officer brought in coffee for you and the professor. You go off to the cupboard for a bottle of Benedictine, of which you will spoon a measure into each cup. But as soon as you turn around from the cupboard you find the duty officer in the doorframe again, with Second Lieutenant Kočí waiting there beside him. The report was ready and edited, so you just slopped some of the liqueur into the professor's cup and pushed him, confused, cup in hand, through the door, where he passed the private eye. You were ablaze with impatience.

I've got it. I know — and you can rely on it — I know where Lieutenant Láska is.

Where?

Don't be angry, Comrade Major, but we need actions, not words. I'm not going to tell you where, I'm going to go down and get him.

You understood that he wanted to hand Láska over to you, literally. And in the eyes of that private eye you could see that he really did know where to find him — they were abrim with unshakable certainty. You felt a stone fall from your heart, and so you forgave him his irregular behaviour.

You want to take someone along with you? I can give you four armed comrades.

I'll handle it myself. Just let me be off.

But then he cast an eye at that bottle of Benedictine that you still had in your hand, after having splashed a bit into the professor's cup. And so you reached into the cupboard for shot glasses, clinked with him, and the private eye burped loudly — something that you just can't bear from any other of your subordinates. But you would have forgiven the private eye at that moment even if he had relieved himself otherwise.

And Second Lieutenant Kočí gave a waggish salute and left. It was twenty-three minutes after midnight.

On a prominent place on your desk you left a card with information as to where you might be found in the event that Second Lieutenant Kočí returned in the meantime with his prey.

Svoboda Square was as submerged in darkness as a bathyscaphe in the Black Sea. Not a soul down below — only up there on the scaffolding of the building next to the Klein Palace, the night shift of the masons were sitting. They pass around a bottle and smoke, flinging little fragments of brick, which they call quantums, at the unlit lanterns. Ah, you little shits! you say, turning loving eyes upon those four high-spirited bricklayers. You head towards the train station and pass it by, passing under the viaduct and then through the intersection to Křenová St. You're on your way to a little cuddle, which today you need like never before.

I have to admit, Ivanek, that I wasn't expecting you today. I'm in a hurry. Early in the morning I'm off with my class, haymaking somewhere in the Šumava. But as for you, you can't be serious. This little itch of yours, we can't do much about that. Sorry.

Sorry yourself. I had a really screwed-up day today. And now, a screwed-up night.

Don't be angry, Ivanek, but it can't be just like that. What's going on with you? We tell each other everything, no?

No. You know that. You know that there are things I can't talk about. I shouldn't have come.

Sure. I'm nothing but a little snitch you fuck when you've got a hard-on. (Pause) Sorry. I'm stupid. Can you forgive me that?

Then you both got dressed and Darya suddenly laughs and says Wait a bit, and runs off to the kitchen, from which she returns with two pastry jewels: one white and one black, from the pastry shop U Čtyř Mamlasů. Lovingly. She pushes a portion of the chocolate cake into your open mug. It was supposed to be a reward for a nice shag, but every good teacher knows that encouraging weak pupils is just as important as handing out awards for first place.

You stand there gazing at the picture above the chest of drawers. You're thinking that Yes, something indeed has happened to you. The world has spun backwards. The picture above the chest of drawers depicts a junk on some lake or another beneath snow-covered mountain summits.

You return to Běhounská. But before you even get to the midpoint of Svoboda Square, you're ill again. You bend down over a rubbish bin, you retch, and here they come again, in a hurry, slightly digested: a chocolate cake and a whipped cream roll. Then someone's at your side. He punches you from behind — so hard, that you double over in pain. Go home to puke, you ox! You lift your eyes to have a look at him. It's a night patrolman, a uniformed SNB officer. He didn't recognise you from behind. If only you so desired, you could turn the course of that little fellow's life with a flick of your finger, and he'd never see his wife or children again, if he has any. But you've never made use of your authority for personal reasons, and you won't do so now. Even though you've got the itch, really, to send an evil dart of fate flying after that chap. But don't forget — you have a good heart (yes, a heart just like that sublime chestnut tree).

Second Lieutenant Kočí hasn't yet returned, Comrade Director.

As soon as he shows up, you'll write up a detailed protocol with him. I still need to go somewhere. Perhaps I won't be back until morning. And if Kočí brings Láska along with him, Lieutenant Láska, you keep an eye on him until I get back. You answer for him, comrade. I want him right here in this chair. Understand? What's your name, comrade? You know, I once knew this Sosna, he was a chemist on Cejl St. No, no, just joking. Listen, you didn't happen to be on duty, like, twenty minutes ago? On Svoboda Square? You were? Aha. Then you're lucky, because I don't have a vindictive bone in my body. No, no, forget about it, you wouldn't understand. I'm off to Prague early today. I want that driver — the best one. Try to have him here at five. What is it? Why are you looking at me like that?

Forgive me, Comrade Director, but maybe you need a little rest.

What? Why — what are you trying to say?

Sorry, I beg your pardon. I wasn't trying to say anything at all.

Purposefully, you pass through the interrogation room as you depart, to have a look at your reflection in the huge see-through mirror that takes up one whole wall of the space. You walk up close and see that you're as green as spinach. With disgust, you stick out your tongue at your reflection. But you shouldn't have done that — your tongue is fairly as green as poison.

Straight to the train station. You're in luck: in eight minutes, the night train to Tišnov is departing from platform three. The wagon is empty. You stand out in the corridor, watching the sparse lights of the seemingly dead city, here and there, rush off into the distances behind you. The city seems covered by a black cowl, blacked-out as if awaiting some nightly raid of the NATO air forces. You're on your way home, to Vysočina. In Tišnov you'll wait for the train to Žďár, but suddenly it occurs to you that perhaps you've gone insane. You're on your way home to talk it all over with Mama and Father, to tell them everything, how today you killed, how today you had to shoot a man dead. But it's like you've completely forgotten that there is no home awaiting you anymore. Mama died just before the war, from cervical cancer, and your father, who literally depended on her — and he was a fellow who could support a house frame with his shoulder and bring any tavern brawl to an end with a single, forceful word — committed suicide shortly thereafter.

What's going on with me? you ask yourself. Up until today, you'd never experienced anything of the sort. Every man, perhaps, has limits inside him, and today you've overstepped yours. You sit on a bench in front of the Tišnov station, waiting for the train that will take you back to Brno. Your eyelids grow heavy and only the rain will wake you up. Upon which you go to find the stationmaster. You pound on the door with the glass pane, through which you show your official I.D. Then you ring up Běhounská to send a car for you.

It's now three in the morning and still neither hide nor hair of Kočí. And he's well aware of how impatiently you're awaiting his report. And if he's had to go off somewhere, why, he could still phone in. Or maybe not? Again, another unforgivable mistake. You shouldn't have let him go by himself. Or at least you should have made sure of what he knows concerning Láska, and where he's going to fetch him from. Then someone knocks at the door.

You leap out of your seat: Kočí?

The door opens, but there you see just one of the SNB officers from the night shift.

I wanted to ask you, Comrade Director, if there was anything you might need? I could brew some coffee…

What's your name, comrade?

Paseka.

So that's a mistake. It ought to be Snooper Kominsky. Or Pushy Snoopovich. Or…

And Officer Paseka withdraws quickly backwards and closes the door softly behind him.

But now, after Paseka has shaken you out of that deadened immobility, from that statue-like catatonia into which you'd fallen upon returning from Tišnov, you decide to do something about it. You could at least talk it through with your wife.

Yes, that's it. You need a confession. Obviously, the ideal person would be Valentin Petrovich. The Soviet consul is just about the same age as your father would be, and you feel secure in his parental authority too. But now, at night, he's unavailable. You've got to make do with what's on offer.

Officer Paseka's more than happy to be of use. He runs off to the garage for the Tatraplán he'd just parked there, but when he's about to get in behind the wheel you push him aside and slam the door in his face. The Tatraplán shudders twice, as if jerking in the spasms of a death-seizure, before setting off on an unexpected adventure.

Even during the new régime Pisárky at night has preserved its character of a residential quarter. Here, the hour of lights-out is not observed so strictly, for the personnel will not be heading off in the early morning to lathe and mill, forklift and crane, or handloom. The lights of the classical, Neo-Baroque, Neo-Renaissance, Rustic and Art Nouveau villas sparkle through the thick greenery of their gardens, or are shielded behind high walls with belting and so-called diamond bossage. And despite the fact that the possessions have changed hands, their original owners and renters, the proprietors of the textile mills and manufactories, the aristocracy of this 'Austrian Manchester' who built the quarter at the turn of the twentieth century, have vanished into the so-called abyss of history, still and all, intimate dramas and rococo amusements still go on here, for satyrs and nymphs continue to reside in the crowns of these trees, nestling in the currant and raspberry bushes, carrying on their gleeful capers even in the new social environment, for, after all, everyone — lord or churl, moralist or scoundrel — is outfitted with the same equipment of desire and lust that leads us along by the nose or other appropriate appendage.

It's three thirty in the morning and Valentin Petrovich, the Soviet consul, is surprised indeed — he has no idea how woodsmen from Vysočina react to such situations — so surprised is he that he falls — covering his privates with a pillow, into his mother tongue: Gaspada, shto eto takoye? Eto stranno, eto… dazhe sverkhyestestvenno…[39] After which he stumbles naked out of your bedroom.

You slam the door and rush out of the house. Behind the wheel once more, back to town. Now your whole world has a crumbled. Even your home isn't your home anymore.[40] The foxes have their holes, the birds of the air nests, only you feel now just like what, fifty years later, we'll call a *houmlesák*. A homeless man in a luxury car. We understand one another, don't we?

You still don't have an inkling of where you're headed right now. But then it slowly begins to dawn on you while the Tatraplán is speeding through the city centre, across the Green Market — the Zelný rynk (25th of February Square) and begins to climb upwards toward the cathedral.

Uneasily you open the door; the Tatraplán is squeezed into a narrow street. You're not even sure if you're ringing the right doorbell.

Reverend Father, the Comrade Policeman's here…

And the old woman who keeps house for Father Mrch has you wait in the foyer while she scurries off to help the old man out of bed.

You're never really sure whether Father Mrch is giving to Caesar what belongs to Caesar, or whether he's just good at pretending. But he's the only clergyman in your region that you respect. All the rest of them are just snitches in dog collars, sweaty with zeal.

You're here to take me away, Major sir? Am I to get dressed?

Father Mrch had nothing on but a white nightshirt, but in the poor light of the hallway he seemed to be wearing a shimmering chasuble. And when he began tottering with the uncertain steps of an old man and waving his hands, it looked as if he wanted to bestow a blessing on Comrade Sluk.

So come on in, whatever you're here for.

The housekeeper, who's still lurking there, wondering what's still to be done and how and whom to serve, now runs off to light the grand chandelier, quietly glancing about to see what else she needs to tidy up so as not to bring shame upon the reverend father.

....

[39]   Russian: My dear sirs , what is it? This is weird, it is; it's even supernatural.

[40]   Perhaps a pun here; the word used in Czech is *domov*, which can also signify fatherland, as in the first line of the Czech national anthem: *Kde domov můj* [Where is my Fatherland?].

On a table in the corner of the room you see, in a sort of strange solidarity, a cross of rose-coloured glass and a stuffed animal (a dog sitting on his haunches). You glance around yourself completely confused. You're from a family of atheists and up until now the only times you've ever met with priests was when you were on official business, and you took them for merchants of the opium of the people. So you don't know what you're supposed to do now, you look around confused, while outside one more summer night is coming to an end and it won't be long before Lieutenant Sosna wakes up the driver who is to drive you to Prague early in the morning, while deep in the basement Lieutenant Kal, whom you've forgotten to relieve of his duty, still sits on his stool with his ear to the wall.

WHAM BAM

I was lying in bed reading Balzac's story Sarrasine, which Dr Štefl had recommended to me — that once fashionable gynaecologist, author of detective stories and smooth connoisseur of French literature. It was an old translation on yellowed paper, printed long ago in the Otto's World Library series, a translation in an impressively elaborate diction such as had an unparalleled attraction for Dr Štefl. I had just been savouring the phrase *Before she entrusted the old man to the mysterious watchman, the deliciously attractive girl kissed that walking corpse, and her chaste caress was not without a touch of that graceful playfulness, the secret of which is known to but a few chosen women* — and *He had placed himself unceremoniously alongside one of the most delightful women in Paris, a tasty young beauty of delicate contours; one of those creatures of a nearly childlike freshness, all white and pink, so fragile and almost transparent that the gaze of a man seems to penetrate her like a beam of light through pure ice* — when the telephone rang. So I set off barefoot through two rooms, conscious of the fact that in this manner I was running the risk of repeating that painful lesson I learnt once when a stray tack on the carpet bit into my heel with its one tooth so viciously, that I emitted an undignified whimper.

I'm glad I caught you, she said.

So then, I'm pleased to note that nothing extraordinary has happened to you, for as at this time, although I am not at the moment in the presence of a certain lady whose name there's no need to mention, by a fortunate, blissful coincidence she is to be found at the other end of the telephone line…

What are you babbling about? Has something happened? You're drinking again, aren't you!

Nothing of the sort. I've just been reading an old translation of Balzac.

　　　　　　　　　　　　　　　　　

Well, I just wanted to remind you, love, that I'll be coming over tomorrow with Dr Venhoda of the regional court. Comrade doctor's quite curious about you.

Wait a second. He wasn't supposed to be here until next week. You've given me a nice surprise, you have.

Do you have any idea how much work it took us to convince the old louse in the first place? Your career in the palace of justice —

Not on the telephone, please!

So then, till tomorrow, love. Hugs and kisses.

And she hung up. In my mind I went over what was waiting for me on the morrow. Well then. I'll have to scrape up a cold supper. What about a Swedish platter? Right! That's all I need — some sort of capitalist spread. To say nothing of the fact that the ingredients for such a platter are out of my reach, even if I sweated blood to get them. Maybe I could buy some pierogi somewhere, and cook up a good borscht? I could have some borscht brought over from U Stopků. They're known for that too, after all. But the pierogi? Yes — there on the corner of Victory Blvd, U Padovce, right? And some good wine, it goes without saying. Red, certainly, following the borscht. But it's not so easy as all that — I need to consult Hugs-and-Kisses again. But I'm not going to call her back today.

And so, still barefoot, I'm walking around the flat, near the glass-paned bookshelves when my good guardian angel turns my head in that direction and — what do I see but — horror of horrors! Masaryk's *World Revolution*, *The Black Band* of that émigré Hostovský, Beneš's *Memoirs* and all the books from the Anglo-American Bookstore. What, as if I didn't know how Venhoda flits his eyes about? I don't know that just one book of that sort could turn my life upside-down, and after Venhoda's visit, the next guests to show up at my door might be some SNB goons, just as it happened at the Kratochvils? No, I definitely can't play around with that. And so I immediately set my hand to the task.

I began removing troves of saboteur titles from my library, such as Lockhart's *Retreat from Glory*, Sartre's *Roads to Freedom*, Camus' *Stranger*, Huxley's *Point Counterpoint*, Hemingway's *For Whom the Bell Tolls*, Sinclair Lewis's *Timberlaine*, the short stories of James Thurber, and a whole bunch of other bourgeois literary rascality. Just to be safe, I tossed on the pile some detective books by Dr Štefl: *Murder by Courtesy*, *The Case of Professor Roch*, and *A Murderer of the Soul*, as he once told me that he's done with writing now, as they consider his detective stories to be decadent rubbish.

Tomorrow I've got to stock up on all sorts of Pavel Kohouts and *Young Guards* to plug up the holes left by the eviction of the saboteurs. But now, where am I to stow all those books? I dare not take the risk of offering them to an antiquary, because there are snitches among the used book sellers these days too. I tried to hide them under my bed and chest of drawers. But when I walked a bit away from the furniture, I could see them lying there. Of course, there was no reason to invite Comrade Venhoda into my bedroom, but, as I've already said, he's a crafty bastard. Wherever I won't lead him myself, he'll wriggle in on his own somehow. Sorry, he'd say. Got lost looking for the bathroom. But what do you know? You've even got bookshelves under your bed! No, I've got to get those books out of my flat altogether. To the basement, of course. There's no reason, I reckon, to take the comrade down there.

And so I wrapped up the books in two large parcels, making big enough loops in the knots to carry them from.

And now that I've got everything prepared, I take a peek out into the hallway and give a listen for a moment. After ten o'clock, all of Brno is fast asleep, except for the night shifts in the factories. And here, it's already after eleven! We've been living here a long time already as if under martial law, or in a reformatory. People have already got used to a situation in which to show yourself on the street after ten is, at the very least, suspicious. And from the early morning hours, 'labour, the mother of progress' will be waiting upon them. Work, the supreme governess of our lives. So I might grab my bundles and be off without fear.

I go downstairs and, placing the parcels on the floor at the entrance to the cellar, slide my key into the lock. And here — someone's forgotten to lock the door. I open it and see, right away, that someone's also forgotten to switch off the light. But now I also find that I won't be alone in the cellar. It's eleven thirty at night, and somebody's making a racket down there. At first, it gave me the creeps. I had no idea who it might be. But then it occurred to me that, whoever it was, the explanation for his presence there must be quite ordinary. Somebody, just like me, had ferreted away some books in the cellar, and now he'd come down to fetch Huxley's *Brave New World*. But that wouldn't quite explain the strange noises that the person in question is making. And on the other hand, I have to take into consideration what that other person, whoever it might be, might think of me, should we meet — what I might be doing down there at midnight.

The loops of the twine were cutting into my fingers by now, as I'm standing there on the staircase trying to decide what I should do. It seems as if the whole basement is pulsing with that rhythmic noise, and I just don't know whether it's mere curiosity, or shame at my indecisiveness, or something quite different from both, but whatever it is, at least it sets me in motion. I start descending that long and steep staircase, which turns in spirals upon itself now and again, as if it weren't a staircase at all, but an auger drilling into the depths. The sound is getting louder and somehow I seem to recognise it, though I can't yet place my finger upon it, quite.

And now I'm right in front of my portion of the cellar. I unlock it, turn on the light, and toss my books inside. And now I'm hesitating no longer, but moving on boldly. And that — that's the part of the cellar belonging to Modráček the architect! The light's on inside, and the slatted door is wide open. I call out, but I probably can't be heard over the clatter. So I step inside. And barely have I taken a step or two, hardly do I pass down the little pathway cleared among the basement clutter, than I find myself standing in front of the entrance to some much larger chamber. Some lightbulbs are hanging from the barrel vault, and I see, quite clearly, this huge gilded cage dominating the interior. And inside it, there's somebody lying on a couch, or what have you. A gilded cage, a gigantic vaulted chamber disappearing somewhere into the dark depths — all of this seemed like some kind of fairy-story apparition.

I don't know what to focus on first: the sleeper there in the cage, or architect Modráček in his blue coveralls. He's standing there at a mason's cement-mixer. That's what's making the noise I heard as soon as I opened the door leading to the basement. I can see that he's building some sort of wall. In that great space, that vaulted chamber that you enter through his cellar compartment, in that vast chamber, the end of which cannot be seen, he's building some sort of room around that cage with the weird sleeper. And then he turned around and caught sight of me. He turned around and fairly leapt out of his skin seeing me there. He was so startled that he shouted out something I couldn't understand. I tried to say something to him, to explain my nocturnal presence there, but he didn't hear a word I said. For all that, he acted quite quickly. He jumped aside somewhere, rummaged around for something, and then came my way. Those jumps of his took me so by surprise that I was unable even to put up any resistance. I stood there like a scarecrow, upon which he might set any sort of mask — a rooster, a dog, an elk, a grouse, a turkey, or any sort of tosser. But architect Modráček just took me nicely from behind and placed a rag soaked in chloroform over my face, or something like that. I lost consciousness immediately; everything around me dissolved, wantonly, and my knees buckled…

When I came to, I was in the gilded cage as well. I was sitting there with my back resting against the couch, on which someone was sleeping. It took me a while until I became completely aware of the what and the how. At first I was upset that someone was snoring right in my ear. I gave a loud clap with my hands and only then did I remember what had happened to me. I shot to my feet and saw that there was indeed a thick chain at the door of the cage, with a large padlock hanging from it, but the padlock wasn't fastened. I understood in a moment that I had to take a powder, and the quicker the better. I crept out of the cage. Architect Modráček was nowhere to be seen. I hurried over to the hole through which I'd slipped in in the first place, but there I came up against a locked door. I struggled to open it in vain. So I retreated to the gilded cage. The slumberer awoke at that moment and sat up. I asked him who he was and how he came to be there. That was one of the stupidest questions I'd ever posed, but all the same I'd hoped to receive some sort of stupid answer to it. Yet none was forthcoming. The sleeper didn't pay the slightest attention to me. He just lay down again and went back to sleep.

It occurred to me that at the other end of the vault, which I couldn't make out (there was just one lightbulb shining over the cage) there might be another exit. So I ran off in that direction, since I also understood that I didn't have much time. It also became clear to me that Mr Modráček, whom up until then I'd considered quite a pleasant fellow, and one of the greatest architects of Brno, was above all one of her greatest nut-jobs.

There probably wasn't any other exit at the far end of the vault, but still I crept along that humid wall, purblind, my body flat against it and my arms spread wide. For all that there was something there — like a furniture depot. My hands came in contact with some sort of chest, then I found a whole

host of chairs and a range of beds. It was as if Modráček were preparing
to outfit a whole regiment down here. It all seemed crazier and crazier to
me. But then I heard someone opening those metal doors out front. I knelt
down and rummaged around with my hands until I lit upon some sort of
girder — perhaps it was a leg broken off a metal bed frame, and a tall one at
that. So, am I to face Modráček with that in hand, like some heroic Captain
Korkorán? As if I were unaware of the fact that lunatics are possessed of
simply superhuman strength. He'd snap that rod I was holding in my hand
like a toothpick, and then I'd be lucky if he didn't go on and snap my arm in
two as a punishment for standing up to him. You can choose which arm it's
going to be. But you know what? On second thought I'll break both of them,
so that the one won't be jealous of the other. Then a saving thought flashed
through my mind. I have a certain talent for spatial orientation, which while
it is certainly as useful to a lawyer as knowledge of the languages of New
Guinea to a toreador, at that moment it was just what the doctor ordered.
I realised that behind the right hand wall ought to be found the basement
of the SNB station next door. And it was there, for sure, in the middle of
a sweltering summer, where five cops might well be filling the coal scuttle
with coke and briquettes. And it also flashed upon me how, just after the
war, I met a young Gypsy girl in the train to Zvolen, who foretold me that I
would one day find myself in a very bad situation, from which my knowledge of the morse alphabet would extricate me. So I picked up that rod and
began knocking against the wall, rapping out, twice, the desperate cry for
help: S — O — S, Save Our Souls!

Modráček trained his lantern on me. I spun around with the rod in
my hand. But he was already quite close, armed with some sort of cudgel
himself, so I put the rod down on the ground, cried out something in his
direction, and raised my hands, waiting, prepared for him to cover my face
with the mask of a rooster or a kangaroo. But, mercifully, Modráček merely
covered my face with some sort of wool soaked in chloroform. And at that
very moment I heard four shots spatter against the other side of the wall.
The fourth shot, if that's what it was, rang out after a brief pause. But that
was also the very last thing I heard.

DOUBLE OR NOTHING

I went down into the cellar every morning and evening, in order to satisfy the ever more ravenous Lieutenant Láska. It seemed as if he had decided to compensate for what had befallen him by a fantastic gluttony. And to punish me for having imprisoned him by devouring all of my grain and meat stores. I still couldn't quite figure out whether or not something had happened to his brain, or whether it was all a trick with which he was assailing my compassion and polite upbringing. Some days he said nothing at all, while on others he babbled on endearingly before falling into some quite incomprehensible tongue. But even if he was in the clutches of who knows what sort of mental illness, all the same I could do nothing with a lieutenant of the State Security Services but keep him right where he was, locked up. And so, even though he behaved quite calmly, not only did I keep him in that cage, but I was also able to close off the passage from the underground to my part of the cellar with a metal door. And finally, I got hold of some chloroform, so that I might pacify him quickly, if he took it in mind to try any funny business.

I think I've already mentioned that I bought myself an old Škoda in which to transport my building materials. You, who have forgotten what it was like back then, when all of us were held fast in tight pincers, can't even imagine how unimaginable it was for anyone to venture to do what I was actually doing. After ten in the evening, when the whole city was asleep (or toiling away at the night shift in the factories) I was secretly building something in the underground spaces. From the Škoda, parked close by, I would lug in bricks and sacks of lime and cement. Two doors down from the SNB station. I placed all of my chips on the old saying 'It's darkest right under the candle.' When the SNB and the StB goons buzzed out of the nest in the wee hours before morning, flying off all across the region, they apparently didn't give a thought to Běhounská — so magical a power that saying possesses.

And still I think that I'd gone a bit too dangerously far. As if I wanted them to catch me at it, actually. But what am I saying? How would that explain the fact of my bringing even a cement mixer there? Dragging that heavy beast out of the auto into the building at night, and further, stage by stage, transporting that monster of a thing, so like a petrified pear from some giant garden, down the steep stairs at the risk of placing a foot wrong and, as the machine begins to totter, reaching out to steady it, just to tumble down with it in a fatal lovers' embrace! I had to widen the aperture in the wall so that I could take it into the underground from my cubby hole. Explain all that? To say nothing of the racket made by the mixer, which probably made the whole sleeping building to vibrate, so that the dreams of those unfortunate wretches my neighbours were probably peopled by lashing and flopping whales. But as I didn't intend to warm the whole underground cathedral for the sake of one StB goon, I had no choice but to wall off the space around the gilded cage, enclosing it in some sort of larger prison cell. Now, to take bricks in hand and mix mortar is not exactly how I earn my daily bread. There was always a firewall of sorts between me and the construction work itself. Whenever I did schlep over to a site for a control visit, I only oversaw the men who were overseeing the construction — I was only the overseer of the overseers. It's true, over the last few months I had been at home on the construction site. Those huge blocks of flats on Botanická had only come about thanks to my daily, direct participation. I knew all of the masons and bricklayers as well as if I belonged to their union. During the day at Botan-ická, at night in the underground, where I didn't even have an assistant to pass me the bricks. Of course, I was exaggerating here, too — I was literally fit to fall on my face. But it was a way to stop thinking about my sister for a bit, about her last days and what had really happened to her.

At first I wanted to enclose it with thirty-fives, that is, the perimeter wall, but then it broke upon me that for one underground dungeon I'd have to cart down as much material as if I were building a little underground city. So in the end I decided on an economical sort of enclosure: a more modest brick construction with similar thermal properties. I left some cavities to be insulated with cinder.

While the mixer was doing its job, I sat down at my pile of bricks and made a careful selection. I discarded all the bricks with cracks, even fine ones, for such would absorb moisture, and all the bricks with deeper chipping, for these would cause depressions in the wall and be prone to the formation of mould, especially in these underground conditions. Then, suddenly, I heard someone behind me, calling to me. It gave me a fright and I spun around quickly. There was Dr Pešek, on the floor, below me. I had no idea what he was looking for down here in the middle of the night, but I immediately understood that I couldn't leave things as they were. As a matter of fact, there was no question of any sort of reflection here; I acted automatically — not with reflection but reflexively. I jumped aside to a little depression in the stone wall, where I kept a cleaning rag and the bottle of chloroform. And then I leapt in the direction of that pleasant chap Dr Pešek, grabbed him from behind, and pressed the rag over his nose and mouth. He fought back, tussling in my embrace, but then he suddenly went limp and slipped to the floor. I took him under his arms, dragged him into the cage, and there I propped him up against Lieutenant Láska's divan. But just to be certain, I gave him another dose.

There's no doubt about it — I couldn't have done otherwise. He'd seen too much and despite the best of neighbourly relations that existed between us, and the fact that it was my wife who took care of his choppers and, therefore, that he was favourably disposed to us, I couldn't be confident that he wouldn't begin revolving in his mind what he'd seen, over and over, so that my explanations would never convince him that everything's all right and that the man in the gilded cage that he thought he saw was just some laughable cavern fata morgana.

I went out into his portion of the cellar. The light was shining, the gate was open, and beyond it lay two great parcels of books. I pushed these farther in, shut off the light, closed the gate, hooked the latch, locked the padlock, and thrust the key into my pocket. And it was only then that I was gripped with terror. It was more than clear that the game had slipped out from under my control, and had now taken an unexpected turn leading I knew not where. In the wink of an eye, as soon as Dr Pešek appeared on the scene, suddenly, everything was different. At the same time I knew that I had to play my hand to the end. Already in the coming days, perhaps even in the next few hours, things will occur over which I'll have no control. Because if he had been at home with his girlfriend (a slender brunette with eyes of turquoise and a cascade of hair that always fell down in front of her face like a flag of mourning — we once played poker at the Pešeks' late into the night) and if he had told her that he had to go down into the cellar with something or for something, and if that girlfriend (now I remember: Klára!) woke up in the middle of the night and slid out of bed and ran about the flat barefoot in search of her lover of whom neither hide nor hair is to be found, and if she wounded her foot on a thumbtack — because for some reason which at the moment I am unable to specify, I imagine and can even plainly see on the sapphire rug in the living room of Doctor Pešek's flat a lurking thumbtack suddenly flash. (Pardon me, I hasten to correct myself: Jolana!) But it's a proven fact with me that in my states of anxiety my imagination reacts with various bizarre details. So, is it just that I'm able to imagine such specific things?

I went back to my own portion of the cellar, where I closed and locked the metal door leading to the underground, and there I felt that I needed some fresh air.

I'm standing in front of the main door to our building (Once more I beg your pardon; once more I must correct myself: Květa!) Along the opposite pavement a stray city cat comes padding. She pauses and glances over at me, as if she wanted to tell me something, but she says nothing and just runs on. I reach into my pocket, take a few steps toward the drain, and toss the key to Pešek's cellar-space into the sewer. (It's embarrassing, but I have to correct myself again. I was right the first time. Klára!) This is perhaps the last of my summer nights here. In the future, I'll be spending them in quite a different vault. What was I thinking, after all? That I'd be able to cheat fate?!

I close the front door and return to the basement and at the very same moment that I'm opening the metal doors to the underground I hear something deep in the distance. I turn on all the lights and use my spotlight as well, training its beam into the far reaches of the chamber, and there I see Doctor Pešek, in that German furniture dump, rapping the wall with an iron rod. And what's he tapping out? Of course — SOS in Morse code — Save Our Souls! I'd forgotten to lock the cage, Pešek had awakened from his narcosis, and here — now you see what happens. I run up with the cone of light and Pešek turns around, waiting for me there with the rod in his hand. And at that very moment I hear something like four shots somewhere beyond the wall; three in quick succession and the fourth after a brief pause.

As if someone had rapped against the gate of misfortune four times, quick. Is it even possible? I reach down and pick up some kind of stick from the ground, ready to fight to the death if need be. But then Doctor Pešek caught sight of the flames of determination in my eyes, I guess, because he threw his rod away, raised his hands, and shouted to me Please, don't kill me, sir, please…!

So Doctor Pešek is back in the cage, locked up and pacified with another whiff of chloroform. I don't quite know how often I dare put him out like that without causing him harm. And just look what sort of kind, considerable thoughts occupy my mind at the very moment when it's become quite clear that before long it'll all be up for me, and I'll end up just like my little sister, and the vault I discovered will most likely soon be attached to the police station by the SNB for use as emergency holding cells.

But before I'm able to quite process everything I've just experienced, here comes the next surprise. It seems I haven't learned from my little adventure with Doctor Pešek the importance of closing the door leading to the cellar, and so I run into another night visitor. And here he is. Again I spin around only to catch sight of the smiling face of my new guest.

But we've already met! says the chappie with the poorly knotted necktie. What a small town, really, this Brno of ours! The twelfth of June. Sedlákova St, the second-hand goods shop in the basement! That's where you bought that bear cage. I helped you load it onto your car. Remember? And you presented me with a Cuban cigar. A fine one it was! And I enjoyed it right after indulging in just as fine a bout of lovemaking. Don't worry — I won't go into details or reveal the name of my mistress.

Then he goes up near the cage and, with that pleasant smile ever on his face, points to the personnel: Look here! That one on the couch is without a doubt Lieutenant Láska. His mates have been crying their eyes out with longing for him for some time now. But the one sitting there — I don't recognise in that gentleman anyone I ought to know. Which reminds me — I haven't introduced myself. I'm Second Lieutenant Koči — the very same one who, just a short while ago, was a private eye going by that monicker. I've come to arrest you for the kidnapping of Lieutenant Láska. Now, now, let's not try anything funny, Mr Architect. Any sort of resistance would be a real bad move on your part.

But Second Lieutenant Kočí hadn't the foggiest notion of the shit I was in at the moment, right up to the neck, so that it was all the same to me whether he should shoot me full of holes at that very moment, or send me off to rot in gaol. So he wasn't expecting me to burst at him like a cannon ball (or a ball of lightning?) and knock him off his feet. And while he began, somewhat groggily, to struggle to his feet, I gave him a little taste of chloroform.

Ah… oh… I sigh, and, unlocking the padlock, I take the second lieutenant nicely under his arms, drag him inside, and prop him up at Láska's legs, next to Doctor Pešek. Then I take a few steps back and gaze at that still life before returning to adjust it a bit. There we go. Now it's finished.

Whatever happens over the next few days, today I can declare myself satisfied with my work and sign it with confidence.

(For the last time I beg your pardon: Pešek's sweetheart is called Veronica, for heaven's sake!)

(No, no; this is so embarrassing. Klára. Klára!)

◆

PART THREE

SO HERE IT IS, SAID DOCTOR ŠTEFL THE MESSENGERS HAVE ARRIVED,

and I knew that by messengers he meant the occasional contractions announcing that the birth was imminent, and so when he says that they've arrived, that means that the delivery has begun, after all the waters burst this morning, and so you deigned to be present at a delivery once, my dear madame? and I said yes, when my sister-in-law was giving birth, but that was during the war, right at the end, we were living on Jezuitská St at the time, and one street over, on Geisgasse, so that'd be Kozí, a couple of bombs fell, O, that was a rumble for you, doctor, you simply can't imagine O but I can Alžbětka, I used to live on Křenová and those pleasant fellows our allies also tossed a few over that way, so you had to deliver the child? I didn't have to do anything at all, the birth went like clockwork, the little boy popped out of my sister-in-law like it was nobody's business, a strapping little chappie and outside iron raining down from the sky and fire and clouds of dust, such a twenty-one-gun salute for one little life coming into the world, yeah, yeah, Štefl interrupted me, you've already been present at a delivery so now you'll give me a hand here, run along and get Mrs Modráčková ready, get her bladder empty and give her an enema, shave her and clean her up nice, I've known the doctor for many years, he used to visit us at our watchmaker and jeweller's shop on Česká, once he used to even follow me around, yeah, or maybe it was just a joke him saying that he'd like to get me in bed, but even though we're quite familiar with one another he never ever laid a hand on me, just picked out some jewellery for his wife and his mistresses, and I was a good adviser to him in delicate matters, he only needed to describe a girl to me a bit and I knew right away what would please her, a button-brooch of pearl or a golden loop or a lady's watch with a dial so tiny you'd need a magnifying glass to read it, so I was really pleasantly surprised when Modráček also hunted me down, with you, here, my dear lady, it'll all be one splendid garden party, but now this is an abuse of my person, the architect's wife has already been transferred to the maternity ward so to speak and that's where he shooed me off to her in her wake, I'd never before seen a hospital ward so perfectly kitted out, it can be adapted to any need, from a comfortable private recovery room to an operating theatre, the architect himself surely planned it like that, this whole underground house, this underworld gaol of ours is, it goes without saying, an architectural masterpiece, at least a masterpiece of underground architecture, and every Friday Modráček lectures us on architecture, this cycle he calls the Brno Architectural Adventure, trying as he does to prove that if Brno is most often characterised in architectural terms as a city of horizontal rationality in contrast to Prague, the city of magic, mysticism and conic verticality, that is nothing but a gross simplification, but during one of those lectures of his he broke away from the cycle and devoted the entire time to these underground quarters of ours, at the moment of their conception he was faced with challenges such as no architect had ever before had to deal with, it seems, to mention but the reliably operating and yet extremely complex ventilation system, combined with an immaculate acoustical isolation, such as even were we to set off a cannon down here, nobody outside would hear it unless he knelt down on the street and pressed his ear to the pavement, and then it would only sound like the buzzing of a timid fly, I managed, the architect said, to squeeze into an area that is none too large everything that you need for a comfortable life, and I did everything that was in my power, I really like it when you say things like that to us, Dan Kočí said at that, we worked like slaves at this avant-garde architectural opus of yours, just like the slaves that built the pyramids while you just strolled about with a pistol at your hip and we considered ourselves fortunate that you didn't urge us on with whips and cat-o-nine-tails, after all there's no harm in that, Alžbětka, Štefl insisted, for you to broaden your qualifications a bit past watchmaking and jewellery to midwifery, there's twelve chaps down here and nine ladies, so I doubt not that we'll see some babies born, and so that's how you see it, doctor, for God's sake, it'll be so long before we return from this little bughouse of ours to the great world above, why me, for the love of God?! I say, carrying off the out-enemaed contents of Mrs Modráčková's bowels, because down here you, doctor, are the most normal of us all, evidently, all of us are a little bit buggy, make no mistake about it, and I am too, but now Mrs Modráčková, now Modráčice has started screaming, nothing's going on yet, the birth canal is merely widening, that's all, dilating, Alžbětka, it's the first wave of pain, and I don't have any proper anaesthetic down here — that's something our friend the architect couldn't get his hands on, so just let her scream, let all of Běhounská St hear her, but of course he knew very well that even if she howled like a whole pack of wolves, roaring like a drill sergeant in boot camp, not a peep of that would escape our 'cathedral of quiet' as Mr Architect once called it, I repeat — but it's important to know that before Modráček set about constructing this avant-garde architectural wonder of his, he locked up the first five of his tenants in that golden cage, so that they wouldn't be constantly underfoot, after which he devoted himself to a long and careful process of walling up the interior of the underground with soundproofing, pierced nowhere save by that complex system of ventilation and then, when he let those first five lodgers out of the cage, they had no chance whatsoever of reaching anyone's ears no matter how hard they rapped and tapped, Madame the Architect's wife meanwhile had caught her breath, she stopped moaning and the doctor immediately took the opportunity to kneel down and listen carefully to the echoes following each contraction, feeling her belly with both hands, after which he turned around and said that everything's going just fine and the birth is progressing per vias naturales, the baby is oriented with its head toward the pelvic cavity, its little head straight at the perineum, there won't be any complications, we all know quite well that Dlask the actor is something of a Kapo, the architect comes by twice daily, morning and evening, and it wasn't only me who realised that first thing he always takes Dlask aside and spends a little time with him alone, Dlask is certainly providing him with detailed reports about how the night passed, and when he comes in the evening about what happened during the day, Dlask used to be one of the best actors on the Brno stage, I saw him myself in Molière's *Don Juan* and Shakespeare's *Macbeth*, and both of those roles, how different, were as if written expressly with him in mind, tailor-made, I won't deny it, I was one of his biggest fans, whenever I went to see a production where he excelled I simply tingled all over, goose-flesh at that enchanting beauty, and here I am disgusted to my very soul at the role he's currently playing: Modráček's ever-eager arse-licker but even so Mr Architect doesn't fully trust him, Modráček doesn't trust anyone here nor will he ever, and yet a good two thirds of us have come to terms with it, with our life down here, accepting the status quo, two thirds, that is, fourteen tenants, for example all of the girls except for me and Irena, and after all there are still some authentic rebels amongst us, among whom first of all Dan Kočí, even though he's one of the 'original settlers' (he was among the first ones here, one of the first that Modráček locked up in the gilded cage), and he's always trying to steal a march on Modráček, to get the better of him, trip him up, he's always trying to organise a resistance, to think up little traps for our gaoler sometimes just to keep the momentum going, to keep talking, so that the architect had to convince him that he was deadly serious when he warned us that he wouldn't hesitate to shoot anyone who tried to attack him or to escape, and indeed during one of Kočí's sad attempts he did shoot him in the left leg, Štefl instructed Modráček what he had to buy in Chirana on Cejl St, from stethoscope to scalpel so that he could operate on Kočí, but among all of the medical supplies that Modráček collected thanks to the doctor's prescriptions at the very start, running around to all of the chemists in Brno, as well as the drugstores in the nearby suburbs, he couldn't come by any anaesthetic, no analgesic, nothing to soothe the pain, but then this omission came in handy to Mr Architect, as he wished all of us, not only Dan Kočí, to take good advantage of this exemplary punishment, for Dan Kočí, that tough lad, bellowed like ten bulls and thrashed about like twenty eels, we had our hands full to hold him down as the doctor bored into his leg until he was able to get his pincers on that bullet from the Walther, then on 1 June, the International Day of the Child, when the Communist state decided to pauperise the family by carrying out a drastic currency reform, despite the fact of the president having assured everyone just one day before that nothing of the sort was in the offing, and that such rumours were nothing but propaganda from the American radio, Mr Architect informed us about it all with great pleasure and satisfaction, bringing us newspapers with the official version, and also a flyer which was circulating in Brno, and described how a demonstration of workers was marching through Svoboda Square with a banner reading Stop Stealing from Workers' Families! and how a certain female comrade stood in their way as they marched shouting Comrades! For God's sake, stop! Don't stab socialism in the back! but the host of demonstrators just blew her aside like so much chaff, how people literally lost everything overnight, everything they had in savings banks, hidden under mattresses and stuffed in slippers, and all the protests were liquidated with such severity, the people took such a nice wallop to the schnozzle, and Modráček told us all about it with such pleasure and satisfaction, because none of that affected us at all, we're living in our underground luxury just the same as before, no change at all as far as we are concerned, the plummeting currency didn't hurt him at all, he'd exhausted all of his financial means in the construction of this 'horizontal subterranean city' as early as the beginning of 1953, and we have been living now on all those fancy trinkets that the Germans had taken from the Jewish families of Brno as they were transporting them to the gas, and which they'd stowed down here when they went off to face their own fate, I'm sitting at the feet of the mother to be, with her legs spread open, waiting until I'm needed to hand the doctor something or to hold on to something, the little child's head is ploughing its path like a battering ram that wants to knock down the walls separating it from the outside world, (ah if only that little battering ram knew that it wasn't pounding its way to some world with a sky full of sun and stars, but only to one more, this time cavernous, womb!) and Madame the Architect's Wife stopped screaming again just as if you'd cut a cord and now she's starting to react obediently to Štefl's guiding touches and instructions, she raises herself up a bit, (a basin with a roll of cloth is placed near her, below) and she bends her chin down to her chest and pulls at her shins with her hands just under her knees and between contractions she breathes deeply, disciplined, making an honest effort with her abdominal presses, a shock-worker of a mother, I watch as the doctor extracts the little head with his left hand gently submerged, and all the while gently protecting the edges with his right hand, and now he's extracted the head entirely, gently bending closer and fishing out one arm, and then slightly lifting the little head up and extracting the other arm, and now he's taken the child under both arms, and he pops right out like a cork and here we are, it's a boy, it's a boy Mrs Modráčková! and joy breaks in upon Staré bělidlo![41] what, will it kill you to have a little chuckle? so, what, will it work? now here, Bětka, tie off the cord — here, and up here too — and just so you won't be sorry, here, suck the mucous out of his nose and his mouth, but no, for God's sake dear lady, not with your mouth, if you just turn around there's a suction flask behind you there, and some alcohol for disinfection and don't forget to treat the conjunctiva, do we understand each other? and Štefl washes his hands and begs our pardon, he's going off for a little smoke and Mr Architect comes over to consult with me, he knows that I'm an expert, after all, he also once bought something at my shop for that mistress of his, if my memory serves me correctly, it was a charm bracelet for a charming redhead, he shows me his jewellery box, a little basket still quite full of shiny things, I dip both my hands into Modráček's treasure chest and draw them out laden with brilliant gems, I'm able to picture how difficult they are to peddle when a person doesn't understand the business, and every mother's son is lurking, waiting to pull a fast one on you, and you don't have the foggiest idea, how on earth can you be sure that you're not holding deceptive trash in your hands, or vice versa, that maybe you're about to sell something unique and valuable way below price, something that for example the goldsmiths and jewellers of Vienna would be so eager to snatch from your grip that they'd tear off your hands along with it, and at the same time you emphasise that it's in the interest of everyone here to sell at the best possible price, if we're to preserve a certain standard of living here, I spill the jewels back into the box and at last I trot out with: It's a shame to sell any of it, really, since there is another way to come up with significant resources, but, but, he stutters, his eyes wide, out with it then, Madame Alžběta, don't be shy, where did you ever hear that I could be shy, I'd be quite happy to give you a little shock concerning what's waiting on you, well go right ahead, shock away, well then, I reached into my pocket and when I pulled it out and opened my fist I said See that? What is it? Why, that's a rivet of pure gold, I've taken your whole bear cage apart, piece by piece, it can be unscrewed and unriveted, and I made a little assay of the gold, please don't be upset with me, and guess what? That's not a gilded cage at all, it's a golden cage, entirely of gold, Now

....

[41]   A jocular reference to the novel *Babička* [Grandma] by Božena Němcová (1820–1862), as is the reference to Mad Viktorka later.

                                          JIŘÍ KRATOCHVIL

don't you get upset with me, but you're off your rocker, for heaven's sake they used to keep a bear in it and it was just shoved there into a corner of the yard, right next to a shed leading to the garden, I told you after all how I came by it, that whole golden cage, that's nothing but rubbish what you're saying, On the contrary, sir, it was very cleverly thought out, they poured their entire wealth into that cage, it wasn't the cage keeping the bear but the bear keeping the cage, just like a story from *The Thousand and One Nights Entertainments*, who would have hit upon it since it even fooled you, and all those who robbed the Jews of their wealth didn't give a flip for the cage, they just got rid of it at the second-hand shop, and yet the weight of it alone might have clued them in, but all of them, including that antiques dealer, were struck blind, what a failure of the human imagination, they couldn't even imagine it that someone might keep a cage of pure gold out in the garden, I'll take the cage apart completely and you'll have so much gold that you'll be able to clothe us all in silk satin and poplin and feed us nothing but caviar and lobster and shrimp and fit out a stable of Lipizzaners for us to trot around on down here or a sea aquarium with live sharks, and I reached into the jewellery box again, and you just trick out your girlfriends with these delightful luxuries, but I don't have any girlfriends, Mr Architect lamented, I don't have any privacy whatsoever all of my time for heaven's sake is split between you all down here and the socialist projects up there and then the third phase of the delivery commenced, the birth of that which Dr Štefl calls the jelly-fish, the placenta emerged along with the membranes, the ligaments and the blood vessels and the last bit of umbilical cord, but here too all went on without any complications and it was all over in the space of just a few minutes, Mrs Modráčková didn't even make a peep now, she just gazed at her son and at us with the eyes of Mad Viktorka, if I had to guess, I'd say that Lieutenant Láska didn't just pump his semen into her, but along with that he squirted three or four drops of his lunacy too, I bathed the newborn, dried him carefully and presented him to his meshugga mama, then Koláček the teacher, whom nearly all of us call Professor Cimprlich, you know, Mealymouth, amused me a bit by following me around (I'm nothing special here, he follows everybody around) and he started off with the idea that in these educational evening courses of ours he should also be allowed to lecture on Marxism, because up there, and here he pointed up toward the ceiling of the cavern, up there Marxism is being debased and abused, whereas 'Marxism with a human dimension' as he calls it continues to be the future of humanity, and as soon as we return up there, we might become his emissaries, apostles and missionaries, now first, comrade teacher, don't be an ass, we're never going to return up there, and second, comrade teacher, why should the future of humanity be your Marxism with a human dimension rather than voyeurism with a powerful telescope? Shame on you Madame Alžběta, he huffed in indignation and turned on his heel and marched away, Lieutenant Láska certainly surprised no one when he looked at the fruit of his loins with all the interest a shellfish has for a nasty word, the former bus-driver Kučera suggested that we place the baby in Láska's arms, that direct contact with the newborn child might awaken a fatherly instinct in him, but all of us were opposed to that, because we couldn't know what Láska would do, chiefly, above all, what he might do to the child, Father Klenovský is all hot and bothered for a baptism and is trying to squeeze out of Madame the Architect's Wife a Christian name for her little son, because without that there can be no Christening, but right now at the moment when he's already given up on that and starts to urge us all to pitch in and come to a consensus on what the name should be, right at that moment Mrs Modráčková pulls herself together and says something softly that at first we all took for a loud sigh, but Zuzana the florist knelt down near her and putting her ear to her lips, actually, asked her to repeat it and lo and behold she said the name Eda, so, Eduard, each of us has his own quite comfortable apartment down here, but callouses on our hands as well, since we all of us lent a hand inseparably almost to the common task of building the house, which stretches down the long cavern like dysentery, like typhus, like puerperal fever and all of us have callouses on our brains after those first few weeks of racking them to think up plans of how to take a powder, how to break out of here, how to get the better of Modráček, at the time nothing had been set up down here yet, nothing but the wall encircling the golden cage, and we camped out here like colonists on the threshold of a new land, like the Pilgrim Fathers sleeping on straw mattresses that were rotting already, and on fold-out couches and wooden and metal-framed beds, and on mattresses spread out on the ground, all of that stuff that remained here where the Germans had carted it all down, hiding out, supposedly, from the Red Army, and all of us have callouses on our souls from the time in those first weeks when we had to come to terms with it in the end, that we're going to have to live down here now, literally right under the feet of passers-by rushing about and dawdling, right beneath that world where all of us have our real homes, friends, loves, that evening in honour of Eduard's birth Modráček took us all into the so-called auditorium, the architect never drinks anything himself, as the wretch must be constantly on the watch lest some one of us take advantage of the opportunity, lest the rebels among us attack him, lest anyone get around behind him or jump him, so he lifted a glass of water in toast while we opened champagne, good champagne, from somewhere on the black market, which still has its clientele up there above us, Mr Architect made a short speech about how we should take the birth of our first child as a joyful sign that we have accepted our new tasks as passengers on Noah's Ark, at which Dan Kočí said out of the side of his mouth Vivat! The child of a crazy SNB goon and Modráček's loopy wife! Modráček pretended not to hear that, and finished his toast despite the fact that some of the rebels provocatively poured the contents of their glasses out on the ground, and Fr Klenovský piped up and said Don't be upset, sir, but you really are going too far when you bring Noah's Ark into it like that, when you allow yourself to bring in the Bible, even though you provide for us in this reality here, the fact remains that we are in a prison, which is, let us assume, merely one pocket in the straitjacket of that much greater prison, into which the entire Czech nation has been thrust, but we needn't understand a prison within a prison as some sort of enclave of freedom, unless of course we admit Hegel's negation of negation, the birth of children here I would take as a different sort of sign, even if, like it or not, we were to accept the fact that we ourselves are to spend a certain amount of time here, that doesn't mean that you have the right to imprison children as well, you cannot justify such an act in any way, the birth of that child, that should be the key that unlocks that armoured door over there, after all, in Christian symbolism the birth of a child is of paramount significance, but Modráček had already stepped down off the platform and, crossing through the auditorium, placed his hand upon the shoulder of the Reverend Father Klenovský, I'd love to talk this all over with you, but don't start spinning your philosophical-theological webs about us here, now, all right? the fact is, now this isn't Modráček or Klenovský talking, but me, the fact is, we already started to get into a groove with all this, something which more than anything else bore witness to the fact that now even here in these abnormal conditions, we were beginning to live, as unbelievable as it sounds, to live something resembling a normal life, you might well say that here, day and night, a sort of erotic drama or melodrama was being carried out, with ugly little scenes of jealousy occurring as partners are being exchanged down here at a much quicker tempo than up there in the world above our heads, because time has somehow thickened appreciably down here, sometimes when I glance at the face of my watch I have the feeling that the hands are spinning faster, and there are days here when it seems like we succeed in forgetting that there exists any world other than this 'horizontal subterranean city' of ours, just as the inhabitants of our planet are sometimes completely unaware of the fact that there exists anything beyond our little earth, something of which we are merely an insignificant little portion, at such times the most ordinary days pass along with the extraordinary ones, we experience whole long chains the links of which are forged of bullshit and idiocies, but also real events, or at least such as we wish to consider events, Modráček is constantly trying to engage us somehow, the rhythms of labour here below mirroring after a fashion the rhythms of construction somewhere up above our heads, we're constantly living on a construction site, we always have something to do, in order to bring Modráček's avant-garde architectural opus to its conclusion, that home forced upon us, and constantly there are found amongst us people such as cooperate with Mr Architect, and as time — measured by the lighting and extinguishing of the lamps, which here mechanically divide day from night and night from day — as time passes, as the number of those who have come to terms with life in this jug, this slammer, increases, in the evenings Modráček and Doctor Pešek and the newsagent Tuček arrange these evening courses, everybody is to share with the others what he or she arrived with, what they came down with, and even games are organised and then there's the bread, which Mr Architect delivers each evening in a travelling bag along with tinned food, marmalade, jam, my neighbour is a chef from the U Jakuba hotel, unfortunately there's only one transverse partition separating us, that chef is a real blusterer, he's capable of stomping around the room for hours on end, raging at or to someone absent, I'm certain that he was no different before Modráček snatched him, that doesn't concern me at all, but I'm wildly concerned with this, I'm certain that our furious chef is spitting into the sauce and, in general, what he does with everything he later dishes up on our plates, well, but I haven't yet told you the sort of Renaissance dining room we've been provided with, with copies of famous Renaissance paintings in narrow dark brown frames on the wall surrounding our dining table, which isn't one of those pieces of furniture left behind by the Germans, Modráček had it made to order for us, it cost him a silver ring with a beautiful sapphire eye, the table, naturally, in segments, which he carried down to us in pieces over the space of three days, after which he and Dlask put it together in the dining room, that's a table such as you rarely come across, my father was a carpenter so I know something about it, but to go back a bit, there was something else that I wanted, you see, I wanted something rather impossible, to talk with that chef and ask him if he wouldn't mind switching apartments with Dan Kočí, but when that bastard caught wind of what I was getting at, right away he up and laughs straight into my puss, I thought for a moment of going straight to Modráček or to someone from the so-called organisational self-government, so that the switch might be imposed from above, but as a matter of fact I didn't even know if Dan would agree to it, whether he might think I was looking to get my hooks into him, trying to stake my claim to him, I am after all the least shy of all beasts here covetous of some male meat, certainly because I'm something of an intellectual, since right after the war when they were putting on Sartre's play *No Exit* I didn't give a fig for all the warnings but ran off to see it as fast as my legs would carry me, and what's worse, I read some thirty pages of Husserl's *Cartesian Meditations*, you could say I'm already infected, I'm something of a cursed soul, Mr Architect sometimes has these seizures of touching concern, the human sometimes peeks out of him, like yesterday when he carried into the dining room on his own back all by himself this wall-clock, a so-called 'Viennese Regulator', it's operated by a pendulum and strikes every quarter hour, he called me over and asked me to set it up, he didn't buy it at any bazaar, but carried it down from the attic, I was afraid it might be nothing more than a heap of junk with an irreparably damaged mechanism, but when I opened the cover I was pleasantly surprised, the moving parts with the Graham anchor escarpment were in the best order, all it needed was a good cleaning, I oiled all the bearings, hung the drive-weights on the pully-wires, polished the Biedermeier cabinet, Samuel Hutka hammered two large staples into the wall and with keyhole mounts fastened the clock securely, and when dinner-time came round everybody at table lifted their eyes from their plates in surprise, because the clock had just begun festively to strike noon, and everyone waited patiently until the last chime before once more bending over their plates, but that only happened on the very first day, when it took them by surprise, and it had to happen someday that it would occur to someone that if Lieutenant Láska were to die, why, that would be the very key to unlock that armoured door, all of us of course were well aware of Mr Architect's vow, and that the obligation to keep Lieutenant Láska imprisoned here ends with the StB goon's demise, and so all of us are imprisoned here only by that vow of Modráček's, upon which all else has been raised like a crystal palace on a sugar cone, so that if we just take care of that cone, that is, with your leave, if we devour it, then the whole spectacular edifice will come tumbling down, and we'll be free again, that is, as free as a person can be in the circumstances provided us by that most just of all human governmental systems, the dictatorship of the proletariat, in other words, to put the matter simply, is it not, at bottom, the case that Mr Architect is simply lacking the courage to punish that crazy copper as he deserves to be punished? After all, he's got the murder of Modráček's sister on his conscience and who knows what else, after all, murder is a part of the StB job description, so if we were to take care of the matter on behalf of Mr Architect, we wouldn't be doing anything wrong, we'd merely be executing a just verdict, but no one ever expressed that thought aloud, it just hovered there in the air, so to speak, so that it could be read by the rector, Fr Klenovský, as well, and that thought progressed even further: does an insane StB goon, whose hands are thickly soaked with blood, possess any human dignity? Have we not, therefore, the right to kill one worthless creature, in order thereby to win the freedom of twenty-one people, the life of one bonkers and criminal StB goon in exchange for the freedom of twenty-one quite honest, semi-virtuous and even maybe a little bit righteous people, but Fr Klenovský read that thought hanging there in the air like laundry pinned to a clothesline, twice over, certainly, so it was all too familiar to him, but he immediately also understood that this was merely a seed, a tuft of round seed-head hovering in the windless air here underground, set in motion only now and then by the ventilation system, but he knew that he couldn't allow such seeds to germinate, and for that reason he devoted one of his Sunday sermons to the text Thou Shalt Not Kill, striving to engraft in us the knowledge that as soon as we let ourselves consider such things, that'll be the end of us, we'll never be free, because all we'll do is to unleash Hell, Fr Klenovský enjoys the sympathies of us all, even though the majority are unbelievers, or like me, people who, to speak metaphorically, make the sign of the cross with one hand while picking fleas from the devil's fur with the other, nevertheless nearly all of us attend Mass on Sunday, we built a real church here according to Modráček's plan and design, no mere chapel now, the church takes up the independent forward wing of what Modráček calls the 'horizontal subterranean city,' it's very colourful inside, windowless of course, but even so we have some backlit stained-glass windows, just partially dividing the apse from the rest of the area, the nave, but chiefly we've got a good bit of artificial light here, and everything that was needed, Modráček commissioned from the best experts in the given field and transported it all here, gradually, when the client's paying in precious gems and gold, people will break their backs to satisfy him, especially in times like these, when money has lost all its value and savings can vanish at any time, Fr Klenovský enjoys everyone's sympathies, or at least almost everyone's, and over the following days we tried to show him that he was mistaken, and that none of us have ever thought such things, really, so that there's really no need for him to move in with Lieutenant Láska to personally protect him from our ugliest thoughts, it's nearly inconceivable but the very same thought occurred to Dan as well, even though I said nothing to him at all about my intentions, but he got no farther with the chef than I did, so he went straight to Modráček himself, and this is something that I really do appreciate, seeing how that gimpy leg of his is still bothering him, the one where Modráček shot him, it's possible he'll be limping for the rest of his life, I can't imagine what that conversation of theirs must have been like, but I'm sure of one thing, Dan didn't approach him hat in hand, and he didn't abase himself in any way before him, nor did he promise him anything, and here what do you know but Modráček is capable of being fair, he acceded to our request and went and spoke to the chef himself and probably offered him something as compensation because to our surprise the chef packed up without a whimper and moved off to the far end of the house where Dan had been living up till now, without exchanging a single word with us, yet here I ought to say that the seemingly simpler solution, that we'd be living together in one apartment, wasn't even taken into consideration, especially as any person can see how serious a fellow Dan is, how often he needs to be alone by himself, quite often as a matter of fact, it was hard for me to come to terms with it, but he has inside him some sort of unassuaged longing for something (or rather someone!) that (or whom) he'd left behind up there, and about which (or whom) he didn't want to speak with anyone, which is none of my business, it's night (just a moment ago Modráček switched off the day's allotment of light), I'm sitting with Dan on the steps, on the stoop, but there's no stars above us, of course, just the black vault of the cavern, and so we turn towards that lit-up Mondrianesque wall in the far transverse wing, where some colourful and cleverly composed rectangles of different sizes meet, I won't deny it, give credit where credit is due, sometimes something turns out well for Modráček, I'm sure this underground architecture of his would meet with repugnance and offence up there above, but just a little farther on, past this barb-wired-in world of ours it would excite interest and even awe, not only among experts, perhaps we are here residing, living in something that is at the moment but the music of the future, perhaps an awe-inspiring architectural symphony, in such nocturnal hours as now alongside Dan on the stoop of the 'horizontal subterranean city' I'm actually able to forget that up top there is still something else, our real, true world, are you listening to me, Dan? more than once it's seemed to me that there are some strange nocturnal insects flying about down here, of course, I'm not an entomologist, to say for sure, but I have this feeling, that I've never come across anything like that outside, a nocturnal insect? and Dan starts laughing what do we know about nocturnal insects down here? when is it night down here anyway? When Modráček says Let there be night? And what if it's not an insect at all? Hrach the writer and Dr Štefl and Dlask the actor wrote a play at the encouragement of Mr Architect, and at first they wanted to choose from people who had already done some amateur play-acting, but since they found no one fitting that description, they decided on a clever move, and tearing up what they'd already written they started over from scratch and this time they're not going to be choosing anyone, they just wrote three short plays for sixteen non-actors, excepting themselves and Lieutenant Láska and Mrs Modráčková, who is still laid up after giving birth (but in the end they were just acting themselves anyway), and Hrach and Štefl explained to us that this is all going to be something quite different from Jirásek's *Lucerna* or Klicpera's *Hadrian of Rome*, here everyone is going to be playing him or herself, supposedly these characters are gentle caricatures of us as observed from our daily commerce with one another and it all depends on each of us alone, how we'll approach it, how we'll take it, and the only one who didn't agree to act was Vlasta, who sings with the Army artistic group Ondráš, she was irritated at the unprofessionalism of the whole thing, and then Mr Neužil, a proofreader from the Rovnost printery, who couldn't understand how he is to play himself, I am myself, and so I don't have to play myself, please don't be upset with me, but this is all for the birds, but the rest of us really got into it and as we were working at it and rehearsing it, well, perhaps those were the best days we'd spent down here so far, and here I am exaggerating again, but as Zdena told me — a bookkeeper from the Starobrněnské Brewery — it's really odd, but for the first time I've really felt like myself, playing myself, all of us were a little coy at the start, but then we all fell to it, I liked the chef the best, he acted with passion, stomping around the stage and bellowing that he's going to grind us all up into hamburger, especially that slut from next door, meaning me, even though we're no longer neighbours, and more and more people are continually badgering Modráček to carry on with his hunting expeditions, which requests are of two types, as different from one another as the inhabitants of Greenland from those of the Solomon Islands, as some of them want him to snatch one of their friends or family members, someone dear to them, lovers, sons, daughters, parents, aunts, uncles, or fellow canasta players, while the others want him to drag down here people that don't deserve to be walking about in freedom, so that he'd punish them by imprisoning them in this delightful Alcatraz of ours, and it's hard to say which of these motivations is more deserving of contempt or admiration, Mr Architect isn't about to comply with either, his 'hunting season' has ended, he has, if, you can put it this way, reached his quota, Modráček never hunted for the love of hunting, or for pleasure or gratification, Modráček was a melancholy hunter, if he hadn't vowed what he had vowed, nothing of what had happened next would have happened at all, he wouldn't ever have started hunting in the first place, I'd understood that already, this morning he came hurrying in, rubbing his hands, So listen, apricot season's in full swing, there's gigantic bushels of apricots now at the Greens Market, what if I went ahead and loaded up the car with apricots and hauled them down here, you could make preserves until you keeled over, but somehow none of us were taken with the thought, Váša the lifeguard from the Zábrdovice baths said What, when you were a little boy, did you experience a big apricot boil at your grandmama's and now you want to spread the joy among us? My dear sir I said to Modráček, how do you imagine us making preserves down here anyway, as we don't have any mason jars or those whacking big iron pots or any of the necessary ingredients, All you need do is ask, Mr Architect defended his idea, just tell me what you need and I'll bring it all down here for you, I'd be delighted to, who would've ever thought that someday I'd find myself sitting four fathoms beneath the pavement on a little stool pitting apricots while Dan Kočí's kneeling behind me sliding his arms under mine and trying to pit me, what I really miss horribly down here are trees, Mr Architect indulged us with a little grass down here and some shrubs, even tulip beds, just about everything that can bear this hothouse regimen of ours without sky and much space, but beneath this low cavern vault some days I feel that I'd be happy to trade Dan Kočí for a walk lined with chestnut trees or a gigantic kingly walnut or an even grander holm-oak of the sort I used to go visit in Lužánky, over fifty metres tall, its crown jam-packed with puckish birds, or say the plane trees near the Red Church or 'my' hornbeam on Špilberk, up there above Brno up over our heads, permeated with trees and surrounded by forests, how can I ever forget the scent of resin, how my father's gum-filled carpentry shop smelled so of resin, the broad and tall logs of beechwood from which Dad would make bentwood furniture for the Thonet company, or how I was with him there in Pisárky at the villa of Herzog the factory owner, where he was building him a Finnish sauna of poplar wood, beekeepers from all around would come to us for linden frames for the inner partitions of their hives, nearly all of my toys were wooden and came from that workshop, I shared my bed for nearly ten years with a witch made of lime wood, I loved Brno, what am I saying, I love Brno, because it has the most trees of all of our cities, take a careful look for yourself, before you enter in any place, and if you don't see any trees, turn right around and beat it, fast, Fr Klenovský's already set the date for Eduard Láska's christening, Modráček's confirmed the date and the silent, so to speak dumb until now Madame the Architect's Wife has suddenly started up such a chattering that we'd rather she just shut up again

◆

FROM A DISTANCE

AT BREAKFAST

Petra awakens and gives a quick, curious glance at the sleeping Luděk, over whose face a dream of some sort is flickering. Then it occurs to her that it's a little shameless to be doing that. So she leaps out of bed and trots over to open the double window that gives out onto Kotlářská St. But as soon as she opens it, the sound of the street awakens him.

Don't be a jerk. Close that window! You can only open it here after midnight. And people say that back in the early 50s, Kotlářská was quite a peaceful street. Only here and there a car. And from time to time a horse and wagon.

What? I can't hear you. Wait'll I close the window. So how do you air the place out?

After midnight. Always.

Petra opens the fridge.

We have eggs, sardines, a piece of ham, and what's that? Something wrapped up carefully…

Cousin Rujbr's a forester. He always brings me some game. It's in thick red paper bound with wire, right?

Yeah, that's it. But you're telling me that there are still foresters around these days? I'll make us some ham and eggs. All right? You want instant coffee, or Turkish style?

If you open the cupboard above the sink… See there? A nifty drip coffee maker. Forester is what he calls himself. So I let him, you know? He's some kind of wilderness administrator. He buys the game at a supermarket, wraps it up in some ugly paper, binds it up with wire and brings it over. Like he's poached it himself.

You've got a tray here somewhere, right?

Stop joking. I'm getting up now. Luděk sits up, has a look at the black nail on his big toe, then thrusts his feet into slippers and shuffles off to the bathroom where he concentrates on urinating, running some water into the tub to encourage his lazy pisser.

So I'll set the table. Aha. Here we have a table-cloth with a whale pattern. You a Greenpeacer or something?

Hold on, I can't hear you. I'll be right there. With a strikingly thick thumb and just as strikingly slim a middle finger (Sancho Panza and Don Quixote?), he gives his Johnson a shake or two and then wipes the tip carefully with toilet paper. And then he shuts off the water.

They eat loudly, smacking their lips. Then Luděk stops chewing, and sticks that thumb and middle finger into his mouth (you guessed it — that same Sancho Panza, that same Don Quixote) to extract something.

What is it?

Nothing. And he shows Petra.

Sorry. So far they aren't laying eggs without shells. (Pause.) I'd like to go somewhere today… somewhere there's trees. And you don't have any proper parks hereabout.

What are you, crazy? And Špilák? We even have the first public park in all of the Czech crown lands. Long before Stromovka in Prague. The old Jesuit cloister gardens. The imperial gardeners planted a splendid wood there of rare trees. It's right here, just past the corner. We'll go have a look this afternoon. You'll see.

Coffee in these alabaster cups? And did you read about that Klara Mauerová yesterday? How she murdered her own children down in the cellar? Or that Fritzl in Austria. How he kept his daughter in the cellar for like a hundred and five years, fucking her. And nobody in the house suspected a thing. Blind and deaf. Discovered by chance. Have a look at the Internet. There's like videos of it. How can people see nothing, hear nothing?

You said it yourself. Blind and deaf.

That one tore open the sack of cellar perverts.

Next to them that architect Modráček's a kind old duffer.

Please. He was no pervert. He was forced into what he did by time and circumstance. He was a kind old duffer.

Well, did I say otherwise? Where'd we leave off? Toward the middle of 1953 he already had twenty-one lodgers down there.

Let's count them up. Here goes. Lieutenant Láska, alias Rudolf Švarčsnupf.

Ah, I'd like to be Countess Medusa, alias Diana Manuela Peralta Medinaceli!

Let's move on. Doctor Vlastimil Pešek, lawyer. Doctor Jiří Štefl, physician and author of detective novels. Private eye Daniel Kočí. The writer Libor Hrach, author of *The Adventures of the Wise Badger*. Josef Čepelák, who worked the counter in that store with board games and non-board games, Modráček's wife.

He even locked up his 'invisible wife' down there?

How many have we counted?

Seven.

Irena. Don't know her last name. And Julius Dlask, the actor.

I happen to remember him.

What?

Not so much me as my grandmother. She once told me how he suddenly vanished from the Mahen Theatre. He was her favourite actor. She was really devoted to him. He was all set to appear in this play… it's on the tip of my tongue… *The Chimes of the Kremlin*!

Yes, that's right. *The Chimes of the Kremlin*. It was a play about Lenin. Second Part of the Lenin Trilogy of Pogodin, Nikolai Fyodorovich. *A Man with a Rifle*, *The Chimes of the Kremlin*, and *The Third: Pathetic*.

What rubbish you carry around in your head…

I studied Russian literature. When I was at uni, Pogodin was still read — like Harold Pinter is these days. But let's get back to your grandmother. So, she was nuts for Dlask.

She ate him right up. She went to see *The Chimes of the Kremlin*, smouldering all the way there like a wick.

But he wasn't in that play then.

Right. Somebody took his place. He vanished and no one ever heard anything more about him ever again. Grandma was certain that he had emigrated and headed straight for L.A., to Hollywood, and that he'd come back to us in some American film at last. Like Jiří Voskovec in *Twelve Angry Men*. Such a talent, she said, couldn't just dissolve into thin air.

Well, she was right about that, Luděk confirmed. Not about Hollywood, but he did have a role in that play by Libor Hrach that the Badger-scribbler wrote for Modráček's underground theatre. He and Štefl worked on the scenography.

You're kidding!

And the theatre wasn't all of it. Mr Architect had twenty-one people down there to take care of. He was obsessed with not only keeping them occupied, but creating a self-sufficient world for them, with everything. A difficult enough task. But he tried to do something, at least. For example, he organised lectures on the architecture of Brno.

How uplifting.

Everybody had to pitch in. Dr Štefl lectured too, on popular science and medicine. And Dr Pešek offered legal counselling. He helped everyone down there settle their old civic disputes. For they'd not only been torn from their old life, but also from ongoing legal matters. Every one of us is tangled up in something, and down there they had the chance to extricate themselves from it, slowly and peacefully…

Well then, he really was helpful to them…

I think so. And Modráček even scoured old book stores for good reading material for them. And he brought the daily news down to them, so they'd know how bad it was going on up here, in this evil, fucked-up world, which they could be happy to be well out of.

I'd like to mention, Petra said, clearing the dishes and cups from the table, that we haven't yet counted quite up to ten.

OK, the tenth: Alžběta Hajná, a jeweller and watchmaker. Eleven, Karel Klenovský. He's a very important character, who in the end was to play an important role there. A monk. Not the kind in the barometer, who comes out of his cell with an umbrella when rain is on the way.…

So, a priest, too. Well, that's a real set for you. A cop, a priest, a doctor, a private eye, a lawyer, a writer who's also a labourer at the armaments factory, an actor, a jeweller and watchmaker, Modráček's 'invisible wife' was also a dentist after all, right? A merchant of board games and not only… But I still don't know who that Irena was.

A whore. A slut. A real bitch.

Now hold on there, tap the breaks. It took some guts to be a prostitute back then in the early 50s, during those years of puritanical Communist totalitarianism. Not everybody'd do that.

Just the opposite. They did — as never before, or since. The whole nation — except for a few outsiders and freaks and those in the labour camps — the whole nation prostituted itself. But you're asking about streetwalkers and hotel sluts. There were just as many of them back then as there are today. A statistical rule — the Gaussian Curve: in every age, in every statistically measurable society, you'll find the same percentage of geniuses, idiots, and whores. It's just that it functioned differently then. Most of the whores were collaborating with the StB. They gave the foreigners a good time, while simultaneously serving their Socialist fatherland.

Luděk lights up the morning's first cigarette and then sits down at his computer to look through his mail and delete his spam. It looks like it's going to be a beautiful day.

AT LUŽÁNKY

They passed around the tennis courts and entered Lužánky, greeted by milk-maple and coast Douglas fir.

Just so we understand one another, Luděk explained, Irena wasn't a whore in the sense that she received an honorarium for shagging. She was an official of the National Commission in Brno, in the Buildings Department. But she was outfitted from tip to toe as an evil monster. Inhumanely attractive and at the same time of above-average intelligence, her emotional side had been erased and its place had been taken by moral insanity. To top it all off, she was bi. In other words, Sodom and Gomorrah and then some. And if we're speaking of sex, what interested her was not sex itself, but rather the death instinct — that's what I reckon a psychoanalyst would say. Modráček and Hrách had thought up something like *The Decameron*. They all gathered together each Tuesday and took turns revealing something about their lives. When it came time for Irena, what she said sent shivers down everyone's spine — as if you came across a loose bull in an open field.

The sound of the balls popping on the tennis courts was deadened here by the thick crowns of the beeches, ironwoods, maples, plane trees, firs, oaks, ashes, elms, chestnuts, spruces, yews, walnuts, lindens, poplars, and whole lots of noble trees set in ordered ranks here, scattered in swarms there, which gave the place the appearance of a battlefield map or the image of some immortal, mythical scene that had played out at the dawn of human history, reappearing again and again in the manifestations of the natural world — now in a cluster of clouds on high, now in a bird's eye view of a great city park.

Today — Luděk let out a sigh — for most people, sex is just some light-hearted, titillating game, ah, that unbearable lightness of fucking, whereas back then, at the beginning of the 1950s, when the old religious taboo still functioned simultaneously with the new, puritanical, Communist taboo, back then, sex was something as serious as Fate. For the last time in our history, for most people. Taboo, that is, transformed sex into a fiery, molten lava bubbling just below the surface, and the world fairly trembled above this volatile lava flow...

Watch out, Luděk! Petra cried. Too late. Here. Wipe your shoe here.

O, that human cattle! Luděk griped. They can't bend down to clean up after their beloved beasts! And Luděk's forehead contracted into furrows. Or ruts, to speak Czech. Where was I?

Petra: The hot molten lava of sex flowing just below the trembling crust of the earth.

Exactly. Let's set aside for the moment what Freud and Jung too would indicate as symptoms of the presence of the molten lava of sex, that is, the hysteria of the political trials. But you know, of course, it's no coincidence that the worst Czech sexual offender, the murderer Václav Mrázek, is inextricably bound up with that very period. He rolled on his merry way in the early fifties, and if it had not been for the proverbial coincidence, they wouldn't have caught him. Now, it might seem to us as if we've never heard of so many dangerous sexual perverts as there are these days. But back then, there was simply the strictest embargo imposed on information concerning unexplained sexual delinquencies. You didn't dare disturb the people at their constructive labour with such anxiety. And again, quite simply, the great majority of murders of a sexual nature were, in the early fifties, never solved. And on the other hand, at the time, for our folk sex was the only available route to freedom that the puritanical comrades (and their street gangs) weren't able to control. Let me just remind you of Daniel Kočí and that Brighty of his, that kitten with the highlights in her hair. And let me also remind you of the fact that she was married — and what is more, came of a very strict Catholic family. As for Daniel, well, he had a little harem of a few other lovers besides. In this way, they had the chance to push the limits of their sexual freedom further and further beyond bounds undreamt-of. They knew nothing of Tantrism, yet all the same were capable of passing through the gate of obscenity to the very threshold of mystical experience. Among the intellectuals of the time, a very popular read was the biography of the poet Mayakovsky, which Jindřich Štyrský wrote before the war, entitled *A Cloud in Trousers and Without* — which title was a paraphrase of one of Mayakovsky's well-known verses. Mayakovsky was a revolutionary Soviet libertine, who experimented his whole life long with sex and erotic combinations, just as he did in his early Futuristic poetry. This was a fascinating 'game for real,' for which he paid with his life in that monstrous necrocacy, which set itself up in opposition to any sort of freedom, including sexual. And in the early fifties, he had his epigones among us, and not only in poetry. But such a thing will never happen again. Today, you can sleep around however you please. The first half of the 1950s was the golden age in the history of our sexuality.

That's nice, Petra nodded, but let's get back to Modráček. How did it come about that he wasn't satisfied with settling scores with the murderer of his sister, with Lieutenant Láska, but started hunting down his other 'lodgers?'

Well, at first he wasn't thinking about hunting anyone down. That wasn't his idea at all. Doctor Pešek waltzed in there on his own. That couldn't be helped. And the private eye came creeping up like a mouse — or maybe a louse. And Modráček's 'invisible wife?' It makes sense if you think that it would have been impossible to keep her from sniffing something out. Modráček reckoned that if he let her remain on the loose, well, he'd be taking too big of a risk.

So he gave her a whiff of the chloroform and dragged her down under the armpits into the cellar? And then he began his hunting?

Well, yeah, if you want to put it like that. He netted Hrach at the Bellevue Café. That was the hangout of all the writers and poets in Brno who didn't dare publish their works — until they ended up in a labour camp or, like Hrach, tossed into some factory or handed a shovel. Modráček showed up there as if by pure coincidence: Ah, I'm so happy to see you; I've just remembered that I have something for you, something that should interest you as a writer. You don't mind if I pull you off to the side here for a moment? As luck would have it, Modráček had no idea who was seated there in the vicinity when he made that happy little manoeuvre — a slightly lumpish stool-pigeon, whose knees were a little sore just that day from scouring the parquet at home with a wire brush, and so he couldn't react quickly enough and shift himself closer to them, otherwise Modráček would've had to welcome him as well into his underground boarding house. And so, Hrach got the same story as Lieutenant Láska before him with a slight modification: I've uncovered an entrance in my cellar that leads to an underground chamber where the Krauts holed up towards the end of the war; they left a lot of strange gear behind, which ought to be of interest to a writer like you.

All right, that's how he got him there, but what did he need Hrach for?

It's quite simple. Modráček went paranoid. Almost overnight. Look, when you start locking people up in the cellar, paranoia's just waiting to pounce. This writer was a danger to him, all the more so, as Modráček couldn't be sure what he told him or didn't tell him, back when they had that feast at U Stopků. What if he put two and two together and didn't keep it to himself? And so from then on he couldn't get Hrach out of his mind. It was probably the same thing with that fellow from the shop with board games and not only.

The shopkeeper as well?

Ding-dong bell, the shopkeeper as well. During their conversation he'd let slip the name of Vladimir Nabokov. And so that was a dangerous loose end, too. And so, bang, he bags the shopkeeper. But he needed to think up a reason to lure him there.

OK, I might even be able to understand that. But what about the rest of them, who weren't even slightly initiated into it all?

Well, now that he had several people down there, he needed a doctor. Especially when his 'invisible wife' had a bun in the oven.

But you said that Modráček hadn't been shagging her for years. So she had a lover? Well? Down there? But that's not hard to unravel, right? The playboy, Dan Kočí.

Wide of the mark. It was the loverboy lieutenant, Láska, my love.

Gross. We know he was insane, right? Or at least fairly loopy.

We don't know anything. We merely infer. Modráček's wife also might've wanted to stick it to her architect husband. Or maybe she was fascinated with nut-jobs. Or maybe she just needed to scratch that itch already.

All right, I'll buy it. She gets Lieutenant Láska to scratch her itch. But in that gold cage, right in front of everybody?

　　　　　　　　　　　　　　　　　　　　　　　　

Well, not quite. But let's let that be for now.

All right, so let's keep to Dr Štefl. They knew and trusted each other, correct, him and Modráček?

That reciprocal trust was quite conditional. Conditio sine qua non, as all well-educated doctors said back then.

Let me continue, Petra interrupted: Hello there, Doctor, I'm happy to see you, sir. Or were they on familiar terms?

They were. I haven't yet mentioned this, but right after the war, Štefl was the proud owner of one of Modráček's kitschy villas.

Petra: So, here we go then: Hey, Doc! Glad to see you, chum! Listen — I've got something to show you that ought to be of interest to a writer of detective fiction. I know that they're not printing detective novels any more, but you're not ready to pawn your typewriter yet, are you? Better days will come along, right? So come have a look. Your eyes'll fairly pop out of your head! That the way it went?

Luděk shook his head. I've just got done telling you that he needed a doctor in the underworld. And so he called on Štefl to fetch him to his gravely ill wife's beside. Štefl took a prescription pad and stamp with him, so as to write out the necessary prescriptions as soon as he'd have examined her. And as they were leaving the surgery, Mr Architect slipped a whole packet of prescription slips into his pocket. And so — now he'd have doctor, prescriptions, and rubber stamp at his disposal.

And?

What do you mean and? What could be simpler than that? As soon as they entered the building at Běhounská 3/5, the architect pricked his ears to make sure that there was no one coming down the stairs, and then he said Go on ahead, Jiří, I'll just have a quick look in my letterbox.

But he didn't do that.

For as soon as the doctor had turned his back on him, Modráček fished the bottle out of his breast pocket, along with the rag he used to block up the nostrils of his endearing victims and stepped up, or, hop! pounced, if you prefer, upon the detective writer from the rear. And then he took him under the armpits and dragged him down into the cellar…

But then — like a safecracker wielding a skeleton key, Luděk sniffed the air with his own flaring nostrils. There, where Lužanecký Park gives out onto Lužanecká Street, there is a cosy little wine shop with garden seating.

And right now the scent of frying potatoes was wafting from there. From of old, Luděk's culinary tastes were of the plebeian sort, and Petra had never succeeded in re-training him toward a preference for something more acceptable, like couscous for example, or sushi. And so they sat themselves down to those fried potatoes and, at first, a glass of wine, followed by a whole bottle of red. They sat in silence for a while. And then it was Petra who said: OK, let's assume.

OK, let's assume that's how it went. But, Luděk, if my count is correct, we still have a good ten lodgers to account for. Complete strangers, who weren't let in on anything concerning Modráček's secrets. And so, people who are neither dangerous nor useful to him, right? People he just picked up off the street. But what for? Why?

Luděk wiped his greasy mug on a paper napkin, which he then crumpled into a tight little ball. Then, setting it on his open palm, he sent it flying up into the crown of a nearby ginkgo biloba with a flick of his finger. Petra clapped her hands and the people at the nearby tables glanced over in their direction.

You forget that he was an architect, who had not yet constructed his masterpiece. Of course, there was that little villa in Olomouc and also that house on Eliška Machová that he built for his sister, but the chef-d'oeuvre was still lacking, which would set his name alongside those of Gočár, Krejcar and Fuchs. And his conscience was still nagging him on account of all those postwar architectural gewgaws of his. But now, at last, he had his opportunity.

I don't understand.

But of course you do. Up aboveground at this time it was impossible to construct anything proper. Socrealism was the order of the day. And so, he had to take his dreams down below. Underground. Follow me? The architects of Brno were all great admirers of the gifted Franco-Swiss architect Le Corbusier. Without his abundant influence, those functionalist buildings and entire functionalist developments would never have sprung up in Europe. The whole architectural postwar world had its eyes fixed on Marseilles, where in 1946 Le Corbusier began to construct his Unité d'habitation. In 1952, he finished it, and among the architects of Brno there began to circulate, from hand to hand, that number of a certain Swiss publication in which the Unité d'habitation was featured. It was a building conceived as a 'vertical garden city' — a comfortable and elegant human apiary. It enjoyed a somewhat cultish status among the architects. And now, have a look at our Modráček. He's stunned! Sitting there in his underground chamber alongside his little cement mixer, which is churning the mortar with which he'll construct that circuitous wall enclosing the gold bear cage, crowded now with Lieutenant Láska, Doctor Pešek, Hrach the writer and Dan Kočí the private eye, like hens jostling in a dovecote. That wall was supposed to bring it all to a conclusion — just a little house surrounding the gold cage, so that he wouldn't have to heat the entire grandiose cavern. And now, as he was sitting by that cement mixer, there hatched an idea, inspired by that very building of Le Corbusier's. Obviously, no 'vertical garden city' concept fit here, but just the opposite: a building conceived as a 'horizontal subterranean city.' Still, this was something just as titanic, if in a different way. He was seized by the idea of filling that entire 'cathedral of silence,' as he also began to refer to the cavern, as the acoustics down there were poor — it was as if someone had stuffed the whole, wide-spreading area full of some sort of transparent and impalpable cotton, and only the walls were a good conductor of sound, whereas anyone's speech immediately melted in these regions as fast as snowflakes in a torrid draught... Wait a second, where was I...? Yep, Modráček decided to fill the entire cavernous space with an avant-garde architectural, residential aggregate of autonomous living-units, the prototype of a great underground building à la a 'horizontal subterranean city.'

And so now he begins snatching tenants for his 'horizontal subterranean city?' The only thing that concerned him now was what he had stumbled onto, where he had been led by his paranoia?

Quite simply, that's how it came about. An initial intention, and then chance and circumstance, one thing leads to another, and lo and behold: a simple settling of accounts with the murderer of his little sister grows, in the end, into a grand architectural and, actually, philanthropic, humanistic, project. After all, it was no longer just an experimental subterranean structure with autonomous living units.

For God's sake, what else?

I'm almost embarrassed to say it — an island Utopia. A subterranean, utopian island! In the end, Modráček understood it all as a vocation, a mission. On the one hand, he kept the promise he had made to his dead sister, his vow to snatch her murderer and punish him with a sentence of life imprisonment, while on the other, by a chance set of circumstances, and random motivations, he broadened that mission of his by degrees: to preserve some sort of pattern of humanity from that which threatened them up above. And so, he augmented those twenty-one lodgers of his with individuals chosen from various social classes and professions. Thus, they were to fulfil varied roles there underground, and at the same time, to constitute the model of a better society of the future.

Noah's ark?

Exactly. Until what was going on up above should pass away, until the floodwaters should ebb and it would be time to return with those whom he had been able to preserve. You understand — up above there was one gigantic Marxist Utopia, and down below, beneath the pavement, and right in the very vicinity of an SNB station, there was another, small, private Utopia.

But that means that Modráček was loopy, too. Now, I still don't understand how he was able to keep control of those twenty-one lodgers — why they didn't rise up in revolt against him.

By force, obviously. Every Utopia is a concentration camp. Should any of his lodgers escape, that would threaten the imprisonment of Lieutenant Láska. In order for him to fulfil his vow, his sacred promise, he was capable of anything — and he made sure that his tenants were quite aware of that. He was very open about it. Let us not forget that, among the items he had discovered in that subterranean German hodge-podge there were also two pistols: a 7.65mm Walther and a 9mm Smith and Wesson. He did his best to remove any doubt from their minds that he would not hesitate to use them. But with the passage of time, it all smoothed out, as usually is the case with such hermetically-sealed societies. They even began co co-operate with him, eagerly. Even though Modráček never really trusted his collaborators. It's really very curious the way in which, with the passage of time, such a small community (because, after all, there were twenty-one of them!) takes on the characteristics of much larger societies. There must be some sort of 'societal gene' in people, which prompts them to assume certain roles and, in cooperation with others, pattern each and every society, always, according to structures statistically identical. This is most obvious and comprehensible in enclosed groups, which it wouldn't be proper to call societies. There, such structures appear with the greatest clarity. You can't miss them. And such was the case with Modráček's subterranean island.

The first, heavy drops of rain began to spatter on the tables and slide over the surface. The waiter began bustling among the patrons, raising the sun-shade umbrellas. But then the rain stopped just as suddenly as it had started. Meanwhile, Petra and Luděk had paid their bill, got up, and hurried back home.

IN A SLOW ELEVATOR

The block of flats in which Luděk lives has perhaps the slowest lift in the world. It is perhaps for this reason that the owner, who regained possession of the building after the transformations returned to their rightful owners all that had been confiscated from private persons by the Communist authorities, had a mirror installed. While the lift slowly levitates, the ladies can make up their face. But Luděk made use of the slow elevator to add a few strokes to his sketch of Modráček the architect:

Mr Architect's behaviour might appear quite odd to us today. To make such an absurd vow, and then to fulfil it!

It was an absurd time, Petra noted. And so people too acted absurdly, no?

For sure. But in all this, there was something else as well. As is well known, wars speed up the pace of technological progress. To what do you think we owe so rapid a development of information technology, huh? The war against terrorism is a completely different type of war, different from any up until now, and the most important weapon in it is information. But totalitarian régimes are just the same sort of evil as war. So we shouldn't be surprised that they too bring about something good. So destructive is the pressure that totalitarian régimes exert on people — of course, I'm speaking here about small groups of people, outsiders and freaks and prisoners in the labour camps — that they mobilise immense ethical potential in them, the sort of thing from which we in the sixties began to draw vital strength. From today's perspective, the fifties were much more spiritual a time than the present, for in order to preserve your dignity you had to rely on something within. And in this regard, the 1950s saw a revival of ethics, intensifying and fortifying the moral consciousness — of course, only among that handful of people one calls the salt of the earth — but then the destructive pressure is released, and the liberating ideas gradually begin to materialise and affect even the better ones among those who, up until now, had served the régime.

Do you mean to say that the 1950s were our fairy godmother?

That would be like saying that wars pay off in the long run to humanity in the way of technological progress. Now, the profit derived from totalitarian dictatorships is indeed huge: in a flash, as soon as the totalitarian pressure is released, the first signs of civil society begin to spontaneously make their appearance. In our case, the art world brought forth a fantastic harvest and literature soared to such great heights as subsequently it never achieved again. But the price we paid for this profit was so terrifyingly great that it's really hard to speak of any profit at all. And yet on the other hand — our nation, at least, needs this totalitarian pressure from time to time, like a pig needs a good scratch. We need our martyrs and heroes, otherwise we would melt away in the mire of despair — like today — transformed into a heap of shit.

So I'm to understand Modráček as a martyr and hero?

Luděk lifted his hands in horror: For God's sake, no! It's true that he was capable of devoting his life to the service of something greater, something which brought him no personal profit, but, on the contrary, forced him to live on the edge, risking his existence every day, risking his life. A typical life in service of something greater than himself. In other words, all of this had the formal characteristics of self-sacrifice, and it was a resistance of a sort in the face of total destruction. You can't deny Modráček a certain moral consciousness and ethical potency. But since the days of the ancients, vengeance has been listed among the very worst things a man can fall into. And so it's no wonder that in time his vow led to a whole series of bad things. That crazy idea of creating an 'underground city' and hunting down people in order to protect them from the outside world! In effect, the creation, down below, of a sort of mirror image of what was up above, so that later…

But Luděk didn't finish his thought, as the lift had now been kept standing for quite a while on his floor, and someone down below began furiously pounding on the elevator shaft. Luděk, who since childhood could be sent into a terrified panic by aggressive noises (after all, he kept his windows shut till after midnight) quickly pushed Petra out of the lift and ran out behind her, just as the doors closed behind him and the elevator began its slow descent.

POST COITUM

In the dark of night there is no light save the blinking of the control button on the monitor, and nothing can be heard save the growling of the refrigerator in the kitchen. Petra sits up. She takes the huge pillow that Luděk had slid beneath her to raise her hips and places it behind her back.

What is it? What's wrong?

Nothing. But I did want to ask you: the trick that Mr Architect used to snatch his lodgers wouldn't have worked when he was hunting women. They wouldn't have been too keen to have a peep into some cavern.

That's what's bothering you? Well then, for example, Milada the seamstress ran a black market tailor shop from her flat. When she would get home from work in the textile factory on Cejl St, she would sew some things on the side for the ladies of socialism. Now, Modráček called her over with the story that his wife needed some evening clothes, but hadn't the time to pop over to Horní Heršpice, where Milada had that 'fashion shop' of hers. That's how he got her to Běhounská, and once in the foyer he had his way with her as he did with all his male prey. And he knew that there was no risk of her telling anyone where she was going and why, because she didn't brag about her black market business.

Well, what about Irena?

She worked in the Buildings Department. He spied out where and when she passed by. And once, when she was walking down Běhounská, because that street links Svoboda Square with Jakubské Square, and so sooner or later she had to use it, he ran into her as if by chance and mentioned that he was working on his next neo-classical socialist housing estate. But this time, he was collaborating with the National Artist Medal laureate, the architect Jiří Kroha. A first-class project. It's going to be an event in socialist architecture. Those capitalist beggars are going to go green with envy when they see what we're capable of accomplishing! I've got it all spread out on my draughting table here at home, yeah, I live right here, it's somewhat of a secret you know, top secret as a matter of fact, but you know, if you wanted to see it, like right now, comrade, as the first one really to have a glance…

But I'm still flummoxed at how smoothly it all went.

But that's how it always went, and still does go! We've already mentioned that Austrian chap Jozef Fritzl, the one who had a real fortress for his incestuous delight down in his cellar. And besides that, the socialist cops back then, the SNB goons? They really didn't know how to do anything except lock up class enemies. They were blind and deaf to everything else.

Luděk, it's eight minutes after midnight. Can I open the window?

Sure.

And Petra got up out of bed naked, and trotted over to the window. But the narrator, who's already taken a liking for this, has set a thumbtack on her path. Sharp end pointing upwards.

◆

FATUM FATUUM

There sits Fr Klenovský with his hands resting on his knees, palms upward, staring off into the distance over Modráček's shoulder, as if he couldn't hear a word the latter was saying. But after all, Modráček had been speaking now for quite a while, actually repeating himself. For the third time. Or the fourth. But there's nothing wrong with that, actually; it's good to repeat such an exact, detailed, really perfect, plan.

I say perfect, even though I'm aware of the fact implied by the very title of this chapter, that he's taking the whole thing for granted in a bad way. But still and all, and I'll stand by this, the plan is perfect, charming in its own way. And recently, everything had been falling into place so, according to Mr Architect's thinking, that he himself was beginning to get somewhat suspicious.

Have a good night's sleep, Reverend Father, Modráček says, hesitating a moment — was the priest even listening to what he was saying? — but then he just gave Fr Klenovský's arm a friendly squeeze, and quickly exited the place.

Now he had to pass through the crowd gathered before the experimental structure that he calls his 'subterranean city.' He too must leave his masterwork behind, abandoning his 'subterranean city' which, however, he will always carry around with him. For this construction, realised under such extraordinary conditions, has led him to a knowledge of many things — not only of a technical nature. But after all, in the end, he could rebuild it anywhere, anytime. For he has acquired such solid knowledge, on the basis of which he could perform miracles, literally.

Everyone parts to let him pass, in silence; everyone knows that their days down here are coming to an end now, and soon they will return to the world from which they had been torn. And even if that world is just as hostile to free human existence, still and all — that's where their near and dear ones live — that's where the spruce trees and apple trees grow, where walks are lined with chestnut trees, where fields are full of poppies and the sun shines during the day, the stars can be seen at night.

It strikes Modráček that he ought to bid each and every one of them an individual, heartfelt farewell, shaking everyone's hand in turn. Such would only be proper, for more than one reason. Yet something holds him back. Who was he, really, for all of these people down here? Now, at the end, it would be really good to know. With wonted care, he locks the armoured door and draws down over it what he calls the blind, which is actually a clever curtain that securely hides, masks, the entrance to the underground cavern. He ascends the stairs, halting at the little statue of the saint sunk into the wall opposite the entrance to the cellar. He ponders whether he's overlooked anything important. And then he goes out in front of the building for a breath of fresh air.

It was a warm September night. At this time, day after tomorrow, he would find himself in Vienna, and there would be no problem, he reckoned, getting to the western zone of Austria. He was standing there near the entranceway, not far from where his Škoda was parked — a large sedan known as the Popular — leaning against the display case of the fruit and vegetables store. A little girl came out of the U Cajpla tavern across the street with a pitcher of beer — surely for her daddy's supper. Catching sight of Modráček, she sent a smile his way. But because good girls hardly ever smile at strange men loitering across the street, Modráček understood that someone was merely using the girl to send another favourable sign his way through that smile of hers. Perhaps Fate herself, in friendly fashion, was extending her visiting card to him across the street. Oh, how full the world is of such signs of fate, such semiotic will-o'-the-wisps!

When he closed the door of his flat behind him, and carefully went through each and every room, every place, conscious of the fact that in three or four days men from the StB would be pawing through it all, he was certain that everything was in order there, that they wouldn't find a single thing that would help them understand it all, no key to his soul, whatsoever. Of course, it's another thing altogether that no one's interested in understanding anything, and that souls are not opened up by keys, but rather by crowbars and nitroglycerine.

It was clear to him that, in order not to raise any suspicions at the border, he had to be going there as if on a one-day excursion. In other words, without taking anything along with him. But there was nothing in the whole flat that he would really miss, anyway.

Everything fit together perfectly, like the gear-wheels of a precisely-tuned clockworks (a Swiss chronometer, for example, with Breguet hair-spring and lever regulation). For after all, they were allowing him to travel to Vienna right at the very moment that he needed to go there. All of a sudden, as if his unimpressive staff profile didn't matter a rap. Perhaps it had to do with the sudden disappearance of Lieutenant Láska, whose inexplicable vanishing saw him fall out of favour, and, along with him, all of his work to date was cast in an unfavourable light. And so, the protocols from Lieutenant Láska's interrogations of Modráček the architect were set aside ad acta, while on the contrary, there now came to the fore the fact that the lion's share of socialist living-spaces in Brno were due to Modráček's industry. The private trip to Vienna (supported by the thesis that 'the comrade architect is to examine the postwar reconstruction of living-spaces in Vienna'), at a time when only carefully organised excursions, always outfitted with snoops and chaperones, were being let out of the country, was something so extraordinary, that it indicated at the very least that all of his sins heretofore had been absolved. And also, as if the case of his little sister had been forgotten as well, and so exceptional a grace had been accorded him — even though it was clear to him that there were some strings attached to it all, and that the Party and StB clergy would be expecting something more from him in return once he got back from Vienna, than merely consistent attendance at divine service. And yet, O dear Party archbishops and StB cardinals, my return ticket on the Brno-Vienna-Brno train will expire long before you pounce upon my soul… At least, so Modráček speculated.

Early in the morning, Fr Klenovský waited, by appointment, and they worked together quickly, for the atmosphere in the 'subterranean city' was thickening, the flame was already racing down the long fuse. That's the way it always is — the narrator dares suggest — when the ice begins to crack into floes after a long hard winter. Everyone knew that they would be getting out of there soon, but their concrete resignation might turn into an explosive impatience as night turned into day.

Fr Klenovský, as one of the more physically fit (three years in the mines), took up the coffin from the front, with his back to it. For as we know, coffins are just as difficult to bear as heavy crates. And when they had borne it out of the cooling area (the 'ice pocket,' which also served them as a refrigerator for their foodstuffs), Modráček saw how the crowd parted before the coffin, and how it closed again behind it. Up until then, he had never been in such a dangerous situation, with his back to them and defenceless. Up until then, whenever he came among them, he always made sure to have his back nicely covered, so as to face any unpleasant surprise that might occur. But now, if anyone had jumped him from the rear, that would be a signal for all the rest to pile on, knocking him to the ground; the coffin would topple onto its side, maybe it'd even fall open, but no one would give that a second thought, nor pay any attention to Fr Klenovský, who would do his best to convince them that all of this is unnecessary, for in two or three days they'd be free anyway, but Modráček would be lying beneath this pile of bodies by then, with hands tearing at his pockets to grab the keys to the exit. Yes, that all might easily happen, and Modráček felt his skin tingle all over his back, as if they were about to hurl themselves upon him at any moment. But somehow at the same time he know that this wouldn't happen, that they wouldn't take advantage of the opportunity. And indeed, they just let them pass on through with the coffin; they stood there immobile and silent — the flame running down the fuse hadn't yet arrived.

They set the casket down and Modráček went to undo the complicated locks of the armoured door with its soundproofing; the locks rattled like chains being pulled and then, turning around, standing face to face with the half-circle that the people now formed, he assayed a friendly smile. But that smile didn't quite work. He had sensed that this farewell of his with them wouldn't be worth much, but he had no idea that it would actually be impossible. Right now, he wanted to say something, but his tongue cleft to the roof of his mouth and — why not admit it? — his chin nearly trembled. But on their faces, there was no movement whatsoever.

The most dangerous moment now arrived as they passed with the coffin from the underground and into the basement, and the armoured door stood wide open — the only way out free and clear. But perhaps they were turned to stone there for that space of several minutes? For they stood there, staring into the cellar from the underground, without muttering a word. Again he closed the armoured door with its isolation wall (which didn't let even a decibel pass in or out) and pulled on the 'blind,' that clever curtain that covered everything without giving the slightest hint that anything was behind it.

Now that they found themselves in the narrow passageway in front of the cellar cage-partitions, with the steep cellar steps before them, Fr Klenovský suggested that they switch places so that Modráček would take the casket from the front, as the person lifting the casket up the stairs from the rear would be worse off. But Modráček wouldn't agree to that. And yet, they'd hardly begun the climb when he had the feeling that the contents of the rapidly angled coffin had begun to move — he felt, right away, as if Lieutenant Láska had slid out from inside and right into his arms. That was obviously stupid, since as they'd just pulled the casket out of the 'ice pocket,' he had to be completely stiff, as stiff as an ironing board.

When they were at the cellar door, they waited a moment, listening for any footsteps in the building over their heads. Then, once more, with the door half opened, they checked to make sure that the corridor was unlit. It was indeed the very wee hours of the morning, but some of the tenants would be hurrying off to work before long.

Modráček had unlocked the main door of the building even before he'd descended into the cellar, so now Fr Klenovský just leaned his shoulder against it and they slipped out into the wretchedly lit and — thank God — empty street along with the casket. They set it down on the sidewalk behind the car, but wasted nary a moment. He'd already made room for the coffin in the car, plundering the inside space, but still he had to wrestle with it a while, like fitting a false tooth into resistant gums.

When they'd pulled out of Běhounská and entered Svoboda Square, it had to occur to Modráček in spite of himself just what strange ideas sometimes break the surface of a person's mind, since it suddenly flashed through his head to reach into the casket and fish out Láska's hand to wave with it in the direction of the police station, which they were just then passing, that huge hoosegow on Běhounská (for after all, that wouldn't work, what with rigor mortis and the stiffness from the freezer).

Modráček's Škodovka, that four-door sedan, now rolled into the spreading dawn, leaving the city behind it, driving through Žabovřeska, around the first and second chapels, heading toward Jundrov. The inside of the car stank of the tar with which the casket he'd bought from the underground cabinet maker was smeared. But now the sun is high enough in the sky for us to clearly see that Fr Klenovský is not only dressed in street clothes, but that he's not wearing a collar either, even though he's on pastoral business. But let us not forget that we're still in the first half of the 1950s here, when priests — those morose black-backs — were quite suspect characters, and what SNB goon worth his salt could resist stopping a car if he saw a dog-collar through the window as it approached?

The reasons why Modráček decided to coax the reverend father to accompany him were several. The first of these, obviously, was that he needed his help to bury Lieutenant Láska, to dig a deep grave into which the coffin could be easily lowered. And to tamp down the clay nicely, so as not to catch the eye of any 'gold-digger' who might happen to pass that way later on. And he also wanted it to be a Christian burial, so he might demonstrate that his vow was now completely fulfilled, and the posthumous destiny of the murderer of his little sister was now in the hands of God. And further, he wanted it to be Fr Klenovský who would live in his flat for the next two days, and on the third, when he would most likely be on the other side of the iron curtain, go down into the basement, open the exit from the underground, and lead the rest of them out into the light of God's day. And further, he requested that the reverend father divide up amongst the released citizens of the 'subterranean city' — as a sort of compensation — the rest of the jewels and the gold left over from the bear cage (there still was a full haversack of such things made ready in his flat behind the kitchen door!) at the division of which he was to pay special attention to his wife and Lieutenant Láska's child. A small portion of this treasure he took himself in a tin of Dutch cocoa. He intended to exchange it all still today for cash at a goldsmith's in Královo Pole and then take that off to the Centrálka cemetery to pay down a hundred years' lease on the plot of his sister's eternal rest. And when he'd find himself at the cemetery with the priest, he also wanted to ask him to accompany him to that grave in order to translate into otherworldly speech everything that he now needed to tell his little sister. And finally, he had one more thing in mind: Modráček really wanted (even if he wasn't able to conceive of it in such terms) to make a confession to the reverend father and obtain his absolution.

And because there wasn't much time left for that conversation, he was now driving him straight towards Láska's future grave. But any sort of absolution he might hope for still snagged on one essential and fundamental catch — Modráček obstinately stuck to his guns as far as his vow was concerned: it was his sacred duty to fulfil it. And for this reason he had to keep them all imprisoned until Láska's death. To let even one of them out of there beforehand would mean a gaggle of SNB and StB types showing up, immediately, at the door. And thus, that stubbornness of his finally drove one of the citizens of his 'subterranean city' to murder Lieutenant Láska, just so the gates of that Alcatraz should finally swing open.

They passed through Bystrc and on a sudden impulse, Modráček swung right towards the dam. They rode so close to the reservoir that when he opened the window and spat out, the saliva flew in a great arc, just as fifty years later a well-struck ball would, from the golf course nearby — it was the bitterness of those damned last few years he expectorated from his mouth, after which he pulled the wheel to the right and headed straight uphill in the direction of Rozdrojovice to search for a place there — perhaps something near Vysoká Seč — a peaceful place, shielded from people's eyes, where he, Modráček, could perform that last act, which would at last remove from his back the burden that he had set there himself.

And in this way they arrived at some general remarks concerning guilt and punishment, and also of the presumption of innocence, that legal principle, which means absolutely nothing in a country where the accused party needn't be shown any evidence of his presumed guilt, but on the contrary, the burden is on him to prove his guiltlessness. Where a forced confession was all that was needed to reach a verdict, without any evidence put forward as proof. And then Fr Klenovský explained to him that it was only the New Testament that enshrined the presumption of guiltlessness between God and man. And that it goes on even farther, where human justice can't reach even in the imagination. It's that very last moment in a person's life that decides his guilt or guiltlessness. You know, don't you, the story of the good thief on the cross, who 'even today shall be with me in Paradise?'

So, even today? Modráček asked. Not a chance. In my case not till tomorrow. But tomorrow I'll be there, in the free world.

You new here then, Comrade Missy? Just set right down everything that'll be said here, and then we'll cross it out later together.

According to the report of the comrades from the traffic patrol on Bratislavská, it was an accident. And from the licence plates, it turns out that the Škoda Popular belonged to Modráček the architect. And at this stage, the case was transferred to us here at Běhounská.

But how can we be sure that one of them really is Modráček?

We'll find that out from the teeth. His dental records ought to be in the dentist's office at the health centre right here on Běhounská.

Where all of us go? And as we know, the dentist there is the architect's wife (glancing at the papers) Alena Modráčková.

She was, you mean. Because some time ago Alena Modráčková vanished, and that disappearance is still unexplained.

Nor do we know where she disappeared to. Shouldn't someone have a look into that?

Comrades, if you please. No mixing apples and oranges.

Actually, now that you put it that way, it turns out that Comrade Láska went missing at the same time as... as that Modráčková.

I'd be very glad to know what you're getting at. I'd just asked you not to mix apples and oranges. If that's where you're headed, we might also toss in the disappearance of that... what was his name... that comrade private eye. Because that also occurred at the same time, right? But now let's read that report about the crash that the traffic cops sent us.

You gonna be able to keep up, Comrade?

She'll keep up fine. She's a stenographer. A hundred thirty words a minute.

What? A hundred thirty words a minute? That's not humanly possible.

But it is. So, the report:

According to the tyre tracks on the forest trail, the Škoda Popular automobile was travelling over the crest of the Na Výhoně hill. It continued through the oak woods in the direction of the Trnůvky heights. And so, it was proceeding along a route that presented some difficulties for that sort of vehicle. The accident occurred on the summit of Chlupáč, where the car tipped and rolled. Most likely, a portion of the old quarry wall crumbled with it, and down it tumbled over the steep cliff. The gas tank ignited, resulting in an explosion. The doors were battered shut as the car rolled down the steep slope, and so the people inside didn't have a chance. The tall, dry grass at the bottom of the old quarry burst into flame, as did the saplings thereabout. The fire might have lasted an hour or longer, as the area is remote enough and rather uninhabited. Three charred corpses were found in the car: two in the front and one in the rear, on the floor, where the interior had been cleared of the rear seats.

So now to the summation. Architect Kamil Modráček was to be travelling to Vienna on Tuesday. Our detective, who was to accompany him incognito and keep his eye on him all through that stay in Vienna was waiting on him at the station. But the architect never showed up for his train. Attempts were made to contact him — but quite simply without result. And so, as I see it, one of those carbonised corpses is that of Modráček. As far as the other two are concerned, we admit that it is impossible to identify them, as nothing was found there that would clarify this in any way.

And yet something was found.

I reckon, Comrade, that you have that tin of gold and jewels in mind? The one that was hurled a few metres from the car by the explosion? But I'd also happily link that with Modráček.

But that copper cross-like thing? Which, as far as I know, is sometimes attached to coffin lids?

You surely don't mean to suggest that they had a coffin there with them, which burnt up? You'll pardon my frankness, but that's simply nuts. After all, a coffin wouldn't fit in there.

Let's have a look, Comrade… So this here is shorthand? Hmm? Stenography? So how, Comrade, would you write down in shorthand the word… eh… transformer? And anteater? Giraffe? Destroyer? And henhouse? Bordello? And what about a sentence like… When I was three years old, I had the scarlet fever. Or maybe… Scratch me, darling, on the back. And now, Comrade, write me the sentence, let's see (a long pause, and then he spits it out quickly) Yesterday I knocked over my mother's sideboard, and when she appeared in the door, she went weak in the knees…

All right, enough of the jollies, Comrades, let's get back to work. Because I'm finding here some things that don't quite add up, so I'll be sending some chaps over to Modráček's flat to have a look around.

They fetched the keys from the concierge and went up to the third floor where they opened the door with the little brass plate reading *Eng. Arch. K. Modráček.* Comrades Kudláček and Slín complemented each other well. Kudláček had a photographic memory, and Slín, on his part, a copper's intuition. Whenever they were sent out somewhere, Slín led his intuition on a leash like a bloodhound and later, Kudláček, after the place had been turned upside down, could sit himself down in peace somewhere and walk through each room once more, from place to place, by heart, glaring long at each and every suspicious detail.

They had a look around the foyer. Just past the coatrack there was a door leading to a little room that earlier had certainly served as a servant's quarters. Slín and Kudláček pawed through the coats hanging on the hooks and hangers hung about on roads of Duralumin. We needn't follow them at their boring task, as they go through pockets and pat down linings. Past the closet was the WC, which had a window at eye-level, giving out onto the inner shaft of the building. Carefully, Kudláček climbed up on the toilet seat, opened the window and felt about with his hand along the wall of the shaft. Sometimes, class enemies would hang packets of subversive materials in the shafts behind WC windows. The flat had double doors leading to the main rooms. The layout of these rooms formed an 'L' shape. The largest of these, the one with a draughting table standing at the window giving out onto Běhounská, formed the base of the letter, with the two adjoining rooms making up the vertical arm. Kudláček and Slín began to work over the room systematically. They pulled all of the things and nothings out of all of the chests, commodes and table drawers, and then arranged them carefully on the floor, covering the entire space, as if it were some gigantic game of solitaire in which some of the objects had to be placed face up and some face down. They pulled chairs close to the chests of drawers and climbed up to have a look at their tops, and then examined their dirty hands (Modráček the architect was something of a swine, his flat a sty, which no one dusted ever since he moved his wife down to the underground cavern). And then they scuttled over the floor like crabs, using their specially adapted flat palms to sweep about underneath the chests of drawers and armoires, after which they probed mattress and upholstery with things that looked like knitting needles. They rolled up rugs and tapped each slat in the parquet floor, one by one, after which they examined the walls with the same professional skill.

Oy — you see that nog up there in the ceiling? said Kudláček, nodding upwards.

Don't get all hot and bothered, Slín calmed him down. You see those kind of blocks everywhere. Those are outlets for gas lighting. In old rental blocks like this one there used to be gaslit chandeliers. But still he built a pyramid of chairs and stools and tested out one of the blocks with a screwdriver. Directly across from the doors a window gave out onto a balcony. Kudláček opened the door and found piles of pigeon droppings. Above the balcony, the canopy was literally sagging under the weight of it. He shut the balcony door and retreated quickly, having no desire to muck about in that. Across from the balcony was the bathroom. No windows, but a big bathtub and an undulating ceiling. Slín and Kudláček installed themselves there and had at it with their probing tools like men possessed — but without any result. But when Kudláček opened the door to the kitchen with a jerk of fury (he was pissed off, because his intuition told him that a big haul was waiting on them there, as soon as he slipped the key into the lock beneath that brass plate with Modráček's name, and here — how d'you like that? — pigeon shit…) right behind it he found a haversack, stuffed to bursting, on the floor. That it was full was obvious at first glance, but then, when he tried to lift it, he found it to be as heavy as a porker ready for the slaughter.

And as soon as he opened it and had a look inside, he knew that he had the rabbit by the ears.

Hey, give me a hand with this! Kudláček called out in a joyous voice. They dragged the pack into the middle of the kitchen floor so as to be able to dance a little two-step of victory around it — a *rejdovák* or maybe a *třesák*, but certainly no sarabande. Until at last they got dizzy from it all and fell into one another's arms, and immediately, comradely — who could resist? — they hugged each another and kissed.

I reckon that we've gravely underestimated Modráček, Comrades. It's high time we said it aloud. All the evidence points to him having a plan to copperfield, to book it.

I'd like to point out that not all of the comrades here are from Brno, so we'll have to tap the brakes on the local jargon.

I apologise. I wanted to say that, most likely, Modráček had a plan to hoof it.

But if that's the case, I still don't understand how he figured on dragging with him that haversack full of jewels and gold that was found in his kitchen. And how he could get it past our man following him.

Anybody who's clever enough to amass a satchel like that, a gold mine like that, behind the back of the working class, would be clever enough to find a way to vasquez it. Pardon me. I mean, to abscond with it. Let us not underestimate our class enemies, Comrades. He had his sack all ready, and if not for that accident, he'd have it with him now, somewhere in Canada, probably. Let us not forget the words that Stalin spoke to us, heart to heart: that in these times when the construction of socialism is being carried out, the class struggle doesn't ebb, rather, it intensifies, it spreads. Did you get that, Comrade Stenographer?

So, I'd be interested in learning what sort of contact Modráček had with the Kratochvils. After all, they lived in the same building, on the same floor. If they opened their doors, they could spit into each other's soup. Anyone here have anything to say about that?

I suppose I can. There was practically no contact between them at all. We had our eyes on the Kratochvils all the while. And even though we induced Modráček to spy on them for us, he avoided them like everyone else in the building. We've got it all written down in detail.

Well, now it's clear, I figure, that we got it all backwards. Surveilling the Kratochvils was boring. No contacts, nothing special there at all. In short, it was the other flat we ought to have been watching — Modráček's!

The question remains, who do those other two burnt corpses belong to? We haven't any such equipment as might help us identify them.

Socialist science is hard at work on that. Someday, all you'll need is a little piece of a human body to tell you who it came from.

Even pieces burnt to a crisp?

Even pieces burnt to a crisp, Comrades. Did you get that, Comrade Stenographer?

Now, show me how you'd write, for example, the name of Comrade Skočdopole here, eh? And do you know how to write khozrashchot, Comrade? Or maybe, maybe… lipocarapus?

What, what? There's no such thing as lupo… carabus or whatever. Stop teasing her, you ape! Don't give him a second thought, Comrade… But hold on, I'll dictate something beautiful to you… Let me just make sure I can remember… Aha, I have it, Comrade! May I? So —

> Born at a time when thunderous storm-clouds roll,
> We march through storms with grim determination,
> Boldly, towards our elevated goal,
> Bowing before no one except the nation…
> Along with that nation, so bright and pure,
> As if it just emerged now from the hand
> Of God, bearing an image, firm, secure,
> Ancient, eternal, to plant in this land!

Did you get that, Comrade? Show me. Astounding, right?! That always grabs me right by the heart. Those lumps over there are laughing at me, but you — you get me, Comrade, right? Stenography, you say? I'm going to make sure my wife learns how to do that…

(But no one was laughing at all. All of them, rather, were standing or sitting there, deeply, deeply touched.)

THE DETOURS OF PETR LUŇÁK
EDITOR OF RADIO PROGRAMMES

Tomáš called me over first thing in the morning. In his left hand he was holding an unlit cigarette, which he slowly lifted to his lips; then, just as slowly, he raised his lighter towards it. But then he pulled it back out of his lips with his left hand, and, just as slowly, set the lighter down on the desk next to the keyboard of his laptop. He slid the cigarette back into the packet, only to pull it back out after a little while and hold it like that in his hand, unlit, before setting it once again upon his lips. And he will be repeating this complex little manoeuvre all throughout our conversation. Maybe he'll even be doing it all day long, from waking until falling sleep. I can even imagine those hands of his repeating their tiny journeys with cigarette and lighter while he's snoring in bed.

How's it going, Petr? You want a cigarette too?

You know I don't smoke.

Well then, have a seat. You see, I've got two bits of bad news for you. What do want to hear first, the bad news, or the bad news?

You're not making the choice any easier. Well, fuck it. Let's have the bad news.

Well then. As you may know, there's nobody in the Music Section today. And we've got an interview scheduled with Anna Fraccaroli, the composer. Nope. It can't wait till tomorrow. Tomorrow she'll already be in Prague.

She's an Italian, right? But you also know I'm no good with languages. And I don't know shit about music.

It's not as bad as you think. Anna Fraccaroli was born right here in Brno. And she'll be doing a huge interview about music this afternoon on TV. So your job is just to get her to talk about her life. But you'll have to trot off to her little abode. She'll be waiting there for you before ten.

And, dare I ask, where this little abode of hers is located?

At the Autonomous Ward of the Epidermal Faculty of the Military Hospital. You may not be aware of the fact that, ever since the army went totally professional and shrank, the Military Hospitals have begun admitting civilian patients as well. Her little abode is directly across from the baths in Zábrdovice. Anna Fraccaroli had an operation there. She happened to run across a friend of hers from school here in Brno, who happens to be a dermatologist, and he happened to notice that she has a lot of birthmarks. He ran some tests on her at his surgery, and it turned out that she had basal cell carcinoma. It's a benign skin condition, but it can turn malignant. What are you gawking at me like that for? I got all this information from phone calls and e-mails. You see, I've done a good chunk of your work for you already. So, get a move on and finish the job. She's being released at ten.

And the bad news?

Aha, yes, we can't forget that. So, Martinková from the news desk is on Mallorca, and Slavíčková, also from the news desk, is in hospital with appendicitis. So you'll have one more detour on your route. You're scheduled for a chat with someone about the collection systems beneath the historical centre of Brno.

Collection systems? You mean sewers?

Not exactly, but, yes, they're underground too.

Listen, chief, we're still the Literature Section, I believe?

You guessed it! We certainly are. My, you are a sharp one. But that doesn't matter.

The little abode looked just like a little abode. I couldn't find any doorbell or intercom. But then, by chance, one of the employees was returning from shopping and he let me in. While I was waiting on Madame Fraccaroli, who was — they told me — still in the recovery ward on the first floor (but who supposedly already knew of me!), I had a look around the ground floor. Consulting rooms, nurses' stations, an operating room, baths, and something like a rehabilitation room, and then, near a pair of black doors without any handles, a coffee machine. I fished ten crowns out of my pocket, punched some buttons, and waited for the cup to fill.

I'll have one too, please.

I spun around. She stretched out her hand. In it was a hundred crown note. I shook my head. No, no, Madame Fraccaroli, I'm paying for this round. I was holding the cup in my hand — a café Vienna, allegedly, and suddenly I felt a little queer.

There must be a café hereabout. Perhaps you'll permit me to invite you for a real cup of coffee?

I'm sorry, but that just won't work. If you want to interview me, let me have one of those, because I'm really on the clock, you see.

And so she took a cup from me and led me off to that place I'd glanced at before, the one I took to be an operating room. And indeed it was. A tall operating table was there, and above it, a large bright lamp, a chest with medical instruments, a sink and a washtub on a wheeled stand. On the wall there was a little shelf as well as two illustrations in drypoint: reeds on the edge of a fishpond, and a snail crawling over a large leaf. But into this otherwise minimalist area someone had introduced two large, comfortable, I would say classicist chairs, with a matching table. Where they were stored in this little, economical house is anyone's guess. But then one of the employees poked his head in and asked us if everything was to our liking and whether we needed anything else. Madame Fraccaroli nodded that everything was OK, and the head disappeared once more from the half-opened door, which then closed behind it.

I remained silent for a while at the outset, gazing with interest at the lady; I guessed her to be a bit over fifty (later, I was to learn that she was nearing sixty). She had a peculiar, narrow face, which was nearly hidden in thick rings of copper-coloured hair. She was wearing a short coat, open, with large baggy pockets that protruded over the hem; beneath this was a trouser skirt. Everything was in olive and deep orange. She wore no jewellery except for a heavy art-nouveau ring on the middle finger of her left hand, with an eye that must have been sapphire. I set this all down in my memory so that I could describe her to my listeners — especially my female listeners — before the recorded conversation should begin. And then it hit me — how on earth are you behaving, glomming at her any-thing-but-everyday face like that, at the whole uncommon phenomenon of her. But then Madame Fraccaroli caught the look of despair on my face and shooed it away with a smile.

I've already been told that I'm not supposed to speak with you about music, for the time for that will come this afternoon when I'll be interviewed for the television. So we'll leave Janáček and Alois Piňos off to the side.

I wanted to object, but Fraccaroli stifled the comment with a graceful gesture.

Don't apologise. Serious music, as it's called today, is a rather sectarian proposition. But I won't be able to avoid a tiny musical overture, as it were. About how I came to live in Italy. So, it was 1966 — April, to be precise, and here in the Brno Palace of Arts my third symphony had premiered. Quite by chance, an Italian composer from Salerno happened to be present. No, don't get ahead of yourself — his name wasn't Fraccaroli. But my work had a profound effect on him. So strong a one, in fact, that he wanted to meet me. And then, in the Slavia café he announced to me that he had a Latin title for my symphony — Prima digestio fit in ore, which in Czech would be: Digestion begins in the mouth. And here I must explain that through the lips of my composition the whole digestive process speaks, or rather, engages in conversation — each constituent part of it. So you can hear the stomach, the gall bladder, the kidneys, the intestines. But we'd agreed not talk about music. I'm sure you know that musical talent almost always goes hand in hand with linguistic talent. And Italian is by far the language of musicians. Basile Bernardo, the musical composer from Salerno, spent a whole month in Brno, after which he took me off to Italy. But before he could arrange a wedding, I ran away from him with Federico Fraccaroli, the musical producer. But let's get back to Brno, and at last to what's of interest to you and your listeners.

Madame Fraccaroli got up and slowly went over to the window, through which she gazed towards the Zábrdovice baths across the way. She was standing with her back to me, so I had to get up as well and move close behind her in order to record her monologue. That's not good, because trams were running past under the windows, along with delivery vans and heavy trucks. I'll have a fine time getting a clear recording of this, I thought. But Madame Fraccaroli didn't give me too much time to dwell on such things — she went on speaking and I stood there listening, with my jaw on the floor.

My maiden name was rather horrid — Švarcšnupf. My father, Rudolf Švarcšnupf, was an StB lieutenant. Like everybody else in the StB, he had his own official pseudonym. In public, he was known as Lieutenant Láska.

He had his office in this big police station on Běhounská St. We lived in an old apartment block with a balconied courtyard on Pekařská. The flat used to belong to a musical composer named Maňoušek, who emigrated in forty-nine. I never heard anything more about him, even though I searched for him throughout the musical world. You see, I was convinced of the fact that he had been an extraordinary composer, even though I had nothing solid on which to base that supposition. I simply just knew that he was an extraordinary composer and basta. I frequently thought of him, however, after my Italian marriage, when I would meet up with musicians and musical journalists in Rome, Madrid, Paris, Amsterdam, New York, Tokyo, or Rio de Janeiro — I was always trying to catch the scent of a trace of him. But then again, maybe he hadn't been successful in his attempts to cross the border after all. Maybe the border guards let loose their dogs on him and they tore him apart, or something like that. And yet, still and all, I keep thinking that maybe one day I'll finally run across him somewhere and I'll be able to tell him how much I owe him. Because in that flat of his, of ours, he'd left behind a piano. Well, actually, an upright — you know, with the vertical soundboard and strings. And here we go. When I was three or four years old, that's the time I'm speaking of here, I was a noticeably backward child, and if it hadn't have been for music, I would never have emerged from that. And that piano, well, it was the lifeline that pulled me ashore. Dad didn't know a thing about music, and the very sort of music that moved me was something far from what my parents understood music to be, as far as possible. And so it took them quite a while to see that I was something of a musical savant — an idiot savant, as the term used to be. Well, my Dad never actually came to see that, because one day he simply disappeared. The same thing happened to him as happened to that composer I was telling you about, with this one difference — that in the case of Maňoušek it was at least known that he'd emigrated, or tried to emigrate. My Dad just vanished into thin air one day, dissolved, entered some other dimension or was swallowed by the earth at his feet. My mother simply couldn't explain it otherwise.

Fraccaroli turned away from the window and fished a packet of cigarettes out of her purse. You won't be upset with me if I drag you off somewhere I can have a smoke?

I followed her like a lamb. We passed down a hallway, to the very end of it, where Madame Fraccaroli turned into an empty space, which might have been a sauna once, or a large bath, but now was bare, with pipes sticking from the walls and tiles falling off here and there. We passed through this and then through some other doors leading to an inner courtyard. Here there were three benches for the patients, and some great clay flower-pot from which a stunted tree of some sort emerged. Except for that, the place was empty.

We sat down. Before us the vista opened on to just the sort of interior courtyard balconies she remembered from her childhood, spreading around us in a half-circle, enclosing the area in which we were sitting. Madame Fraccaroli lifted an opened tin from the ground, which served her as an ashtray here, and set it down on the bench next to her. Before she lit up, she performed a little ritual with her cigarette and matches, which yet was nothing so elaborate as that which Tomáš had been performing with his smoke and his lighter. She struck her match and went on.

I've said a lot, without, most likely, saying anything of the sort you're expecting of me. Who cares these days that my father, an StB lieutenant, suddenly vanished as if he had been sucked in by a cosmic black hole. Mama would often speak of him to me. At the time, he was very concerned with one thing. He had been dealing with a certain architect from here in Brno. And with his sister, who was accused of some sort of anti-state activity. They locked her up, after which we moved into her little villa in Žabovřeska. But we only spent a week there, it seems. Because Dad decided that we had to return to that little, second-class flat in the old building on Pekařská. For something terrible had happened. Dad was interrogating the sister of this architect by turns with another officer. The interrogations took place at night, and one morning, after the other interrogator had been with her, they found her hanged in her cell. That sort of thing happened sometimes, I hear. Sometimes it was the fault of those whose job it was to keep their eyes on the cells, and sometimes it was intentional — an intentional oversight. And sometimes it was just plain murder. But later, nobody was made to answer for it. My Dad, though, wanted to start an investigation into how it could have happened. Everybody there was surprised at this — nobody expected anything of the sort from him. And of course, no such investigation was ever seriously taken into consideration. But Dad kept insisting, stubbornly. And when he refused to live any longer in the villa that had belonged to the architect's sister, and returned to the old building on Pekařská, this was not only considered something eccentric, but actually a breakdown of sorts. And it went even further. Supposedly, Dad reported that the entire case against the architect's sister had been fabricated, and he kept on insisting that this was murder, categorically demanding an investigation. He was taken off the case, and a few days later he vanished completely. So, it's all quite clear, isn't it? A word to the wise suffices.

Madame Fraccaroli grew quiet, but I continued to wait on what would come next, even though I was doubtful that this was the sort of thing I wanted to share with the listeners of Radio Brno. So I didn't say a word. Then someone had a peek into the courtyard.

Pardon the interruption, but your car is waiting.

Madame Fraccaroli glanced at her watch. She leapt to her feet and apologised for completely forgetting the time, saying that she had to be off.

I was left sort of high and dry here. What I'd just listened to and recorded was certainly interesting — no doubt — but I was still none too certain what was expected of me after having met with a famous composer from our own Brno.

I accompanied her to her car. It frosted me a bit that, despite the car being practically empty — there was just her and the driver — it never occurred to her to offer me a lift back to the centre of town. But then I saw the car turn round and, instead of heading toward the city centre, it set off, rather, in the direction of Židenice.

So I packed up my official satchel (or rather, pouch; the radio recorder is small enough to fit into my breast pocket), and weighed anchor myself. And then, to my utter disgust, I became aware of the fact that I didn't have my monthly tram ticket on me. But how could I expect to have, as an image flashed through my head: it's laying on the desk in my room next to the second volume of Kočí's *Research Encyclopaedia*, which I'd pulled off the shelf. Why I set it there and left it there was something I couldn't comprehend. So I set off towards the nearest kiosk to buy myself a single-fare ticket. But the kiosk was shuttered. A sign read: 'This news kiosk is for sale.' And then I realised that I hadn't all that much time to spare, as I was supposed to be on my way to my second detour of the day. At 11:30 I was supposed to be meeting with the foreman of those workers who blast or rather dig the underground collectors of Brno, that is, their galleries. So I jumped onto the next tram and, of course, right at the next stop two ticket-auditors got on and made right towards me with such infallible certainty, it was as if they were being led on a leash by some lousy god of misfortune. I showed them my radio ID and said I'd like to record a chat with them about ticket-auditors in Brno. Why not? they smiled. But first, your fine. But the talk wasn't going to be just for Radio Brno. You can stick your chat, partner, you know where, one of them said. And so, these fellows are tough guys I'm dealing with, the sort that even golden-tongued St John Chrysostom himself wouldn't be able to charm. And then I remembered that horrifying story of a certain law-abiding and peaceful citizen who wasn't able to pay his fine immediately, which then grew to an astronomical figure until, in the end, the bailiffs came round, and the god-fearing citizen in question, who was famed far and wide for his kindness and openheartedness even towards the homeless, hanged himself on the spot after the repossession was executed. At least he was lucky enough that they left him some rope. I pulled out a thousand crown note. So you see, editor, sir, that wasn't so painful, was it? Go to hell you ticket-punching ass, you! I growled (in spirit).

I was to meet with that foreman of the blasters or the diggers at the Potrefená husa. Which used to be the famous café-restaurant Bellevue, in which an even more famous scene from Kundera's story 'I the Mournful God' was played out. Unfortunately, there exists no memorials-law of the sort that would protect the names of celebrated municipal objects.

As I turned onto Běhounská St from Svoboda Square, I recalled immediately what Fraccaroli had told me about her father with that ugly last name, and the unforgettable pseudonym Láska. The police station is still standing on the street corner, from which, during the Communist days, I imagine, the StB goons would spill out like swarms of wild African bees. Just now, some policeman stuck his snobby nose out of the front door, only to cagily retract it again. But here I almost ran into someone — literally — someone whom I recognised immediately. Indeed, it took only a second for me to realise that I knew him from the radio. He had worked in the literary section in the nineties, but was just about to retire when I was taken on. It was the writer Jiří Kratochvil. Fuck, but did he get old! His head was as white as if lime had been dumped on it, and I noticed that he was limping on one leg. I'm not sure now if he wasn't already limping back then, or whether that limp wasn't a sort of, so to say, epiteton constans of his. Unfortunately, he recognised me too.

He grumbled something, nodded, and stepped aside. But he took me so by surprise that I stopped in my tracks. Immediately he made a furious gesture with his hand for me to follow him. I took a few steps into a narrow alley behind the retreating Kraťas, who continued to direct me with his hands as if I were manoeuvring a truck in a tight space. And then he stopped and turned his head to the right. We were standing before the entrance to some sort of building.

Whenever I walk past here, I always have to stop in, he said. In this building, I spent the ugliest years of my life after my father's emigration. Despite the fact that I haven't lived here for over forty-five years, I just can't get rid of the place. It's a trap for me, this building. He fixed his eyes on me, waiting for me to say something. I didn't say anything.

I'm just returning from hospital, he continued. And while I was being operated on, my mother died and they buried her before I was released. I've already been to have a look at her grave in the Centrálka. There's a hill of clay piled on top. Before I go back there next year, her casket will have sunk and disintegrated and the hill of clay will have sunk as well. And then he gave his head a furious scratch. And again he looked at me, waiting for me to say something. I didn't say anything. He ran his tongue over his lips. Listen, we still friends? I was just in the old book shop on Kapuciňák. They have Rushdie's *Midnight's Children* there for only a hundred fifty crowns. I'll pay you back next week — I'll leave the dough at the porter's at Brno Radio. If I don't come to know that novel, I can just go fuck myself as a writer.

I forked over the one-fifty.

And because I had to expect the foreman of the blasters or diggers would want a beer, I had to head off down Česká now, because there's an ATM machine there.

The foreman of the blasters and diggers sat at a window overlooking the square. I had no doubt about it being him — that fluorescent yellow vest of his set himself apart from everyone else. Except the other yellow vest sitting next to him, who was certainly a corpsman or a doorman or longshoreman.

The foreman made a face. Wasn't the interview person supposed to be a lady? Oh well. Whatever. We're not gonna make a tragedy out of it. I see it like this: over dinner, we'll tell you everything you need to know about the collectors in Brno. Then we've got a hat for you and a vest and you'll come

　　　　　　　　　　　JIŘÍ KRATOCHVIL

along with us and have a gander down below. And you'll see — there, it's all something else.

Of course, they ordered the most expensive thing on the menu — fallow-deer ragoût. At first I was horrified, but then I thought — This isn't coming out of my pocket. Unlike the fine in the tram and the alms to Kratochvil, this here is a business expense. A write-off. The radio'll be footing the bill for dinner at the Potrefená husa, at least I dare trust they will. I myself chose something a bit more common: Vienna goulash, so that when I presented the bill to Tomáš, he'd see that I wasn't abusing his trust.

The foreman and the longshoreman waited patiently for the waiter to bring their dinner. So far they were talking among themselves, as if I weren't there at all. But as soon as the ambidextrous waiter set their chow down in front of them, the foreman took a taste and then smiled encouragingly, nodding at his pal. They went at it with gusto, chewing and turning the morsels over in their mouths to get them all juicy with saliva, and then they began talking the way people do when their mouths are full, so that a fair third of what they said was lost to me, disappearing down their gullets with the fallow-deer ragoût. And in the meantime, while they were spluttering, they would squirt small bits of venison my way, salvos of Lilliputian shrapnel which I didn't dare wipe off my face for fear of insulting them, as if I held the intimacy of their gobs in disdain, for then I wouldn't get what I needed from them, or, on the contrary, maybe they'd be so amused at it that they'll do it all the more, training their artillery full on me, until my whole face would be covered in a thin mask and only my continually blinking eyelids would keep the peepholes open, through which my eyes would stare out like terrified chicks. And it was then that it occurred to me, as it had already several times over the past few days, that I have an undeniable literary talent and I should be writing my own stories and novels and not mucking about in the literary section with texts written by others.

Are you even listening to us? the foreman asked. But my diligent little recorder had already taken note of the fact that the whole operation of building the collectors in Brno had commenced in 1973, at Dornych. And furthermore, the recorder learned that there are two sorts of collector, the primary ones, such as carry water from waterworks, heat from heating plants, electricity from power plants, gas from gasworks and telephone conversations from central switchboards. And that these collectors average five metres in diameter and are found some twenty to thirty metres underground. Secondary collectors are those that carry their loads to individual buildings. They average three metres in diameter and are found six to seven metres underground. Utility networks lacking in such collectors — now it was the other fellow speaking — crashed every other moment. Yet collectors are outfitted with sensors and detection systems, so problems can be avoided.

The whole task of constructing collectors — said the foreman, carefully sopping up the deer-sauce — arises from existing utility networks, and the course of individual constructions is directly calibrated to the network of streets in a given municipal area.

But what about the historical vaults? I asked. Brno is supposedly built over underground vaulted chambers.

Agreed, said the foreman. And to a much greater extent than had been suspected up till now. He pushed aside the cleaned plate and reached for the wine list. In the end, his choice fell upon a Sauvignon 'of late vintage.' Brno has an underground. Who would know that if not us? To a certain degree, the depths of the collector-galleries matches the average depth of the historical underground areas. Often, the edge of our gallery runs up against such a vault, and then we use them as auxiliary maintenance spaces. And sometimes we need to fill in those historical spaces for engineering reasons, with a mix of concrete and gravel. And then sometimes we run across the curiouser curiosities.

May I, chief? the other piped up.

You certainly may, the foreman nodded. But only after you wipe your greasy mug. And he handed him a paper napkin.

So, we ran into one of the curiousest curiosities right here on Běhounská St. We call it the big pocket.

Or sleeve, or muff, the foreman corrected. If you know what that is.

By chance I do, I said. When I was so high (here I stretched my hand out above the floor at about table height), we had two such sleeves — one of caracul, the other of some other sort of fur, hanging in our wardrobe. I remember being somewhat afraid of them, well, more than somewhat, actually, since someone told me that the souls of my two dead grandmothers were living in them. One in each muff.

But this whacking big muff of ours is sewn up at both ends, the foreman noted. And what am I getting at? And the foreman nudged his companion. Don't be shy. Tell 'im.

What he's getting at, the other said, pointing towards the foreman, is that we have here a long underground gallery, closed off at both sides, simply inaccessible. It's the size of a primary collector, well, even a little larger. It starts at Běhounská right beneath number 3/5 and stretches all the way to Svoboda Square. And the fact that it's carefully sealed at both ends is something quite unusual. We tried to probe it, all sorts of ways, but no dice. And then it occurred to us that there must be an access point to the gallery from the cellar of Běhounská 3/5. And yet we found nothing there, either. How to get inside is gonna be a tough nut to crack, because that there sleeve is well fortified from within.

But in the end, none of this is our worry. When the time comes, we'll find a way to open it up, the former commented.

But what can that be down there? I asked, though actually I wasn't fascinated in the least.

Well, most likely some sort of naturally refrigerated pantry. A sort of gigantic mediaeval fridge. They probably preserved meat down there. Of course, the mystery is — why is it so impenetrably sealed? It's possible that somebody wanted to conceal his property there from looting invaders.

But then why did this person keep it sealed? Why didn't he ever open it later on?

If the invaders couldn't get at his stuff, maybe they could get at him, and gobbled him up. And maybe we've got a three-hundred-year-old vacuum down there, which has preserved everything perfectly. When we open it up, the butcher shops of Brno will be filled to overflowing with pork, beef, veal, mutton, and all sorts of game. After all, back then the woods around Brno were full of hare, pheasant, partridge, boar, deer, stags and — above all, fallow deer.

We laughed.

And then the bottle of Sauvignon arrived. The foreman took a taste and we looked out through the window on to the moving pictures of Moravské Square. Two deaf people were standing in front of the Scala Cinema, gesticulating energetically. A gaggle of nuns processed through the crossroads, the last two carrying a large basket of laundry. A tram rumbled by with a large advert for bottled beer on its side. The beer bottles were decked out in tails and walking sticks. Time suddenly stood still and I realised that these blasters or diggers or what have you were quite nice chaps.

They gave me a helmet and a vest. Outside a van was waiting, which took us to the nearest entrance to a primary collector on Josefská. We descended into the great gallery, which was lit up with fluorescent lamps. The blue of the load-bearing structures fixed to the walls, stretching out into the distance, prepared to house the utility network, was the dominant colour. There was a hum and a rushing sound, which diminished, rather than increasing, the deeper we progressed. When we had gone on for a while the foreman asked me if I had any idea where we were. Right under the crossroads where Bratislavská and Koliště meet, he said, pointing to a little blue post on which a plate was affixed reading 'U12AR6.' There are such orientational plates down here every fifty metres, so we always know exactly what's above our heads at any given moment. You're lucky to be down in a collector that's not yet all kitted out. Next week you'd be tripping over cables, ducts, and boxes. But I figure we should go back now. And so we went back.

GHOSTSCRIPT
OR, FUR MUFFS

I hasten to assure you that it didn't turn out at all as you might be fearing it did. I've already led them all out of Modráček's fur muff, and set them into happier chapters of other novels of mine, though under somewhat different aliases. As for the fur muff, I've extracted it from the underground and hung it up in Petr Luňák's wardrobe — that fellow from Radio Brno. When he first notices it there, he'll be startled, maybe, but then he'll recall a jovial thirtieth birthday party and how he told someone there about his childish terror of those things, about ghosts living in them — and he'll chuckle at the practical joke. So the muff is there indeed, safe and sound, perhaps he'll give it to his girlfriend, and when the hard winter comes round again, it'll make a peep in her direction, and who knows but that'll be the start of a new trend in Brno — the winter streets will be filled with girls with muffs! And then maybe somebody will remember that ugly old novel about the evil 1950s, and recall that it also had a charming story about a fur muff. And what more can a novelist hope for?

Added 30 November 2008

ACKNOWLEDGEMENT

From the bottom of his heart, the author thanks Jan Šlesinger, MD, who assisted at the delivery of Eduard Láska.

◆

BIBLIOGRAPHY

SOURCE TEXT:

Kratochvil, Jiří: *Slib*. Brno: Druhé město, 2009.

SECONDARY SOURCES

BRABEC, Jiří, et al. (eds.) *Slovník českých spisovatelů. Pokus o rekonstrukce dějin české literatury 1948–1979* [Dictionary of Czech Writers. An Attempt at a Reconstruction of the History of Czech Literature 1948–1979]. Toronto: 68 Publishers, 1982.

FIŠER, Zbyněk. 'Fantastično a postmoderna: role fantastična v díle Jiřího Kratochvila' [The Fantastic and the Postmodern: the Role of the Fantastic in the Work of Jiří Kratochvil], in Tereza Dědinová (ed.), *Na rozhraní světů. Fantastická literatura v mezioborovém zkoumaní* [At the Interface of Worlds. Interdisciplinary Research into Fantastic Literature]. Brno: Filozofická fakulta Masarykovy univerzity, 2016, pp. 269-274.

GALUSKOVÁ, Ladislava. *Poetika míst v díle Jiřího Kratochvila* [The Poetics of Place in the Work of Jiří Kratochvil]. Brno: Filozofická fakulta, Ústav hudební vědy Masarykovy univerzity (Bakalářská diplomová práce), 2010.

JAMES, Petra. 'The Trauma of "Enforced Disappearance" as a Topic in Central European Fiction after 1989,' in Florin Abraham and Réka Földváryné Kiss (eds.), *Remembrance and Solidarity. Studies in 20th Century European History*, No. 6 (2018), pp. 61-84.

KINDL, *Martin. Proměny vztahu českého katolického exilu v Římě po roce 1948 k marxismu a komunismu* [Changes in the Relationship of the Czech Catholic Exile Community in Rome to Marxism and Communism After 1948]. Prague: Fakulta Humanitních Studií Katedry Obecné Antropologie (Diplomová práce), 2014.

MACHALA, Lubomír. 'Petrovské prozaické kvarteto jako zrcadlo současné literární situace (Nad knihami Jiřího Kratochvila, Petra Ulrycha, Alexandry Berkové a Michala Viewegha)' [The Petrov Prose Quartet as a Mirror for the Contemporary Literary Situation (on the Books of Jiří Kratochvil, Petr Ulrych, Alexandra Berková and Michal Viewegh), *Česká literatura*, Vol. 49, No. 6 (2001), pp. 645-654.

RÓŻEWICZ, Tadeusz. *Zawsze fragment: Recycling* [Always a Fragment: Recycling]. Wrocław: Wydawnictwo dolnośląskie, 1998.

SEGEL, Harold B. *The Columbia Guide to the Literatures of Eastern Europe since 1945.* New York: Columbia University Press, 2003.

SEGEL, Harold B. *The Columbia Guide to the Literatures of Eastern Europe since 1945.* New York: Columbia University Press, 2008.

WRONOVÁ, Michaela. 'Fantastické momenty v české metafyzické detektivce' [Fantastic Moments in Czech Metaphysical Detective Writing], in Tereza Dědinová (ed.), *Na rozhraní světů. Fantastická literatura v mezioborovém zkoumaní* [At the Interface of Worlds. Interdisciplinary Research into Fantastic Literature]. Brno: Filozofická fakulta Masarykovy univerzity, 2016. pp. 301-312.

ABOUT THE TRANSLATOR

Charles S. Kraszewski (b. 1962) is a poet and translator, creative in both English and Polish. He is the author of three volumes of original verse in English (*Diet of Nails*; *Beast*; *Chanameed*), and one in Polish (*Hallo, Sztokholm*). He also authored a satirical novel *Accomplices, You Ask?* (San Francisco: Montag, 2021). He translates from Polish, Czech and Slovak into English, and from English and Spanish into Polish. He is a member of the Union of Polish Writers Abroad (London) and of the Association of Polish Writers (SPP, Kraków).

WHERE WAS THE ANGEL GOING?

by Jan Balaban

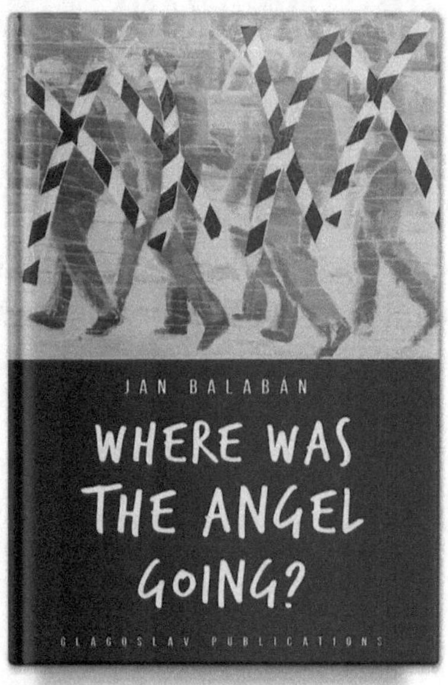

'Somewhere in the cosmos there are happier places,' muses Martin Vrána, the hero of Jan Balabán's novel *Where was the Angel Going?*. 'People are transported to the planet Earth for punishment. Part of the punishment is their ignorance of the fact. We've forgotten that we've forgotten.' Yet, as this very reflection implies, in Martin's case, part of his 'punishment' is his ever-present memory of an Eden from which he had been expelled. The prototypical outsider, a member of a minority community within a minority community (a Protestant in the overwhelmingly agnostic Czech Republic), Martin, like the survivor of a shipwreck, strives to shore up his vital resources amidst the billows of an inimical world, which constantly advance and threaten to wash away everything he holds dear.

Where was the Angel Going? is a novel made up of forty-six linked stories. As always, Balabán's prose is so vivid that the reader can practically taste the 'honey and dust,' which are the characteristic flavours of Ostrava. And yet, in its lyrical message of love and friendship as basic human needs no less critical than air and water, *Where was the Angel Going* is nonetheless an eminently universal novel. Everyone will find him or herself in these pages, as we are all of us descended from that first pair of exiles, Adam and Eve.

Buy it > www.glagoslav.com

FOREFATHERS' EVE
by Adam Mickiewicz

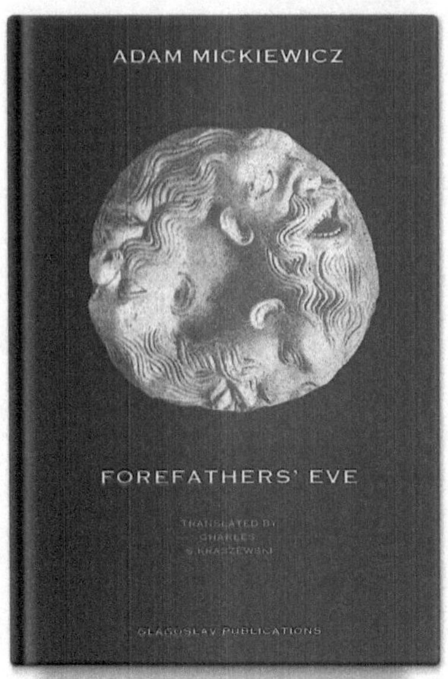

Forefathers' Eve [*Dziady*] is a four-part dramatic work begun circa 1820 and completed in 1832 – with Part I published only after the poet's death, in 1860. The drama's title refers to *Dziady*, an ancient Slavic and Lithuanian feast commemorating the dead. This is the grand work of Polish literature, and it is one that elevates Mickiewicz to a position among the "great Europeans" such as Dante and Goethe.

With its Christian background of the Communion of the Saints, revenant spirits, and the interpenetration of the worlds of time and eternity, *Forefathers' Eve* speaks to men and women of all times and places. While it is a truly Polish work – Polish actors covet the role of Gustaw/Konrad in the same way that Anglophone actors covet that of Hamlet – it is one of the most universal works of literature written during the nineteenth century. It has been compared to Goethe's Faust – and rightfully so...

Buy it > www.glagoslav.com

MAYBE WE'RE LEAVING

by Jan Balaban

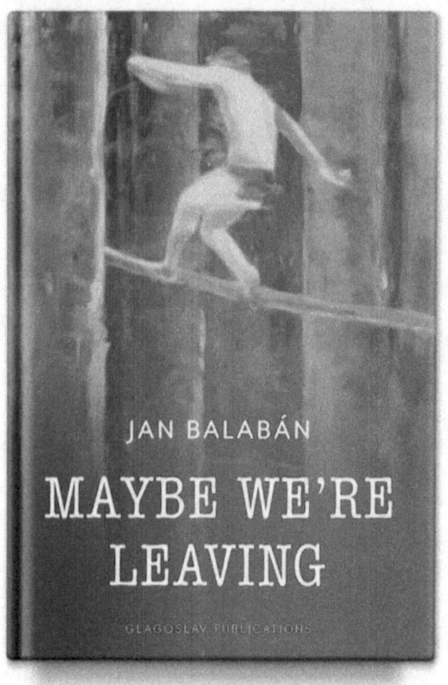

A young boy from the housing estates comes across a copse of old oaks to which he can escape, as to an oasis of calm. Although he may forget about it once he becomes an adult and "puts aside the things of childhood," it will remain a locus of balance, decades later, for a single mother struggling with the difficulties of raising the child she loves. A husband, on the lip of an ugly divorce, drives across town in the middle of the night to rescue his wife, abandoned by her lover, and then — as she falls asleep in the car — takes the long way home, to prolong a moment such as he has not experienced in years. An elderly doctor, self-diagnosed with Alzheimer's disease, makes use of the few precious moments of consciousness granted him each morning to pass on to his grandson what he has learned about life and living responsibly. Loss, and permanence, the ephemeral and the eternal, are common themes of Jan Balabán's collection of short stories *Maybe We're Leaving*, presented here in the English translation of Charles S. Kraszewski. With psychological insight that rivals the great novels of Fyodor Dostoevsky, the twenty-one linked narratives that make up the collection present us with everyday people, with everyday problems — and teach us to love and respect the former, and bear the latter.

Buy it > www.glagoslav.com

THE VILLAGE TEACHER AND OTHER STORIES

by Theodore Odrach

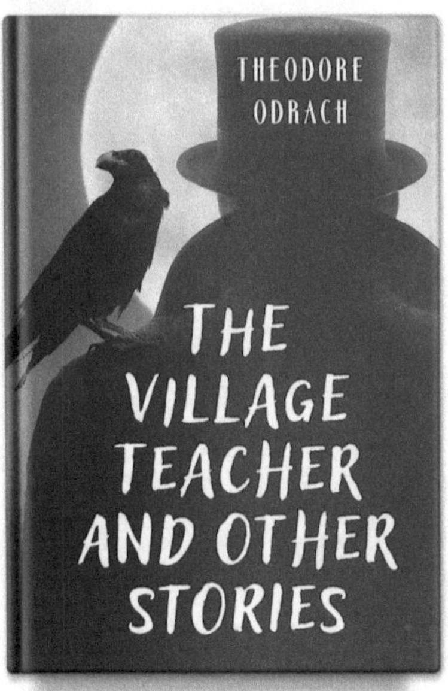

The twenty-two stories in this collection, set mostly in Eastern Europe during World War Two, depict a world fraught with conflict and chaos. Theodore Odrach is witness to the horrors that surround him, and as both an investigative journalist and a skilful storyteller, using humor and irony, he guides us through his remarkable narratives. His writing style is clean and spare, yet at the same time compelling and complex. There is no short supply of triumph and catastrophe, courage and cowardice, good and evil, as they impact the lives of ordinary people.

In "Benny's Story", a group of prisoners fight to survive despite horrific circumstances; in "Lickspittles", the absurdity of an émigré writer's life is highlighted; in "Blood", a young man travels to a distant city in search of his lost love; in "Whistle Stop", two German soldiers fight boredom in an out-of-the-way outpost, only to see their world crumble and fall.

A BURGLAR OF THE BETTER SORT

by Tytus Czyżewski

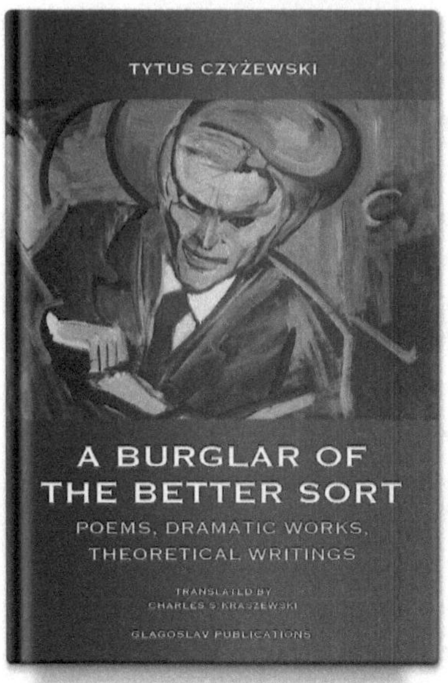

The history of Poland, since the eighteenth century, has been marked by an almost unending struggle for survival. From 1795 through 1945, she was partitioned four times by her stronger neighbours, most of whom were intent on suppressing if not eradicating Polish culture. It is not surprising, then, that much of the great literature written in modern Poland has been politically and patriotically engaged. Yet there is a second current as well, that of authors devoted above all to the craft of literary expression, creating 'art for art's sake,' and not as a didactic national service. Such a poet is Tytus Czyżewski, one of the chief, and most interesting, literary figures of the twentieth century. Growing to maturity in the benign Austrian partition of Poland, and creating most of his works in the twenty-year window of authentic Polish independence stretching between the two world wars, Czyżewski is an avant-garde poet, dramatist and painter who popularised the new approach to poetry established in France by Guillaume Apollinaire, and was to exert a marked influence on such multi-faceted artists as Tadeusz Kantor.

Buy it > www.glagoslav.com

- *A History of Belarus* by Lubov Bazan
- *Children's Fashion of the Russian Empire* by Alexander Vasiliev
- *Empire of Corruption: The Russian National Pastime* by Vladimir Soloviev
- *Heroes of the 90s: People and Money. The Modern History of Russian Capitalism* by Alexander Solovev, Vladislav Dorofeev and Valeria Bashkirova
- *Fifty Highlights from the Russian Literature* (Dutch Edition) by Maarten Tengbergen
- *Bajesvolk* (Dutch Edition) by Michail Chodorkovsky
- *Dagboek van Keizerin Alexandra* (Dutch Edition)
- *Myths about Russia* by Vladimir Medinskiy
- *Boris Yeltsin: The Decade that Shook the World* by Boris Minaev
- *A Man Of Change: A study of the political life of Boris Yeltsin*
- *Sberbank: The Rebirth of Russia's Financial Giant* by Evgeny Karasyuk
- *To Get Ukraine* by Oleksandr Shyshko
- *Asystole* by Oleg Pavlov
- *Gnedich* by Maria Rybakova
- *Marina Tsvetaeva: The Essential Poetry*
- *Multiple Personalities* by Tatyana Shcherbina
- *The Investigator* by Margarita Khemlin
- *The Exile* by Zinaida Tulub
- *Leo Tolstoy: Flight from Paradise* by Pavel Basinsky
- *Moscow in the 1930* by Natalia Gromova
- *Laurus* (Dutch edition) by Evgenij Vodolazkin
- *Prisoner* by Anna Nemzer
- *The Crime of Chernobyl: The Nuclear Goulag* by Wladimir Tchertkoff
- *Alpine Ballad* by Vasil Bykau
- *The Complete Correspondence of Hryhory Skovoroda*
- *The Tale of Aypi* by Ak Welsapar
- *Selected Poems* by Lydia Grigorieva
- *The Fantastic Worlds of Yuri Vynnychuk*
- *The Garden of Divine Songs and Collected Poetry of Hryhory Skovoroda*
- *Adventures in the Slavic Kitchen: A Book of Essays with Recipes* by Igor Klekh
- *Seven Signs of the Lion* by Michael M. Naydan

- *Forefathers' Eve* by Adam Mickiewicz
- *One-Two* by Igor Eliseev
- *Girls, be Good* by Bojan Babić
- *Time of the Octopus* by Anatoly Kucherena
- *The Grand Harmony* by Bohdan Ihor Antonych
- *The Selected Lyric Poetry Of Maksym Rylsky*
- *The Shining Light* by Galymkair Mutanov
- *The Frontier: 28 Contemporary Ukrainian Poets - An Anthology*
- *Acropolis: The Wawel Plays* by Stanisław Wyspiański
- *Contours of the City* by Attyla Mohylny
- *Conversations Before Silence: The Selected Poetry of Oles Ilchenko*
- *The Secret History of my Sojourn in Russia* by Jaroslav Hašek
- *Mirror Sand: An Anthology of Russian Short Poems*
- *Maybe We're Leaving* by Jan Balaban
- *Death of the Snake Catcher* by Ak Welsapar
- *A Brown Man in Russia* by Vijay Menon
- *Hard Times* by Ostap Vyshnia
- *The Flying Dutchman* by Anatoly Kudryavitsky
- *Nikolai Gumilev's Africa* by Nikolai Gumilev
- *Combustions* by Srđan Srdić
- *The Sonnets* by Adam Mickiewicz
- *Dramatic Works* by Zygmunt Krasiński
- *Four Plays* by Juliusz Słowacki
- *Little Zinnobers* by Elena Chizhova
- *We Are Building Capitalism! Moscow in Transition 1992-1997* by Robert Stephenson
- *The Nuremberg Trials* by Alexander Zvyagintsev
- *The Hemingway Game* by Evgeni Grishkovets
- *A Flame Out at Sea* by Dmitry Novikov
- *Jesus' Cat* by Grig
- *Want a Baby and Other Plays* by Sergei Tretyakov
- *Mikhail Bulgakov: The Life and Times* by Marietta Chudakova
- *Leonardo's Handwriting* by Dina Rubina
- *A Burglar of the Better Sort* by Tytus Czyżewski
- *The Mouseiad and other Mock Epics* by Ignacy Krasicki
- *Ravens before Noah* by Susanna Harutyunyan

- *An English Queen and Stalingrad* by Natalia Kulishenko
- *Point Zero* by Narek Malian
- *Absolute Zero* by Artem Chekh
- *Olanda* by Rafał Wojasiński
- *Robinsons* by Aram Pachyan
- *The Monastery* by Zakhar Prilepin
- *The Selected Poetry of Bohdan Rubchak: Songs of Love, Songs of Death, Songs of the Moon*
- *Mebet* by Alexander Grigorenko
- *The Orchestra* by Vladimir Gonik
- *Everyday Stories* by Mima Mihajlović
- *Slavdom* by Ľudovít Štúr
- *The Code of Civilization* by Vyacheslav Nikonov
- *Where Was the Angel Going?* by Jan Balaban
- *De Zwarte Kip* (Dutch Edition) by Antoni Pogorelski
- *Głosy / Voices* by Jan Polkowski
- *Sergei Tretyakov: A Revolutionary Writer in Stalin's Russia* by Robert Leach
- *Opstand* (Dutch Edition) by Władysław Reymont
- *Dramatic Works* by Cyprian Kamil Norwid
- *Children's First Book of Chess* by Natalie Shevando and Matthew McMillion
- *Precursor* by Vasyl Shevchuk
- *The Vow: A Requiem for the Fifties* by Jiří Kratochvil
- *De Bibliothecaris* (Dutch edition) by Mikhail Jelizarov
- *Subterranean Fire* by Natalka Bilotserkivets
- *Vladimir Vysotsky: Selected Works*
- *Behind the Silk Curtain* by Gulistan Khamzayeva
- *The Village Teacher and Other Stories* by Theodore Odrach
- *Duel* by Borys Antonenko-Davydovych
- *War Poems* by Alexander Korotko
- *Ballads and Romances* by Adam Mickiewicz
- *The Revolt of the Animals* by Wladyslaw Reymont
- *Poems about my Psychiatrist* by Andrzej Kotański
- *Liza's Waterfall: The hidden story of a Russian feminist* by Pavel Basinsky
- *Biography of Sergei Prokofiev* by Igor Vishnevetsky

  More coming . . .